"Rod Serling is surely one of the most familiar figures in the annals of broadcasting, and was the possessor of one of the screen's most distinctive voices: a sometimes wry, sometimes somber voice that, even today, is instantly recognizable. You can hear it in every line he wrote. . . .

"Many elements of his fantasies are, inevitably, universal . . . yet there is also something uniquely American in these tales. . . . And, like fairy tales, his stories are not afraid to teach a moral lesson—many of them focus on such modern concerns as ethics, brotherhood and the everpresent threat of nuclear war. . . ."

—T. E. D. Klein,
from his *Introduction*

STORIES FROM THE TWILIGHT ZONE

ROD SERLING

Introduction by T.E.D. Klein

BANTAM BOOKS
TORONTO · NEW YORK · LONDON · SYDNEY · AUCKLAND

For my brother Bob,
the first writer of the Serling clan

RL 6, IL age 13 and up

STORIES FROM THE TWILIGHT ZONE
A Bantam Spectra Book / October 1986

*This collection was first published in three separate
volumes:* Stories From the Twilight Zone, More Stories
From the Twilight Zone, *and* New Stories From the
Twilight Zone

Library of Congress Cataloging-in-Publication Data

Serling, Rod, 1924–1975
 Stories from the Twilight zone.

 1. Fantastic fiction, American. 2.
Supernatural—Fiction. I. Twilight zone (Television
program) II. Title.
PS3537.E654S7 1986 813'.54 86-47578
ISBN 0-553-34329-7

Published simultaneously in the United States and Canada

PRINTED IN THE UNITED STATES OF AMERICA

FG   0 9 8 7 6 5 4 3 2 1

CONTENTS

INTRODUCTION

If you were born in the twentieth century and, some time during the past thirty years, happened to pass within viewing distance of a television set, you're probably acquainted with the man who wrote this book. Rod Serling—who died, age fifty, in 1975—is surely one of the most familiar figures in the annals of broadcasting, and was the possessor of one of the screen's most distinctive voices: a sometimes wry, sometimes somber voice that, even today, is instantly recognizable. You can hear it in every line he wrote.

In fact, if you've seen a single episode of TV's original *Twilight Zone*, chances are you'll never get that voice out of your head, with its echoes of daddy, wise uncle, camp counselor, professor, and network anchorman all rolled into one. Thanks to that voice, and to the series's continued popularity in syndicated form, the tales in this book are coming to you with certain uncommon advantages—ready-made faces to go with the characters' names, the presence of an expert storyteller speaking into memory's ear—and a certain disadvantage: you may be less likely to approach them as stories that can stand on their own.

And that would be a shame. Because even if the series had never graced the airwaves and Rod Serling had never stepped onto America's television screens, hands folded gravely before him, the phrase "The Twilight Zone," as this book demonstrates, would still signify something special: a world of "what if?" where wishes come true (sometimes horribly), where illusion reigns and magic really works (but only so long as you believe), where little guys are blessed with the strength of titans, where miraculous machines spell our salvation—or our doom—and where the most frightening monsters of all turn out to be ourselves.

It's also a world whose coordinates are ever-so-slightly askew: where, on the railroad line between Stamford and Westport, you'll find a town called Willoughby that isn't on the map; where a transatlantic jumbo jet is liable to arrive at the right destination but in the wrong year; and where, according to "The Mighty Casey," the Brooklyn Dodgers played not at Ebbets Field but at Tebbet's. Baseball aficionados may quibble; but then, the Twilight Zone has always enjoyed its own unique geography.

TV aficionados may do likewise, noting that, in the televised version of "Casey," the team was not the Dodgers but a ragtag bunch known as the Hoboken Zephyrs. There are many such changes in each of the stories that follow, from initial script to TV show to printed page, right down to the way you distinctly remember seeing the show when you were twelve. But these and a thousand other tiny alterations and elaborations are merely the stuff of late-night arguments among trivia buffs. While you're sure to discover lines of familiar dialogue in the pages ahead, and even patches of the original narration, they are simply the skeletons on which Serling hung the tales.

What matters is that, lovingly expanded and embellished, the stories have been given a new life here. For every character who wears a perfunctory description pulled straight from the teleplay, like the "attractive widow in her thirties" in "The Big, Tall Wish," we have others who reveal a recognizable humanity, such as the construction foreman in "Escape Clause," warily approaching the scene of a gruesome accident: "He covered his eyes because of a normal reluctance to view mangled bodies. He also peeked between two fingers, because of the equally normal trait of being fascinated by the horrible."

The short-story format has also allowed Serling the room to indulge a gift for language and imagery:

It was night when Martin Sloan returned to Oak Street and stood in front of his house looking at the incredibly warm lights that shone from within. The crickets were a million tambourines that came out of the darkness. There was a scent of hyacinth in the air. There was a quiet rustle of leaf-laden trees that screened out the moon and made odd shadows on cooling sidewalks. There was a feeling of summer, so well remembered.

That's from my favorite story of the lot, "Walking Distance." I get a lump in my throat each time I read it, even when proofreading the script version for the first issue of *Twilight Zone* magazine. (Maybe that was why I missed so many typos.) It also held a special meaning for Serling himself, who was careful to set the short story in upstate New York near Binghamton, his boyhood home—just the sort of personal note that TV leaves out.

And television can't convey the scent of those hyacinths or the cool of those sidewalks.

Or the fact that the doctor's feet hurt in "Escape Clause."

Or, in another tale, the hint of John Dillinger in a small boy's freckled face. (That Serling identifies the outlaw, whose middle name was Herbert, as "John J. Dillinger" may simply be further proof that things are awry in the Twilight Zone.)

Or another tale's conclusion, as dry as if penned by John Collier, in which a minor character, having had his fill of mystery, enjoys "a Brown Betty for dessert" and goes happily to bed.

We'd miss that Brown Betty on TV.

We'd also miss the occasional aside—"His volume of business was roughly that of a valet at a hobos' convention"—and the rhythm of this simile: "Beasley was a little man whose face looked like an X ray of an ulcer."

And we'd miss the description of the bloated, sadistic Oliver Misrell in "A Stop at Willoughby," sitting at the conference table and "blinking like a shaven owl."

Misrell, whose name suggests a wedding of "dismal" and "miserable," exemplifies Serling's relish for colorful Dickensian names—Luther Dingle, Mouth McGarry, the snobbish Bartlett Finchley, the gunslinger Rance McGrew—and, indeed, this book features a gallery of memorably grotesque characters that might almost have stepped from the pages of Dickens: the complete hypochondriac, Walter Bedeker; the thin-lipped, narrow-shouldered, prune-faced Franklin Gibbs, "a sour-faced little man in a 1937 suit"; Harvey Hennicutt, the silver-tongued con man who can even sell a Sherman tank; and Henry Corwin, the drunken department-store Santa. One larger-than-life character, the swinishly avaricious Peter Sykes, even sports a Dickens villain's name.

It's clear, in fact, that Serling was a Dickens fan. His TV play *Carol for Another Christmas* updates Dickens's *A Christmas Carol*, and he consciously echoes the latter's opening lines in his story "The Night of the Meek." There's also a reference to Scrooge in "Where Is Everybody?" and, though not by name, in "The Odyssey of Flight 33," when a distraught airline pilot, face-to-face with the impossible, decides, "It was a bad dream that followed a late lobster snack and an extra quart of beer."

Yet Serling's real inspirations were a lot closer to home. If many elements of his fantasies are, inevitably, universal—superheroes and saviors, pacts with the devil, wishes with unexpected consequences, magic spells and several Deadly Sins, characters who overreach themselves and meet ironic but appropriate dooms, a modern-day jetliner whose mysterious fate recalls the lost ships in sea legends of old, extraterrestrials who drift in and out of the tales at will, meddling in human affairs like the gods of Greek myth—there is also something uniquely American in these tales. Presided over by a pantheon of home-grown heroes—baseball stars, Hollywood stars, astronauts, gunfighters, and ingenious inventors, as well as such lesser figures as snake-oil salesmen, soda jerks, admen, shady small-time politicians, and a handful of endearing losers—they are set amid classic American locales: suburbia, the wild West, the seductive glitter of Las Vegas, the Mexican border, the ballpark, the prizefight ring (which provided the background for his celebrated *Requiem for a Heavyweight* and which Serling knew from the inside, having boxed during his army days), and the corporate boardroom (another territory he'd explored before, in the TV play *Patterns*). While, like fairy tales, his stories are not afraid to teach a moral lesson, many of them focus on such modern American concerns as business ethics, brotherhood, and the everpresent threat of nuclear war.

They are also invincibly democratic, displaying a typical American irreverence for stuffed shirts and snobs. At times they approach the tall tale in their penchant for exaggeration and slapstick. Characters in "Casey" blunder into water buckets and swallow lit cigars, and a nervous young pitcher throws the rosin bag instead of the ball. ("As it turned out, this was his best pitch of the evening.") The inept cowboy hero of "Showdown with Rance McGrew," unable to extricate his gun from its holster, eventually sends it flying over his shoulder to shatter a barroom mirror.

You have a sense of Serling enjoying himself in these scenes, adding a bit of wise-guy humor to the story out of sheer high spirits: "The sigh Bertram Beasley heaved was the only respectable heave going on within a radius of three hundred feet of home plate." And:

> The three pitchers that scout Maxwell Jenkins had sent over turned out to be pitchers in name only. One of them, as a matter of fact, had looked so familiar that McGarry swore he'd seen him pitch in the 1911 World Series. As it turned out, McGarry had been mistaken. It was not he who had pitched in the 1911 World Series but his nephew.

One hears, in the rhythm of that passage, echoes of Runyon and Twain.

There's even a hint of the later, bitter Twain—the Twain of "The Man That Corrupted Hadleyburg"—in "The Rip Van Winkle Caper" and "The Fever," with their bleak view of the human species in extremis. You'll find it, too, in Serling's three cynical end-of-the-world fantasies. "The Shelter" (with its hero "suddenly realizing that underneath . . . we're an ugly race of people"), "The Midnight Sun" (in which man's darker nature emerges only briefly), and "The Monsters Are Due on Maple Street" (with its deliberate parallels to the Communist witchhunt of the fifties.)

Serling resembles Twain, as well, in his love-hate relationship with that modern American god, the machine—a god on whom we've come to depend, but of whose disposition we're a little uncertain. Serling's fascination, so apparent in the TV series as well as in this book, dates back to the early fifties, to a youthful radio script, *A Machine to Answer the Question*, about a computer that "can break down every human problem into a mathematical equation"—and provide the answer to whatever question it's asked, even as to the prospect of an alien invasion. (Says the script's pre-*Twilight Zone* narrator: "Man's small mind can only project so far. . . . What's needed is a device to explain the mystery, to probe the void—a machine.")

In fact, Serling himself seems to have had, in the words of
the title of one of his stories, "A Thing About Machines." That
particular tale—the paranoid fantasy of a man whose relation to
mechanical objects is one of, at best, uneasy coexistence—ascribes
to machines a distinctly human will, and a pitiless one at that. So
does "The Fever," in which a fiendishly inimical machine defeats
a mere mortal . . . or helps him, rather, to defeat himself. The
inhabitants of "Maple Street" prove ripe for conquest because of
their reliance on modern conveniences (to conquer them "just
stop a few of their machines and radios and telephones and lawn
mowers"); one suspects that the passengers and crew of "Flight
33" are similarly undone by their unquestioning trust in machinery and the known laws of the universe. Robots, a constant presence in Serling's TV series, come to humanity's aid in "The
Mighty Casey" and "The Lonely"; though the mannequin in
"Where Is Everybody?," like the impersonal voice at the end of
the phone ("This is a recording"), makes the hero's agony all the
greater as he longs for the touch of a fellow human being.

This last aspect of modern American life—its underlying
loneliness and sense of dislocation—provides an even more fun-
damental theme. Like so many of the televised episodes, the tales
in this book are pervaded by a fear of being alone; it is presented,
in fact, as the most unbearable of punishments. In "Escape
Clause," "The Lonely," and "Where Is Everybody?" (in which
the ubiquitous presence of brand names and advertising slogans
proves to be of little comfort), the anguish of isolation can drive a
man to madness or death. Characters in this unsettling world are
perpetually in danger of getting lost (sometimes at the most un-
likely moments), disconnected from their fellows, disoriented in
time as well as space. "Showdown with Rance McGrew" is a
comic nightmare about being yanked willy-nilly into the past;
"The Odyssey of Flight 33" is the same nightmare on a grander
and more horrifying scale (if tempered by a boyish excitement at
the idea of seeing real dinosaurs). "The Rip Van Winkle Caper" is
a cautionary tale about travel in the opposite direction.

But for an unhappy few, traveling in time seems the only
way out—because the sense of dislocation, which in some tales
appears as the most hellish of fates, is depicted, in others, as an
inescapable condition of modern American life. Lost in a world
of high pressures, power plays, and false values, the alienated
heroes of "Walking Distance" and "A Stop at Willoughby" yearn

for the simplicity and serenity of the past: in the former tale, for the hometown, Homewood, of the hero's own past; in the latter, for the quintessential small town of America's past. (Though Willoughby itself is an idealized construction found only in Currier-&-Ives-induced dreams, the story, like "Walking Distance," must have had a personal meaning for Serling, who'd spent the early days of his career commuting from Connecticut to New York on the New Haven line.) Of Homewood we read, "Somewhere at the end of a long, six-lane highway . . . Martin Sloan was looking for sanity," while Willoughby, too, is described as "a doorway that leads to sanity." Clearly both towns offer solace in the same achingly desirable form—a return, through time, to the timelessness of childhood—and both, typically, are stumbled upon in the full flush of summertime. Perhaps, as a character observes, "There's only one summer to a customer," but Serling, it seems, got more than his share.

T.E.D. Klein

THE MIGHTY CASEY

There is a large, extremely decrepit stadium overgrown by weeds and high grass that is called, whenever it is referred to (which is seldom nowadays), Tebbet's Field and it lies in a borough of New York known as Brooklyn. Many years ago it was a baseball stadium housing a ball club known as the Brooklyn Dodgers, a major league baseball team then a part of the National League. Tebbet's Field today, as we've already mentioned, houses nothing but memories, a few ghosts and tier after tier of decaying wooden seats and cracked concrete floors. In its vast, gaunt emptiness nothing stirs except the high grass of what once was an infield and an outfield, in addition to a wind that whistles through the screen behind home plate and howls up to the rafters of the overhang of the grandstand.

This was one helluva place in its day, and in its day, the Brooklyn Dodgers was one rip-roaring ball club. In the last several years of its existence, however, it was referred to by most of the ticket-buying, turnstile-passers of Flatbush Avenue as "the shlumpfs!". This arose from the fact that for five years running, the Brooklyn Dodgers were something less than spectacular. In their last year as members of the National League, they won exactly forty-nine ball games. And by mid-August of that campaign a "crowd" at Tebbet's Field was considered to be any ticket-buying group of more than eighty-six customers.

After the campaign of that year, the team dropped out of the league. It was an unlamented, unheralded event pointing up the fact that baseball fans have a penchant for winners and a short memory for losers. The paying customers proved more willing to travel uptown to the Polo Grounds to see the Giants, or crosstown to Yankee Stadium to see the Yankees, or downtown to any movie theater or bowling alley than to watch the Brooklyn Dodgers stumble around in the basement of the league season after season. This is also commentative on the forgetfulness of baseball enthusiasts, since there are probably only a handful who recollect that for a wondrous month and a half, the Brooklyn Dodgers were a most unusual ball club that last season. They didn't start out as an unusual ball club. They started out as shlumpfs as any Dodger fan can articulately and colorfully tell you. But for one month and one half they were one helluva club. Principally because of a certain person on the team roster.

It all began this way. Once upon a time a most unusual event happened on the way over to the ball park. This unusual event was a left-hander named Casey!

It was try-out day for the Brooklyn Dodgers and Mouth McGarry, the manager of the club, stood in the dugout, one foot on the parapet, both hands shoved deep into his hip pockets, his jaw hanging several inches below his upper lip. "Try-out days" depressed Mouth McGarry more than the standing of his ball club, which was depressing enough as it stood, or lay—which would be more apt, since they were now in last place, just thirty-one games out of first. Behind him, sitting on a bench, was Bertram Beasley, the general manager of the ball club. Beasley was a little man whose face looked like an X ray of an ulcer. His eyes were sunk deep into his little head, and his little head was sunk deep in between two narrow shoulder blades. Each time he looked up to survey McGarry, and beyond him, several gentlemen in baseball uniforms, he heaved a deep sigh and saw to it that his head sank just a few inches deeper into his shoulder blades. The sigh Bertram Beasley heaved was the only respectable heave going on within a radius of three hundred feet of home plate. The three pitchers that scout Maxwell Jenkins had sent over turned out to be pitchers in name only. One of them, as a matter of fact, had looked so familiar that McGarry swore he'd seen him pitch in the 1911 World Series. As it turned out, McGarry had been mistaken. It was not he who had pitched in the 1911 World Series but his nephew.

Out on the field McGarry watched the current crop of try-outs and kept massaging his heart. Reading left to right they were a tall, skinny kid with three-inch-thick glasses; a seventeen-year-old fat boy who weighed about two hundred and eighty pounds and stood five-foot-two; a giant, hulking farm boy who had taken off his spike shoes; and the aforementioned "pitcher" who obviously had dyed his hair black, but it was not a fast color and the hot summer sun was sending black liquid down both sides of his face. The four men were in the process of doing calisthenics. They were all out of step except the aging pitcher who was no longer doing calisthenics. He had simply sat down and was fanning himself with his mitt.

Beasley rose from the bench in the dugout and walked over to McGarry. Mouth turned to look at him.

"Grand-looking boys!"

"Who were you expecting?" Beasley said, sticking a cigar in his mouth. "The All Stars? You stick out a try-out sign for a last division club—" he pointed to the group doing the calisthenics, "and this is the material you usually round up." He felt a surge of anger as he stared into the broken-nosed face of Mouth McGarry. "Maybe if you were any kind of a manager, McGarry, you'd be able to whip stuff like this into shape."

McGarry stared at him like a scientist looking through a microscope at a bug. "I couldn't whip stuff like that into shape," he said, "if they were eggs and I was an electric mixer. You're the general manager of the club. Why don't you give me some ball-players?"

"You'd know what to do with them?" Beasley asked. "Twenty games out of fourth place and the only big average we've got is a manager with the widest mouth in either league. Maybe you'd better get reminded that when the Brooklyn Dodgers win one game we gotta call it a streak! Buddy boy," he said menacingly, "when contract time comes around, *you* don't have to." His cigar went out and he took out a match and lit it. Then he looked up toward home plate where a pitcher was warming up. "How's Fletcher doing?" he asked.

"Are you kidding?" Mouth spat thirty-seven feet off to the

left. "Last week he pitched four innings and allowed only six runs. That makes him our most valuable player of the month!"

The dugout phone rang and Beasley went over to pick it up. "Dugout," he said into the receiver. "What? Who?" He cupped his hand over the phone and looked over at Mouth. "You wanta look at a pitcher?" he asked.

"Are you kidding?" Mouth answered.

Beasley talked back into the phone. "Send him down," he said. He hung up the receiver and walked back over to Mouth. "He's a lefty," he announced.

"Lefty Shmefty," Mouth said. "If he's got more than one arm and less than four—he's for us!" He cupped his hands over his mouth and yelled out toward the field. "Hey, Monk!"

The catcher behind home plate rose from his squat and looked back over toward the dugout. "Yeah?"

"Fletcher can quit now," Mouth called to him. "I've got a new boy coming down. Catch him for a while."

"Check," the catcher said. Then he turned toward the pitcher. "Okay, Fletch. Go shower up."

Beasley walked back over to sit on the bench in the dugout. "You got the line-up for tonight?" he asked the manager.

"Working on it," Mouth said.

"Who starts?"

"You mean pitcher? I just feel them one by one. Whoever's warm goes to the mound." He spat again and put his foot back up on the parapet, staring out at the field. Once again he yelled out toward his ballplayers. "Chavez, stop already with the calisthenics."

He watched disgustedly as the three men stopped jumping up and down and the old man sitting on the ground looked relieved. Chavez thumbed them off the field and turned back toward the bench and shrugged a what-the-hell-can-I-do-with-things-like-this kind of shrug.

Mouth took out a handkerchief and wiped his face. He walked up the steps of the dugout and saw the sign sticking in the ground which read: "Brooklyn Dodgers—try-outs today." He pulled back his right foot and followed through with a vicious kick which sent the sign skittering along the ground. Then he went over to the third-base line, picked up a piece of grass and chewed it thoughtfully. Beasley left the dugout to join McGarry. He kneeled down alongside of him and picked up another piece of grass and began to chew. They knelt and lunched together until McGarry spit out his piece of grass and glared at Beasley.

"You know something, Beasley?" he inquired. "We are so deep in the cellar that our roster now includes an infield, an outfield and a furnace! And you know whose fault that is?"

Beasley spit out his own piece of grass and said, "You tell me!"

"It ain't mine," McGarry said defensively. "It just happens to be my luck to wind up with a baseball organization whose farm system consists of two silos and a McCormick reaper. The only thing I get sent up to me each spring is a wheat crop."

"McGarry," Beasley stated definitely, "if you had material, would you really know what to do with it? You ain't no Joe McCarthy. You ain't one half Joe McCarthy."

"Go die, will you," McGarry said. He turned back to stare down the third-base line at nothing in particular. He was unaware of the cherubic little white-haired man who had just entered the dugout. Beasley *did* see him and stared wide-eyed. The little old man came up behind Mouth and cleared his throat.

"Mr. McGarry?" he said. "I am Dr. Stillman. I called about your trying out a pitcher."

Mouth turned slowly to look at him, screwed up his face in distaste. "All right! What's the gag? What about it, Grampa? Did this muttonhead put you up to it?" He turned to Beasley. "This is the pitcher, huh? Big joke. Yok, yok, yok. Big joke."

Dr. Stillman smiled benignly. "Oh, I'm not a pitcher," he said, "though I've thrown baseballs in my time. Of course, that was before the war."

"Yeah," Mouth interjected. "Which war? The Civil War? You don't look old enough to have spent the winter at Valley Forge." Then he glared at him intently. "Come to think of it— was it really as cold as they say?"

Stillman laughed gently. "You really have a sense of humor, Mr. McGarry." Then he turned and pointed toward the dugout. "Here's Casey now," he said.

Mouth turned to look expectantly over the little old man's shoulder. Casey was coming out of the dugout. From cleats to the button on top of his makeshift baseball cap there was a frame roughly six feet, six inches high. The hands at his sides were the dimensions of two good-sized cantaloupes. His shoulders, McGarry thought to himself, made Primo Carnero look like the "before" in a Charles Atlas ad. In short, Casey was long. He was also broad. And in addition, he was one of the most powerful men either McGarry or Beasley had ever seen. He carried himself with the kind of agile grace that bespeaks an athlete and the only jarring note in the whole picture was a face that should have been handsome, but wasn't, simply because it had no spark, no emotion, no expression of any sort at all. It was just a face. Nice teeth, thin lips, good straight nose, deep-set blue eyes, a shock of sandy hair that hung out from under his baseball cap. But it was a face, McGarry thought, that looked as if it had been painted on.

"You're the lefty, huh?" McGarry said. "All right." He pointed toward the home plate. "You see that guy with the great big mitt on? He's what's known as a catcher. His name is Monk. Throw a few into him."

"Thanks very much, Mr. McGarry," Casey said dully.

He went toward home plate. Even the voice, McGarry thought. Even the voice. Dead. Spiritless. McGarry picked up another long piece of grass and headed back to the dugout, followed by Beasley and the little old man who looked like something out of Charles Dickens. In the dugout, McGarry assumed his familiar pose of one foot on the parapet, both fists in his hip pockets. Beasley left the dugout to return to his office which was his custom on days the team didn't play. He would lock himself in his room and add up attendance figures, then look through the want ads of *The New York Times*. Just Stillman and Mouth McGarry stood in the dugout now, and the elderly little man watched everything with wide, fluttering eyes like a kid on a tour through a fireworks factory. McGarry turned to him.

"You his father?"

"Casey's?" Stillman asked. "Oh, no. He has no father. I guess you'd call me his—well, kind of his creator."

Dr. Stillman's words went past McGarry the way the super-chief goes by a water tank. "That a fact?" he asked rhetorically. "How old is he?"

"How old is he?" Stillman repeated. He thought for a moment. "Well, that's a little difficult to say."

Mouth looked over toward the empty bench with a see-the-kind-of-idiocy-I-have-to-put-up-with kind of look. "That's a little difficult to say," he mimicked fiercely.

Stillman hurriedly tried to explain. "What I mean is," he

said, "it's hard to be chronological when discussing Casey's age. Because he's only been in existence for three weeks. What I mean is—he has the physique and mind of roughly a twenty-two-year-old, but in terms of how long he's been here—the answer to that would be about three weeks."

The words had poured out of Dr. Stillman's mouth and McGarry had blinked through the whole speech.

"Would you mind going over that again?" he asked.

"Not at all," Dr. Stillman said kindly. "It's really not too difficult. You see I made Casey. I built him." He smiled a big, beatific smile. "Casey's a robot," he said. The old man took a folded and creased document from his vest pocket and held it out to Mouth. "These are the blueprints I worked from," he said.

Mouth swatted the papers out of the old man's hand and dug his gnarled knuckles into the sides of his head. That goddamn Beasley. There were no depths to which that sonofabitch wouldn't go to make his life miserable. He had to gulp several times before he could bring himself to speak to the old man and when finally words came, the voice didn't sound like his at all.

"Old friend," his voice came out in a wheeze. "Kind, sweet old man. Gentle grandfather, with the kind eyes, I am very happy that he's a robot. Of course, that's what he is." He patted Stillman's cheek. "That's just what he is, a nice robot." Then there was a sob in his voice as he glared up at the roof of the dugout. "Beasley, you crummy sonofabitch!" A robot yet. This fruity old man and that miserable ball club and the world all tumbling down and it just never ended and it never got any better. A robot!

Dr. Stillman scurried after Mouth who had walked up the steps of the dugout and out on to the field. He paused along the third-base line and began to chew grass again. Over his shoulder Casey was throwing pitches into the catcher at home plate, but Mouth didn't even notice him.

"I dunno," he said to nobody in particular. "I don't even know what I'm *doing* in baseball."

He looked uninterested as Casey threw a curve ball that broke sharply just a foot out in front of home plate and then shrieked into the catcher's mitt like a small, circular, white express train.

"That Beasley," Mouth said to the ground. "That guy's got as much right in the front office as I've got in the Alabama State

Senate. This guy is a nothing, that's all. Simply a nothing. He was born a nothing. He's a nothing now!"

On the mound Casey wound up again and threw a hook that screamed in toward home plate, swerved briefly to the left, shot back to the right, and then landed in the catcher's mitt exactly where it had been placed as a target. Monk stared at the ball wide-eyed and then toward the young pitcher on the mound. He examined the ball, shook his head, then threw it back to him, shaking his head slowly from side to side.

Meanwhile Mouth continued his daily analysis of the situation to a smiling Dr. Stillman and an empty grandstand. "I've had bum teams before," he was saying. "Real bad outfits. But this one!" He spat out the piece of grass. "These guys make Abner Doubleday a criminal! You know where I got my last pitcher? He was mowing the infield and I discovered that he was the only guy on the club who could reach home plate from the pitcher's mound on less than two bounces. He is now ensconced as my number two starter. That's exactly where he's ensconced!"

He looked out again at Casey to see him throw a straight, fast ball that landed in Monk's glove and sent smoke rising from home plate. Monk whipped off the glove and held his hand agonizedly. When the pain subsided he stared at the young pitcher disbelievingly. It was then and only then that picture and sound began to register in Mouth McGarry's mind. He suddenly thought about the last two pitches that he'd seen and his eyebrows shot up like elevators. Monk approached him, holding his injured hand.

"You see him?" Monk asked in an incredulous voice. "That kid? He picks up where Feller left off, I swear to God! He's got a curve, hook, knuckler, slider and a fast ball that almost went through my palm! He's got control like he uses radar. This is the best pitcher I ever caught in my life, Mouth!"

Mouth McGarry stood there as if mesmerized, staring at Casey who was walking slowly away from the mound. Monk tucked his catcher's mitt under his arm and started toward the dugout.

"I swear," he said as he walked, "I never seen anything like it. Fantastic. He pitches *like nothing human!*"

Mouth McGarry and Dr. Stillman looked at one another. Dr. Stillman's quiet blue eyes looked knowing and Mouth McGarry chewed furiously down the length of a piece of grass, his last bite taking in a quarter inch of his forefinger. He blew on it, waved it in the air and stuck it in his mouth as he turned toward Stillman, his voice shaking with excitement.

"Look, Grampa," Mouth said, "I want that boy! Understand? I'll have a contract drawn up inside of fifteen minutes. And don't give me no tough talk either. You brought him here on a try-out and that gives us first option."

"He's a robot, you know," Stillman began quietly.

Mouth grabbed him and spoke through clenched teeth. "Grampa," he said in a quiet fury, "don't ever say that to nobody! We'll just keep that in the family here." Then suddenly remembering, he looked around wildly for the blueprint, picked it up from the ground and shoved it in his shirt pocket. He saw Stillman looking at him.

"Would that be honest?" Stillman said, rubbing his jaw.

Mouth pinched his cheek and said, "You sweet old guy, you're looking at a desperate man. And if the baseball commissioner ever found out I was using a machine—I'd be dead. D-E-D! Dead, you know?" Mouth's face brightened into a grimace which vaguely brought to mind a smile when he saw Casey approaching. "I like your stuff, kid," Mouth said to him. "Now you go into the locker room and change your clothes." He turned to Stillman. "He wears clothes, don't he?"

"Oh, by all means," Stillman answered.

"Good," Mouth said, satisfied. "Then we'll go up to Beasley's office and sign the contract." He looked at the tall pitcher standing there and shook his head. "If you could pitch once a week like I just seen you pitch, the only thing that stands between us and a pennant is if your battery goes dead or you rust in the rain! As of right now, Mr. Casey—you're the number one pitcher of the Brooklyn Dodgers!"

Stillman smiled happily and Casey just looked impassive, no expression, no emotion, neither satisfied nor dissatisfied. He just stood there. Mouth hurried back to the dugout, took the steps three at a time and grabbed the phone.

"General Manager's office," he screamed into it. "Yeah!" In a moment he heard Beasley's voice. "Beasley?" he said. "Listen, Beasley, I want you to draw up a contract. It's for that left-hander. His name is Casey. That's right. Not just good, Beasley. Fantastic. Now you draw up that contract in a hurry." There was an angry murmur at the other end of the line. "Who do you think I'm giving orders to," Mouth demanded. He slammed the phone down then turned to look out toward the field.

Stillman and Casey were heading toward the dugout. Mouth rubbed his jaw pensively. Robot-shmobot, he said to himself. He's got a curve, knuckler, fast ball, slider, change of pace and hallelujah—he's got two arms!

He picked up one of Bertram Beasley's cigars off the ground, smoothed out the pleats and shoved it into his mouth happily. For the first time in many long and bleak months Mouth McGarry had visions of a National League pennant fluttering across his mind. So must John McGraw have felt when he got his first look at Walter Johnson or Muller Higgins, when George Herman Ruth came to him from the Boston Red Sox. And McGarry's palpitations were surely not unlike those of Marse Joseph McCarthy when a skinny Italian kid named DiMaggio ambled out into center field for the first time. Such was the bonfire of hope that was kindled in Mouth McGarry's chest as he looked at the blank-faced, giant left-hander walking toward him, carrying on his massive shoulders, albeit invisibly, the fortunes of the Brooklyn Dodgers and Mrs. McGarry's son, Mouth!

It was a night game against St. Louis forty-eight hours later. The dressing room of the Brooklyn Dodgers was full of noise, clattering cleats, slammed locker doors, the plaintive protests of Bertram Beasley who was accusing the trainer of using too much liniment (at seventy-nine cents a bottle), and the deep, bullfrog profanity of Mouth McGarry who was all over the room, on every bench, in every corner, and in every head of hair.

"You sure he's got the signals down, Monk?" he asked his catcher for the fourteenth time.

Monk's eyes went up toward the ceiling and he said tiredly, "Yeah, boss. He knows them."

Mouth walked over to the pitcher who was just tying up his shoes. "Casey," he said urgently, wiping the sweat from his forehead, "if you forget them signals—you call time and bring Monk out to you, you understand? I don't want no cross-ups." He took out a large handkerchief and mopped his brow, then he pulled out a pill from his side pocket and plopped it into his mouth. "And above all," he cautioned his young pitcher, "—don't be nervous!"

Casey looked up at him puzzled. "Nervous?" he asked.

Stillman, who had just entered the room, walked over to them smiling. "Nervous, Casey," he explained, "ill at ease. As if one of your electrodes were—"

Mouth drowned him out loudly, "You know 'nervous,' Casey! Like as if there's two outs in the ninth, you're one up, and you're pitchin' against DiMaggio and he comes up to the plate lookin' intent!"

Casey stared at him deadpan. "That wouldn't make me nervous. I don't know anyone named DiMaggio."

"He don't know anyone named DiMaggio," Monk explained seriously to Mouth McGarry.

"I heard 'im," Mouth screamed at him. "I heard 'im!" He turned to the rest of the players, looked at his watch then bellowed out, "All right, you guys, let's get going!"

Monk took Casey's arm and pulled him off the bench and then out the door. The room resounded with the clattering cleats on concrete floor as the players left the room for the dugout above. Mouth McGarry stood alone in the middle of the room and felt a dampness settle all over him. He pulled out a sopping wet handkerchief and wiped his head again.

"This humidity," he said plaintively to Dr. Stillman who sat on the bench surveying him, "is killing me. I've never felt such dampness—I swear to God!"

Stillman looked down at Mouth's feet. McGarry was standing with one foot in a bucket of water.

"Mr. McGarry," he pointed to the bucket.

Mouth lifted up his foot sheepishly and shook it. Then he took out his bottle of pills again, popped two of them in his mouth, gulped them down and pointed apologetically to his stomach. "Nerves," he said. "Terrible nerves. I don't sleep at night. I keep seeing pennants before my eyes. Great big, red, white and blue pennants. All I can think about is knocking off the Giants and then taking four straight from the Yanks in the World Series." He sighed deeply. "But for that matter," he continued, "I'd like to knock off the Phillies and the Cards, too. Or the Braves or Cincinnati." A forlorn note crept into his voice now. "Or anybody when you come down to it!"

Dr. Stillman smiled at him. "I think Casey will come through for you, Mr. McGarry."

Mouth looked at the small white-haired man. "What have

you got riding on this?" he asked. "What's your percentage?"

"You mean with Casey?" Stillman said. "Just scientific, that's all. Purely experimental. I think that Casey is a superman of a sort and I'd like that proven. Once I built a home economist. Marvelous cook. I gained forty-six pounds before I had to dismantle her. Now with Casey's skills, his strength and his accuracy, I realized he'd be a baseball pitcher. But in order to prove my point I had to have him pitch in competition. Also as an acid test, I had to have him pitch with absolutely the worst ball team I could find."

"That's very nice of you, Dr. Stillman," Mouth said. "I appreciate it."

"Don't mention it. Now shall we go out on the field?"

Mouth opened the door for him. "After you," he said.

Dr. Stillman went out and Mouth was about to follow him when he stopped dead, one eyebrow raised. "Wait a minute, dammit," he shouted. "The worst?" He started out after the old man. "You should have seen the Phillies in 1903!" he yelled after him.

An umpire screamed, "Play ball!" and the third baseman took a throw from the catcher then, rubbing up the ball, he carried it over to Casey on the mound, noticing in a subconscious section of his mind that this kid with the long arms and the vast shoulders had about as much spirit as a lady of questionable virtue on a Sunday morning after a long Saturday night. A few moments later, the third baseman cared very little about the lack of animation on Casey's features. This feeling was shared by some fourteen thousand fans, who watched the left-hander look dully in for a sign, then throw a side-arm fast ball that left them gasping and sent the entire dugout of the St. Louis Cardinals to their feet in amazement.

There are fast balls and fast balls, but nothing remotely resembling the white streak that shot out of Casey's left hand, almost invisibly toward the plate, had ever been witnessed. A similar thought ran through the mind of the St. Louis batter as he blinked at the sound of the ball hitting the catcher's mitt and took a moment to realize that the pitch had been made and he had never laid eyes on it.

This particular St. Louis batter was the first of twenty-five men to face Casey that evening. Eighteen of them struck out and only two of them managed to get to first base, one on a fluke single that was misjudged over first base. By the sixth inning most of the people in the stadium were on their feet, aware that they were seeing something special in the tall left-hander on the mound. And by the ninth inning when Brooklyn had won its first game in three weeks by a score of two to nothing, the stadium was in a frenzy.

There was also a frenzy of a sort in the Brooklyn dugout. The corners of Mouth McGarry's mouth tilted slightly upward in a grimace which the old team trainer explained later to a couple of mystified ballplayers was a "smile." Mouth hadn't been seen to smile in the past six years.

Bertram Beasley celebrated the event by passing out three brand new cigars and one slightly used one (to McGarry). But the notable thing about the Brooklyn dugout and later the locker room was that the ball team suddenly looked different. In the space of about two and a half hours, it had changed from some slogging, lead-footed, aging second-raters to a snappy, heads-up, confident looking crew of ballplayers who had a preoccupation with winning. The locker room resounded with laughter and horse play, excited shouting drifted out from the showers. All this in a room that for the past three years had been as loud and comical as a funeral parlor.

While wet towels sailed across the room and cleated shoes banged against locker doors, one man remained silent. This was the pitcher named Casey. He surveyed the commotion around him with a mild interest, but was principally concerned with unlacing his shoes. The only emotion he displayed was when Doc Barstow, the team trainer, started to massage his arm. He jumped up abruptly and yanked the arm away, leaving Barstow puzzled. Later on Barstow confided to Mouth McGarry that the kid's arm felt like a piece of tube steel. McGarry gulped, smiled nervously and asked Doc how his wife had been feeling. All this happened on the night of July 1st.

Three weeks later the Brooklyn Dodgers had moved from the cellar to fifth place in the National League. They had won twenty-three games in a row, seven of them delivered on a platter by one left-handed pitcher named Casey. Two of his ball games were no-hitters and his earned run average was by far the lowest not only in either League, but in the history of baseball. His name was on every tongue in the nation, his picture on every sports page, and contracts had already been signed so that he would be appearing on cereal boxes before the month was out. And as in life itself, winning begot winning. Even without Casey, the Dodgers were becoming a feared and formidable ball club. Weak and ineffectual bat-slappers, who had never hit more than .200 in their lives, were becoming Babe Ruths. Other pitchers who had either been too green or too decrepit were beginning to win ball games along with Casey. And there was a spirit now— an aggressiveness, a drive, that separated the boys from the pennant-winners and the Brooklyn Dodgers were potentially the latter. They looked it and they played it.

Mouth McGarry was now described as "that master strategist" and "a top field general" and, frequently, "the winningest manager of the year" in sports columns which had previously referred to him as "that cement-headed oaf who handles a ball club like a bull would handle a shrimp cocktail." The team was drawing more customers in single games than they'd garnered in months at a time during previous seasons. And the most delightful thing to contemplate was the fact that Casey, who had begun it all, looked absolutely invulnerable to fatigue, impervious to harm, and totally beyond the normal hazards of pitchers. He had no stiff arms, no sore elbows, no lapses of control, no nothing. He pitched like a machine and while it was mildly disconcerting, it was really no great concern that he also walked, talked and acted like a machine. There was no question about it. The Dodgers would have been in first place by mid-August at the very latest, if a shortstop on the Philadelphia Phillies had not hit a line ball directly at Casey on the mound which caught him just a few inches above his left eye.

The dull, sickening thud was the shot heard all around the borough and if anyone had clocked Mouth McGarry's run from the dugout to the mound where his ace left-hander was now sprawled face downward, two guys named Landy and Bannister would have been left in eclipse. Bertram Beasley, in his box seat in the grandstand, simply chewed off one quarter of his cigar and swallowed it, then fell off his seat in a dead faint.

The players grouped around Casey and Doc Barstow motioned for a stretcher. McGarry grabbed his arm and whispered at him as if already they were in the presence of the dead.

"Will he pull through, Doc? Will he make it?"

The team doctor looked grim. "I think we'd better get him to a hospital. Let's see what they say about him there."

Half the team provided an escort for the stretcher as it moved slowly off the field. It looked like a funeral cortège behind a recently deceased head of state with Mouth McGarry as the principal mourner. It was only then that he remembered to motion into the bullpen for a new pitcher, an eager young towhead out of the Southern Association League who had just been called up.

The kid ambled toward the mound. It was obvious that at this moment he wished he were back in Memphis, Tennessee, sorting black-eyed peas. He took the ball from the second baseman, rubbed it up, then reached down for the rosin bag. He rubbed his hands with the bag then rubbed the ball, then rubbed the bag then put down the ball, wound up and threw the rosin bag. As it turned out, this was his best pitch of the evening. Shortly thereafter he walked six men in a row and hit one man in the head. Luckily, it was a hotdog vendor in the bleachers so that no harm was done in terms of moving any of the men on base. This was taken care of by his next pitch to the number-four batter on the Philadelphia Phillies squad, who swung with leisurely grace at what the kid from Memphis referred to as his fast ball, and sent it on a seven-hundred-foot trip over the center field fence, which took care of the men on the bases. The final score was thirteen to nothing in favor of the Phillies, but Mouth McGarry didn't even wait until the last out. With two outs in the ninth, he and Beasley ran out of the park and grabbed a cab. Beasley handed the driver a quarter and said, "Never mind the cops. Get to the hospital."

The hackie looked at the quarter then back toward Beasley and said, "This better be a rare mint, or I'll see to it that you have your baby in the cab!"

They arrived at the hospital twelve minutes later and pushed their way through a lobby full of reporters to get to an elevator and up to the floor where Casey had been taken for observation. They arrived in his room during the last stages of the examination. A nurse shushed them as they barged into the room.

"Booby," McGarry gushed, racing toward the bed.

The doctor took off his stethoscope and hung it around his neck. "You the father?" he asked Mouth.

"The father," McGarry chortled. "I'm closer than any father."

He noticed now for the first time that Dr. Stillman was sitting quietly in the corner of the room looking like a kindly old owl full of wisdom hidden under his feathers.

"Well, gentlemen, there's no fracture that I can see," the doctor announced professionally. "No concussion. Reflexes seem normal—"

Beasley exhaled sounding like a strong north wind. "I can breathe again," he told everyone.

"All I could think of," Mouth said, "was there goes Casey! There goes the pennant! There goes the Series!" He shook his head forlornly, "And there goes my career."

The doctor picked up Casey's wrist and began to feel for the pulse. "Yes, Mr. Casey," he smiled benevolently down into the expressionless face and unblinking eyes, "I think you're in good shape. I'll tell you though, when I heard how the ball hit you in the temple I wondered to myself how—"

The doctor stopped talking. His fingers compulsively moved around the wrist. His eyes went wide. After a moment he opened up Casey's pajamas and sent now shaking fingers running over the chest area. After a moment he stood up, took out a handkerchief and wiped his face.

"What's the matter?" Mouth asked nervously. "What's wrong?"

The doctor sat down in a chair. "There's nothing wrong," he said softly. "Not a thing wrong. Everything's fine. It's just that—"

"Just that what?" Beasley asked.

The doctor pointed a finger toward the bed. "It is just that this man doesn't have any pulse. No heart beat." Then he looked up toward the ceiling. "This man," he said in a strained voice, "this man isn't alive."

There was absolute silence in the room marred only by the slump of Beasley's body as he slid quietly to the floor. No one paid any attention to him. It was Dr. Stillman who finally spoke.

"Mr. McGarry," he said in a quiet, firm voice, "I do believe it'll have to come out now."

Beasley opened his eyes. "All right, you sonofabitch, McGarry, what are you trying to pull off?"

Mouth looked around the room as if searching for an extra bed. He looked ill. "Beasley," he said plaintively, "you ain't gonna like this. But it was Casey or it was nothing. God, what a pitcher! And he was the only baseball player I ever managed who didn't eat nothing."

Stillman cleared his throat and spoke to the doctor. "I think you should know before you go any further that Casey has no pulse or heart beat . . . because he hasn't any heart. He's a robot."

There was the sound of another slump as Bertram Beasley fell back unconscious. This time he didn't move.

"A *what?*" the doctor asked incredulously.

"That's right," Stillman said. "A robot."

The doctor stared at Casey on the bed who stared right back at him. "Are you sure?" the doctor asked in a hushed voice.

"Oh, by all means. I built him."

The doctor slowly removed his coat and then took off his tie. He marched toward the bed with his eyes strangely wide and bright. "Casey," he announced, "get up and strip. Hear me? Get up and strip."

Casey got up and stripped and twenty minutes later the doctor had opened the window and was leaning out breathing in the evening air. Then he turned, removed his stethescope from around his neck and put it in his black bag. He took the blood pressure equipment from the night-stand and added this to the bag. He made a mental note to check the X rays as soon as they came out, but knew this would be gratuitous because it was all very, very evident. The man on the bed wasn't a man at all. He was one helluva specimen, but a man he wasn't! The doctor lit a cigarette and looked across the room.

"Under the circumstances," he said, "I'm afraid I must notify the baseball commissioner. That's the only ethical procedure."

"What do you have to be ethical about it for?" McGarry challenged him. "What the hell are you—a Giant fan?"

The doctor didn't answer. He took the twenty or thirty sheets of paper that he'd been making notes on and rammed them in his pocket. He mentally ran down the list of medical societies and organizations that would have to be informed of this. He also devised the opening three or four paragraphs to a monumental paper he'd write for a medical journal on the first mechanical man. He was in for a busy time. He carried his black bag to the door, smiled and went out, wondering just how the

American Medical Association would react to this one. The only sound left in the room was Beasley's groaning, until McGarry walked over to Casey on the bed.

"Casey," he said forlornly, "would you move over?"

The Daily Mirror had it first because one of the interns in the maternity ward was really a leg man for them. But the two wire services picked it up twenty minutes later and by six the following morning the whole world knew about Casey—the mechanical man. Several scientists were en route from Europe, and Dr. Stillman and Casey were beleaguered in a New York hotel room by an army of photographers and reporters. Three missile men at Cape Canaveral sent up a fabulous rocket that hit the moon dead eye only to discover that the feat made page twelve of the afternoon editions because the first eleven pages were devoted exclusively to a meeting to be held by the commissioner of baseball, who had announced he would make a decision on the Casey case by suppertime.

At four-thirty that afternoon the commissioner sat behind his desk, drumming on it with the end of a pencil. A secretary brought him a folder filled with papers and in the brief moment of the office door opening, he could see the mob of reporters out in the corridor.

"What about the reporters?" the secretary asked him.

Mouth McGarry, sitting in a chair close to the desk, made a suggestion at this point as to what might be done to the reporters or, more specifically, what they could do to themselves. The secretary looked shocked and left the room. The commissioner leaned back in his chair.

"You understand, McGarry," he said, "that I'm going to have to put this out for publication. Casey must definitely be suspended."

Bertram Beasley, sitting on a couch across the room, made a little sound deep in his throat, but stayed conscious.

"Why?" Mouth demanded noisily.

The commissioner pounded a fist on the desk top. "Because he's a robot, Goddamn it," he said for the twelfth time that hour.

Mouth spread out his palms. "So he's a robot," he said simply.

Once again the commissioner picked up a large manual. "Article six, section two, the Baseball Code," he said pontifically.

Dodgers, I want to tell you, and since I was the man who discovered Casey—"

The reporters rapidly left the room followed by the commissioner and his secretary, followed by Casey and Stillman.

"It behooves me to tell you gentlemen," Mouth continued,
wetting his lips over the word "behooves" and wondering to himself where he got the word. "It behooves me to make mention of
the fact that the Brooklyn Dodgers are the team to beat. We've
got the speed, the stamina," he recollected now the Pat O'Brien
speech in a Knute Rockne picture, "the vim, the vigor, the
vitality—"

He was unaware of the door slamming shut and unaware
that Bertram Beasley was the only other man in the room. "And
with this kind of stuff," he continued, in the Knute Rockne voice,
"the National League pennant and the World Series and—"

"McGarry," Beasley yelled at him.

Mouth started as if suddenly waking from a dream.

Beasley rose from the couch. "Why don't you drop dead?"
He walked out of the room, leaving Mouth all by himself, wondering how Pat O'Brien wound up that speech in the locker room
during the halftime of that vital Army–Notre Dame game.

How either McGarry or Bertram Beasley got through the
next twenty-odd hours was a point of conjecture with both of
them. Mouth emptied his bottle of nerve pills and spent a sleepless night pacing his hotel room floor. Beasley could recall only
brief moments of consciousness between swoons which occurred
every time the phone rang.

The following night the team was dressing in the locker
room. They were playing the first of a five-game series against
the New York Giants and McGarry had already devised nine different batteries, then torn them all up. He now sat on a bench
surveying his absolutely silent ballplayers. There was not a
sound. At intervals each pair of eyes would turn toward the
phone on the wall. Beasley had already phoned Dr. Stillman's
residence seven times that evening and received no answer. He
was on the phone now, talking to the long-distance operator in
New Jersey.

"Yeah," Beasley said into the phone. "Yeah, well thank you
very much, operator."

Mouth and the rest of the players waited expectantly.

"Well?" Mouth asked. "How is he?"

Beasley shook his head. "I don't know. The operator still can't get an answer."

Monk, the big catcher, rose from the bench. "Maybe he's right in the middle of the operation," he suggested.

Mouth whirled around at him, glaring. "So he's in the middle of the operation! Whatsa matter, he can't use one hand to pick up a phone?" He looked up at the clock on the wall then jutted his jaw fiercely, his eyes scanning the bench. "We can't wait no longer," he announced. "I got to turn in a battery. Corrigan," he said pointing toward one of the players, "you'll pitch tonight. And now the rest of you guys!" He stuck his hands in his back pockets and paced back and forth in front of them in a rather stylized imitation of Pat O'Brien.

"All right, you guys," he said grimly. "All right, you guys!" He stopped pacing and pointed toward the door. "That's the enemy out there," he said, his voice quivering a little. "That's the New York Giants." He spoke the words as if they were synonymous with a social disease. "And while we're out there playing tonight"—again his voice quivered—"there's a big fellah named Casey lying on a table, struggling to stay alive."

Tears shone in Monk's eyes as the big catcher got a mental picture of a courageous kid lying on a hospital table. Gippy Resnick, the third baseman, sniffed and then honked into a handkerchief as a little knot of sentiment tightened up his throat. Bertram Beasley let out a sob as he thought about what the attendance record was, six weeks B.C.—before Casey—and did some more projecting on what it would be without Casey. Mouth McGarry walked back and forth before the line of players.

"I know," he said, his voice tight and strained. "I know that his last words before that knife went into his chest were—'Go up there, Dodgers, and win one for the big guy!'"

The last words of this speech were choked by the tears that rolled down McGarry's face and the sob that caught in his own chest.

The street door to the locker room opened and Dr. Stillman came in, followed by Casey. But all the players were watching Mouth McGarry, who had now moved into his big finale scene.

"I want to tell you something, guys! From now on"—he sniffed loudly—"from now on there's gonna be a ghost in that dugout. Everytime you pick up a bat, look over to where Casey used to sit—because he's gonna be there in spirit rooting for us, cheering for us, yellin', 'Go Dodgers, go!'"—McGarry turned and looked at Casey, who was smiling at him. Mouth nodded perfunctorily. "Hello there, Casey," he said and turned back to the team. "Now I'm gonna tell you something else about that big guy. This fellah has a heart. Not a real heart, maybe, but this fellah that's lyin' there with a hole in his chest—"

Mouth's lower jaw dropped seven inches, as he turned very slowly to look at Casey. He had no chance to say anything, however, because the team had pushed him aside as they rushed toward the hero, shaking his hand, pounding him on the back, pulling, grabbing, shouting at him. Mouth spent a moment recovering and then screamed, "All right, knock it off! Let's have quiet! Quiet! QUIET!" He pulled players away from Casey and finally stood in front of the big pitcher. "Well?" he asked.

Stillman smiled. "Go ahead, Casey. Tell him."

It was then that everyone in the room noticed Casey's face. He was smiling. It was a big smile. A broad smile. An enveloping smile. It went across his face and up and down. It shone in his eyes. "Listen, Mr. McGarry," he said proudly. He pointed a thumb at his chest and Mouth put his ear there. He could hear the steady tick, tick, tick.

Mouth stepped back and shouted excitedly. "You got a heart!"

There was a chorus of delighted exclamation and comment from all the players and Beasley, poised for a faint, decided against it.

"And look at that smile," Stillman said over the shouting. "That's the one thing I couldn't get him to do before—smile!"

Casey threw his arm around the old man. "It's wonderful. It's just wonderful. Now I feel—I feel—like—togetherness!"

The team roared their approval and Bertram Beasley mounted a rubbing table, cupping his hands like a megaphone, and shouted, "All right, Dodgers, out on the field. Let's go, team. Casey starts tonight. The new Casey!"

The team thundered out on to the field, pushing Mouth McGarry out of the way and blotting out the first part of the speech which had begun, "All right, you guys, with vim, vigor and vital—" He never got to finish the speech because Monk, Resnick and a utility infielder had carried him with their momentum out the door and up to the dugout.

When Casey's name was announced as the starter for the

Dodgers that night the crowd let out a roar that dwarfed any thunder ever heard in or around the environs of New York City. And when Casey stepped out on the field and headed toward the mound, fifty-seven thousand eight hundred and thirty-three people stood up and applauded as one, and it was only the second baseman who, as he carried the ball over to the pitcher, noticed that there were tears in Casey's eyes and an expression on his face that made him pause. True, he'd never seen *any* expression on Casey's face before, but this one made him stop and look over his shoulder as he went back to his base.

The umpire shouted, "Play ball," and the Dodgers began the running stream of chatter that always prefaced the first pitch. Monk, behind the plate, made a signal and then held up his glove as a target. Start with a fast ball, he thought. Let them know what they're up against, jar them a little bit. Confuse them. Unnerve them. That was the way Monk planned his strategy behind the plate. Not that much strategy was needed when Casey was on the mound, but it was always good to show the big guns first. Casey nodded, went into his windup and threw. Twelve seconds later a woman in a third-floor apartment three blocks away had her bedroom window smashed by a baseball that had traveled in the neighborhood of seven hundred feet out of Tebbet's Field.

Meanwhile, back at the field, the crowd just sat there silently as the leadoff batter of the New York Giants ambled around the base path heading home to the outstretched hands of several fellow Giants greeting him after his leadoff home run.

Mouth McGarry at this moment felt that he would never again suffer a stab of depression such as the one that now intruded into his head. He would recall later that his premonition was quite erroneous. He would feel stabs of depressions in innings number two, three and four that would make that first stab of depression seem like the after effect of a Miltown tablet. That's how bad it got forty-five minutes later, when Casey had allowed nine hits, had walked six men, and thrown two wild pitches, and had muffed a pop fly to the mound, which, McGarry roared to the bench around him, "could have been caught by a palsied Civil War veteran who lost an arm at Gettysburg."

In the seventh inning Mouth McGarry took his fifth walk over to the mound and this time didn't return to the bench till he'd motioned to the bullpen for Casey's relief—a very eager kid, albeit a nervous one, who chewed tobacco going to the mound and got violently sick as he crossed the third-base line because he swallowed a piece. Coughing hard, he arrived at the mound and took the ball from Mouth McGarry. Casey solemnly shoved his mitt into his hip pocket and took the long walk back toward the showers.

At ten minutes to midnight the locker room had been emptied. All the players save Casey had gone back to the hotel. Bertram Beasley had left earlier—on a stretcher in the sixth inning. In the locker room were a baseball manager who produced odd grunts from deep within his throat and kept shaking his head back and forth—and a kindly white-haired old man who built robots. Casey came out of the shower, wrapped in a towel. He smiled gently at Mouth and then went over to his locker where he proceeded to dress.

"Well?" Mouth shouted at him. "Well? One minute he's three Lefty Groves, the next minute he's the cousin to every New York Giant who ever lived. He's a tanker. He's a nothing. All right—you wanna tell me, Casey? You wanna explain? You might start by telling me how one man can throw nine pitched balls and give up four singles, two doubles, a triple and two home runs!"

The question remained unanswered. Stillman looked toward Casey and said very softly, "Shall I tell him?"

Casey nodded apologetically.

Stillman turned toward McGarry. "Casey has a heart," he said quietly.

Mouth fumed. "So? Casey has a heart! So I know he's gotta heart! So this ain't news, prof! Tell me something that is!"

"The thing is," Casey said in his first speech over three sentences since McGarry had met him. "The thing is, Mr. McGarry, I just couldn't strike out those poor fellahs. I didn't have it in me to do that—to hurt their feelings. I felt—I felt compassion!" He looked toward Stillman as if for confirmation.

Stillman nodded. "That's what he's got, Mr. McGarry. Compassion. See how he smiles?"

Casey grinned obediently and most happily, and Stillman returned his smile. "You see, Mr. McGarry," Stillman continued. "You give a person a heart—particularly someone like Casey, who hasn't been around long enough to understand things like competitiveness or drive or ego. Well," he shrugged, "that's what happens."

Mouth sat down on the bench, unscrewed the bottle of pills and found it was empty. He threw the bottle over his shoulder. "That's what happens to *him*," he said. "Shall I tell you what happens to me? I go back to being a manager of nine gleeps so old that I gotta rub them down with formaldehyde and revive them in between innings." He suddenly had a thought and looked up at Casey. "Casey," he asked, "don't you feel any of that compassion for the Brooklyn Dodgers?"

Casey smiled back at him. "I'm sorry, Mr. McGarry," he said. "It's just that I can't strike out fellahs. I can't bring myself to hurt their careers. Dr. Stillman thinks I should go into social work now. I'd like to help people. Right, Dr. Stillman?"

"That's right, Casey," Stillman answered.

"Are you going?" Casey asked McGarry as he saw the manager head for the door.

Mouth nodded.

"Well good-by, Mr. McGarry," Casey said. "And thank you for everything."

Mouth turned to him. The grin on his face was that of dying humanity all over the world. "Don't mention it," he said.

He sighed deeply and walked out to the warm August evening that awaited him and the black headlines on a newspaper stand just outside the stadium that said, "I told you so" at him, even though the lettering spelled out, "CASEY SHELLED FROM MOUND." A reporter stood on the corner, a guy McGarry knew slightly.

"What about it, McGarry?" the reporter asked. "What do you do for pitchers now?"

Mouth looked at him dully. "I dunno," he sighed. "I just feel them one by one and whoever's warm—"

He walked past the reporter and disappeared into the night, a broken-nosed man with sagging shoulders who thought he heard the rustle of pennants in the night air, and then realized it was three shirts on a clothesline that stretched across two of the adjoining buildings.

From Rod Serling's closing narration, "The Mighty Casey," *The Twilight Zone,* scheduled for telecast March 25, 1960, CBS Television Network.

A BASEBALL FIELD—LONG ANGLE SHOT
It is empty and in absolute quiet.

NARRATOR'S VOICE
Once upon a time there was a major
league team called the Brooklyn
Dodgers who during the last year
of their existence as a ball team
wound up in last place and shortly
thereafter wound up in oblivion.
They are rarely if ever mentioned
in these parts again. Rumor has
it that a ball club on the West
Coast is the residue of what was
left of the original ball club.
(a pause)
And on occasion in a dark bar off
Flatbush Avenue, someone might
whisper the name of a certain pitcher
with an exceptional left hand. Somebody else will softly murmur the
question—whatever happened to the
mighty Casey?
(a pause)
No, you won't find any of the answers
in the records. Though they are
available should anyone be interested
by checking under "B" for baseball
in The Twilight Zone!

FADE TO BLACK

ESCAPE CLAUSE

Walter Bedeker lay on his bed waiting for the doctor. He wore a heavy, wool bathrobe over heavy wool pajamas, and had a heavy wool scarf wrapped tightly around his head and knotted under the chin in a giant bow. On the nightstand next to him was a tray full of bottles. There were pills, lotions, antibiotics, nasal sprays, throat sprays, ear drops, nose drops, three boxes of Kleenex and a book titled, *How To Be Happy Though Bedridden*. He stared dourly up at the ceiling then cocked an irritated eye toward the bedroom door, beyond which he could hear his wife's footsteps walking from kitchen to living room.

Ethel his wife was healthy. Oh God, she was healthy! Like a horse was Ethel. Never even had a cold. But he, Walter Bedeker, went from crisis to crisis, ailment to ailment, agonizing pain to agonizing pain.

Walter Bedeker was forty-four years old. He was afraid of the following: death, disease, other people, germs, drafts and everything else. He had one interest in life, and that was Walter Bedeker; one preoccupation, the life and well being of Walter Bedeker; one abiding concern about society, if Walter Bedeker should die, how would it survive without him. In short, he was a gnome-faced little man who clutched at disease the way most people hunger for security.

Ethel entered his room for the fifth time that hour to even out his blankets, fluff up his pillow. He looked at her jaundice-eyed and didn't say anything except to groan slightly when she helped him put his head back down on the pillow.

"Head still ache, darling?" Ethel asked him.

"Ache, Ethel, is not the word for it," he told her through a taut mouth. "Ache is a mild inconvenience. What I have is an agony. What I have is a living torture!"

Ethel made a brave attempt at a sympathetic smile. Walter never talked of his ailments in anything less than superlatives and this was his fifth stay-in-bed that month. The door chimes rang and she was unable to keep the look of relief from crossing her features. Walter recognized it instantly.

"Can't stand being in the room with me, can you," he said to her. "Sick people bore you, don't they?" He turned away to look at the wall to his right. "That is the tragedy of illness," he said to the wall. "The fleeting compassion of your so-called loved ones!"

"Oh, Walter—" Ethel began, and then stopped. She shrugged resignedly and went to answer the front door.

The doctor was waiting there with his black bag and he followed Ethel into the bedroom.

"Well, how are you feeling today, Mr. Bedeker?" he asked. The doctor was tired and his feet hurt. He hated house calls unless they were emergencies and Walter Bedeker's beckonings were never emergencies. He had difficulty keeping the tiredness out of his voice.

"How do I look?" Bedeker barked at him.

The doctor smiled at him and said, "Rather well, as a matter of fact."

Bedeker's face screwed up like a persimmon and mimicked him fiercely. "Rather well, as a matter of fact, huh? Well I can assure you, doctor, I'm not rather well. I'm not in the least bit well. I'm a very sick man. Which you'll soon discover once you examine me. But I want you to tell me the worst. I don't want any cushioning. I'm not a coward, doctor."

"I'm sure you aren't. Hold your arm out, Mr. Bedeker. I'd like to take your pressure first."

Bedeker thrust out a remarkably well muscled arm for a man his age and the doctor wrapped the pressure cloth around it.

Ten minutes later he was putting most of his impedimenta back in the bag while Bedeker stared at him glumly.

"Well, doctor?"

The doctor closed the bag and turned to Bedeker without speaking.

"I asked you a question, doctor. How bad is it?"

"It isn't bad at all," the doctor said. "As a matter of fact, it's quite good. You have no temperature. Pressure normal. Respiration normal. Heart action normal. No infection. Throat clear. Nasal passages clear. Ears clear."

"What about the pains in my back and side? What about four sleepless nights in a row? What about *that*?" Bedeker shouted triumphantly.

The doctor shook his head. "What about that? 'That,' Mr. Bedeker, is psychosomatic!"

Bedeker's eyes grew large. "Psychosomatic? You're trying to tell me that I'm sick only in the mind?"

"Something like that, Mr. Bedeker," the doctor answered quietly. "There's nothing wrong with you, really, except the ailments you manufacture for yourself. Your pains, Mr. Bedeker, are imaginary. Your inability to sleep is a case of nerves—but nothing more. In short, Mr. Bedeker, you're a very healthy man!"

Walter Bedeker smiled sadly at his favorite confidant, the wall on the right, and talked to it, occasionally jerking his head toward the doctor.

"See? This is a doctor. Four years premed. Four years medical school. Two years internship. Two years residency. And what is he? I ask you, what is he?" Then he shouted, "A quack!"

The doctor had to smile in spite of himself. Ethel came in on tiptoe, and whispered to the doctor, "What's the prognosis?"

Bedeker shouted, "Don't ask *him*. The man's an idiot!"

"Walter, darling," Ethel said patiently, "don't excite yourself."

"Don't whisper," Bedeker shouted. "You're looking at half of my troubles right there," he said to the doctor. "This woman. This awful woman who runs around whispering all day long to make me *think* I'm sick even if I'm not. And I *am*," he added quickly. "I'm lying here at death's door and who's ushering me out? A quack and this whispering woman without a mind!"

"I'll call tomorrow, Mrs. Bedeker," the doctor said jovially.

"There'll be no need to call," Bedeker answered. "Just come on over with the death certificate and fill it out."

"Oh, Walter—" Ethel said piteously.

"Don't drench me with those crocodile tears of yours, idiot," Bedeker screamed at her. "She'd be so happy to get rid of me, doctor, I just can't tell you!"

The doctor was no longer smiling as he went out, followed by Ethel. At the front door he looked at her very closely. She must have been a very attractive woman in her day. God, to be married to that man for as long as she'd been married to him!

"How is he, doctor?" Ethel asked.

"Mrs. Bedeker," the doctor said, "your husband is one of the healthiest patients I have. If he were up in front of me for an exam to get into the combat Marines, I'd pass him with flying colors."

Ethel shook her head dubiously. "He's sick most of the time. He won't let me open a window in the house. He says for every cubic foot of air there are eight million, nine hundred thousand germs."

The doctor threw back his head and laughed. "He's probably right."

Ethel said worriedly, "And he's just quit his job. The fifth job he's quit since the first of the year. He says they make him work in a draft."

The doctor stopped laughing and looked at this small, comely woman in front of him. "Mrs. Bedeker," he said softly, "there isn't a thing in the world I can do for your husband. Or any other doctor for that matter—except, perhaps, a psychiatrist."

Ethel's hand went to her mouth in a shocked gesture. "A psychiatrist," she said.

The doctor nodded. "His trouble is in his mind. This awful fear of disease. This phobia about death. I suppose I'm oversimplifying it when I say there's nothing wrong with him because in a sense there really is. This constant worrying about himself is an illness of a sort. Has he always been this frightened?"

"Ever since I can remember," said Ethel. "When he was courting me he told me he was in the last stages of T.B. and only had a week to live." She looked away reminiscently and sadly. "I only married him because I felt so sorry for him—!" She bit her lip. "What I meant, doctor—"

The doctor patted her on the arm and said, "I understand. I'll give you a call tomorrow." He looked closely at her again, reached in his pocket for a pad and scribbled down a prescription. "Here," he said, handing it to her. "You look a little run-down yourself. This is for vitamins."

Bedeker's voice came shrieking from the bedroom. "Ethel! There's a draft in here and I feel a coma coming on!"

"Yes, darling," Ethel hurriedly called. "I'll be right in."

"Don't forget about the vitamins," said the doctor, wincing a little at the sound of Bedeker's voice. "Good-by, Mrs. Bedeker."

Ethel shut the door behind him and rushed back into the bedroom.

Bedeker lay on the bed, his head off the pillow, and waved weakly toward the window to his left. "Ethel," he whined at her, "there's freezing air blasting into the room!"

The window was open about a fifth of an inch. As she put it down, Bedeker half rose in bed.

"Do you know how many germs come in one cubic foot of air, Ethel?"

Under her breath she repeated the figure as he called it out.

"Eight million, nine hundred thousand!" He lowered his head back to the pillow. "I know you want me gone and that's why you leave windows open all over the place, but as a point of decency, Ethel, couldn't you do it more subtly?"

Ethel smoothed out his blankets. "The doctor said you needed some air. He said it was stuffy in here." She patted his hand which he drew away sharply.

He suddenly saw the prescription in her other hand. "What's this?" Bedeker said, yanking it out of her fingers. "Where'd you get this? I'm not sick, but he gives you a prescription for medicine for me. Nothing wrong with me and while I lie here helpless, he's out there telling you that I've got a life expectancy of twenty minutes." He puckered up his mouth like a prune. "Don't deny it, Ethel. Kindly don't deny it. I smelled the collusion the moment he left the room!"

Ethel's eyes closed as a wave of weakness hit her. Then she took a deep breath. "It is for vitamins, Walter, for *me*."

Bedeker bolted upright in bed. "Vitamins? For *you*." Then he turned to the wall and spoke to it, nodding familiarly at it. "I lie here while the life seeps out of me, and that quack prescribes medicines for my wife. See? I'm dying and she gets vitamins!"

He broke into a spasm of coughing. When Ethel tried to pat his back he pushed her away, then very limply and weakly he lay back down on the bed, shook his head and closed his eyes.

"Never mind, Ethel. Go on, get out of here. Let me die in peace."

"All right, Walter," Ethel said softly.

"*What?*" Bedeker shouted.

This time it was Ethel's eyes that closed. "I meant," she whispered, "I'll let you alone, Walter, so you can take a little nap."

He lay there quietly for a moment and then suddenly jumped up and sat on the edge of the bed. "I can't nap," he squealed. "Why does a man have to die anyway? I asked you a question, Ethel. Why does a man have to die?" He got out of bed and went to the window, feeling the sash at the bottom for any errant air that might intrude. "The world goes on for millions and millions of years and how long is a man's life?" He held up two fingers. "This much! A drop. A microscopic fragment. Why can't a man live five hundred years? Or a thousand years? Why does he have to die almost the minute he's born?"

"I'm sure I don't know, dear."

"No, you wouldn't. Go on, get out of here, Ethel."

"Yes, dear," she said, and escaped into the living room with the tremendous sense of relief she always felt after getting out of Walter Bedeker's presence. Today had been one of the worst days. He had called the doctor four times that morning, then had Ethel phone the hospital to check on the availability of an oxygen tent. He had insisted right after lunch that she phone the janitor to come and check the heating pipes. The janitor had arrived and Walter had immediately engaged him with a running broadside from the bed as the janitor pounded on the hot water pipes and steam and damp heat floated into the room.

"You want heat, Mr. Bedeker?" the janitor had said to him gleefully. "In about twenty minutes, it'll be about a hundred and five in here. So heat you'll get!"

Livid with rage at the noise of the janitor's pounding, Bedeker had shouted at him, "Ape! Get out of here. If I'm to die, at least I'll die in comfort and peace. Go on, get out of here!"

The janitor surveyed his principal irritation in an apartment house of eighty-three families. "Well, if you do die, Bedeker," he'd said, "—and you go where you're goin'—as far as the temperature goes, you ain't gonna be able to tell the difference!"

Now Ethel felt the result of the janitor's promise. The apartment was stuffy beyond belief. She opened up one of the living room windows and let the cool, fall air ripple over her hot, tired flesh. But she could still hear Walter Bedeker's running monologue from the bedroom.

"It's a crime for a man to live such a short span of years. An absolute crime," Bedeker's muffled voice said.

Ethel went into the tiny kitchen, shut the door and poured herself a cup of coffee.

Walter Bedeker sat propped up in bed looking at his reflection in the dresser mirror across the room. "A crime," he repeated. "What I wouldn't give! What I wouldn't give to live a decent number of years. Two hundred. Three hundred." He heaved a deep sigh and shook his head.

A voice, deep, resonant, with a chuckle in it, said, "Why not five or six hundred?"

Bedeker nodded agreeably. "Why not? Or a thousand. What a miserable thing to contemplate. A handful of years, then an eternity in a casket down under the ground. The dark, cold ground!"

"With worms yet," the voice answered him.

"Of course, with worms," Bedeker said. Then his eyes grew wide as suddenly across the room, materializing rather rapidly in the bedroom chair, he saw a large, fat man in a dark suit. Bedeker gulped, gaped, blinked his eyes and then just stared.

The gentleman smiled and nodded. "I subscribe to your views wholly, Mr. Bedeker," he said. "I mean wholly."

Bedeker continued to stare at him and said, "I'm delighted. And who might you be?"

"Cadwallader's my name," the gentleman answered. "At least I'm using it this month. It has a nice feeling on the tongue."

Bedeker surreptitiously looked around the room, checking the door, the window, then took a quick look under the bed. Then he looked at the man accusingly. "How did you get in?"

"Oh, I've never been gone," Cadwallader said. "I've been here for some time." Then he leaned forward in the manner of a man about to start his business. "I'll be brief, Mr. Bedeker," he said. "You look like a man with a nose for a bargain. I'd like to make a proposition to you. We each have something the other wants, and that seems a relatively solid basis for a bargain."

Bedeker's voice was coolly appraising. "Do we? What in the world do you have that I could possibly want?"

The fat man smiled and lit a cigarette, then he sat back comfortably. "Oh, many things, Mr. Bedeker," he said. "You'd be surprised. Many things. Varied and delightful."

Bedeker studied the man's face. An odd face, he reflected. Fat, but not unpleasant. Nice white teeth, even though the eyes were a little shiny and wild. Bedeker scratched his jaw thoughtfully.

"What do I have that could remotely interest you?"

Cadwallader's smile was deprecating. "Actually a minor item," he said. "Smaller than minor. Insignificant. Microscopic." He held up two fat, little fingers. "Teensy weensy!"

The two men's eyes locked.

"What did you say your name was?" Bedeker asked.

"What's in a name, Mr. Bedeker?" Cadwallader replied ingratiatingly. "Just a question of semantics—language. A stretch of words, really. For example, what is it you want? You want an extended life span. You want a few hundred years to play around with. Now some people would call it immortality of a sort. But why give it that kind of description? Why make it sound so imposing. Let's call it—the two of us—let's call it some additional free time! After all what are a few hundred years or a few thousand years?"

Bedeker swallowed. "A few . . . *thousand*?"

"Or five thousand or ten thousand—" Cadwallader threw the numbers into the breach like a used car salesman bringing up his heavy artillery. "The world will go on ad infinitum, so what's a few thousand years more or less, give or take, add or subtract."

Bedeker rose warily from the bed and studied the fat man. "This little item, Mr. Cadwallader, that I am to give you in exchange—what do you call that?"

Cadwallader gave him a little Santa Claus wink. "What *do* we call that?" he asked. "Let's see! We can call it a little piece of your make-up. A little crumb off the crust of your structure. A fragment of an atom from your being." His smile persisted, but it never quite reached his eyes. "Or, we might call it a—"

"Or a soul!" Bedeker shrieked at him triumphantly.

The smile on Cadwallader's face was positively beatific. "Or that," he said softly. "After all, what is it? And when you're gone, thousands of years hence—what do you need it for?"

Walter Bedeker stood up and pointed a wavering finger in the direction of Mr. Cadwallader. *"You're the Devil,"* he announced.

Cadwallader bowed slightly from the giant equator that was his waist and said modestly, "I'm at your service. How about it, Mr. Bedeker? Why not? A partnership of a sort. You deed me over your so-called soul and I give you immortality. Life everlasting—or as long as you want it to be everlasting. And indestructibility, Mr. Bedeker. Think of it! Complete indestructibility. Nothing can ever hurt you!"

Bedeker looked off dreamily. "Nothing can hurt me? And I can live forever?"

Cadwallader smiled and said, "Why not? Certainly forever. Again, Mr. Bedeker, just terms. And everything's relative. For you, it's forever. For me, it's just a walk around the block. But we're *both* satisfied."

Bedeker stood there lost in thought and Mr. Cadwallader walked over to his elbow. His voice was soft and gentle, but also rich with promise.

"Think of it," Cadwallader said, "to be without fear of dying. To be indestructible. Invincible. Not to have to worry about disease. Accidents. Pestilence. War. Famine. Anything. Governments and institutions disintegrate. People die. But Walter Bedeker goes on and on!"

Bedeker, his head tilted, a smile playing on his puckish, gnome-like face, walked over to the mirror and studied his reflection. "Walter Bedeker goes on and on," he said thoughtfully.

Mr. Cadwallader stepped up behind him so that his reflection joined Bedeker's.

"Mr. Cadwallader," Bedeker said, "about this soul. You say I won't miss it?"

"Why, you'll never know it's gone."

"And I'll go on and on quite unable to die, you say?"

"Quite."

"No tricks?" Bedeker asked. "No hidden clauses? I'll just live as long as I want to live, is that it?"

Cadwallader chuckled at him. "That's it. That's precisely it."

Mr. Cadwallader went back over to his chair and sat down again. Bedeker remained at the mirror studying his face, running a questioning finger over it.

"How about my appearance?" he asked.

"I'm afraid I can't do much about that," Cadwallader said thoughtlessly, but he glided over the slip. "What I mean is—you should look pretty much the same."

"But in five hundred years," Bedeker insisted, "I don't want to look like any dried up old prune."

Cadwallader looked up toward the ceiling, and shook his head at the enormity of the competition. "Oh, Mr. Bedeker," he said, "you drive a mean bargain. A most difficult bargain. But," he made a gesture of resignation, "you'll find me a co-operative"—he smiled apologetically while he searched for the right word—"man?—And we'll throw this into the bargain. Whatever aging takes place on your features will be more or less imperceptible."

Bedeker turned to him from the mirror. "Cadwallader, I believe we're close to making a deal."

Cadwallader began to rub his hands together and then quickly put them behind his back. "Mr. Bedeker," he said happily, "you'll never regret this. Not to your dying day!"

Bedeker looked at him sharply. "Which by rights," Cadwallader added hurriedly, "should not be for several thousand years. However, there is something, Mr. Bedeker—"

Bedeker waggled a finger at him. "Ah ha. Ah ha. Ah ha! Now it comes out, huh?"

"It's for your benefit, I can assure you." Cadwallader took a large, thick document from his pocket and thumbed through it. "Article 93," he exclaimed. "Here it is, right here." He pointed to the page and turned it around so that Bedeker could see it.

"What about it?" Bedeker asked warily. "Read it to me."

The fat gentleman cleared his throat. "It's in the nature of an escape clause," he said. "*Your* escape clause. Whereas the party of the first part upon due notification to the party of the second part—" Cadwallader mumbled. "Oh, this is tiresome. I'll just give it to you thumb nail. It's simply this. If you ever get tired of living, Mr. Bedeker, you can exercise this clause by calling on me and requesting your—" He smiled. "Oh there go the semantics again. Your demise? At which point I shall see to it that you are given a rapid and uncomplicated—" he held up his hands and wiggled his fat fingers—"departure?"

Bedeker puckered up his mouth in a wise, elfish little look, snapped his fingers and beckoned for the document. Cadwallader handed it over with a flourish, then loosened his tie as Bedeker riffled through the pages. Mr. Cadwallader took a large crimson handkerchief from his pocket and wiped his face.

"You sure keep it hot in here!" he murmured.

Bedeker finished the last page, then handed the document back to the fat man.

"It appears to be in order, Mr. Cadwallader, but I can assure you that I'm not the sort of man to kill the goose that lays the golden egg. When you talk immortality to me, brother, I *mean* immortality! You're going to have a long, long, long wait!"

Again Cadwallader bowed his assent. "Mr. Bedeker," he said, "nothing would please me more!"

Bedeker said, "Then I think you've got a deal."

This time Mr. Cadwallader couldn't restrain himself from rubbing his hands together. His eyes positively glittered and it struck Bedeker that he was looking at a two-holed opening into a furnace. He could reflect no longer upon this because Mr. Cadwallader reached into the air and pulled out what appeared to be a smoking rubber stamp. This he swung in a wide arc and brought it down on the front page of the document. There was a sizzling sound and the document floated to the floor, burning at the edge. Bedeker could see that on the lower right-hand corner was the imprint of a seal. It looked like a circle with horns in the middle. After a moment the fire went out and the paper lay smoking. Bedeker bent over and picked it up.

"Yes, it seems to be pretty much in order," Bedeker said. "Now a few other questions, Mr.—"

But the room was empty. He thought he heard the sound of distant laughter retreating into the night, but he wasn't sure and soon he heard nothing. Bedeker carefully folded the document and shoved it in the dresser drawer. He smiled at himself in the mirror, then went to the window and with an impulsive gesture, he flung it open, letting the cold air rush into the room. He stood beating his chest and breathing deeply. He had never in his life felt so free, so unencumbered, and so absolutely healthy.

This reminded Bedeker of his tray, with all its medicines, bottles, jars, lotions, and his book, *How To Be Happy Though*

Bedridden. He picked them up and hurled them out the window, smiling as after a few seconds, he heard the bottles smash on the pavement fourteen stories below. Turning from the window, he noticed the hot water pipes. A shimmering heat rose from them and they looked brick red in the lamp light. He approached them gingerly, and stood over them, very slowly raising his hands until he could feel the heat pour into his palms and through his fingers. Red hot, he noted. *Red hot.*

"Proof of the pudding," Bedeker murmured, "and no time like the present!"

He slammed both palms down on the pipes, listened to the sizzle of the burning flesh, watched the smoke rise in front of his eyes. But there was no sensation of pain. There was no sensation of any kind. He lifted his hands and stared at them. Not a mark. He looked down at the red hot pipes, and laughed aloud. He continued to laugh, his head back, as he walked across the room and threw himself on the bed. He heard the bedroom door open and Ethel stood there staring at him, frightened.

"Walter," she said nervously. "Is everything all right?"

"Is everything all right?" he repeated. "Everything, Ethel, my love, is delightful. Everything is superb. Everything is perfect."

He got up and went to the dresser. There was a nail file lying alongside a brush set. He picked it up and smiling happily, jammed the point into his palm. Ethel screamed and fell back against the door. Then very slowly she opened her eyes to look at the Cheshire-cat grin on her husband's face. He held out an unscathed palm.

"See, my dear? The hand is quicker than the eye! The proof of the pudding! Witness, my dear . . . the new Walter Bedeker!"

He started to laugh again, a gusty, roaring, uncontrollable laugh and he paraded back and forth across the room like a rooster in a barnyard. Ethel stood still, her face pale, wondering if she dared leave the room to get to the telephone. Or if at any moment the demented man in front of her might get violent. Her eye fell on the nail file on the dresser. She gasped, bit deep into a knuckle, and looked at Walter in horror. There had been blood on the nail file.

In the weeks that followed, Ethel Bedeker was never sure whether or not she preferred the old days to these new ones. Or whether perhaps it had been an irreparable mistake to have been married or even born. The "new" Walter Bedeker turned out to be a mystifying individual. True, he no longer betook himself to his bed five times a month and screamed impossible demands. As a matter of fact, he was rarely home any more. But his new behavior was equally disturbing.

The first indication she got of what might be expected was a phone call from an insurance adjuster attached to a building firm. Walter, it seemed, had been hit by a falling steel "I" beam that weighed about two and a half tons. It had been in the process of being raised by a chain to the tenth floor of an office building under construction. The chain had broken and the beam had fallen three hundred feet to land on Walter's head and smash him down into the sidewalk. The foreman on the job first had been violently ill, then had walked very slowly toward that spot in the sidewalk where the horror was waiting for him. He covered his eyes because of a normal reluctance to view mangled bodies. He had also peeked between two fingers, because of the equally normal trait of being fascinated by the horrible. He was to be disappointed on both scores, because Walter Bedeker had crawled out from underneath the beam, none the worse for being squashed, except that his clothes were ripped and his hair disheveled. He had thundered at the foreman that he'd better contact his lawyer because there was going to be one helluva whopping suit in the offing.

It was to tell Ethel all this that the insurance adjuster had phoned, and to inform her that he was on his way to their apartment.

That afternoon Walter signed a waiver of further claim and collected a check for five thousand dollars.

This happened on a Wednesday and the following Saturday afternoon Walter was alone in the self-service elevator when for some strange reason the main cable broke, and the elevator car shot down the two-thousand-foot shaft to be smashed to smithereens at the bottom. The building superintendent heard his shrieking voice echoing up through the shaft and went down to the basement to pry open the wrecked door. Bedeker lay in the rubble with nothing injured, not even his aplomb. (This affair was settled for thirty-eight hundred dollars and forty-two cents.)

A week later Bedeker was standing in front of a fireworks factory when the building went up in smoke. The newspapers called it the worst fire disaster to occur in the city in twenty-five years. Luckily, it happened after the five o'clock whistle, and only three bodies were found, burnt beyond recognition, in the debris. Bedeker had been buried under a collapsing, burning wall, but had crawled out on his hands and knees right to the foot of a fireman who had fainted dead away upon seeing him. His clothes had been burnt entirely off his body and this accounted for the figure of thirty-nine dollars and fifty cents added to the ten thousand for which the fireworks company settled with him.

In the next five weeks Bedeker was in eight major accidents—a subway collision, a bus overturning, five automobile accidents (in each case the driver swore that Bedeker had stepped out in front of the speeding car), and a decidedly freakish circumstance in a restaurant where Bedeker complained there was glass in his beef stew. It wasn't until after the manager had paid Bedeker two hundred dollars in cash that the waiter showed the manager a half-chewed glass on the table. By this time Bedeker had walked out in a huff, pocketing his two hundred dollars, and was no more to be seen.

It was now New Year's Eve and Ethel had timidly asked Bedeker if they could go out to dinner or to a show or perhaps to a nightclub. Bedeker stood at the window, his back to her, not answering.

"Eleven accidents," he said, "that's what I've been in. Eleven accidents."

Ethel, who had just mentioned that it was a long time since they'd been dancing together, tried another tack.

"That's the point, dear," she said hopefully. "You need recreation. You need to get your mind off things."

Bedeker continued to stare out the window. "Wouldn't you think, Ethel," he asked rhetorically, "that there'd be an element of thrill in eleven accidents? Eleven accidents in which you *know* nothing can happen to you?"

"I guess so, Walter," Ethel answered irresolutely, not understanding a thing he was talking about.

"Well, it's a fact," Bedeker continued. "There should be an excitement in this sort of thing." He walked away from the window. "*Well, there isn't.* It's dull. It's absolutely without the remotest bit of excitement. In short, I'm bored with it."

"Walter, dear," Ethel said softly, "I guess we should count our blessings."

"You, Ethel," Bedeker snapped, "should shut your mouth. You look for all the world like a small gray mouse searching for a piece of cheese."

She let the cold, hurt feeling subside before she answered him.

"Walter, you can be terribly cruel, do you know that?"

Bedeker rolled his eyes upward and said, "Ethel, please shut your mouth!" He paced the room back and forth. "I swear he cheated me! Mortal-shmortal! What's the good of it when there aren't any kicks? Any excitement at all!"

Ethel found herself looking at him in helpless confusion. He was Walter Bedeker all right. He was her husband. But he was totally and distinctly different from the man she married, the hypochondriac she had lived with for so many years.

"Walter," she asked, "do you feel all right?"

Bedeker ignored her. "At least when I was concerned about my health," he said aloud to no one, "there was an element of risk there. But now there is no risk. There is no excitement. There is no nothing!"

He suddenly cocked his head slightly, his eyes grew wide and he ran past her to the bathroom. She heard him fumbling through the medicine chest over the sink. There was the clatter of bottles and of glass.

"Ethel?" he called from the bathroom. "Do we have any starch?"

Ethel walked toward the bathroom door. "Starch?" she asked.

Bedeker said, "Of course, starch."

Ethel looked over his shoulder at the bottles he had lined up. There was iodine, rubbing alcohol and epsom salts. He had one glass into which he was pouring sizable portions from each.

"Starch!" Bedeker repeated impatiently.

Ethel went to the kitchen and got a bottle of starch from a cabinet under the sink. She brought it to Bedeker and he immediately unscrewed the top and poured this last ingredient into the mixture, which foamed and took on a kind of mustard color. Bedeker held up the glass, and with a quick motion, drank it all down. Ethel gaped at him as he smacked his lips, looked at his face in the mirror, stuck out his tongue, then put the glass down disconsolately.

"You see?" he asked.

"See what?" Her voice trembled.

"See what I just drank? Iodine, rubbing alcohol, epsom salts and starch. And what did it do to me, Ethel? I ask you—what did it do to me? It did nothing! Absolutely nothing. I've just drunk enough poison to kill a dozen men and it tasted like lemonade. *Weak* lemonade."

Ethel leaned against the door. Her voice was very steady. "Walter," she said, "I want to know what this is all about!"

Bedeker peered at her elfishly. "What it's all about? You really want to know?"

She nodded.

"All right," Bedeker said, "I'll tell you. I happen to be immortal. I am indestructible. I made a pact with a man named Cadwallader who has given me immortality in exchange for my soul. More succinctly than that, I couldn't put it."

Ethel caught a brief look at her reflection in the mirror and wondered in part of her brain how any woman could look so pale and so frightened.

"I want you to sit down, Walter," she said, collecting herself. "I'm going to make you some tea and then I'm going to call the doctor."

She turned to leave and Bedeker grabbed her arm, yanking her around to face him.

"You will *not* make tea," he commanded. "And you will *not* call the doctor. If you had any imagination at all, Ethel, you *might* tell me what I could do to get a little excitement out of all of this. I've been in subway crashes, bus accidents, major fires and just now I drank poison. You *saw* me." He paused and shrugged. "Nothing! Absolutely nothing. You know what I've been thinking?" He left the bathroom and walked back into the living room. "I have been thinking, Ethel, that I should go up to the roof and throw myself down the light well! Smack dab down the light well. Fourteen stories down just for the experience of it."

Ethel sat heavily down in a chair, close to tears now. "Please, Walter. Please, for goodness' sake—"

Bedeker went toward the door. "Ethel, darling, shut your mouth."

She sprang to her feet and raced to the door, intercepting him just as he started to open it.

"Walter," she beseeched him. "Please, Walter, for God's sake—"

He pushed her out of the way and went out, down the hall, to the rear stairs and started to climb. Ethel followed him, pleading all the way, arguing, cajoling, but he would have none of it. On the roof, he headed toward the light well. It was a big, square hole covered by glass. There was a small concrete shelf around it that stood only about eight inches high. Ethel immediately got between Walter and the concrete strip, and held out her hands to him.

"Please, Walter," she said. "Please, my darling—"

Bedeker said, "Ethel, go drown in the tub and leave me alone. I'm going head first down that light well, and I want you to get out of the way!"

He advanced toward her and she backed away from him.

"Please, darling," she said. "Please come back to the apartment. I'll make you potato pancakes. Remember, you used to love potato pancakes."

Bedeker yanked her arm away from him, pushed her aside. "You, my dear," he said, "are a potato pancake. You look like a potato pancake. You have all the excitement of a potato pancake. You are as tasteless as a potato pancake. Now I've told you for the last time to get out of my way."

She threw herself against him, struggling to push him back and only at the last instant did she realize that her foot was no longer on the level of the roof floor. It dangled over the concrete stoop surrounding the stairwell. In a moment her balance shifted and she had fallen backwards, smashing through the glass, and hurtled fourteen stories down to the concrete courtyard below. Even her scream was a quiet, pathetic noise coming from a quiet, pathetic woman. It was more misery than horror; more a gentle protest than the last utterance of a woman going head first to her death.

Bedeker tiptoed over to the light well and looked down. Lights were going on sporadically on every other floor like the panel board of an elevator announcing the stops. He scratched his jaw, took out a cigarette and lit it.

"I wonder what it felt like," he said softly.

Some place off in the distance he heard a siren. There was a growing mumble and jumble of voices inside the building. Then suddenly he had a thought. It was a wonderful thought. An exciting thought. He hurried to the door leading to the rear stairs, went down them two at a time, trotted into his apartment and picked up the telephone.

"Operator," he said, "get me the police, please. Immediately. It's an emergency." After a moment he heard the voice of a desk sergeant at the local precinct. "Hello? Is this the police station? Well, this is Walter Bedeker, 11 North 7th Street. That's correct. Apartment 12B. Will you please come over here right away. No, no trouble. I just killed my wife. That's right. Yes, I'll stay right here. Good-by."

He put the receiver down, took a deep luxurious drag on his cigarette, flicked the ashes away and said, "Well, let's give the old electric chair a whirl!"

The trial of the State vs. Walter Bedeker was, in the words of the District Attorney, "the most predictable thing to hit town since professional wrestling." The court reporters, spectators, and certainly the jury seemed to share the prosecution's view. In three days of proceedings, the State made one telling point after the other. They established motive. (Six witnesses had testified to the fights between Walter Bedeker and his wife.) They showed premeditation. (The janitor testified that he had heard Bedeker threaten his wife on at least a dozen occasions.) And they did everything but bring in photographs of the actual commission of the crime. (At least ten neighbors had seen Bedeker come down off the roof and hurry back into his apartment.)

So in short, Mr. Walter Bedeker sat alongside of his lawyer on the eve of the last day of trial in a most vulnerable position. You could not have told this, however, by looking at Walter Bedeker. He sat half smiling at the judge, the witnesses, the prosecution. On the stand he openly and freely admitted he had pushed his wife down the light well and had no misgivings about it at all. As a matter of fact, he would do it again.

His lawyer, hired by the State, was a desperately energetic young man who objected on the slightest provocation, who argued, pleaded and thundered throughout the trial, who parried every telling thrust on the part of the prosecution and parried well. But his was a losing cause and he knew it. He became acutely aware of just how losing it was when after sending a penciled note of inquiry over to his client he received the note back with the following scrawl underneath his question: "Go to hell, affectionately, Walter Bedeker." From that point on the defense was reasonably certain that the normal rapport between client and lawyer did not exist in this case. And further, that this was a client whose answers on the stand seemed to suggest collusion between him and the prosecution. Because Walter Bedeker was convicting himself with every answer, every gesture, obviously because he wished to.

On the evening of the third day of trial, Bedeker's lawyer went to see Bedeker in his cell. He arrived during his client's dinner and found himself completely ignored until Bedeker had started his dessert. Then the little man looked up as if suddenly realizing the lawyer was there and nodded perfunctorily.

"Cooper, the legal beagle. What brings you here at this odd hour?"

Cooper sat down on the other chair and studied his client. "Mr. Bedeker," he said grimly, "you may not realize this, but at the rate things are going this case will go to the jury by tomorrow."

Bedeker nodded and continued to spoon down ice cream. "How do you feel, Cooper?" he asked.

Cooper squirmed with frustration and put his briefcase on the floor. "How am I? I'm miserable, Mr. Bedeker. I've been miserable since I took your case. I've had tough clients before, but nobody like you."

"Really?" Bedeker asked insouciantly. "What disturbs you?"

"What disturbs me is that in three days of trial you've acted like a man desperate to get convicted. When I examine you, you shut up like a clam. When the prosecuting attorney examines you, you act as if you were betting on him to win the case." He leaned forward intensely. "Now look, Bedeker, this is the goods here. If this case goes to the jury tomorrow as things stand now, you don't have chance number one."

Bedeker lit a cigarette and leaned back on his cot. "Is that a fact?" he asked.

"That is a fact. Now tomorrow this is what I want us to do!"

He lifted the briefcase and unzipped it. He was diving into it for papers when Bedeker said, "Don't bother, Mr. Cooper. Just don't bother." He waved at the briefcase. "Put it away."

"How's that?" Cooper asked.

"Put it away."

Cooper stared at him for a long, unbelieving moment. "Bedeker, did you get what I was trying to tell you? You're about twelve hours away from a guilty verdict on a charge of first degree murder."

Bedeker smiled and clucked. "And what will the penalty be?"

"The penalty," Cooper said tiredly, "in this State for first degree murder is death in the electric chair."

"Death in the electric chair," Bedeker repeated. He tapped his fingers on the side of the cot and then examined his nails.

"Bedeker," Cooper shouted, almost beyond control.

"Death in the electric chair. And if I were in California?"

"What?" Cooper asked incredulously.

"How would they try to kill me if I lived in California," Bedeker said.

"Capital punishment there is the gas chamber, but I frankly don't see why—"

"And in Kansas?" Bedeker interrupted.

"In Kansas," Cooper answered, "it's hanging. Now I'm going to tell you something, Bedeker—"

Bedeker rose from the cot and surveyed the lawyer who now had a thin covering of perspiration over his face.

"No, Mr. Cooper," Bedeker said mildly. "I'm going to tell *you* something. The only thing they'll get for their trouble if they try to electrocute me is a whopping electricity bill! Now good night, Mr. Cooper. See you in court!"

Cooper sighed deeply. He slowly zipped up his briefcase and rose. "I don't know, Bedeker," he said. "I just don't understand you. The alienist says you're sane and you say you killed your wife. But way down deep I know you didn't. So tomorrow when I sum up for you, I'm going to lead from terrible weakness." He shrugged hopelessly. "But I intend to do the best I can."

He turned and went to the cell door, tapping on it for the guard. After a moment they heard him coming down the corridor. He unlocked the door and Cooper walked out.

"Mr. Cooper," Bedeker's voice came from behind the bars. The defense attorney turned to look at him.

Bedeker smiled at him. "Mr. Cooper," he said. "Really— don't bother!"

The prosecution on the following morning delivered one of the briefest summations in a murder trial ever presented in the history of the State. It lasted only a minute and a half and afterwards the District Attorney walked smiling and confident back to his seat. Mr. Cooper rose for his summation and after about ten seconds of a stumbling if sincere start, he seemed to warm up and a relatively listless jury suddenly seemed very aware of him. Even the judge leaned over on his elbows to listen more intently. A court reporter later described it as one helluva summation—one of the best ever heard in that courtroom.

"Guilty, yes," Cooper roared. "But premeditated? Hardly!" His client, Cooper contended, had *not* led his wife up to the roof. She had followed him. No witness had proven otherwise. Killed her—yes, this he did. Pushed her off the stoop, down the light well—absolutely. No contest. But had he planned to do it? This was a moot point. Twenty-eight minutes later, after an address loaded with moot points, Cooper sat down next to Walter Bedeker and listened to the murmur running through the courtroom. Bedeker smiled vaguely at him. He hadn't been listening. He was busy jotting notes on a pad. Things he intended to do after he got out. Cooper could see a few of his scrawled plans over Bedeker's shoulder. "Land on third rail in subway station." "Jump in front of diesel engine." "Hide in hydrogen bomb testing area." Etc. Etc.

Sixty-three minutes later the jury came back with a verdict of guilty and shortly thereafter Walter Bedeker stood in front of the bench for his sentencing. He leaned against the bench on his elbow, picked his teeth, yawned and looked generally bored. Walter Bedeker had paid little heed to the proceedings in that courtroom. Even now he scarcely heard what the judge was saying. Something to the effect that the court prescribed life imprisonment. It was not the words that jarred him. Rather it was Cooper, grabbing him, hugging him, shaking him.

"Life imprisonment, old man," Cooper screamed into his ear joyfully. "I knew we could do it! I just knew we could do it."

As the turnkey led Bedeker through the side door of the courtroom he became gradually aware of the hum of voices around him. "God, what a summation!" "Life imprisonment—masterful!" "There's one helluva lucky man!"

It wasn't until Bedeker was walking down the corridor outside that he realized what had happened. Cooper had got him off with life imprisonment. He stopped, turned toward the courtroom at the other end of the corridor and screamed out loud,

"Wait a minute! *WAIT A MINUTE!* I can't get imprisoned for life! Don't they understand? Don't they know what this means? *I can't go to prison for life.*"

He began to cry. He was crying when they put him in the black paddy wagon to take him back to jail. He cried all during the trip and that night in his cell he was still crying.

When the cell guard brought him his dinner he noted that Mr. Bedeker's eyes were red-rimmed and that he only toyed with his food.

"You're a lucky guy, Bedeker," the guard said through the cell doors. "Tomorrow they'll be taking you to the penitentiary. That'll be your new home. It's a long way from the death cell."

Bedeker didn't answer. He sat looking down at the tray of food on his lap and felt the rising bubbles of sadness and hopelessness and misery crawl up his body and he had to stifle a sob.

"Look at it this way," the guard said philosophically. "What's life, Mr. Bedeker? Forty years. Fifty years. Hell, you can do that standing on your head." Bedeker could hear him as he went down the corridor. "That's all. Forty, fifty years. Maybe not even that much—"

Bedeker set the tray on the floor and put his head in his hands.

"Forty, fifty years," he murmured to himself. "Forty or fifty years. Or sixty, or seventy, or a hundred, or two hundred."

Numbers drifted across his mind. Five figure numbers. Six figure numbers. And he heard a voice thundering at him from no place in particular.

"After all, what are a few hundred years or a few thousand? Or five thousand or ten thousand? What is it in the scheme of things?" The voice ended on a note of laughter. Big laughter. Resounding, quaking laughter that came from the belly of a fat man.

Walter Bedeker looked up to see the corpulent blue-suited figure of Cadwallader standing in the middle of the cell grinning at him, his white teeth gleaming, his eyes suddenly coal red.

"Mr. Bedeker," he rumbled. "Just think of it! Immortality . . . indestructibility . . . institutions fail, governments disintegrate, people die! But Walter Bedeker goes on and on." His laugh was rolling thunder across the cell. "Walter Bedeker goes on and on. And on and on and on."

Bedeker screamed and buried his face against the pillow on the cot. There was an odor in the cell. A burning odor. Was it brimstone? Very likely.

"Mr. Bedeker?" Cadwallader's voice was soft now, the words arrived on velvet. "About that escape clause. Would you care to exercise it now?"

Bedeker never even raised his head from the pillow. He nodded and a moment thereafter felt a pain sear across his chest, a terrible pain. A pain more agonizing than anything he'd ever felt before. His body twitched convulsively and he fell off the cot to land on his back, his eyes staring lifelessly up toward the cell. Walter Bedeker was a dead body. The thing that had been his soul let out a strangled scream and struggled inside the pocket of a blue suit as it was carried into another dimension.

The guard found Walter Bedeker during bed check that night. He opened the cell door, rushed in and felt for a pulse. Then he'd called the prison doctor and the warden. It was a heart attack and this was written on a cardboard tag that was attached to his chart.

A comment was made by one of the attendants in the prison morgue. It was something to the effect that he'd never seen a look of such utter horror on a man's face as that which Walter Bedeker's wore as they shoved him into a refrigerated compartment and closed the door.

From Rod Serling's closing narration, "Escape Clause," *The Twilight Zone*, November 6, 1959, CBS Television Network.

The CAMERA PANS away from the body and then slowly up the side of the cell until it stops on a shot of the barred window facing the outside.

NARRATOR'S VOICE
There's a saying . . . every man is put
on earth condemned to die. Time and
method of execution unknown.
(a pause)
Perhaps this is as it should be. Case
in point—Walter Bedeker, lately

called him by name, and smiled a quiet, respectful deference when he entered their places.

But the hell of it, the misery of it was that Martin Sloan had an incipient ulcer that at this moment began a slow, raking crawl over his insides. He knew panic a dozen times a day—that convulsive, breath-stopping, ice-cube feeling of doubt and indecision; of being second guessed, of being wrong; the effort to make his voice firm, his decisions sound irrevocable, when deep inside his gut—worse as each day passed—he felt a vague slipping away of all the props he conjured up and took on the stage with him when he faced the president of the agency, the clients, or the other account execs.

And that ulcer! That Goddamned ulcer. He felt it rise in him again and tensed himself like a man going into a cold shower. It burned across his stomach. After it subsided, he lit a cigarette and felt the wetness on his back as the hot June perspiration turned his Hathaway shirt into a clinging, itchy thing and made his palms sodden extensions of himself.

Martin Sloan went to the window to look out at New York. The lights were on along Park Avenue and he remembered the lights of his home town. He often thought about his home town lately. For the past several months he had been coming back to the apartment from the office to sit in the dark living room and drink long, solitary scotches; to think about himself as a boy, and where it had all begun—the chronology of the thirty-six-year-old man who had the world by the short hair, but at least three times a week felt like crying.

Sloan gazed down at the Park Avenue lights and thought about himself as a boy and the main street of his town and the drugstore that Mr. Wilson owned. Sporadic, unrelated remembrances, but part of a bittersweet pattern that made that room, the scotch, the reflection in the mirror so unbearable. Again he felt that urge to cry and pushed it down deep inside of him along with the pain of the ulcer. A thought came to him. Get in the car and go. Get out of New York. Away from Madison Avenue. Away from the blathering, meaningless, mixed-metaphored jargon of his boss; the ratings and the "percentages-of-audience" and the cosmetic accounts and the three-million-dollar gross billings and that sick, ugly façade of good fellowship among strangers.

Some kind of ghostly billy club tapped at his ankles and told him it was later than he thought. He left his apartment, picked up his car, drove out on to Grand Central Parkway. Hunched over the wheel of his red Mercedes-Benz he asked himself very briefly just where the hell did he think he was going and he was undismayed by the fact that there wasn't an answer. He wanted to think, that was all. He wanted to remember. And when he turned off on the New York Throughway and headed upstate he had no further resolves. He just kept driving on into the night and was only dimly aware that old man Wilson's drugstore seemed strangely etched in his mind. It was this picture that sent his brain back on an errand to recapture memories of a time before. Memories of a place called Homewood, New York, a quiet, tree-filled little town of three thousand people. As he drove, he remembered what had been a minute fragment of his life, but God what a fragment! The wondrous time of growing up. Quiet streets on a summer night. The joy of parks and playgrounds. The uninhibited freedom of a child. Memories ebbed back and forth across his mind and left him with a strange, indefinable hunger that subconsciously he realized was not just for a place—but for a time. He wanted to be a boy again. That was what he wanted. He wanted to turn around in his life and go backwards. He wanted to run past the years to find the one in which he was eleven years old.

Martin Sloan, in a Brooks Brothers suit, driving a red sports car, headed out into the night and away from New York. He drove with an urgency and a purpose without really knowing his destination. This was no week-end drive. It was no momentary turning of his back to convention and habit. This was an exodus. This was flight. Somewhere at the end of a long, six-lane highway that stretched out across the rolling hills of upstate New York, Martin Sloan was looking for sanity.

He stopped at a motel near Binghamton, New York, slept a few hours, and was on his way again, and at nine in the morning pulled into a gas station off the State highway. He'd been going fast and the car squealed to a stop sending up clouds of dust. A little of the drive that sustained him in New York, a little of the impatience that pushed him through the days, clung to him now and he honked the horn persistently. The attendant, a nice-looking kid in dungarees, looked up from the tire he was repairing a few yards away, wiped his hands with a cloth and stood listening to Martin Sloan's horn.

"How about some service?" Martin yelled.

"How about some quiet?" the attendant answered him.

Martin bit his lower lip and turned away, gripping the steering wheel, studying the dashboard.

"I'm sorry," he said softly.

The attendant came toward him.

"Would you fill it up, please?" Martin asked.

"Sure."

"I said I was sorry," Martin said.

"I heard you," the attendant answered. "You take high-test in these things, don't you?"

Martin nodded, handed him the keys to the gas tank. The attendant went around to the rear of the car and unlocked the tank.

"How about an oil change and a lube job, too?" Martin asked him.

"Sure," the attendant said. "It'll take about an hour."

Martin said, "I've got plenty of time."

He turned to look across the road at a sign which read, "Homewood, 1½ miles."

"That's Homewood up ahead, isn't it?" Martin asked.

The attendant said, "Yep."

"I used to live there. Grew up there as a matter of fact. I haven't been back in eighteen . . . twenty years."

He got out of the car, reached in his pocket for a cigarette and noticed that it was his last one. There was a cigarette machine in front of the station. Martin got a pack of cigarettes from it and came back, still talking.

"Eighteen . . . twenty years. And then last night I—I just got in the car and drove. Reached a point where I, well—I had to get out of New York. One more board meeting, phone call, report, problem—" He laughed and the laugh sounded hollow and tired.

"New York, is that where you're from?" the attendant asked.

"That's right. New York."

"I see you guys all the time," the attendant said. "Take a drive in the country—gotta go a hundred miles an hour. Stop for a red light, somebody beats you startin' up when she turns green, then your day's ruined. God, how do you guys keep at it?"

Martin turned away and fiddled with the side mirror on his car. "We just do," he answered. "We just keep at it and then there comes a June night—when we suddenly take off." He looked across the road again toward the sign. "A mile and a half," he mused. "That's walking distance."

"For some people," the attendant answered him.

Martin grinned. "But not for New York executives in red sports cars, huh?"

The attendant shrugged.

"I'll come back for the car later on." Martin grinned. "A mile and a half—that's walking distance!"

He took off his coat and slung it over his shoulder and tramped down the road to Homewood, a little over a mile away—and twenty years later.

Martin entered the drugstore and stood motionless near the door in the dark coolness. It was exactly as he remembered it. A narrow, high-ceilinged room with an old-fashioned soda bar on one side, a counter on the other. A wooden stairway that led to a small office off a tiny balcony. This was where Mr. Wilson, the owner, used to take his catnaps, Martin remembered. A thin little man with thick glasses wiped soda glasses and smiled at Martin across the fountain.

"What'll it be?" he asked.

Martin looked at the posters on the walls, the old-fashioned hanging lights, the two big electric fans that hung down from the ceiling. He went to the counter and sat down. The five big glass jars of penny candy were just as he remembered them.

"You still make great chocolate sodas?" he asked the man behind the soda bar. "Three scoops?"

The man's smile looked a little strained. "How's that?"

Martin's laugh was apologetic. "I used to spend half my life in this drugstore," he explained. "I grew up here. The one thing I always remember ordering—that was a chocolate ice cream soda with three scoops. And it was ten cents, too."

The little man looked at him quizzically and Martin studied his face.

"You know," Martin said, "you look familiar to me. Have I seen you before?"

The clerk shrugged and grinned. "I got that kind of a face."

"It's been a long time," Martin said. "Eighteen . . . twenty years. That's when I left." Then he laughed at a collection of secret thoughts that crossed his mind. "I wish I had a buck," he continued, "for every hour I spent at this fountain though. From grammar school right through third-year high." He turned on the stool to look out at the bright, sunny street outside. "Town looks the same too." He turned back to the little man. "You know it's really amazing. After twenty years to look so exactly the same."

The little man in glasses fixed his soda and then handed it to him. "That'll be a dime."

Martin started to fish in his pocket, then stopped abruptly. "A dime?" he asked incredulously. He held up the giant, richly dark glass. "Three scoops?"

The soda jerk laughed. "That's the way we make 'em."

Martin laughed again. "You're going to lose your shirt. Nobody sells sodas for a dime any more."

There was a moment's silence then the little man asked, "They don't? Where *you* from?"

Martin started to spoon down some of the chocolate ice cream. "New York," he said between gulps. "Hey, you make a great soda!"

The little man leaned on the counter with his elbows. "Taste okay?" he asked.

"Wonderful." He finished the ice cream and slurped up the last of the soda water. He grinned. "Like I never left home. That was great." He turned to scan the room. "Funny," he said, "how many memories you connect with a place. I always thought if I ever came back here, it'd all be changed."

The store looked back at him. The counters and shelves and posters and lights. The electric fans. They looked back at him like old friends. "It's just as if—" Martin said thoughtfully, "—as if I'd left yesterday." He got off the stool and stood twirling it. "Just as if I'd been away overnight." He smiled at the soda jerk. "I'd almost expect Mr. Wilson to be sitting up there in the office and sleeping away his afternoons just the way he always did before he died."

He didn't see the soda jerk start at this.

"That's one of the images I have," he continued. "Old Man Wilson sleeping in his big comfortable chair in his office up there. Old Man Wilson—may his soul rest in peace."

He reached in his pocket, took out a dollar bill and put it on the counter. The soda jerk stared at it, surprised.

"That's a buck!"

Martin smiled at him, tapped the glass with a finger.

"That—" he looked around the room—"and all of this, they're worth it."

He went back out into the hot summer. The soda jerk leaned on the counter, wondering about Martin, then lifted up the top of the chocolate syrup container and peered inside. He replaced it, came around from behind the counter, climbed the stairs, and tapped gently on a door. A muffled, sleepy voice responded.

"Yes?"

The soda jerk opened the door a few inches. "Mr. Wilson," he said to the white-haired old man, sitting in the heavy leather chair, one eye open, "we need more chocolate syrup."

The old man winked, nodded and closed his eyes again. "I'll order some this afternoon."

In a moment he was fast asleep again. The soda jerk went back to the counter. He took Martin Sloan's glass and started to wash it. Funny guy, he thought. Lose your shirt if you sell three scoops for a dime. He chuckled as he was drying the glass. Nobody sold three scoops for a dime any more. Then he shrugged and put the glass away. You met all kinds. You sure met all kinds. But this guy, this one was odd. This one had a look on his face. How would you describe the look? He was so . . . so *happy*. Just being in the dingy old drugstore, he looked happy. A woman came in with a prescription and the soda jerk didn't think of Martin Sloan any more that day.

Martin walked down Oak Street—the street he'd grown up on. It stretched out ahead of him flanked by big, full-leafed maple trees that cast sharp black shadows against the brilliant whiteness of the sunshine. Big, two-story Victorian houses set back behind long, green lawns were old friends to him. He rattled off names of their owners as he walked slowly down the sidewalk. Vanburen. Wilcox. Abernathy. He looked across the street. Over there, Dr. Bradbury, Mulrooney, Grey. He stopped and leaned against a tree. The street was exactly as he remembered it. He felt the bittersweet pang of nostalgia. He remembered the games he'd played with the kids on this street. The newspapers he'd delivered. The small-boy accidents on roller skates and bicycles. And the people. The faces and names that fused in his mind now. His house was on the corner and for some reason he wanted to save this for last. He could see it ahead of him. Big, white, with a semi-circular porch running around it. Cupolas. An iron jockey in front. God, the things you remembered. The things you tucked away in an old mental trunk and forgot. Then you opened the trunk and there they were.

"Hi," a little boy's voice said.

Martin Sloan looked down to see a four-year-old with syrup on his face, shooting marbles. "Hi," Martin answered and sat down on the curb beside him. "You pretty good?" He pointed toward the boy's marbles.

"At aggies?" the little boy said. "I'm not so bad."

Martin picked up one of the marbles and looked through it. "I used to shoot marbles, too. We gave them special names. The steel kind, the ballbearings we took off old streetcars, we called them steelies. And the ones we could see through—we called them clearies. Still call them names like that?"

"Sure," said the little boy.

Martin pointed across the street toward a telephone pole marked up by a thousand jackknives. "That's where we used to play hide-and-seek," he said to the boy. He grinned. "Draw a circle around the old man's back and who's to punch it." He laughed aloud as the thought warmed and delighted him. "Right on this street, every night in the summer we used to play that. And I used to live in that corner house down there," he pointed. "The big, white one."

"The Sloan house?" the little boy asked.

Martin's eyes grew a little wider. "That's right. You still call it that?"

"Still call it what?"

"The Sloan house. My name's Sloan. I'm Martin Sloan. What's your name?"

He held out his hand but the boy backed away, frowning at him.

"You're not Marty Sloan," the boy said accusingly. "I know Martin Sloan and you're not him."

Martin laughed. "I'm not, huh? Well, let's see what the driver's license says."

He reached into his breast pocket for his wallet. When he looked up the little boy was running down the street and then across a lawn to the house opposite his. Martin got slowly to his feet and began to walk again. It was the first slow walk, Martin reflected, that he'd taken in a long, long time. The houses and lawns went by and he drank them all in. He wanted this slow. He wanted to relish it all. In the distance he could hear children's laughter and the tinkle of an ice-cream wagon bell. It all fitted, sight and sound and mood. He got a tight feeling in his throat.

He didn't know how long he had walked but later he found himself in the park. Like the drugstore, like the houses, like the sounds—nothing had changed. There was the pavilion with the big, round, band-concert stand. There was the merry-go-round, loaded with kids, the brassy, discordant calliope music still chasing it round and round. There were the same wooden horses, the same brass rings, the same ice-cream stands, cotton candy vendors. And always the children. Short pants and Mickey Mouse shirts. Lollipops and ice-cream cones and laughter and giggling. The language of the young. The music—the symphony of summer. The sounds swirled around him. Calliope, laughter, children. Again the tight feeling in his throat. Bittersweet again. All of it he had left so far behind and now he was so close to it.

A pretty young woman walked by him, wheeling a baby carriage. She stopped, caught by something she saw in Martin Sloan's face, as he watched the merry-go-round. She'd never seen a look quite like that before. It made her smile at him, and he smiled back.

"Wonderful place, isn't it?" he said.

"The park? It certainly is."

Martin nodded toward the merry-go-round. "That's a part of summer, isn't it? The music from the merry-go-round. The calliope."

The pretty woman laughed. "And the cotton candy and the ice cream and the band concert."

There was no smile on Martin's face now. It had been replaced by an intensity, a yearning. "There isn't anything quite as good ever," he said softly. "Not quite as good as summer and being a kid."

The woman stared at him. What was there about this man? "Are you from around here?" she asked.

Martin said, "A long time ago. I lived just a couple of blocks from here. I remember that bandstand. God, I should. I used to sneak away at night, lie over there on the grass staring up at the stars, listening to the music." His voice took on an excitement now. "I played ball on that field over there," he continued. "Third base. And I grew up with that merry-go-round." He pointed to the concert pavilion. "I carved my name on that post

over there one summer. I was eleven years old and I carved my
name right on—" He stopped abruptly and stared.

There was a small boy sitting on the railing of the pavilion
carving something on the post with a jackknife. Martin Sloan
walked slowly toward him. He felt a sensation he had never felt
before. It was cold and heat and excitement. It was shock and
surprise and a mystery he couldn't fathom. He looked up at the
small boy and saw his own face of twenty-five years ago. He was
looking at himself. He stood shaking his head from side to side,
squinting up against the sun and then he saw what the boy was
carving on the post. It was a kid's printed scrawl, the letters uneven. It read, "Martin Sloan." Martin caught his breath and
pointed at the boy who was suddenly aware of him.

"Martin Sloan! *You're Martin Sloan.*"

The boy slid down from the railing. He looked frightened.
"Yes, sir, but I didn't mean nothing, honest. Lots of kids carve
their names here. Honest. I'm not the first one—"

Martin took a step closer to the boy. "You're Martin Sloan.
Of course you're Martin Sloan, that's who you are. That's the
way I looked."

He was unaware that his voice had suddenly become loud
and of course he couldn't know how intense his face looked. The
boy backed off and then scurried down the steps.

"Martin!" Sloan's voice followed him. "Martin, please—
come back. Please, Martin."

He started to chase him and the boy disappeared in the multicolored crowd of shorts and Mickey Mouse shirts and mothers'
cotton dresses.

"Please, Martin," Sloan called again, trying to find him.
"Please—don't be frightened. I don't want to hurt you. I just
wanted to—I just wanted to ask you some questions.

"I just wanted to tell you," Martin continued gently, now
more to himself, "I just wanted to tell you what is going to happen."

He turned to see the pretty woman beside him again. He
closed his eyes and ran a hand over his face, confused, bewildered.

"I don't know," he said vaguely. "I really don't know." He
opened his eyes and dropped his hand. "If it's a dream—I suppose I'll wake up."

He was conscious of the laughter once more, the calliope

music, the voices of the children. "I don't want it to be a dream," he said. "Oh, God, I don't want it to be a dream."

When he looked at the young woman there were tears in his eyes. "I don't want time to pass, do you understand? I want it to be the way it is now."

The young woman didn't understand what there was about this man that made her feel such pity. She wanted to comfort him, but did not know how. She watched him turn and walk out of the park, and she wondered about him all the rest of the day, this strange man with the intense look, who stood in the middle of the park, in love with it.

Martin knew where to go now. It was all he knew. Except that something odd was happening to him. Something unreal. He was not frightened. Merely disquieted. He went back to Oak Street and stood in front of his house. Again he felt memories sweep over him. He went up the front walk, up the steps and rang the bell. He was trembling and did not know why. He heard footsteps approaching, the door opened and a man looked at him through the screen.

"Yes?" the man inquired.

Martin Sloan didn't answer. For a moment he couldn't speak. Eighteen years ago he'd attended his father's funeral on a rainy, cold, wind-swept March afternoon and now he was looking into his father's face on the other side of a screen door. The square jaw, the deep-set blue eyes, the wonderfully etched lines that gave him a look of both humor and wisdom. His father's face. A face he loved. And it was looking at him through the screen.

"Yes?" His father stopped smiling and the voice became edged with impatience. "Whom did you want to see?"

Martin's voice was a whisper. "Dad! Dad!"

From inside the house he heard his mother's voice. His mother was dead fourteen years, but there was her voice. "Who is it, Robert?" his mother asked.

"Mom?" Martin's voice shook. "Is that Mom?"

Robert Sloan's eyes narrowed and his lips compressed. "Who are you?" he asked. "What do you want here!"

Mrs. Sloan arrived at her husband's elbow, took one look at her husband's face and then stared out at Martin.

"Why are you both here?" Martin asked. "*How* can you be here?"

Questioning and concerned, Mrs. Sloan looked from Martin to her husband. "Who is it?" she asked. "What do you want, young man?"

Martin shook his head in disbelief, feeling every part of him yearn toward the man and woman who stood before him. He wanted to touch them, feel them, embrace them.

"Mom," he said finally. "Don't you know me? It's Martin, Mom. It's Martin!"

The woman's eyes grew wide. "Martin?" She turned to her husband, whispering, "He's a lunatic or something."

Robert Sloan started to close the door. Martin tried the handle. It was locked.

"Please, Dad, wait a minute. You mustn't be frightened of me. My God, how can you be frightened of me?" He pointed to himself as if he represented all the logic in the world. "I'm Martin," he repeated. "Don't you understand? I'm Martin. I grew up here."

He saw the coldness on both faces, the fear, the rejection. He was like a little boy now. He was like a little boy who had been lost and then come home and been stopped at the front door.

"I'm your son," he said. "Don't you recognize me? Mom? Dad? Please—look at me."

The door slammed shut in his face and it was several minutes before he could walk down the steps. Then he paused to look back at the house. Questions assaulted him, questions without form. Questions that made no sense. What in God's name was happening here? Where was he? When was he? Trees and houses converged on him and he felt the street coming up at him. Oh God, he didn't want to leave. He had to see his parents again. He had to talk to them.

The sound of a car horn intruded upon him. In the next yard, there was a kid who seemed familiar. He was standing beside a roadster with a rumble seat.

"Hi," the boy shouted at him.

"Hi," Martin answered. He went toward the car.

"Nice, huh?" the boy asked. "First one of its kind in town. My dad just bought it for me."

"What?" Martin asked.

"New car," the boy's smile was persistent. "First one of its kind. Beauty, huh?"

Martin looked from the front bumper to the rear light. "Got a rumble seat," he said softly.

The boy tilted his head questioningly. "Sure, it's got a rumble seat. It's a roadster."

"I haven't seen a rumble seat in twenty years."

There was a silence and the boy's face tried to recapture the enthusiasm of a moment before. "Where you been, mister? Siberia?"

Martin Sloan didn't answer him. He just stared at the roadster. First one of its kind in town, the boy had said. First one. Brand new. A 1934 automobile and it was brand new.

It was night when Martin Sloan returned to Oak Street and stood in front of his house looking at the incredibly warm lights that shone from within. The crickets were a million tambourines that came out of the darkness. There was a scent of hyacinth in the air. There was a quiet rustle of leaf-laden trees that screened out the moon and made odd shadows on cooling sidewalks. There was a feeling of summer, so well remembered.

Martin Sloan had walked a lot of pavements and thought a lot of thoughts. He knew now with a clear and precise clarity that he was back twenty years in time. He had somehow, inexplicably, breached an unbreachable dimension. He was no longer disturbed nor apprehensive. He had a purpose now and a resolve. He wanted to put in a claim to the past. He went toward the front steps and his foot hit something soft. It was a baseball glove. He picked it up, slipped it on his hand, pounded the pocket as he had years ago. Then he discovered a bicycle propped up in the middle of the yard. He rang the bell on the handlebar and felt a hand enclose his and muffle the ring. He looked up to see Robert Sloan beside him.

"Back again, huh?" his father said.

"I had to come back, Pop. This is my house." He held up the glove in his hand. "This is mine, too. You bought it for me on my eleventh birthday."

His father's eyes narrowed.

"You gave me a baseball, too," Martin continued. "It had Lou Gehrig's autograph on it."

His father stared at him for a long, reflective moment.

"Who are you?" he asked softly. "What do you want here?" He struck a match, lit his pipe, then held the match out while he studied Martin's face in the brief flame.

"I just want to rest," Martin said. "I just want to stop running for a while. I belong here. Don't you understand, Pop? I belong here."

Robert Sloan's face softened. He was a kind man and a sensitive one. And wasn't there something about this stranger which gave him an odd feeling? Something about him that—that looked familiar?

"Look, son," he said. "You're probably sick. You've got delusions or something, maybe. I don't want to hurt you and I don't want you to get in any trouble either. But you'd better get out of here or there *will* be trouble."

There was the sound of the screen door behind him opening and Mrs. Sloan came out.

"Who are you talking to, Rob—" she began to call. She stopped abruptly when she saw Martin.

He ran over to the porch and up the steps to grab her. "Mom," he shouted at her. "Look at me! Look into my face. You can tell, can't you?"

Mrs. Sloan looked frightened and tried to back away.

"Mom! *Look at me.* Please! Who am I? Tell me who I am."

"You're a stranger," Mrs. Sloan said. "I've never seen you before. Robert, tell him to go away."

Martin grabbed her again and turned her around to face him. "You've got a son named Martin, haven't you? He goes to Emerson Public School. The month of August he spends at his aunt's farm near Buffalo, and a couple of summers you've gone up to Saratoga Lake and rented a cottage there. And once I had a sister and she died when she was a year old."

Mrs. Sloan stared at him wide-eyed. "Where's Martin now?" she said to her husband.

Again Martin tightened his grip on her shoulders. "*I'm Martin,*" he shouted. "I'm your son! You've got to believe me. I'm your son Martin." He released her and reached into his coat pocket to pull out his wallet. He began to tear out cards. "See? See? All my cards are in here. All my identification. Read them. Go ahead, read them."

He tried to force the wallet on her and his mother, desperate and frightened, lashed out and slapped him across the face. It was an instinctive action, done with all her strength. Martin stood stock still, the wallet slipping out of his fingers to fall to the ground, his head shaking from side to side as if a terrible mistake had been made and he was amazed that the woman couldn't perceive it. From the distance came the sound of the calliope. Martin turned to listen. He walked down the steps past his father to the front walk. He stood there for a moment listening to the calliope again. Then he began to run down the middle of the street toward the sound of the music.

"Martin," he shouted, as he raced toward the park. "Martin! Martin! Martin, I've got to talk to you!"

The park was lit up with lanterns and street lights and colored electric signs on the stands. A moving path of light from the merry-go-round went round and round and played on Martin's face as he looked wildly around to find an eleven-year-old boy in a night filled with them. Then suddenly he saw him. He was riding the merry-go-round.

Martin raced over to it, grabbed a post as it whirled past and catapulted himself on to the moving platform. He started a running, stumbling journey through a maze of bobbing horses and a hundred little faces that moved up and down.

"Martin," he shouted, colliding with a horse. "Martin, please, I have to talk to you!"

The little boy heard his name, looked over his shoulder, saw the man with the disheveled hair and perspiring face coming toward him. He climbed off the horse, threw his box of popcorn away and started to run, threading his way expertly among the rising and dipping horses.

"Martin!" Sloan's voice called after him.

He was getting closer. He was only ten or fifteen feet away now, but the boy continued to run from him.

It happened suddenly. Martin came within an arm's length of the boy and reached out to grab him. The boy looked over his shoulder and, unseeing, stepped over the edge of the platform and fell headlong into whirling, multicolored space. His leg caught on a protruding piece of metal that extended from under the platform, and for a shrieking, agonizing moment he was dragged along with the merry-go-round. The boy screamed just once before the attendant, his face a pale mask, reached for the clutch and pulled it back. No one noticed then or remembered later that two screams joined the calliope music as it died away in a dissonant, premature finale. Two screams. One from an eleven-year-old boy, descending through a nightmare, before he blacked out. One from Martin Sloan who felt a piercing agony shoot through his right leg. He clutched at it, almost falling. There were shouts now from mothers and children as they raced toward the little boy lying a few feet from the merry-go-round, face down in the dirt. They collected around him. An attendant pushed his way through and kneeled by the boy. He gently lifted him in his arms and a little girl's high-pitched voice rose over the crowd.

"Look at his leg. Look at his leg."

Martin Sloan, aged eleven, was carried out of the park, his right leg bleeding and mutilated. Martin tried to reach him but already they had carried him off. There was a silence and then a murmur of voices. People began to drift out of the area to their homes. Concession stands closed up. Lights went off. Within a moment Martin found himself alone. He leaned his head against one of the guard poles of the merry-go-round and closed his eyes.

"I only wanted to tell you," he whispered. "I only wanted to tell you that this was the wonderful time for you. Don't let any of it go by without—without enjoying it. There won't be any more merry-go-rounds. No more cotton candy. No more band concerts. I only wanted to tell you, Martin, that this is the wonderful time. Now! Here! That's all. That's all I wanted to tell you."

He felt a sadness well up inside of him. "God help me, Martin, that's all I wanted to tell you!"

He went over to the edge of the platform and sat down. Wooden horses stared lifelessly at him. Shuttered concession stands surveyed him blindly. The summer night hung all around him and let him alone. He didn't know how long he had sat there when he heard footsteps. He looked up to see his father walk across the merry-go-round platform to reach his side. Robert Sloan looked down at him and held out a wallet in his hand. Martin's wallet.

"I thought you'd want to know," Robert said. "The boy will be all right. He may limp some, the doctor told us, but he'll be all right."

Martin nodded. "I thank God for that."

"You dropped this by the house," Robert said, handing him the wallet. "I looked inside."

"And?"

"It told quite a few things about you," Robert said earnestly. "The driver's license, cards, the money in it." He paused for a moment. "It seems that you *are* Martin Sloan. You're thirty-six years old. You have an apartment in New York." Then, with a question in his voice—"It says your license expires in 1960. That's twenty-five years from now. The dates on the bills—the money, those dates haven't arrived yet, either."

Martin looked straight in his father's face. "You know now then, don't you?" he asked.

Robert nodded. "Yes, I know. I know who you are and I know you've come a long way from here. A long way and—a long time. I don't know why or how. Do you?"

Martin shook his head.

"But you know other things, don't you, Martin? Things that will happen."

"Yes, I do."

"You also know when your mother and I—when we'll—"

Martin whispered, "Yes, I know that, too."

Robert took the pipe out of his mouth and studied Martin for a long moment. "Well, don't tell me. I'd appreciate not knowing. That's a part of the mystery we live with. I think it should always be a mystery." There was a moment's pause. "Martin?"

"Yes, Dad."

Robert put his hand on Martin's shoulder. "You have to leave here. There's no room for you. And there's no place. Do you understand?"

Martin nodded and said softly, "I see that now. But I *don't* understand. Why not?"

Robert smiled. "I guess because we only get one chance. Maybe there's only one summer to a customer." Now his voice was deep and rich with compassion. "The little boy . . . the one *I* know, the one who belongs here. This is his summer, Martin. Just as it was yours one time." He shook his head. "Don't make him share it."

Martin rose and looked off toward the darkened park.

"Is it so bad—where you're from?" Robert asked him.

"I thought so," Martin answered. "I've been living at a dead run, Dad. I've been weak and I made believe I was strong. I've been scared to death—but I've been playing a strong man. And suddenly it all caught up with me. And I felt so tired, Pop. I felt so damned tired, running for so long. Then—one day I knew I had to come back. I had to come back and get on a merry-go-round and listen to a band concert and eat cotton candy. I had to stop and breathe and close my eyes and smell and listen."

"I guess we all want that," Robert said gently. "But, Martin, when you go back, maybe you'll find that there are merry-go-rounds and band concerts where you are and summer nights, too. Maybe you haven't looked in the right place. You've been looking behind you, Martin. Try looking ahead."

There was a silence. Martin turned to look at his father. He felt a love, an acme of tenderness, a link, deeper than flesh that ties men to men.

"Maybe, Dad," he said. "Maybe. Good-by, Dad."

Robert walked several feet away, stopped, remained there for a moment, his back to Martin, then he turned toward him again. "Good-by—son," he said.

An instant later he was gone. Behind Martin the merry-go-round began to move. The lights were off, there was no noise, only the shadowy figures of the horses going round and round. Martin stepped on it as it turned, a quiet herd of wooden steeds with painted eyes that went around in the night. It went a full circle and then began to slow down. There was no one on it. Martin Sloan was gone.

Martin Sloan went into the drugstore. It was the one he remembered as a boy, but aside from the general shape of the room and the stairway leading to an office off a small balcony, it bore no resemblance to the place he remembered. It was light and cheerful with strips of fluorescent lights, a blaring, garish juke box, a fancy soda bar full of shining chrome. There were a lot of high school kids there dancing to the juke box, poring over the teen mags in the corner near the front window. It was air conditioned and very cool. Martin walked through the smoke of cigarettes, the blaring rock 'n' roll, the laughing voices of the kids, his eyes looking around trying to find any single thing that had familiarity. A young soda jerk behind the counter smiled at him.

"Hi," he said. "Something for you?"

Martin sat down on one of the chrome and leather stools.

"Maybe a chocolate soda, huh?" he said to the kid behind the fountain. "Three dips?"

"Three dips?" the soda jerk repeated. "Sure, I can make one with three dips for you. It'll be extra. Thirty-five cents. Okay?"

Martin smiled a little sadly. "Thirty-five cents, huh?" His eyes scanned the room again. "How about old Mr. Wilson," he asked. "Used to own this place."

"Oh, he died," the soda jerk said. "A long time ago. Maybe fifteen, twenty years. What kind of ice cream you want? Chocolate? Vanilla?"

Martin wasn't listening to him.

"Vanilla?" the soda jerk repeated.

"I've changed my mind," Martin said. "I guess I'll pass on the soda." He started to get off the stool and half stumbled as his stiff right leg was thrust out momentarily in an awkward position. "These stools weren't built for bum legs," he said with a rueful grin.

The soda jerk looked concerned. "Guess not. Get that in the war?"

"What?"

"Your leg. Did you get that in the war?"

"No," said Martin thoughtfully. "As a matter of fact I got it falling off a merry-go-round when I was a kid. Freak thing."

The soda jerk snapped his fingers. "The merry-go-round! Hey, I remember the merry-go-round. They tore it down a few years ago. Condemned it." Then he smiled sympathetically. "Little late I guess, huh?"

"How's that?" Martin asked.

"A little late for you, I mean."

Martin took a long look around the drugstore. "Very late," he said softly. "Very late for me."

He went out into the hot summer day again. The hot summer day that appeared on the calendar as June 26, 1959. He walked down the main street and out of the town, back toward the gas station, where he'd left his car for a lube job and oil change so long ago. He walked slowly, his right leg dragging slightly along the dusty shoulder of the highway.

At the gas station he paid the attendant, got into his car, turned it around and started back toward New York City. Only once did he glance over his shoulder at a sign which read, "Homewood, 1½ miles." The sign was wrong. He knew that much. Homewood was farther away than that. It was much farther.

The tall man in the Brooks Brothers suit, driving a red Mercedes-Benz, gripped the wheel thoughtfully as he headed south toward New York. He didn't know exactly what would face him at the other end of the journey. All he knew was that he'd discovered something. Homewood. Homewood, New York. It wasn't walking distance.

From Rod Serling's closing narration, "Walking Distance," *The Twilight Zone*, October 30, 1959, CBS Television Network.

LONG ANGLE SHOT

Looking down as the car slowly starts onto the highway. Over the disappearing car we hear the Narrator's Voice.

> NARRATOR'S VOICE
> Martin Sloan, age thirty-six. Vice-president in charge of media. Successful in most things, but not in the one effort that all men try at some time in their lives—trying to go home again.
> (a pause)
> And also like all men perhaps there'll be an occasion, maybe a summer night sometime, when he'll look up from what he's doing and listen to the distant music of a calliope—and hear the voices and the laughter of the people and the places of his past. And perhaps across his mind there'll flit a little errant wish—that a man might not have to become old, never outgrow the parks and the merry-go-rounds of his youth.
> (a pause)
> And he'll smile then too because he'll know it *is* just an errant wish. Some wisp of memory not too important really. Some laughing ghosts that cross a man's mind . . . that are a part of The Twilight Zone.

Now the CAMERA PANS down the road to the sign that reads "Homewood, 1½ miles."

FADE TO BLACK

THE FEVER

It was this way with Franklin Gibbs. He had a carefully planned, precisely wrought little life that encompassed a weekly Kiwanis meeting on Thursday evening at the Salinas Hotel; an adult study group sponsored by his church on Wednesday evening; church each Sunday morning; his job as a teller at the local bank; and about one evening a week spent with friends playing parchesi or something exciting like that. He was a thin, erect, middle-aged, little man whose narrow shoulders were constantly kept pinned back in the manner of a West Point plebe and he wore a tight-fitting vest which spanned a pigeon chest. On his lapel was a Kiwanis ten-year attendance pin and, above that, a fifteen-year service pin given him by the president of the bank. He and his wife lived on Elm Street in a small, two-bedroom house which was about twenty years old, had a small garden in back, and an arbor of roses in front which were Mr. Gibbs's passion.

Flora Gibbs, married to Franklin for twenty-two years, was angular, with mousy, stringy hair and chest measurements perhaps a quarter of an inch smaller than her husband's. She was quiet voiced though talkative, long, if unconsciously, suffering and had led a life devoted to the care and feeding of Franklin

Gibbs, the placating of his sullen moods, his finicky appetite, and his uncontrollable rage at any change in the routine of their daily lives.

This background explains at least in part Franklin Gibbs's violent reaction to Flora's winning the contest. It was one of those crazy and unexpected things that seem occasionally to explode into an otherwise prosaic, uneventful life. And it had exploded into Flora's. She had written in to a national contest explaining in exactly eighteen words why she preferred Aunt Martha's ready-mix biscuits to any other brand. She had written concisely and sparingly, because her life was a concise and spare life without the frills or the little, flamboyant luxuries of other women, a life of rationed hours and budgeted moments; thin, skimpy, unadorned, unpunctuated, until the contest, by the remotest hint of variance or color. And then she got the telegram. Not the first prize—that would have been too much. (It happened to be fifty thousand dollars, and Franklin, with thin-lipped impatience, suggested that perhaps had she tried harder she might have won it.) It was the third prize, which involved a three-day trip for two, all expenses paid, to Las Vegas, Nevada, a beautiful room in a most exceptionally modern and famous gambling hotel, with shows, sightseeing tours, and wonderful food all thrown in, along with an airplane flight there and back.

The announcement of the trip fell into Flora's life like a star shell bursting over a no-man's-land. Even Franklin was momentarily taken aback at the suddenly animated appearance of his normally drab-faced wife. It gradually dawned on him that Flora was quite serious about wanting to take the trip to Vegas. There was a scene over the breakfast table the morning after the telegram's arrival. Franklin told his wife in no uncertain terms that gambling in Las Vegas was for the very rich or the very foolish. It was not for the stable or the moral and since morality and stability meant a great deal to Mr. Gibbs, they would have to telegraph back to the contest people (collect, Mr. Gibbs parenthetically noted) to acquaint them with their decision about Las Vegas, Nevada, and, as Mr. Gibbs put it, "its decidedly questionable roadhouse vice-dens."

When Mr. Gibbs returned from the bank that noontime for lunch, there wasn't any. Flora was crying in her room and, for the first time in a rooster-pecked, subservient, acquiescent life, she took a stand. She had won the trip to Las Vegas and she was going, with or without Franklin. This information was imparted through heavy sobbing and a spasmodic rendition of a biblical quotation—something about whither thou goest I shalt go; something some lady in the Old Testament had said to another lady, but sufficiently close in its application here to cover a husband not accompanying his wife on a trip to Las Vegas. But actually it was a combination of a long Memorial Day weekend and the fact that the trip was free that finally made Franklin Gibbs change his mind.

A week later, Franklin, in his shiny, tight, blue Kiwanis Officer's Installation suit with vest and lapel button, and Flora, in a flower-patterned cotton dress with a big green sash and a flowerpot hat with a large feather, took the six-and-a-half-hour flight to Las Vegas, Nevada. Flora spent the entire six-and-a-half hours gurgling excitedly; Franklin remained petulantly silent with only an occasional remark about any state government so totally immoral as to permit legalized gambling.

They were met at the airport by a hotel car which drove them to the Desert Frontier Palace—a gaudy, low-slung, sweeping structure emblazoned with nude girls in neon. Flora spent the automobile trip telling the driver all about Elgin, Kansas, in a high-pitched, ludicrously girlish way. Franklin remained silent except for a single comment on a platinum blonde who passed in front of the car when it stopped for a light. This was to the effect that she seemed typical of a town of decidedly questionable virtue.

Their room was air-conditioned, very modern and comfortable in a highly chromed way. The management had left a bowl of fruit and a vase of flowers which Flora nervously rearranged three or four times, while she chattered at her husband. Franklin sat glumly reading a Chamber of Commerce booklet from the City Fathers of Las Vegas, punctuating the few silences with negative comparisons between Vegas and much more solid, if smaller, Elgin, Kansas.

An hour later there was a knock on the door and the hotel public relations man entered with a photographer. His name was Marty Lubow and he wore the professional greeter's smile with competence.

"Well, Mr. and Mrs. Gibbs," Lubow asked, "is your room comfortable? Is there anything at all you need? Anything I can do for you?"

Flora's voice trilled nervously as her hands darted around her dress, pulling up, yanking down, straightening, smoothing. "Oh, it's lovely, Mr. Lubow. Just lovely. You make us feel—well, you make us feel important!"

Lubow laughed jovially back at her, "Well, after all, you are important, Mrs. Gibbs. It isn't every day we can entertain a celebrated contest winner!"

The photographer at his elbow looked glum and whispered over his shoulder, "Not every day—maybe every *other* day."

Lubow's laugh covered the photographer's voice and pushed its way through the room. There was something enveloping about Mr. Lubow's laugh. It was his own special weapon for every emergency.

"I think," he said, "we should take our pictures right here. I think standing in the middle of the room would be best, don't you, Joe?"

The photographer heaved a deep sigh which was a combination of agreement and resignation. He stuck a bulb in the flash section of the camera, then leaned against the door lining up the shot. Lubow ushered Flora to a spot in the center of the room, then beckoned to Franklin who remained silently dour in his chair.

"Right over here next to your lovely missus, Mr. Gibbs," he said happily.

Franklin let out a long-suffering sigh, rose and walked over to stand close to Flora.

"Wonderful," gushed Lubow, looking at the two of them with amazed eyes, as if by joining them in the center of the room he had performed a feat only a degree less amazing than climbing the Matterhorn all alone. "Just wonderful," he repeated. "All right, Joe, how's that look?"

The photographer responded by taking the picture and left both Flora and Franklin blinking in the aftermath of the flash— Flora with her fixed, nervous smile, and Franklin staring malevolently and challengingly toward the photographer. Again Lubow's laughter shook the room. He pounded on Franklin's back, wrung his hand, patted Flora's cheek and somehow, in the same motion, headed toward the door. The photographer had already opened it and was on his way out.

"Now you folks just keep in touch with us—" Lubow was saying as he left.

"It's *The Elgin Bugle*, Mr. Lubow," Flora called after him. Lubow turned. "How's that?" he inquired.

"That's our home town paper," Flora answered. *"The Elgin Bugle."*

"Of course, of course, Mrs. Gibbs. *The Elgin Bugle*. We'll send a copy of the picture right out to them. Enjoy yourselves, folks, and welcome to Las Vegas and the Desert Frontier Palace."

He winked happily at Flora, grinned manfully at Franklin and was only momentarily nonplussed by the frozen petulance on Franklin's face. He recovered sufficiently to wave as he walked away. His laughter was a twenty-one-gun salute honoring nothing in particular, but in an odd way pulling the curtain down on the meeting.

It was another fifty-five minutes before Flora could persuade her husband to go out to the gambling room and see what it was like. It took the bulk of those minutes for her to persuade him that there was nothing immoral in just *watching* people gambling. And in the intervals between argument she was forced to listen to Franklin's own personal critique on the miserable weakness of human beings who threw away money on dice, cards and machines. In the end he suffered himself to be put into his Kiwanis Officer Installation coat once again and led by Flora into the main building of the hotel, and then into the principal gambling room. It was a plush, noisy, people-loaded room, crowded with crap tables, a long bar, roulette wheels and three rows of one-armed bandits. It was a room full of noises that rose up from the heavily carpeted floor, touched the acoustical ceiling, and though softened by both, nonetheless hung in the air. The noises were gambling noises. There was the spinning clatter of roulette wheels. The tinkle of glasses. The metallic clack, clack, clack of the one-armed bandit levers being pulled down. There were the droning voices of the croupiers calling out numbers, red and black, and underneath all of this the varied pitch of human voices—the nervous squeals of the winners, the protesting groans of the losers. The sounds fused together and hit Franklin and Flora Gibbs with the force of an explosion as they entered the room and stood there on the periphery of the activity, staring into the strange, gaudy and noisy new world.

The two of them stood at the door trying to feel at ease, conscious for the first time of how they looked—Flora, a fluttery woman, in an unfashionable dress with a corsage that did nothing but emphasize dullness; Franklin, a little man in a 1937 suit, with slicked-down hair, pointed shoes and a look of midwestern primness, worn defensively like a badge. They were two foreign elements at this moment, joined together in a bond of inferiority closer, perhaps, than they ever shared in Elgin, Kansas.

They stood there like that for ten minutes, watching the tables, the games, the stacks of chips and silver dollars; the glamorous-looking women and the impeccable men. Flora's eyes grew wider and wider. She turned to Franklin.

"It has such a flavor, this place!"

He looked at her, fishy-eyed, then turned up his nose. "Flavor, Flora? I'm surprised at you. You know how I feel about gambling."

Flora smiled appeasingly. "Well, this is different though, Franklin—"

"It is neither different nor moral. Gambling is gambling! It's *your* vacation, Flora. But I must, in good conscience, repeat to you what I have been saying all along—that it's a tragic waste of time. Hear me, Flora? A tragic waste of time!"

Flora's lower lip trembled and she reached out to touch his arm. "Please, Franklin," she said quietly, "try to enjoy it, won't you? We haven't had a vacation in such a long time. Such a very long time. A vacation—or even a good time together."

Franklin's left eyebrow shot upward and his voice was that of a wounded Congressional Medal of Honor winner who had suddenly been told he had to go back on the line. "It is a matter of record, Flora," he announced, "that I work desperately hard and I have very little time—" It was the opening paragraph to a tailor-made speech that Franklin delivered at least once a month. It was when he branched off into a new tack, alleging that he felt unclean in this kind of room with semi-clad girls and dice throwers, that he realized Flora was no longer listening to him.

Across the room a one-armed bandit had lit up, a bell clanged, and a woman screamed hysterically. After a moment, a long-legged blonde in tights, carrying a basket of money, walked over to the woman by the machine, called out its number to a floor manager and then handed the woman the basket of money. She was immediately surrounded by members of her party who took her to the bar, all chattering like happy squirrels.

Flora left Franklin's side and went to the one-armed bandits spread along one whole side of the room. From where she stood it looked like a forest of arms yanking down levers. There was a continuous clack, clack, clack of levers, then a click, click, click of tumblers coming up. Following this was a metallic poof sometimes followed by the clatter of silver dollars coming down through the funnel to land with a happy smash in the coin receptacle at the bottom of the machine.

Franklin was studying the long-legged blonde with sour disapproval, and was unaware that Flora had taken a nickel out of her purse until she dropped the coin into one of the machines. Flora was reaching for the lever when she realized that Franklin was glaring at her. She flushed, forced a smile and then looked supplicatingly at him.

"Franklin, it's—it's only a nickel machine, dear."

His high-pitched voice sandpapered against her. "Just a nickel machine, Flora? *Just* a nickel machine! Why don't you just go out and throw handfuls of nickels into the street?"

"Franklin, darling—"

He moved closer to her, his voice low, but full of a carefully closeted fury. "All right, Flora, we go to Las Vegas. We waste three days and two nights. We do it because that's your idiotic way of enjoying yourself. And it doesn't cost us anything. But now you're spending our money. Not even spending it, Flora— you're just throwing it away. And it's at this point, Flora, that I have to take a hand. You are obviously not mature enough—"

There was the suggestion of pain in Flora's eyes. Her face was edged with a nervousness that Franklin recognized as a prelude to several hours of quiet handwringing, and deep, spasmodic sighs. It was Flora's only defense over the years.

"Please . . . please, Franklin, don't make a scene," she whispered. "I won't play. I promise you—" She turned to the machine and then, with a kind of hopeless gesture, back to him. "The nickel's already in."

Franklin heaved a deep, resigned sigh and looked up toward the ceiling. "All right," he said. "Throw it away. Pull down the lever or whatever it is you do. Just throw it away."

Flora kept her eyes on Franklin as she pulled the lever down, listening to the sound of the tumblers and then the empty poof and then the silence. The corners of Franklin's mouth twitched in a righteous smile, and for one fleeting moment Flora hated him. Then habit took over for her, and she stood quietly at her husband's elbow and heard him declare that he was going back to the room to get ready for dinner.

"I guess I'm not very lucky," she said softly.

He didn't answer. At the door she looked straight into his face.

"Franklin, it was only a nickel."

"Twenty of them make a dollar, Flora, and I work hard for those dollars!"

He was about to open the door when a drunk standing by a dollar machine turned and saw him. The drunk grabbed Franklin, pulled him over to the machine. Franklin recoiled as if exposed to something infective, but the drunk held Franklin firmly with one hand, a glass in the other.

"Here, old buddy," the drunk said, "—you try it." He put down his glass and took a silver dollar from his pocket. "Here, go ahead. I'm one hour and thirty minutes on this miserable, crummy, money-grabbin'—!" He forced the silver dollar into Franklin's hand. "Go ahead, old pal. It's yours. You play it."

A woman at the bar waved frantically at them. "Charlie," she screamed, "are you gonna come over here or am I gonna come over there and get you?"

"I'm coming, honey, I'm coming," he answered. He smiled at Franklin, burped out a shaft of Johnny Walker-flavored air, patted Franklin on the back and then guided his hand, still holding the silver dollar, into the slot on top of the machine.

Franklin looked like a small animal caught in a trap. He looked wildly left and right, searching for aid, embarrassed, discomfited, frightened.

"Really," Franklin said, "I'm not at all interested. Please— I'm in a hurry—"

The drunk chortled happily as the silver dollar was deposited in the slot, then walked unsteadily toward the bar.

Franklin glowered at the machine. His first thought was the possibility of getting the silver dollar back without having to play it. He studied the machine intently. It was like all the others. Big, gaudily lit, with a glass-covered compartment in the center, showing an incredible number of silver dollars inside its big metal gut. Two lights over this compartment had an odd similarity to eyes and the slot at the bottom filled out the picture of a monstrous neon face. Franklin raised his right hand to the lever.

Over his shoulder he saw Flora smiling hopefully. Then, as if taking a big decisive step, he yanked down the lever, watched the whirling tumblers that one after another came to a stop, showing two cherries and a lemon. There was a loud metallic clack and then the sound of the coins as they arrived in the receptacle at the bottom—ten of them.

Franklin was only faintly aware of Flora's delighted squeal. He looked down at the coins and slowly, one by one, took them out. A strange, warm sensation was running through him; an odd excitement that he'd never experienced before. He saw his reflection in the chrome strip on the machine and was surprised at what he saw—a flushed, bright-eyed little face, cheek muscles twitching, lips stretched tight in a thin smile.

"Oh, Franklin, you *are* lucky."

He looked at Flora, manufacturing a grimness of face and tone, and held up the silver dollars in his palm. He said, "Now, Flora, you'll see the difference between a normal, mature, thoughtful man and these wild idiots around here. We will take these, put them in our room, and we will go home with them."

"Of course, dear."

"These baboons here would throw it away. They'd compulsively put it back into the machine. But the Gibbses don't! The Gibbses know the value of money! Come on, my dear, it's late. I'd like to shave for dinner."

Without waiting for her, he turned toward the door. Flora padded after him like a diffident pet. A look of pride was on her face as she watched the tiny, erect figure ahead of her pushing his way through the crowd with a resolution and a strength that seemed to reaffirm the status of Elgin, Kansas. Neither of them saw the drunk return to the machine and put in another silver dollar. But Franklin heard the sound of coins landing in the receptacle.

He whirled around, startled. He had heard coins all right, but he had heard something else too. He had distinctly heard his own name, a metallic, raspy jumbled rendition—but, nonetheless, his name. The coins had landed in the receptacle and had called out, "Franklin." He rubbed nervously at his jaw and turned to Flora.

"Did you say something?" he asked.

"What, dear?"

He turned to stare at her, taking a moment to identify her, having to reach back into his subconscious to reconstitute a world that he had left several hours before and which no longer seemed very real to him.

"Stay here, Flora," he said. "I have to get some more silver dollars. Don't let anybody use this machine, understand?"

"Franklin, dear—" her voice half-heartedly chased him, and then died out as he left her behind.

She watched him take a bill out of his wallet, hand it to the cashier, and get a large stack of silver dollars in return. He carried them back, brushed past her and started to feed them into the machine, one by one. He'd gone through five of them with no result when Flora touched his arm again, this time much more positively, and with a grip sufficiently tight to keep him from depositing yet another silver dollar.

"Franklin!" her voice carried a rising concern. "How much money have you lost? Have you been playing this machine all night?"

Franklin's voice was terse. "I have."

"You've lost a great deal of money then, haven't you?"

"Very likely."

Flora wet her lips and tried to smile. "Well, darling, don't you think you ought to stop?"

He looked at her as if she'd just suggested that he drink a bucket of paint. "Stop?" he half shouted. "How can I stop, Flora? How in God's name can I stop? I've lost a great deal of money. A great deal of money! Look! Look at this."

He pointed to the big sign over the machine. "Special jackpot $8,000," it read.

"See that?" he said. "When it pays off, you make eight thousand dollars!" He turned to the machine again, speaking more to it than to his wife. "Well, it's got to pay off. If a person stands here long enough, it *must* pay off."

As if to emphasize the logic of his remark, he slammed another silver dollar in the slot, pulled down the lever and stared intently at the tumblers as a cherry came up with two lemons and three silver dollars dropped into the receptacle. Again he lost himself with the machine and became oblivious to Flora. He lost five more silver dollars and felt the gnawing bite of irritation that comes with defeat.

"Franklin, darling," Flora began, "you know how awful you

feel in the morning when you've been up too late at night—"

He whirled around at her and screamed, "Flora, why don't you shut your mouth."

She drew back, white-faced, feeling the shriveling shame that was always caused by Franklin's temper. He noticed it and it egged him on. It always gave him a kind of perverse satisfaction to yell at Flora. She was so plain and so weak; she was such a piece of dough to be pulled and kneaded and pounded. And she was worth screaming at, because she would react. Not like the machine that had been his enemy for so many hours, his tormentor. He wanted to kick the machine, to scratch it, gouge it, make it feel pain. But the machine was impassive and invulnerable. Flora wasn't. Flora with her mousy little face. For a passing, exploding moment he wanted to hit her, to smash his fist into her face. But it was almost as good to scream at her and get a reaction.

"I hate a shrew, Flora," he shouted.

Several people turned to stare at them.

"I can't stand a woman who hangs over your shoulder and sees to it that you have miserable luck."

He heard her sobbing intake of breath and it poured kerosene on the fire that flared inside of him.

"That's what you're doing to me now, Flora—you're giving me miserable luck. You and your Las Vegas. You and your God-damned contests. Get out of my sight, will you? Will you get out of my sight now!"

She made one more weak, pitiful protest, "Franklin, please, people are watching—"

"The hell with people," he shouted. "I'm not concerned with people. People can go to hell."

He turned and, with sweaty palms, clutched at the sides of the machine, his lips compressed. Burning on his face was the anger of frustration, mixed with the high fever of the bad gambler.

"This is what I'm concerned with," he said. "This machine! This damned machine." His anger burned hotter, his frustration took over. He pounded his knuckles against it. "It's inhuman the way it lets you win a little and then takes it all back. It teases you. It holds out promises and wheedles you. It sucks you in. And then—" He slammed another silver dollar into the slot, pulled down the lever with both hands, then watched as two plums and a lemon showed up on the tumbler and there was the dull click once again, with silence following it.

He was unaware of Flora now, unaware of the people who stood watching him behind her. He was unconscious of the noises, the lights, the sweat on his body, the fact that his mouth twitched. There was this machine in front of him. There was this machine that had a face on it and it had been cheating him and he had to pay it back. He had to revenge himself on it and the only weapons he could use were silver dollars. He put them in, pulled down the lever, watched, listened, waited.

He didn't see Flora, handkerchief to face, walk away from the machine and disappear out the door. He didn't hear a man in a cashmere sport coat comment loudly to his wife that, "the little prune-faced guy was a real nut with that machine." A waiter asked him if he wanted a drink and he didn't look at the waiter or answer him. There were only two things left in Franklin Gibbs's world. Himself and the machine. Everything else had ceased to exist.

He was a sour-faced little man in an old-fashioned suit and he stood at the machine gorging it with silver dollars, trying to make it vomit back at him. He was a dope addict now, in the middle of a long and protracted needle, and he never really knew, even at five in the morning when the room was empty save for one blackjack game, one dice table still operating and himself, that in every clinical sense, he'd lost his mind.

Everything that he'd used to sustain himself through his lifetime—his willfulness, his pettiness, his self-delusions, his prejudices—he'd whipped together like a suit of armor and this is what he wore as he battled the machine on into the morning. Slip in the coin, pull down the lever. Slip in the coin, pull down the lever. Slip in the coin, pull down the lever. Keep it up. Don't stop. Don't break the routine of hand and arm and eye and ear. This was the new chronology of his life function. Sooner or later the machine would pay off. It would surrender to him. It would acknowledge his superiority by suddenly spewing out eight thousand silver dollars. This was all he thought about as he stood there, oblivious to the dawn outside, to anything except that he was alone in the world with a one-armed bandit that had a face.

When the night cashier left and yawned a good morning to his replacement, he made mention of the funny little duck by the machine who'd been there something like seven hours.

"I seen them get hooked before," he said to his replacement, then shook his head, "but never like him. Never like that buggy little guy over there!"

That was the epitaph to Franklin Gibbs's first night at Las Vegas, but only to that night. At eight-thirty in the morning, when Flora came in to find him, he was still at the machine.

Marty Lubow had a brief talk with the resident manager of the hotel about eleven in the morning. They talked in passing of a couple of public relations stunts in the offing, the nature of the ad campaign for Sammy Davis, Jr., who would start at the hotel two weeks hence, and, just before Lubow left, the manager asked him about Franklin Gibbs whom several people had mentioned. There is a grapevine of no mean proportions in the Las Vegas hotel circuit. Let a man make seven straight passes at a crap table and within five minutes the information is known all over town. Or let a movie star drop a bundle and make a scene and a gossip columnist has phoned it in within an hour. But even in a town full of characters and caricatures, there was always room for one more. And a sour-faced little man in a 1937 suit was obviously setting a new record for time spent and money lost at one silver buck machine. The manager queried Lubow as to the nature of the beast and Lubow laughingly told him that if Gibbs could hold out till six that evening they could probably set up some picture stuff. This might be a natural for *Life* magazine.

But at three o'clock that afternoon, after Lubow had seen Franklin, he was no longer interested in any kind of press coverage. Quite the contrary. One look at the little man's face was quite sufficient to have him phone the house physician to inquire somewhat obliquely how long a man could live without sleep.

At five-thirty, Franklin Gibbs had lost three thousand, eight hundred dollars, cashed three checks, downed one glass of orange juice and one half of a boiled ham sandwich, and had come close to striking his wife across the side of the face when, with tears rolling down her cheeks, she had pleaded with him to come back to the room to take a nap.

Franklin Gibbs's life was entirely funneled into the slot machine in front of him. At this point he had no recollection of ever having done anything but feed in coins and pull down levers. He felt neither thirst nor hunger. He knew he was desperately tired and that his vision seemed out of focus, but there was no question of giving up.

It wasn't until nine o'clock that evening, after the hotel manager had told him he would be unable to cash another check and Flora had telegraphed his brother in Iowa—a rambling, incoherent telegram which spoke of disaster—that Franklin Gibbs got an ice-cold, clutching feeling in his gut. He had three silver dollars left and he'd reached the point where he kept mumbling to the machine that it was now time to pay off. He was owed eight thousand silver dollars and there wasn't any question about it. What was the matter with the machine, anyway? Didn't it know the rules? He kept talking to it, urging it, arguing with it— sweaty, sodden, obsessed. It was just twenty-one minutes after eleven when Franklin Gibbs put in the last silver dollar. The machine made a strange kind of whirring noise and the lever stopped halfway down on its arc, clanked noisily and then stuck. Franklin Gibbs stood stock-still for a long, unbelieving moment and it came to him that right then, right at that instant, he was being taken. This was the moment of the big cheat. Obviously this was the coin that was to have brought him the eight-thousand-dollar jackpot. He had no doubt about it at all. He was supposed to have won this time, and the machine, the machine with the ugly face, the machine that had hounded him by calling out his name, had now stooped to the nadir of deceit and was refusing to pay off.

Franklin felt ripples of anger rise up from deep inside him, anger that began as a trickle and built to a coursing flood. Anger that bubbled and seethed and boiled. Anger that suddenly pinched at him and clutched at him and tore at him.

"What's the idea?" he shouted at the machine. "What's the idea, you bastard! Goddamn you. Give me back my dollar. That's my last one, you miserable, crummy, dirty—" His breath caught up with him and for a moment all he could do was wheeze. "Give me back my Goddamned dollar."

He hit the machine. He punched it. He clawed it. He shoved it. Two floor men, a cashier and the assistant manager, headed toward him from opposite points of the room, but not before he had broken the knuckles of his right hand and not before he had pushed the machine off its stand to go crashing down to the floor, and not before he had thrown himself on it, tangling himself up in it, cutting his arm against the broken glass that was its nose and bleeding all over the carpet.

They led him out of the room, screaming, crying, sobbing, shouting and fighting. Flora ran after them, wringing her hands and weeping.

The house physician set and bandaged Franklin's hand, put three stitches in his arm and gave him a sedative. They undressed him, put him to bed, then stood over him while he fell into an uneasy sleep. The doctor told Flora that it would be best to take him home the following day and that Franklin should have a long session with his own physician when he returned to Elgin, Kansas. He even murmured something about the possibility of psychiatric help later on. Flora kept nodding at him, her face pale and tear-stained. After they had gone she sat silently staring at her husband.

Somewhere in the nether land of Franklin Gibbs's subconscious he heard a voice clear and distinct. It was produced by coins rubbing against themselves. It was a metallic, clanking, "Franklin!" that suddenly was shouted into the air. He woke with a start and heard it again. Then again. He got out of bed and walked past a frightened Flora toward the door.

"Franklin!" It came from the hall outside. It mocked him. It assailed him. It spit at him. He flung open the door. There was the machine in the corridor, its eyes blinking on and off.

"Franklin," it cajoled him. "Franklin, Franklin, Franklin."

He screamed and slammed the door.

"Franklin, Franklin, Franklin."

The noise of it filled the room and then he saw it staring at him in the bedroom mirror. He screamed again and turning, saw it behind the chair. He backed against the closet door and mistaking it for an escape route, flung it open. There was the machine inside the closet blinking at him and calling his name. He tripped and sprawled on the floor, banging his head against the corner of the dresser, and there was the machine looking at him from the center of the room.

"Franklin, Franklin, Franklin," it called out to him.

He couldn't scream any more. He had no voice left. All he had to clutch was his terror. A silent, voiceless terror. He scrambled to his feet and ran this way and that way, now bumping against furniture, now falling into the arms of Flora who scrabbled at him, shouting his name. He opened the door to the hall and there was the machine grinning at him.

The last moment of Franklin Gibbs's life was spent in a mad dash across the hotel room toward the window. He went through it, taking most of the glass with him, to land two stories below on the concrete walk that surrounded the big swimming pool. He hit it, forehead first, and the loud snap that separated his vertebrae at the back of his neck bore no relationship to any sound that Flora had ever heard before. But she heard this over the sound of her own screaming as she stood at the broken window and looked down at the crumpled figure of Franklin Gibbs in his pajamas, his head tilted at an odd angle to his body. He was quite dead.

No one was allowed to touch the body. Someone had tastefully and compassionately covered it with a blanket. A sheriff's deputy had phoned for the ambulance and was just now succeeding in getting most of the people out of the pool area.

Mr. Lubow, white-faced with anxiety, was in Flora's room helping her pack. He was telling her there was a much more comfortable little sanitarium at the other end of the town and he was quite certain she'd be able to rest there much more easily. She sat on the edge of the bed while he talked to her in low, nervous gusts about how sad and sorry they were that this had happened. She was a dough-faced, catatonic sphinx whose life had suddenly drained away. She had a vague passing thought that she should telegraph Franklin's brother again and she thought additionally that Franklin hadn't believed in insurance, but both thoughts were dulled and stifled by a blanket of neutral dullness that she let settle over her. She didn't want to think any more. She was too tired.

Down by the pool Franklin Gibbs's body lay cold and broken. One lifeless hand extended from underneath the blanket, resting on the concrete. In the dark shrubbery beyond, there was a rattle of noise. A silver dollar fell to the ground and rolled unerringly across the walk to spin to a stop right next to Franklin Gibbs's hand.

No one in the hotel could explain what the one-armed bandit was doing near the pool where they found it the following morning. It was in pretty bad shape, dented, scratched, with the lever stuck tight and most of its glass broken, but they sent it to the factory for a repair job and it was due back on the line within a week or two. The pool boy found the silver dollar also the following morning and put it in his pocket and Flora Gibbs flew back to Elgin, Kansas, to pick up the broken crockery of her life.

She lived a silent, patient life from then on and gave no one any trouble. Only once did anything unusual happen and that was a year later. The church had a bazaar and someone brought in an old used one-armed bandit. It had taken three of her friends from the Women's Alliance to stop her screaming and get her back home to bed. It had cast rather a pall over the evening.

From Rod Serling's closing narration, "The Fever," *The Twilight Zone*, February 5, 1960, CBS Television Network.

NARRATOR'S VOICE
Mr. Franklin Gibbs, visitor to Las Vegas,
who lost his money, his reason, and
finally his life to an inanimate metal
machine variously described as—a one-
armed bandit, a slot machine or, in
Mr. Franklin Gibbs's words, a monster
with a will all its own. For our
purposes we'll stick with the latter
because we're in The Twilight Zone!

FADE TO BLACK

WHERE IS EVERYBODY?

The sensation was unrelated to anything he'd ever felt before. He awoke, but had no recollection of ever having gone to sleep. And, to mystify him further, he was not in a bed. He was walking down a road, a two-lane black macadam with a vivid white stripe running down the center. He stopped, stared up at a blue sky, a hot, mid-morning sun. Then he looked around at a rural landscape, high, full-leafed trees flanking the road. Beyond the trees were fields of wheat, golden and rippling.

Like Ohio, he thought. Or maybe Indiana. Or parts of up-state New York. Suddenly he was conscious of the words being thought. Ohio. Indiana. New York. It immediately occurred to him that he didn't know where he was. A new thought followed quickly—he didn't know *who* he was, either! He looked down at himself, fingering the green, one-piece set of coveralls he was wearing, the heavy, high shoes, the zippered front that went from neck to crotch. He touched his face and then his hair. An inventory. Trying to piece together items of familiarity. An orientation through the tips of his fingers. He felt a light beard stubble, a nose slightly indented at the bridge, moderately heavy eyebrows, close-cropped hair. Not quite a butch—but close. He was young. Reasonably young, anyway. And he felt good. Healthy. At peace. He was confused as hell, but not at all frightened.

He walked over to the side of the road, took out a cigarette and lit it. He stood there leaning in the shade of one of the giant oaks that flanked the road. And he thought: I don't know who I am. I don't know where I am. But it's summer and I'm out in the country some place and this must be some kind of amnesia or something.

He drew deeply and enjoyably on the cigarette. As he took it out of his mouth and held it between his fingers, he looked at it. King-sized and filtered. Phrases came to him. "Winstons taste good like a cigarette should." "You get a lot to like in a Marlboro." "Are you smoking more now but enjoying it less?" That was for Camels—the kind you used to be willing to walk a mile for. He grinned and then laughed out loud. The power of advertising. He could stand there not knowing his name or where he was, but the twentieth-century poetry of the tobacco company cut across even the boundaries of amnesia. He stopped laughing and considered. Cigarettes and slogans meant America. So that's what he was—an American.

He flipped away the cigarette and walked on. A few hundred yards up the road he heard music coming from around the bend ahead. Loud trumpets. Good ones. There was a drum in the background and then a single, high-flying trumpet that rode an obbligato to the percussion. Swing. That's what it was, and again he was conscious of a word symbol that meant something to him. Swing. And this one he could relate to a specific time. It went with the 1930s. And this was beyond the thirties. This was the fifties. The 1950s. He let these facts pile up on top of one another. He felt like the key piece of a jigsaw puzzle, other pieces falling into place around him, forming a recognizable picture. And it was odd, he thought, how definite the pattern was, once they fell. Now he knew it was 1959. This was beyond doubt. Nineteen fifty-nine.

As he rounded the bend and saw the source of the music, he took a quick inventory of what he had discovered. He was an American, maybe in his twenties, it was summer, and here he was.

In front of him was a diner, a small, rectangular clapboard building with a sign on the front door which read, "OPEN."

Music was pouring out the front door. He went inside and got an impression of familiarity. He'd been to places like this before, this much he knew definitely. A long counter studded with catsup bottles and napkin holders; a back wall plastered with hand-written signs announcing kinds of sandwiches, soups, pie a la mode, and a dozen other items. There were a couple of large posters with girls in bathing suits holding up Coke bottles, and at the far end of the room was what he knew to be a juke box, the source of the music.

He walked the length of the counter, swinging a couple of seats around as he passed. Behind the counter an open swinging door led to the kitchen where he could see a big restaurant stove, a pot of coffee perking on it. The gurgling sound of the coffee was familiar and comforting and sent an aroma of breakfast and morning into the room.

The young man smiled as if seeing an old friend, or better, *feeling* the presence of an old friend. He sat down on the last stool so that he could see into the kitchen. There were shelves laden with canned goods, a big double-door refrigerator, a wooden chopping table, a screen door. He looked up at the signs on the wall. The Denver sandwich. The hamburger. Cheeseburger. Ham and eggs. Again he was aware of the phenomenon of having to associate obviously familiar words with what they repre-sented. What was a Denver sandwich, for example? And what was pie a la mode? Then, after a few moments of reflection, a picture came into his mind along with a taste. He had an odd thought then, that he was like an infant who was being exposed to the maturing process in a fantastically telescoped, jet-propelled way.

The music on the juke box broke through his thoughts, loud and intrusive.

He called out, toward the kitchen, "That loud enough for you, is it?"

There was a silence. Only the music answered him.

He raised his voice, "Can you hear it okay?"

Still no response. He went over to the machine, pushed it out a few inches from the wall and found a small volume-knob near the base. He turned it. The music fell away from him and the room seemed quieter and more comfortable. He pushed the ma-chine back against the wall and returned to his stool. He picked up the cardboard menu that was leaning against the napkin holder and studied it, occasionally looking up into the kitchen. He could see four pies browning nicely through the glass door of the oven and again there was the sense of something familiar, something friendly that he could respond to.

He called out again: "I think I'll have ham and eggs. Eggs up and easy and some hash browns."

Still there was no movement from the kitchen and no answering voice.

"I saw a sign that there was a town up ahead. What's the name of it?"

Coffee bubbled in the big enamelled pot, the steam rising into the air. A light wind moved the screen door in a creaking four-inch arc back and forth, and the juke box continued to play quietly. The young man was getting hungry now and felt a little nudge of irritation.

"Hey," he called out, "I asked you a question in there. What's the name of the town up ahead?"

He waited for a moment and when there was no answer he got up from the stool, vaulted the counter, pushed the swinging door open and went into the kitchen. It was empty. He walked through to the screen door, pulled it open and went outside. There was a big gravel back yard, unpunctuated by anything but a row of garbage cans, one of which had tipped over, littering the ground with a collection of tin cans, coffee grounds, egg shells and some empty cereal boxes; some orange crates; a broken, partially spokeless wheel; three or four piles of old newspapers. He was about to go back inside when something made him stop dead. He looked again at the garbage cans. There was something missing. An element not there that should have been there. He didn't know what it was. It was just a minute tilt to the dial inside his head that registered balance and reason. Something was wrong and he didn't know what it was. It left him with a tiny feeling of disquiet which he pushed into the back of his mind.

He returned to the kitchen, went over to the coffeepot, smelled it again, carried it over to the chopping table. He found a mug and poured himself a cup of hot coffee. He leaned against the back of the chopping table and sipped the coffee, enjoying it, liking its familiarity.

Then he went into the other room and took a large doughnut from a glass jar. He carried it back to the kitchen, and leaned against the jamb of the swinging door so that he could survey both rooms. He munched slowly on the doughnut, sipped at the coffee, and reflected. Whoever ran this place, he thought, is either in the basement or maybe his wife's having a baby. Or maybe the guy's sick. Maybe he's had a coronary or something. Maybe he should look around and find a basement door. He looked over at the cash register behind the counter. What an easy set up for a heist. Or for a free meal. Or for anything, for that matter.

The young man reached in his pocket and pulled out a handful of coins and a dollar bill.

"American money," he said aloud. "That settles that. No question about it. I *am* an American. Two half-dollars. A quarter. A dime. Four pennies and a dollar bill. That's American money."

He went into the kitchen again, looking up at the cereal boxes with the familiar names. The Campbell soup cans. Was that the one with the fifty-seven varieties? Again he reflected on who he was and where he was. On the disjointed *non sequiturs* that passed through his consciousness: his knowledge of music, the colloquialisms he spoke, the menu that he read and understood perfectly. Ham and eggs and hash browns—things he could relate to appearance and taste and smell. And then a phalanx of questions marched by. Exactly who was he? What the hell was he doing there? And where was "there"? And why? That was the *big* question. Why did he suddenly wake up on a road and not know who he was? And why wasn't anyone in the diner? Where was the owner or the cook or the counterman? Why weren't they there? And again the little germ of disquiet that he'd felt outside stirred inside him.

He chewed the last piece of doughnut, swigged it down with what remained of the coffee, and went back into the other room. Once again he vaulted over the counter; tossed a quarter on top of it. At the front door, he turned and surveyed the room again. Damn it, but it was normal, it was real, it was natural looking. The words, the place, the smell, the look. He put his hand on the knob of the door and pulled it open. He was about to step outside when a thought hit him. Suddenly he knew what had disturbed him about the garbage cans. He carried this disquiet with him as he walked out into the hot morning.

He knew what was the missing element and the knowledge

gave him a cold apprehension that he hadn't felt before. It did little jarring things to his nerve endings because suddenly something formed and entered into his thoughts. Something that couldn't be understood. Something beyond the norm. Beyond the word symbols, past the realm of logic that had been supporting him and answering his questions and giving him a link to reality.

There were no flies.

He walked around the corner of the building to stare again at the back yard with its row of garbage cans. There were no flies. There was a silence and nothing stirred and there were no flies.

He walked slowly back toward the highway, suddenly conscious of what was wrong. The trees were real and the highway and the diner with everything in it. The smell of the coffee was real and the taste of the doughnut and the cereals had the right names and Coca-Cola came in a bottle and cost a nickel. It was all right and proper and everything was in its right place. *But there was no life to it!* This was the missing element—activity! This was the thought he carried down the highway past a sign which said, "Carsville, 1 mile."

He entered the town and it spread out in front of him, neat and attractive. A small main street circled a village park that lay in the center of everything. Set back in the middle of this park area was a large school. On the circular main street were a row of stores, a movie theater, more stores and a police station. Further down was a church, a residential street that lay beyond and finally a drugstore on the corner. There was a bookstore, a confectionery, a grocery store and out in front of it, a small sign which read "Bus Stop." It lay there quietly and prettily in the mid-morning sun and it was quiet. There was no sound at all.

He walked down the sidewalk peering into the windows. All of the stores were open. The bakery had fresh cake and cookies. The bookstore was running a special sale. The movie theater advertised a picture out front having to do with war in the air. There was a three-story office building that told of lawyers inside, public notary and a real estate firm. Further down there was a glass-enclosed public telephone and then a department store with a delivery entrance blocked off from the street by a wire mesh fence.

Once again he reflected on the phenomena. There were the stores, the park, the bus stop, the whole works, but there were no people. There wasn't a soul to be seen. He leaned against the side of the bank building and scanned the street left to right, as if somehow he could find something stirring if he looked hard enough.

It was when his eyes reached the fence fronting the department store delivery entrance directly across the street, that he saw the girl. She was sitting in a truck parked inside the yard, plain as day—the very first person he'd seen. He felt his heart jump as he nervously stepped off the curb and started walking toward her. Halfway across the street he stopped, feeling his palms wet. He had an impulse to run like hell over to the truck or to stand there and shout questions at the girl. He forced a matter-of-factness into his tone, made himself smile.

"Hey, Miss! Miss, over here." He felt his voice rising higher and again he made an effort to keep it low and conversational. "Miss, I wonder if you could help me. I was wondering if you knew where everyone was. Doesn't seem to be anyone around. Literally . . . not a soul."

Now he took what he hoped was a sauntering walk across the street toward her, noticing that she continued to look straight at him from inside the cab of the truck. He reached the other side of the street, stopped a few feet from the wire mesh gate and smiled at her again.

"It's a crazy thing," he said. "Crazy, oddball thing. When I woke up this morning—" He stopped and he thought this over. "Well, I didn't exactly wake up," he said. "I just sort of—just sort of found myself walking down the road."

He reached the sidewalk, went through the half-open gate to the passenger side of the truck. The girl inside wasn't looking at him any longer. She was staring straight out through the front windshield and he saw her profile. Beautiful woman. Long blonde hair. But pale. He tried to think where he'd seen features like that—so immobile, so without expression. Bland, yes, but more than bland. Spiritless.

"Look, Miss," he said. "I don't want to frighten you, but there must be somebody around here who could tell me—"

His hand had opened the truck door when his voice was cut off by the girl's body as she slumped over, past the wide, amazed eyes of the young man, and down, hitting the sidewalk with a loud, almost metallic clank. He stared down at the upturned face, then became aware of words on the panel of the truck, "Resnick's Store Mannequins." He looked back at her face—the wooden, lifeless face with the painted cheeks and the painted mouth and the fixed half-smile, with the eyes that were wide open and showed nothing, told nothing. Eyes that looked exactly what they were—holes in a dummy's face. Something of the humor of it struck him now. He grinned, scratched his jaw, then slowly slid down, his back against the side of the truck till he was sitting next to the mannequin who lay there staring up at the blue sky and the hot sun.

The young man nudged her hard wooden arm, winked, clucked his tongue and said, "You'll forgive me, babe, but at no time did I mean to be so upsetting. As a matter of fact"—he nudged her again—"I've always had kind of a secret yen for the quiet type." Now he reached over to pinch the unyielding cheek and laughed again. "Get what I mean, babe?"

He picked up the dummy and carefully deposited her back in the cab of the truck, pulling her dress down to a modest point over the knees. He closed the cab door, then turned and took a few aimless steps away from the truck. On the other side of the mesh gate was the circular main street with the small park in the middle. He went to the fence and let his eyes move left to right once more, taking in every one of the stores, as if by some unique concentration he might find a sign of life. But the street lay empty, the stores were unoccupied, the silence was persistent.

He went toward the service entrance of the department store beyond the truck and stuck his head into a dark hall loaded with mannequins piled nude on top of one another. The thought hit him that it was like World War II pictures of the gas ovens at the concentration camps, the way they were piled on top of one another. He was disturbed by the similarity and hurriedly backed out into the delivery yard. Then he shouted toward the open door.

"Hey! Anybody here? Anybody hear me?"

He went to the truck again and looked inside. There was no key in the ignition. He grinned at the lifeless face of the mannequin.

"How about it, babe? You wouldn't know where the ignition keys would be, would you?"

The mannequin stared straight ahead at the windshield.

It was then he heard the sound. The first he'd heard outside the diner. At first it made no sense to him. It was unrelated to anything he knew or could associate with the stillness. Then he realized what the sound was. It was a phone ringing. He ran toward the fence, slamming himself against it, his fingers gripping the wire strands, his eyes darting around until he found what he was looking for. It was the glass-enclosed public phone booth just across the street, a few yards into the park. The phone was still ringing.

The young man flung himself through the gate and raced across the street. He reached the booth at a dead run, flung open the glass door and almost pulled the phone out by the wire as he grabbed the receiver off the hook. He kicked the door shut behind him.

"Hello. Hello!" He jangled the receiver furiously. "Hello! Operator? Operator?"

The phone was dead. He waited a moment, then slammed the receiver back on the cradle. He reached into his breast pocket and pulled out a dime. He shoved it in the slot and waited. Presently he heard his first voice, the colorless, astringently courteous tone of a telephone operator.

"The number you have reached," the voice said, "is not a working number—"

The young man was angry now. He shouted into the phone. "Are you out of your minds down there? I didn't dial a number—"

"Please be sure you have the right number and are dialing it correctly."

"I didn't dial a number, operator. The phone rang and I answered it." Again he jiggled the hook wildly. "Operator. Operator, will you listen to me, please? All I want to know is where I am. Understand? I just want to find out where I am and where the people are. Please, operator, listen—"

Again the operator's voice, impersonal, cold, as if from another planet. "The number you have reached is not a working number. Please be sure you have the right number and are dialing it correctly."

Then there was a long pause before the voice continued, "This is a recording!"

The young man slowly replaced the receiver and stood there conscious now of the quiet town that surrounded him through the glass, terribly aware of the silences that hung over the place, a silence punctuated by what the operator had said. "This is a recording." The whole damn place was a recording. Sound put on wax. Pictures put on canvas. Things placed on a stage. But only for effect. But a voice—that was a lousy joke.

The inanimate things such as unattended coffeepots, mannequins, stores—these he could wonder at and walk away. But a human voice—he desperately needed to know that this was surrounded with flesh and blood. It was a cheat to have it any other way. It was a promise and then a withdrawal. It made him angry in addition to causing that tiny flutter of frightened concern. The phone book was hanging by a chain. He grabbed it, ripped it open, started to read through the pages. The names sprang up at him. Abel. Baker. Botsford. Carstairs. Cathers. Cepeda.

"Well, where are you people," he shouted. "Where do you hang out? Where do you live? Just in this Goddamned book here?"

Again he riffled through the pages. The Dempseys. The Farvers. The Grannigans. And so on to a man named Zatelli who lived on North Front Street and whose first initial was A. The young man let the book drop from his hands. It swung back and forth on the chain. Slowly his head lifted until he stared out at the empty street.

"Look, boys," he said softly. "Who's watching the stores?" The glass windows looked back at him. "*Who's watching any of the stores?*"

He turned slowly, put his hand on the door and pushed. The door remained stationary. He pushed again. It was stuck tight. And now he had the feeling that it was a gag. A very big, complex, terribly unfunny gag. He pushed hard, throwing his shoulder against the door and still it did not move.

"Awright," he shouted. "Awright, it's a very funny joke. Very funny. I love your town. I love the sense of humor. But now it's not funny any more. Understand? Now it stinks. Who's the wise guy who locked me in here?" Now he kicked, shoved, pushed at the door until the sweat rolled down his face. He closed his eyes and leaned against the glass for a moment and then suddenly looked down to see the door hinge arched toward him. He gently pulled and the door swung open, bent and out of alignment, but open. He'd been pushing on it instead of pulling. It was as simple as that. He felt he should laugh or perhaps apologize to something or someone, but of course, there was no one to apologize to.

He stepped out into the sunlight and went across the park toward a building with a big glass globe in front with lettering on it which read "Police." He smiled to himself as he went toward it. Head for law and order, he thought. But more than just law and order—head for sanity. Maybe that's where to find it. When you're a little boy and lost, your mother tells you to go up to the nice policeman and tell him your name. Well, now he was a little boy and he was lost and there was no one else he could report to. And as to a name—someone would have to tell *him*.

The police station was dark and cool, split in half by a counter which ran the length of the room. Behind it was the sergeant's desk and chair and across the far wall a radio operator's table with microphone and a CW sending and receiving set. To the right was a barred door into a cell block. He went through the swinging door in the middle of the counter to the microphone. He picked it up, studying it, then illogically, as if it were expected of him to go along with the gag, he put on an official radio-car voice.

"Calling all cars. Calling all cars. Unknown man walking around police station. Very suspicious-looking egg. Probably wants to—"

His voice broke off. Across the room by the sergeant's desk, a thin column of smoke drifted lazily up toward the ceiling. He slowly put down the microphone and went to the desk. A big, quarter-smoked cigar was lying in an ash tray, lighted and smoking. He picked it up, then put it down. He felt a tension, a fear, a sense of being watched and listened to. He whirled around as if to catch someone in the act of just that—staring and listening.

The room was empty. He opened the barred door. It creaked noisily. He went into the cell block. There were eight cells, four on each side, and they were all empty. Through the bars of the last cell on the right he could see a sink. Water was running. Hot water. He saw the steam. On a shelf was a razor, dripping wet and a shaving brush, full of lather. He closed his eyes for a moment because this was too much. This was far too much. Show me goblins, he thought, or ghosts or monsters. Show me dead people walking in a parade. Play shrill and discordant trumpet sounds on a funeral horn that jars the stillness of the morning— but stop frightening me with the grotesque normality of things. Don't show me cigar butts in ash trays and water running in a sink and lather-covered shaving brushes. These are what shock more than apparitions.

He slowly entered the cell and went to the sink. He reached out a trembling hand and touched the lather on the brush. It was real. It felt warm. It smelled of soap. The water dripped into the sink. The razor said Gillette, and he thought of the World Series on television and the New York Giants taking four in a row from the Cleveland Indians. But God that must have been ten years ago. Or maybe it was last year. Or maybe it hadn't happened yet. Because now he had no base, no starting point, no date or time or place of reference. He was not conscious of the sound of the creaking cell door, as it slowly closed on him, until he saw the shadow of it on the wall inching across slowly, inexorably.

He let out a sob and flung himself across to the door, squeezing through just before it closed. He hung on to it for a moment, then backed away from the cell to lean against the door on the opposite side, and stare across at the now closed and locked door as if it were a kind of poisonous animal.

Something told him to run. Run. Run like hell. Get out. Take off. Get away. It was a whispered command in his inner ear. It was a last ditch order from an embattled mind, assaulted by nightmarish fear that could at any moment lock him rooted to the earth. It was all his instincts screaming at him in the name of safety and salvation. Get the hell out of here. Run! Run! *RUN!*

He was outside in the sun racing across the street, stumbling over the curb, scratching himself on a hedge as he ploughed head first into it. Then over the hedge and into the park, running, running, running. He saw the school building loom up in front of him and there was a statue in front. His motion carried him up the steps to the statue until suddenly he found himself clutching a metal leg of a heroic looking educator who died in 1911 and whose metal visage loomed up in front of him silhouetted against the blue sky. Then he began to cry. He looked up at the stillness, the stores, the movie theater, and finally the statue, and he cried. "Where is everybody? Please, for Christ's sake tell me . . . where is everybody?"

* * *

The young man sat on the curb in the late afternoon staring down at his shadow and the other shadows that flanked him. A store awning, a bus-stop sign, a streetlight post—formless globs of shadow that stretched across the sidewalk in a line. He slowly rose to his feet, looked briefly at the bus-stop sign and then down the street as if in some halfhearted, half-hopeless expectation of seeing a big red and white bus approach, open its doors, let out a crowd of people. People. That's what the young man wanted to see. His own kind.

The silence had been building all day. It had become an entity all of itself, a pressure on him, an oppressive, hot, itchy, wool-like thing that surrounded and covered him, that made him sweat and squirm and wish he could throw it off and crawl out.

He took a slow walk down the main street—his fortieth or fiftieth walk down that same street since morning. He passed the now familiar stores, looking into the now familiar doors, and it was the same. Counters, goods unattended.

He entered a bank for the fourth time that afternoon, and also for the fourth time, walked behind the tellers' cages, picking up handfuls of money and throwing them aside. Once he lit his cigarette from a hundred-dollar bill and laughed uproariously at it until suddenly, after he'd thrown the half-burnt bill down on the ground, he found himself unable to laugh any longer. All right, so a guy can light a cigarette from a hundred-dollar bill— but so what?

He walked out of the bank and then crossed the street and headed for the drugstore. There was a two-for-one sale announced on signs plastered across the window. Church bells rang from down the street and this jarred him. For a moment he flattened himself against the side of the drugstore staring wildly toward the sound until he realized what it was.

He walked into the drugstore, a big, square room surrounded by high counters and shelves with many glass display cases running in lines across the room. A big, mirror-backed fountain was at the rear, with pictures of floats and frappes and sodas and malts. He stopped by the cigar counter, helped himself to an expensive one, took off its paper and sniffed.

"A good cigar, that's what this country needs," he said aloud as he walked toward the fountain. "A good cigar. A couple of good cigars. And some people to smoke them."

He put the cigar carefully in a breast pocket and went in back of the fountain. From there he scanned the room, the empty booths, the juke box selectors over each one. And felt the stillness of the place that was totally incongruous with what was in it. It was a room poised for action; a room on the verge of coming alive, but never quite doing so. Behind the fountain were the ice-cream containers. He picked up an ice-cream scoop, took a glass dish from a shelf near the mirror and put two large scoops of ice cream in it. He covered this with syrup, then with nuts, added a cherry and some whipped cream.

He looked up and said, "How about it, anybody? Anybody for a sundae?" He paused and listened to the silence. "Nobody, huh? Okay."

He spooned up a large hunk of ice cream and cherry and whipped cream, put it in his mouth and liked the taste of it. For the first time he saw his reflection in the mirror and he was not surprised by what he saw. The face had a vaguely familiar look, not handsome, but not unpleasant. And young, he thought. It was quite young. It was the face of a man well under thirty. Maybe twenty-five or twenty-six, but no older. He studied the reflection. "You'll forgive me, old pal," he said to it, "but I don't recollect the name. The face seems familiar, but the name escapes me."

He took another bite of the ice cream, rolled it around in his mouth, melted it, and swallowed it, watching these actions in the mirror. He pointed the spoon very casually at the image.

"I'll tell you what my problem is. I'm in the middle of a nightmare that I can't wake up from. You're part of it. You and the ice cream and the cigar. The police station and the phone booth—that little mannequin." He looked down at the ice cream and then around at the drugstore, then back to his reflection.

"This whole bloody town—wherever it is—*whatever* it is—" He cocked his head to one side, suddenly remembering something and he grinned at the image.

"I just remembered something. Scrooge said it. You remember Scrooge, old buddy—Ebenezer Scrooge? It's what he said to the ghost, Jacob Marley. He said, 'You may be an undigested bit of beef, a blot of mustard. A crumb of cheese. A fragment of an undone potato. But there's more of gravy about you than grave.'"

He put the spoon down now and pushed the ice cream away. "You see? That's what you are. That's what you all are. You're what I had for dinner last night." Now the smile faded. Something intense crept into the voice. "But I've had it now. I've had it. I want to wake up." He turned from the mirror to the store and the empty booths. "If I can't wake up I've got to find somebody to talk to. That much I've *got* to do. I've got to find somebody to talk to."

For the first time he noticed a card standing on the counter. It was a basketball schedule of Carsville High School, announcing that on September 15th Carsville would play Corinth High. On September 21st, Carsville would play Leedsville. There'd be games on through December with six or seven other high schools—this was all announced matter-of-factly, quite officially, on the large poster.

"I must be a very imaginative guy," the young man said at last. "Very, very imaginative. Everything right down to the last detail. The last little detail."

He left the fountain and crossed the room to where there were several revolving pocket-book racks. Titles on the book covers flicked briefly across his consciousness, then disappeared. Murder stories, introduced on the covers by blondes in negligees, with titles like *The Brothel Death Watch*. Reprints of famous novels and gag books. Something called *Utterly Mad*, with a smiling half-wit face, captioned, "Alfred E. Neuman says, 'What, me worry!'" Some of the books seemed familiar. Fragments of plots and characters made brief excursions into his mind. He absent-mindedly turned the racks as he walked by. They creaked around, sending titles, pictures and covers blurring in front of his eyes, until he saw one that made him reach forward, grab the rack to stop it.

The book's cover depicted a kind of vast desert with a tiny, almost undistinguishable figure of a human being standing in the middle of it, arms akimbo, staring up toward the sky. There was a dim range of mountains beyond and, seemingly rising from the mountaintops, was a single line title, *The Last Man On Earth*.

The young man riveted his eyes to these words, feeling a fusion taking place between mind and sight. *The Last Man On Earth*. There was something especially meaningful—something of particular significance—something that suddenly made him gasp and whirl the rack around, sending the title off into a blurred orbit.

But when the rack slowed down, the book cover took on clarity again and it was then that he discovered there were many of them. There were many books of the last man on earth. Row after row of tiny figures standing, arms outstretched, on vast deserts, each cover staring back at him as the rack slowed and finally stopped moving.

He backed away from the books, unable to take his eyes away from them, until he reached the front door and briefly saw his reflection in the mirror—a white-faced, youngish looking man who stood at the entrance to a drugstore, looking tired, lonely, desperate and—frightened.

He went out, assuming composure while both his body and his mind pulled and yanked at him. Halfway across the street, he stopped, turning round and round and round.

Suddenly he shouted, "Hey? Hey! Hey, anybody? Anybody see me? Anybody hear me? Hey!"

An answer came after a moment. The deep throated, melodic bells of the church pealed out the notice of the passing day. They rang five times and then stopped. The echo lingered, and then this too faded away. The young man went down the street past the now familiar stores, no longer seeing them. His eyes were open but he saw nothing. He kept thinking of the book titles— *The Last Man On Earth,* and it did something to his insides. It was as if a heavy glob of indigestible food had gone protesting down his throat to settle, leaden and heavy, in his gut. *The Last Man On Earth.* The picture and the words stuck with frightening clarity in his consciousness. The tiny figure of the lone man in the desert, hands outstretched. The indistinct, lonely little figure whose fate was spread across the sky, across the mountain ranges beyond it—the last man on earth. He couldn't shake that picture, or the words, as he headed toward the park.

He was quite unaware that the afternoon sun now looked pale and distant as it moved across the sky. It was on its way out for that day.

It was night and the young man sat on a park bench close to the statue in front of the school. He played tic-tac-toe with a stick in the dirt, winning game after game and then wiping out each victory with the heel of his shoe to begin all over again. He'd made himself a sandwich in a small restaurant. He'd walked through the department store and then through a Woolworth five-and-dime. He'd gone into the school, through empty classrooms and had stifled an impulse to scrawl obscenities on a blackboard. Anything to shock or jar or to defy. Anything in the way of a gesture to rip away at the façade of reality that surrounded him. He was sure it was a façade. He was sure it must be just the real quality of the unreal dream and if only he could erase it and reveal what was underneath!—but he couldn't.

A light shone on his hand. He looked up startled. Street lights were going on and lights in the park joined them. Light after light all over the town. Street lights. Store windows. And then the flickering of the marquee lights in front of the theater.

He rose from the bench and went to the theater and stopped by the tiny box office. A ticket was sticking out of the metal slot. He put it in his breast pocket and was about to go inside when he saw a poster announcing the movie inside. On the poster was a large blowup of an air force pilot, profile to the sky, staring up at a flight of jet aircraft that streaked across and over him.

The young man took a step toward the poster. Slowly and unconsciously his hands touched the coveralls he was wearing and very gradually there was a bridge between himself and the man on the poster. And then it came to him. They were dressed alike. The coveralls were almost identical. The young man grew excited, and some of the fatigue washed away, leaving behind it an enthusiasm bordering on exultation. He reached out and touched the poster. Then he whirled around to look toward the empty streets and spoke aloud.

"I'm Air Force. That's it. I'm Air Force. I'm in the Air Force. That's right! I remember. I'm in the Air Force." It was a tiny, insignificant skein to a crazy quilt blanket of unknowns—but it *was* something he could pick up and hold and analyze. It *was* a clue. And it was the first one. The only one.

"I'm in the Air Force," he shouted. He headed into the theater. "I'm in the Air Force!" His voice reverberated through the empty lobby. "Hey, anybody, everybody, somebody—I'm in the Air Force!" He yelled it into the theater, the words banging through the air, over the row after row of empty seats and hitting against the huge, white, motionless screen at the far end.

The young man sat down and found he was perspiring. He felt for a handkerchief, pulled it out, wiped his face. He felt the beard stubble, knowing that there were a thousand closed doors to his subconscious he was close to opening.

"Air Force," he said softly now. "Air Force. But what does that mean? What does 'Air Force' mean?" His head jerked upward. "Was there a bomb? Is that it? That *must* have been it. A bomb—" He stopped, shaking his head. "But if there'd been a bomb, everything would have been destroyed. And nothing's been destroyed. How could it have been a—"

The lights began to dim and a strong beam of light from a projectionist's booth somewhere in the rear of the theater suddenly shone on the white screen. There was the sound of music, loud, blaring, martial music, and on the screen a B-52 bomber headed down a runway and suddenly screamed into the air over his head. There were more big B-52's and now they were in the sky, a flight of them, heading up leaving lines of vapor trails. And always the music blaring out underneath it.

The young man rose to his feet, his eyes wide, disbelieving. The beam of light disappeared into a small, blinking hole high above a balcony.

"Hey!" he screamed. "Who's showing the picture? Somebody must be showing the picture! Hey! Do you see me? I'm down here. Hey, whoever's showing the picture—I'm down here!"

He ran up the aisle, through the lobby, and up the stairs to the balcony. He stumbled across the dark seats, falling several times and finally, not finding an aisle, he simply crawled and jumped and scrambled over the tops of seats toward the small bright hole in the wall at the far end. He threw his face against it, staring directly into the blinding, white light. It sent him reeling back in momentary blindness.

When he could see again he found another opening in the wall, higher than the first. He jumped up, and got a quick glimpse of an empty room, a giant projector and stacks of film cans. He was dimly aware of voices on the screen, loud, giant voices that filled the theater. Once again he jumped up to look in the projectionist's booth and in the brief moment of one-sided combat with gravity, he again saw the empty room, the machine running smoothly, the hum of it heard dimly through the glass.

But when he landed back on his feet he knew there was no one up there. It was a machine running by itself. It was a picture showing itself. It was like the town and everything in it. Machines, items, things—all unattended. He backed away, banged against the back of the top row of seats and, losing his balance, sprawled head first.

The beam of light kept changing intensity as scenes altered on the screen. There was dialogue and music and it reverberated around the theater. Voices of giants. Music of a million-piece band. And something inside the young man cracked. The small compartment in the back of his mind, where man closets his fears, ties them up, controls and commands them, broke open and they surged across brain and nerves and muscles—a nightmare flood in open rebellion.

The young man scrambled to his feet, sobbing, choking, screaming. He raced down the stairs, through the door, down the steps toward the lobby.

It was when he reached the foot of the steps that he saw the other person. He was directly across the lobby and approaching from a flight of stairs the young man hadn't noticed before. The young man didn't see him clearly nor did he try. He just ran toward him, dimly aware that the other person was running toward him at the same time. In the fraction of a moment that it took him to cross the lobby he had only one thought and that was to reach the other person, to touch him, to hold him. To follow him out to wherever he was going. Out of the building, off the streets, out of the city, because now he knew that he must get away.

It was this thought that filled his mind just before he hit the mirror—a full length mirror that hung on the opposite wall. And he hit it with the force of a hundred and seventy pounds, smashing into it at a dead run. The mirror seemed to explode into a thousand pieces. He found himself on the floor looking at little fragments of his reflection in the small and minute sections of mirror that remained on the wall. It was the picture of a hundred young men lying cut and dazed on the floor of a theater lobby, staring up at what was left of a mirror. And then he lurched to his feet and, like a drunken man in a tilting ship in a heavy sea, he stumbled out of the lobby and out into the street.

Outside it was dark and misty; the streets were wet. The

street lights were enveloped in fog and each shone like a dim moon hanging in vapor. He began to run along sidewalks and across streets. He tripped over a bicycle stand and landed on his face, but was on his feet in a moment continuing the mad, headlong, thoughtless, desperate race to no place in particular. He tripped over a curb near the drugstore and again fell on his face, conscious for a moment that he could still feel pain—a jarring, wrenching pain. But only for a moment. He pushed his palms against the sidewalk, forcing himself up and then fell over on his back.

For a moment he lay there, eyes closed. And then he opened them. A nightmare knocked at his head and asked to come in and ice flowed over his body. He started to scream. An eye was looking at him. A giant eye, bigger than the upper trunk of a man. An unblinking, cold-looking eye was staring at him and his scream never let up, even after he had floundered again to his feet and started to run back toward the park. He was like a human siren disappearing into the dark. Behind him the big painted eye on the optometrist's window stared after him—cold, inhuman and unblinking.

He fell, clutching against a street light. There was a panel with a button which his fingers touched, scrabbled at and finally kept pushing over and over again. A sign over it read, "Push to turn green." He didn't know the sign was there. He only knew he had to push the button and this he kept doing, while the light over the intersection turned red, then yellow, then green, over and over again, responding to the bleeding knuckles of the young man who kept pushing a button and moaning to himself in a soft, barely intelligible chant.

"Please—please, somebody—help me. Help me, somebody. Please. Please. Oh dear God—somebody help me! Won't somebody help me. Won't somebody come—can anyone hear me—?"

The control room was dark and the figures of the uniformed men were silhouetted against the light that came from a small viewing screen on which could be seen the face and upper body of Sergeant Mike Ferris, a youngish looking man in coveralls who kept pushing a button to the right of the screen. Ferris's voice babbled out into the darkness of the control room pleading for help, or someone to listen, for someone to show themselves. It was the sobbing, pleading, supplicating voice of a man whose

THE MONSTERS ARE DUE ON MAPLE STREET

It was Saturday afternoon on Maple Street and the late sun retained some of the warmth of a persistent Indian summer. People along the street marveled at winter's delay and took advantage of it. Lawns were being mowed, cars polished, kids played hopscotch on the sidewalks. Old Mr. Van Horn, the patriarch of the street, who lived alone, had moved his power saw out on his lawn and was fashioning new pickets for his fence. A Good Humor man bicycled in around the corner and was inundated by children and by shouts of "Wait a minute!" from small boys hurrying to con nickels from their parents. It was 4:40 P.M. A football game blared from a portable radio on a front porch, blending with the other sounds of a Saturday afternoon in October. Maple Street. 4:40 P.M. Maple Street in its last calm and reflective moments—before the monsters came.

Steve Brand, fortyish, a big man in an old ex-Marine set of dungarees, was washing his car when the lights flashed across the sky. Everyone on the street looked up at the sound of the whoosh and the brilliant flash that dwarfed the sun.

"What was that?" Steve called across at his neighbor, Don Martin, who was fixing a bent spoke on his son's bicycle.

Martin, like everyone else, was cupping his hands over his eyes, to stare up at the sky. He called back to Steve, "Looked like a meteor, didn't it? I didn't hear any crash though, did you?"

Steve shook his head. "Nope. Nothing except that roar."

Steve's wife came out on the front porch. "Steve?" she called. "What was that?"

Steve shut off the water hose. "Guess it was a meteor, honey. Came awful close, didn't it?"

"Much too close for my money," his wife answered. "Much too close."

She went back into the house, and became suddenly conscious of something. All along Maple Street people paused and looked at one another as a gradual awareness took hold. All the sounds had stopped. All of them. There was a silence now. No portable radio. No lawn mowers. No clickety-click of sprinklers that went round and round on front lawns. There was a silence.

Mrs. Sharp, fifty-five years of age, was talking on the telephone, giving a cake recipe to her cousin at the other end of town. Her cousin was asking Mrs. Sharp to repeat the number of eggs when her voice clicked off in the middle of the sentence. Mrs. Sharp, who was not the most patient of women, banged furiously on the telephone hook, screaming for an operator.

Pete Van Horn was right in the middle of sawing a 1 x 4 piece of pine when the power saw went off. He checked the plug, the outlet on the side of the house and then the fuse box in his basement. There was just no power coming in.

Steve Brand's wife, Agnes, came back out on the porch to announce that the oven had stopped working. There was no current or something. Would Steve look at it? Steve couldn't look at it at that moment because he was preoccupied with a hose that suddenly refused to give any more water.

Across the street Charlie Farnsworth, fat and dumpy, in a loud Hawaiian sport shirt that featured hula girls with pineapple baskets on their heads, barged angrily out toward the road, damning any radio outfit that manufactured a portable with the discourtesy to shut off in the middle of a third-quarter forward pass.

Voices built on top of voices until suddenly there was no more silence. There was a conglomeration of questions and protests; of plaintive references to half-cooked dinners, half-watered lawns, half-washed cars, half-finished phone conversations. Did it have anything to do with the meteor? That was the main question—the one most asked. Pete Van Horn disgustedly threw aside the electric cord of his power mower and announced to the group of people who were collected around Steve Brand's station wagon that he was going on over to Bennett Avenue to check and see if the power had gone off there, too. He disappeared into his back yard and was last seen heading into the back yard of the house behind his.

Steve Brand, his face wrinkled with perplexity, leaned against his car door and looked around at the neighbors who had collected. "It just doesn't make sense," he said. "Why should the power go off all of a sudden *and* the phone line?"

Don Martin wiped bicycle grease off his fingers. "Maybe some kind of an electrical storm or something."

Dumpy Charlie's voice was always unpleasantly high. "That just don't seem likely," he squealed. "Sky's just as blue as anything. Not a cloud. No lightning. No thunder. No nothin'. How could it be a storm?"

Mrs. Sharp's face was lined with years, but more deeply by the frustrations of early widowhood. "Well, it's a terrible thing when a phone company can't keep its line open," she complained. "Just a terrible thing."

"What about my portable radio," Charlie demanded. "Ohio State's got the ball on Southern Methodist's eighteen-yard line. They throw a pass and the damn thing goes off just then."

There was a murmur in the group as people looked at one another and heads were shaken.

Charlie picked his teeth with a dirty thumbnail. "Steve," he said in his high, little voice, "why don't you go downtown and check with the police?"

"They'll probably think we're crazy or something," Don Martin said. "A little power failure and right away we get all flustered and everything."

"It isn't just the power failure," Steve answered. "If it was, we'd still be able to get a broadcast on the portable."

There was a murmur of reaction to this and heads nodded.

Steve opened the door to his station wagon. "I'll run downtown. We'll get this all straightened out."

He inched his big frame onto the front seat behind the wheel, turned on the ignition and pushed the starter button. There was no sound. The engine didn't even turn over. He tried it a couple of times more, and still there was no response. The others stared silently at him. He scratched his jaw.

"Doesn't that beat all? It was working fine before."

"Out of gas?" Don offered.

Steve shook his head. "I just had it filled up."

"What's it mean?" Mrs. Sharp asked.

Charlie Farnsworth's piggish little eyes flapped open and shut. "It's just as if—just as if everything had stopped. You better *walk* downtown, Steve."

"I'll go with you," Don said.

Steve got out of the car, shut the door and turned to Don. "Couldn't be a meteor," he said. "A meteor couldn't do *this*." He looked off in thought for a moment, then nodded. "Come on, let's go."

They started to walk away from the group, when they heard the boy's voice. Tommy Bishop, aged twelve, had stepped out in front of the others and was calling out to them.

"Mr. Brand! Mr. Martin. You better not leave!"

Steve took a step back toward him.

"Why not?" he asked.

"They don't want you to," Tommy said.

Steve and Don exchanged a look.

"*Who* doesn't want us to?" Steve asked him.

Tommy looked up toward the sky. "Them," he said.

"Them?" Steve asked.

"Who are 'them'?" Charlie squealed.

"Whoever was in that thing that came by overhead," Tommy said intently.

Steve walked slowly back toward the boy and stopped close to him. "What, Tommy?" he asked.

"Whoever was in that thing that came over," Tommy repeated. "I don't think they want us to leave here."

Steve knelt down in front of the boy. "What do you mean, Tommy? What are you talking about?"

"They don't want us to leave, that's why they shut everything off."

"What makes you say that?" Irritation crept into Steve's voice. "Whatever gave you *that* idea?"

Mrs. Sharp pushed her way through to the front of the crowd. "That's the craziest thing I ever heard," she announced in a public-address-system voice. "Just about the craziest thing I ever did hear!"

Tommy could feel the unwillingness to believe him. "It's always that way," he said defensively, "in every story I've ever read about a spaceship landing from outer space!"

Charlie Farnsworth whinnied out his derision.

Mrs. Sharp waggled a bony finger in front of Tommy's mother. "If you ask me, Sally Bishop," she said, "you'd better get that boy of yours up to bed. He's been reading too many comic books or seeing too many movies or something."

Sally Bishop's face reddened. She gripped Tommy's shoulders tightly. "Tommy," she said softly. "Stop that kind of talk, honey."

Steve's eyes never left the boy's face. "That's all right, Tom. We'll be right back. You'll see. That wasn't a ship or anything like it. That was just a—a meteor or something, likely as not—" He turned to the group, trying to weight his words with an optimism he didn't quite feel. "No doubt it did have something to do with all this power failure and the rest of it. Meteors can do crazy things. Like sun spots."

"That's right," Don said, as if picking up a cue. "Like sun spots. That kind of thing. They can raise cain with radio reception all over the world. And this thing being so close—why there's no telling what sort of stuff it can do." He wet his lips nervously. "Come on, Steve. We'll go into town and see if that isn't what's causing it all."

Once again the two men started away.

"Mr. Brand!" Tommy's voice was defiant and frightened at the same time. He pulled away from his mother and ran after them. "Please, Mr. Brand, please don't leave here."

There was a stir, a rustle, a movement among the people. There was something about the boy. Something about the intense little face. Something about the words that carried such emphasis, such belief, such fear. They listened to these words and rejected them because intellect and logic had no room for spaceships and green-headed things. But the irritation that showed in the eyes, the murmuring and the compressed lips had nothing to do with intellect. A little boy was bringing up fears that shouldn't be brought up; and the people on Maple Street this Saturday afternoon were no different from any other set of human beings. Order, reason, logic were slipping, pushed by the wild conjectures of a twelve-year-old boy.

"Somebody ought to spank that kid," an angry voice muttered.

Tommy Bishop's voice continued defiant. It pierced the murmurings and rose above them. "You might not even be able to get to town," he said. "It was that way in the story. *Nobody* could leave. Nobody except—"

"Except who?" Steve asked.

"Except the people they'd sent down ahead of them. They looked just like humans. It wasn't until the ship landed that—"

His mother grabbed him by the arm and pulled him back. "Tommy," she said in a low voice. "Please, honey . . . don't talk that way."

"Damn right he shouldn't talk that way," came the voice of the man in the rear again. "And we shouldn't stand here listening to him. Why this is the craziest thing I ever heard. The kid tells us a comic-book plot and here we stand listening—"

His voice died away as Steve stood up and faced the crowd. Fear can throw people into a panic, but it can also make them receptive to a leader and Steve Brand at this moment was such a leader. The big man in the ex-Marine dungarees had an authority about him.

"Go ahead, Tommy," he said to the boy. "What kind of story was this? What about the people that they sent out ahead?"

"That was the way they prepared things for the landing, Mr. Brand," Tommy said. "They sent four people. A mother and a father and two kids who looked just like humans. But they weren't."

There was a murmur—a stir of uneasy laughter. People looked at one another again and a couple of them smiled.

"Well," Steve said, lightly but carefully, "I guess we'd better run a check on the neighborhood to see which ones of us are really human."

His words were a release. Laughter broke out openly. But

soon it died away. Only Charlie Farnsworth's horse whinny persisted over the growing silence and then he too lapsed into a grim quietness, until all fifteen people were looking at one another through changed eyes. A twelve-year-old boy had planted a seed. And something was growing out of the street with invisible branches that began to wrap themselves around the men and women and pull them apart. Distrust lay heavy in the air.

Suddenly there was the sound of a car engine and all heads turned as one. Across the street Ned Rosen was sitting in his convertible trying to start it, and nothing was happening beyond the labored sound of a sick engine getting deeper and hoarser and finally giving up altogether. Ned Rosen, a thin, serious-faced man in his thirties, got out of his car and closed the door. He stood there staring at it for a moment, shook his head, looked across the street at his neighbors and started toward them.

"Can't get her started, Ned?" Don Martin called out to him.

"No dice," Ned answered. "Funny, she was working fine this morning."

Without warning, all by itself, the car started up and idled smoothly, smoke briefly coming out of the exhaust. Ned Rosen whirled around to stare at it, his eyes wide. Then, just as suddenly as it started, the engine sputtered and stopped.

"Started all by itself!" Charlie Farnsworth squealed excitedly.

"How did it do that?" Mrs. Sharp asked. "How could it just start all by itself?"

Sally Bishop let loose her son's arm and just stood there, shaking her head. "How in the world—" she began.

Then there were no more questions. They stood silently staring at Ned Rosen who looked from them to his car and then back again. He went to the car and looked at it. Then he scratched his head again.

"Somebody explain it to me," he said. "I sure never saw anything like that happen before!"

"He never did come out to look at that thing that flew overhead. He wasn't even interested," Don Martin said heavily.

"What do you say we ask him some questions," Charlie Farnsworth proposed importantly. "I'd like to know what's going on here!"

There was a chorus of assent and the fifteen people started across the street toward Ned Rosen's driveway. Unity was restored, they had a purpose, a feeling of activity and direction. They were *doing* something. They weren't sure what, but Ned Rosen was flesh and blood—askable, reachable and seeable. He watched with growing apprehension as his neighbors marched toward him. They stopped on the sidewalk close to the driveway and surveyed him.

Ned Rosen pointed to his car. "I just don't understand it, any more than you do! I tried to start it and it *wouldn't* start. You saw me. All of you saw me."

His neighbors seemed massed against him, solidly, alarmingly.

"I don't understand it!" he cried. "I swear—I don't understand. What's happening?"

Charlie Farnsworth stood out in front of the others. "Maybe you better tell us," he demanded. "Nothing's working on this street. Nothing. No lights, no power, no radio. Nothing except one car—*yours*!"

There were mutterings from the crowd. Steve Brand stood back by himself and said nothing. He didn't like what was going on. Something was building up that threatened to grow beyond control.

"Come on, Rosen," Charlie Farnsworth commanded shrilly, "let's hear what goes on! Let's hear how you explain your car startin' like that!"

Ned Rosen wasn't a coward. He was a quiet man who didn't like violence and had never been a physical fighter. But he didn't like being bullied. Ned Rosen got mad.

"Hold it!" he shouted. "Just hold it. You keep your distance. All of you. All right, I've got a car that starts by itself. Well, that's a freak thing—I admit it! But does that make me some sort of a criminal or something? I don't know why the car works—it just does!"

The crowd was neither sobered nor reassured by Rosen's words, but they were not too frightened to listen. They huddled together, mumbling, and Ned Rosen's eyes went from face to face till they stopped on Steve Brand's. Ned knew Steve Brand. Of all the men on the street, this seemed the guy with the most substance. The most intelligent. The most essentially decent.

"What's it all about, Steve?" he asked.

"We're all on a monster kick, Ned," he answered quietly.

"Seems that the general impression holds that maybe one family isn't what we think they are. Monsters from outer space or something. Different from us. Fifth columnists from the vast beyond." He couldn't keep the sarcasm out of his voice. "Do you know anybody around here who might fit that description?"

Rosen's eyes narrowed. "What is this, a gag?" He looked around the group again. "This a practical joke or something?" And without apparent reason, without logic, without explanation, his car started again, idled for a moment sending smoke out of the exhaust, and stopped.

A woman began to cry, and the bank of eyes facing Ned Rosen looked cold and accusing. He walked to his porch steps and stood on them, facing his neighbors.

"Is that supposed to incriminate me?" he asked. "The car engine goes on and off and that really does it, huh?" He looked down into their faces. "I don't understand it. Not any more than you do."

He could tell that they were unmoved. This couldn't really be happening, Ned thought to himself.

"Look," he said in a different tone. "You all know me. We've lived here four years. Right in this house. We're no different from any of the rest of you!" He held out his hands toward them. The people he was looking at hardly resembled the people he'd lived alongside of for the past four years. They looked as if someone had taken a brush and altered every character with a few strokes. "Really," he continued, "this whole thing is just . . . just weird—"

"Well, if that's the case, Ned Rosen," Mrs. Sharp's voice suddenly erupted from the crowd, "maybe you'd better explain why—" She stopped abruptly and clamped her mouth shut, but looked wise and pleased with herself.

"Explain what?" Rosen asked her softly.

Steve Brand sensed a special danger now. "Look," he said, "let's forget this right now—"

Charlie Farnsworth cut him off. "Go ahead. Let her talk. What about it? Explain what?"

Mrs. Sharp, with an air of great reluctance, said, "Well, sometimes I go to bed late at night. A couple of times—a couple of times I've come out on the porch, and I've seen Ned Rosen here, in the wee hours of the morning, standing out in front of his house looking up at the sky." She looked around the circle of faces. "That's right, looking up at the sky as if—as if he was waiting for something." She paused for emphasis, for dramatic effect. "As if he was looking for something!" she repeated.

The nail in the coffin, Steve Brand thought. One dumb, ordinary, simple idiosyncrasy of a human being—and that probably was all it would take. He heard the murmuring of the crowd rise and saw Ned Rosen's face turn white. Rosen's wife, Ann, came out on the porch. She took a look at the crowd and then at her husband's face.

"What's going on, Ned?" she asked.

"I don't know what's going on," Ned answered. "I just don't know, Ann. But I'll tell you this. I don't like these people. I don't like what they're doing. I don't like them standing in my yard like this. And if any one of them takes another step and gets close to my porch—I'll break his jaw. I swear to God, that's just what I'll do. I'll break his jaw. Now go on, get out of here, all of you!" he shouted at them. "Get the hell out of here."

"Ned," Ann's voice was shocked.

"You heard me," Ned repeated. "All of you get out of here."

None of them eager to start an action, the people began to back away. But they had an obscure sense of gratification. At least there was an opponent now. Someone who wasn't one of them. And this gave them a kind of secure feeling. The enemy was no longer formless and vague. The enemy had a front porch and a front yard and a car. And he had shouted threats at them.

They started slowly back across the street forgetting for the moment what had started it all. Forgetting that there was no power, and no telephones. Forgetting even that there had been a meteor overhead not twenty minutes earlier. It wasn't until much later, as a matter of fact, that anyone posed a certain question. Old man Van Horn had walked through his back yard over to Bennett Avenue. He'd never come back. Where was he? It was not one of the questions that passed through the minds of any of the thirty or forty people on Maple Street who sat on their front porches and watched the night come and felt the now menacing darkness close in on them.

There were lanterns lit all along Maple Street by ten o'clock. Candles shone through living-room windows and cast flickering, unsteady shadows all along the street. Groups of people huddled

on front lawns around their lanterns and a soft murmur of voices
was carried over the Indian-summer night air. All eyes eventually
were drawn to Ned Rosen's front porch.

He sat there on the railing, observing the little points of light
spotted around in the darkness. He knew he was surrounded. He
was the animal at bay.

His wife came out on the porch and brought him a glass of
lemonade. Her face was white and strained. Like her husband,
Ann Rosen was a gentle person, unarmored by temper or any
proclivity for outrage. She stood close to her husband now on the
darkened porch feeling the suspicion that flowed from the people
around lanterns, thinking to herself that these were people she
had entertained in her house. These were women she talked to
over clotheslines in the back yard; people who had been friends
and neighbors only that morning. Oh dear God, could all this
have happened in those few hours? It must be a nightmare, she
thought. It had to be a nightmare that she could wake up from.
It couldn't be anything else.

Across the street Mabel Farnsworth, Charlie's wife, shook
her head and clucked at her husband who was drinking a can of
beer. "It just doesn't seem right though, Charlie, keeping watch
on them. Why he was right when he said he was one of our
neighbors. I've known Ann Rosen ever since they moved in.
We've been good friends."

Charlie Farnsworth turned to her disgustedly. "That don't
prove a thing," he said. "Any guy who'd spend his time lookin' up
at the sky early in the morning—well there's something wrong
with that kind of person. There's something that ain't legitimate.
Maybe under normal circumstances we could let it go by. But
these aren't normal circumstances." He turned and pointed toward the street. "Look at that," he said. "Nothin' but candles and
lanterns. Why it's like goin' back into the Dark Ages or something!"

He was right. Maple Street had changed with the night. The
flickering lights had done something to its character. It looked
odd and menacing and very different. Up and down the street,
people noticed it. The change in Maple Street. It was the feeling
one got after being away from home for many, many years and
then returning. There was a vague familiarity about it, but it
wasn't the same. It was different.

Ned Rosen and his wife heard footsteps coming toward their house. Ned got up from the railing and shouted out into the darkness.

"Whoever it is, just stay right where you are. I don't want any trouble, but if anybody sets foot on my porch, that's what they're going to get—trouble!" He saw that it was Steve Brand and his features relaxed.

"Ned," Steve began.

Ned Rosen cut him off. "I've already explained to you people, I don't sleep very well at night sometimes. I get up and I take a walk and I look up at the sky. I look at the stars."

Ann Rosen's voice shook as she stood alongside of him. "That's exactly what he does. Why this whole thing, it's—it's some kind of madness or something."

Steve Brand stood on the sidewalk and nodded grimly. "That's exactly what it is—some kind of madness."

Charlie Farnsworth's voice from the opposite yard was spiteful. "You'd best watch who you're seen with, Steve. Until we get this all straightened out, you ain't exactly above suspicion yourself."

Steve whirled around to the outline of the fat figure that stood behind the lantern in the other yard. "Or you either, Charlie," he shouted. "Or any of the rest of us!"

Mrs. Sharp's voice came from the darkness across the street. "What I'd like to know is—what are we going to do? Just stand around here all night?"

"There's nothin' else we can do," Charlie Farnsworth said. He looked wisely over toward Ned Rosen's house. "One of 'em'll tip their hand. They *got* to."

It was Charlie's voice that did it for Steve Brand at this moment. The shrieking, pig squeal that came from the layers of fat and the idiotic sport shirt and the dull, dumb, blind prejudice of the man. "There's something *you* can do, Charlie," Steve called out to him. "You can go inside your house and keep your mouth shut!"

"You sound real anxious to have that happen, Steve," Charlie's voice answered him back from the little spot of light in the yard across the street. "I think we'd better keep our eye on you, too!"

Don Martin came up to Steve Brand, carrying a lantern. There was something hesitant in his manner, as if he were about to take a bit in his teeth, but wondered whether it would hurt. "I think everything might as well come out now," Don said. "I really do. I think everything should come out."

People came off porches, from front yards, to stand around in a group near Don who now turned directly toward Steve.

"Your wife's done plenty of talking, Steve, about how odd you are," he said.

Charlie Farnsworth trotted over. "Go ahead. Tell us what she said," he demanded excitedly.

Steve Brand knew this was the way it would happen. He was not really surprised but he still felt a hot anger rise up inside of him. "Go ahead," he said. "What's my wife said? Let's get it *all* out." He peered around at the shadowy figures of the neighbors. "Let's pick out every Goddamned peculiarity of every single man, woman and child on this street! Don't stop with me and Ned. How about a firing squad at dawn, so we can get rid of all the suspects! Make it easier for you!"

Don Martin's voice retreated fretfully. "There's no need getting so upset, Steve—"

"Go to hell, Don," Steve said to him in a cold and dispassionate fury.

Needled, Don went on the offensive again but his tone held something plaintive and petulant. "It just so happens that, well, Agnes has talked about how there's plenty of nights you've spent hours in your basement working on some kind of a radio or something. Well none of us have ever *seen* that radio—"

"Go ahead, Steve," Charlie Farnsworth yelled at him. "What kind of a 'radio set' you workin on? I never seen it. Neither has anyone else. Who do you talk to on that radio set? And who talks to you?"

Steve's eyes slowly traveled in an arc over the hidden faces and the shrouded forms of neighbors who were now accusers. "I'm surprised at you, Charlie," he said quietly. "I really am. How come you're so Goddamned dense all of a sudden? Who do I talk to? I talk to monsters from outer space. I talk to three-headed green men who fly over here in what look like meteors!"

Agnes Brand walked across the street to stand at her husband's elbow. She pulled at his arm with frightened intensity. "Steve! Steve, please," she said. "It's just a ham radio set," she tried to explain. "That's all. I bought him a book on it myself. It's just a ham radio set. A lot of people have them. I can show it to you. It's right down in the basement."

Steve pulled her hand off his arm. "You show them nothing," he said to her. "If they want to look inside our house, let them get a search warrant!"

Charlie's voice whined at him. "Look, buddy, you can't afford to—"

"Charlie," Steve shouted at him. "Don't tell me what I can afford. And stop telling me who's dangerous and who isn't. And who's safe and who's a menace!" He walked over to the edge of the road and saw that people backed away from him. "And you're with him—all of you," Steve bellowed at them. "You're standing there all set to crucify—to find a scapegoat—desperate to point some kind of a finger at a neighbor!" There was intensity in his tone and on his face, accentuated by the flickering light of the lanterns and the candles. "Well look, friends, the only thing that's going to happen is that we'll eat each other up alive. Understand? *We are going to eat each other up alive!*"

Charlie Farnsworth suddenly ran over to him and grabbed his arm. "That's not the *only* thing that can happen to us," he said in a frightened, hushed voice. "Look!"

"Oh, my God," Don Martin said.

Mrs. Sharp screamed. All eyes turned to look down the street where a figure had suddenly materialized in the darkness and the sound of measured footsteps on concrete grew louder and louder as it walked toward them. Sally Bishop let out a stifled cry and grabbed Tommy's shoulder.

The child's voice screamed out, "It's the monster! It's the monster!"

There was a frightened wail from another woman, and the residents of Maple Street stood transfixed with terror as something unknown came slowly down the street. Don Martin disappeared and came back out of his house a moment later carrying a shotgun. He pointed it toward the approaching form. Steve pulled it out of his hands.

"For God's sake, will somebody think a thought around here? Will you people wise up? What good would a shotgun do against—"

A quaking, frightened Charlie Farnsworth grabbed the gun from Steve's hand. "No more talk, Steve," he said. "You're going to talk us into a grave! You'd let whoever's out there walk right over us, wouldn't yuh? Well, some of us won't!"

He swung the gun up and pulled the trigger. The noise was a shocking, shattering intrusion and it echoed and re-echoed through the night. A hundred yards away the figure collapsed like a piece of clothing blown off a line by the wind. From front porches and lawns people raced toward it.

Steve was the first to reach him. He knelt down, turned him over and looked at his face. Then he looked up toward the semi-circle of silent faces surveying him.

"All right, friends," he said quietly. "It happened. We got our first victim—Pete Van Horn!"

"Oh, my God," Don Martin said in a hushed voice. "He was just going over to the next block to see if the power was on—"

Mrs. Sharp's voice was that of injured justice. "You killed him, Charlie! You shot him dead!"

Charlie Farnsworth's face looked like a piece of uncooked dough, quivering and shaking in the light of the lantern he held.

"I didn't know who he was," he said. "I certainly didn't know who he was." Tears rolled down his fat cheeks. "He comes walking out of the dark—how am I supposed to know who he was?" He looked wildly around and then grabbed Steve's arm. Steve could explain things to people. "Steve," he screamed, "you know why I shot. How was I supposed to know he wasn't a monster or something?"

Steve looked at him and didn't say anything. Charlie grabbed Don.

"We're all scared of the same thing," he blubbered. "The very same thing. I was just tryin' to protect my home, that's all. Look, all of you, that's all I was tryin' to do!" He tried to shut out the sight of Pete Van Horn who stared up at him with dead eyes and a shattered chest. "Please, please, please," Charlie Farnsworth sobbed, "I didn't know it was somebody we knew. I swear to God I didn't know—"

The lights went on in Charlie Farnsworth's house and shone brightly on the people of Maple Street. They looked suddenly naked. They blinked foolishly at the lights and their mouths gaped like fish's.

"Charlie," Mrs. Sharp said, like a judge pronouncing sentence, "how come you're the only one with lights on now?"

Ned Rosen nodded in agreement. "That's what I'd like to know," he said. Something inside tried to check him, but his anger made him go on. "How come, Charlie? You're quiet all of a sudden. You've got nothing to say out of that big, fat mouth of yours. Well, let's hear it, Charlie? Let's hear why you've got lights!"

Again the chorus of voices punctuated the request and gave it legitimacy and a vote of support. "Why, Charlie?" the voices asked him. "How come you're the only one with lights?" The questions came out of the night to land against his fat wet cheeks. "You were so quick to kill," Ned Rosen continued, "and you were so quick to tell us who we had to be careful of. Well maybe you *had* to kill, Charlie. Maybe Pete Van Horn, God rest his soul, was trying to tell us something. Maybe he'd found out something and had come back to tell us who there was among us we should watch out for."

Charlie's eyes were little pits of growing fear as he backed away from the people and found himself up against a bush in front of his house. "No," he said. "No, please." His chubby hands tried to speak for him. They waved around, pleading. The palms outstretched, begging for forgiveness and understanding. "Please—please, I swear to you—it isn't me! It really isn't me."

A stone hit him on the side of the face and drew blood. He screamed and clutched at his face as the people began to converge on him.

"No," he screamed. "No."

Like a hippopotamus in a circus, he scrambled over the bush, tearing his clothes and scratching his face and arms. His wife tried to run toward him, but somebody stuck a foot out and she tripped, sprawling head first on the sidewalk. Another stone whistled through the air and hit Charlie on the back of the head as he raced across his front yard toward his porch. A rock smashed at the porch light and sent glass cascading down on his head.

"It isn't me," he screamed back at them as they came toward him across the front lawn. "It isn't me, but I know who it is," he said suddenly, without thought. Even as he said it, he realized it was the only possible thing to say.

People stopped, motionless as statues, and a voice called out from the darkness. "All right, Charlie, who is it?"

He was a grotesque, fat figure of a man who smiled now

through the tears and the blood that cascaded down his face. "Well, I'm going to tell you," he said. "I am now going to tell you, because I know who it is. I really know who it is. It's . . ."

"Go ahead, Charlie," a voice commanded him. "Who's the monster?"

Don Martin pushed his way to the front of the crowd. "All right, Charlie, now! Let's hear it!"

Charlie tried to think. He tried to come up with a name. A nightmare engulfed him. Fear whipped at the back of his brain. "It's the kid," he screamed. "That's who it is. It's the kid!"

Sally Bishop screamed and grabbed at Tommy, burying his face against her. "That's crazy," she said to the people who now stared at her. "That's crazy. He's a little boy."

"But he knew," said Mrs. Sharp. "He was the only one who knew. He told us all about it. Well how did he know? How *could* he have known?"

Voices supported her. "How could he know?" "Who told him?" "Make the kid answer." A fever had taken hold now, a hot, burning virus that twisted faces and forced out words and solidified the terror inside of each person on Maple Street.

Tommy broke away from his mother and started to run. A man dove at him in a flying tackle and missed. Another man threw a stone wildly toward the darkness. They began to run after him down the street. Voices shouted through the night, women screamed. A small child's voice protested—a playmate of Tommy's, one tiny voice of sanity in the middle of a madness as men and women ran down the street, the sidewalks, the curbs, looking blindly for a twelve-year-old boy.

And then suddenly the lights went on in another house—a two-story, gray stucco house that belonged to Bob Weaver. A man screamed, "It isn't the kid. It's Bob Weaver's house!"

A porch light went on at Mrs. Sharp's house and Sally Bishop screamed, "It isn't Bob Weaver's house. It's Mrs. Sharp's place."

"I tell you it's the kid," Charlie screamed.

The lights went on and off, on and off down the street. A power mower suddenly began to move all by itself lurching crazily across a front yard, cutting an irregular patch of grass until it smashed against the side of the house.

"It's Charlie," Don Martin screamed. "He's the one." And then he saw his own lights go on and off.

They ran this way and that way, over to one house and then

back across the street to another. A rock flew through the air and then another. A pane of glass smashed and there was the cry of a woman in pain. Lights on and off, on and off. Charlie Farnsworth went down on his knees as a piece of brick plowed a two-inch hole in the back of his skull. Mrs. Sharp lay on her back screaming, and felt the tearing jab of a woman's high heel in her mouth as someone stepped on her, racing across the street.

From a quarter of a mile away, on a hilltop, Maple Street looked like this, a long tree-lined avenue full of lights going on and off and screaming people racing back and forth. Maple Street was a bedlam. It was an outdoor asylum for the insane. Windows were broken, street lights sent clusters of broken glass down on the heads of women and children. Power mowers started up and car engines and radios. Blaring music mixed with the screams and shouts and the anger.

Up on top of the hill two men, screened by the darkness, stood near the entrance to a spaceship and looked down on Maple Street.

"Understand the procedure now?" the first figure said. "Just stop a few of their machines and radios and telephones and lawn mowers. Throw them into darkness for a few hours and then watch the pattern unfold."

"And this pattern is always the same?" the second figure asked.

"With few variations," came the answer. "They pick the most dangerous enemy they can find and it's themselves. All we need do is sit back—and watch."

"Then I take it," figure two said, "this place, this Maple Street, is not unique?"

Figure one shook his head and laughed. "By no means. Their world is full of Maple Streets and we'll go from one to the other and let them destroy themselves." He started up the incline toward the entrance of the spaceship. "One to the other," he said as the other figure followed him. "One to the other." There was just the echo of his voice as the two figures disappeared and a panel slid softly across the entrance. "One to the other," the echo said.

When the sun came up on the following morning Maple Street was silent. Most of the houses had been burned. There were a few bodies lying on sidewalks and draped over porch railings. But the silence was total. There simply was no more life. At four o'clock that afternoon there was no more world, or at least not the kind of world that had greeted the morning. And by Wednesday afternoon of the following week, a new set of residents had moved into Maple Street. They were a handsome race of people. Their faces showed great character. Great character indeed. Great character and excellently shaped heads. Excellently shaped heads—two to each new resident!

From Rod Serling's closing narration, "The Monsters Are Due on Maple Street," *The Twilight Zone*, January 1, 1960, CBS Television Network.

Now the CAMERA PANS UP for a shot of the starry sky and over this we hear the Narrator's Voice.

NARRATOR'S VOICE
The tools of conquest do not necessarily
come with bombs and explosions and
fallout. There are weapons that
are simply thoughts, attitudes, prejudices—to be found only in the minds
of men. For the record, prejudices can
kill and suspicion can destroy and a
thoughtless, frightened search for a
scapegoat has a fallout all of its own
for the children . . . and the children yet
unborn.
(a pause)
And the pity of it is that these
things cannot be confined to . . . The
Twilight Zone!

FADE TO BLACK

MORE STORIES FROM THE TWILIGHT ZONE

THE LONELY

It was like the surface of a giant stove—this desert that stretched in a broiling yellow mat to the scrubby line of mountains on one side and the shimmering salt flats on the other. Occasional dunes and gullies punctuated the yellow sameness with thin, dark purple streaks. But for the most part it looked endless and unchanging; a barren mass of sand that beckoned the heat rays and then soaked them into itself.

The shack was an alien element on the scene. It stood some eighty miles from the nearest mountains. It was built of corrugated metal and had a flat, sloping roof. Alongside it was a 1943 sedan, the metal pitted, windshield without glass, looking as if a wind could blow it apart. And sitting on the metal porch, shaded by the overhang of the roof, was James Corry. He was forty, with a lean, long-jawed face and deep-set, light blue eyes. His hair, once brown, was now a bleached-out thatch that hung dry over his forehead, with streaks of gray at the temples.

Corry was writing slowly and painstakingly in a large diary. Sometimes he paused and squinted out at the desert around him.

In the beginning Corry had been able to lose himself in activities and forget the desert. When he'd put the old car together, for example, he'd been able to work three or four hours at a stretch unmindful of the white orb overhead or even the furnace-like air that sometimes hung heavy and sometimes was thrown at him by the wind in hot gusts.

But that was five years ago when he first was put down here. The old beat-up car had occupied his time. And writing in his diary had done more for him than pass the time. It had been like a survival exercise, in the practice of which a man could train himself to compartmentalize his thoughts, shut out the heat, disregard the loneliness, and somehow make a day go by and then a night and then another day . . . and then another day . . . and then another day . . .

He'd been thirty-five when it happened, on Earth. At odd times it would come back to him, graphic and clear, in actual chronology and vivid, almost unbearable, recall. He could see the dead body of his wife, struck down by a wildly speeding driver. This incredibly beautiful woman, in one violent, shrieking moment, was turned into a thing of horror, to lie, an unrecognizable pulp, on a city street while the drunken maniac responsible careened along to wind up against a lamp post.

Corry saw it happen from his apartment window and dashed out into the street. He took one look at his wife and then ran toward the smashed car. The driver was getting out, his face ashen with a sudden sobriety laced with horror. It had taken only a moment for Corry to do his job. Goaded by a fury, an anger, a hatred, a torment which knew no bounds he strangled the man with his bare hands while onlookers screamed and two large men had been unable to tear him away.

His trial had been brief. The extenuating circumstances surrounding the homicide kept him from the "release pills" that had long ago taken over for gas chambers, gallows, and electric chairs. But often, sitting on the front porch of his desert home, fingers shaking, skin feeling taut, poreless, his whole body somehow mummified and foreign to him, he would reflect that a sentence of thirty-five years on a sandy asteroid could be less compassionate than a swift, painless exit into a black void.

Corry fingered quickly through the pages of his diary from August 1993 back to June of 1990, remembering in another portion of his brain how long that passage of time had taken in actuality.

He looked out toward the distant salt flats. He had started

walking toward them three years ago and collapsed three hours away from the shack. He knew then that the heat and the desert were bars and that the area around his home was a dungeon.

He didn't remember exactly at what point he had become unable to lose himself in writing or doing chores, and the loneliness of the place began to take on an almost physical discomfort. It was an emotional reaction, but it carried with it an ache of body and mind that was deep, real, and constant.

"Banishment" is what they called his punishment. Banishment. Half a lifetime on an asteroid, visited four times a year by a supply ship which stayed, on the average, twelve minutes between landing and taking off. The arrival of the spaceship was like a breath of sanity, a recharging of the mind so that it could function during the next three months.

Corry penciled in the last line of the day's entry, closed the book and thought with relief that it wouldn't be long before the supply ship came again. He went over to the car and leaned against it, feeling the heat press against his back, wishing in some strange, illogical way, that he could perspire. At least this would be a manifestation of his body. It would be a remonstrance against the elements. But as it was, his flesh was like the sand he walked on. It took in the heat uninvited and was incapable of reacting.

He reached through the windowless opening of the door and pressed the horn. It gave off a deep, sludgy, raspy kind of noise and then quickly died away. He pressed it again several times, then turned very slowly, leaning against the door, and let his eyes travel the width of the desert beyond. There was a ritual even to loneliness, he thought. Twice a day he went to his car, to look at it, touch the horn, and sometimes sit in the front seat, staring through a glassless windshield, succumbing to a wishful daydream that the car was on a highway and there was some place to go.

Banished.

The word held little meaning for him before his sentence.

Banished.

It meant something now. It meant a heat that was unbearable. It meant a loneliness beyond rationale. A sobbing hunger for someone of his own kind. A shaky, pulsating yearning to hear a voice other than his own.

He went back to the porch, touching the metal railing. It

had cooled slightly and this meant that night was coming. He looked down at his diary lying on the metal folding chair. He knew exactly what he had written. His mind could pick up anything now and give it back to him because it was uncluttered, almost a desert itself.

"The fifteenth day, sixth month . . . the year five," the entry began. "And all the days and the months and the years the same. There'll be a supply ship coming in soon, I think. They're either due or overdue, and I hope it's Allenby's ship because he's a decent man and he brings things for me."

The words came back to Corry almost as if spoken aloud by his own voice. "Like the parts for that antique automobile. I was a year putting that thing together—such as it is. A whole year putting an old car together."

Corry closed his eyes, touched his hot cheek and the beard stubble.

"But thank God and Allenby for that car and the hours it used up. The days and the weeks. I can look at it out there and I know it's real, and reality is what I need. Because what is there left that I can believe in? The desert and the wind? The silence? Or myself—can I believe in myself any more?"

Corry opened his eyes and stared out toward the salt flats. Disjointed. That described his diary. It was a crazy quilt of unrelated facts, emotions, thoughts and attitudes, opinions that could find no rebuttal because they could not be related to anyone else.

Maybe I'll become like the car, he thought. Inanimate. Just an item sitting in the sand. Then would I feel loneliness? Would I feel misery? He shook his head and closed off the thought process. He'd fix dinner. He had some ice left that he'd made the other day and he'd use it. He'd open up a can of beer and put the ice in it. You never did that on Earth—dilute good beer with ice. But it was something different and anything different here was desirable.

Corry went into the shack. The room was small and square. There were a cot, shelves he had built out of laminated steel, everything studded and knobbed with screws, nuts, and bolts. The bookends he had made out of a magnesium packing case; the chess board from a strip of plastic, with nuts and bolts for men.

There were many pictures drawn in charcoal and then stuck

up on the wall. At first he had sketched city scenes and then, as recollection grew dimmer, he began to draw only that which his eyes could see and his mind contain. There was a whole wall covered with pictures of the desert, the distant mountains, the salt flats, and one or two of the car. There were a few attempts at self-portraiture and in some instances they resembled Corry. Always it was a bold-stroked picture of a man in front of a crowd. Always a crowd. Always a crowd suggested by little formless waves, hints of a multitude of faces and a multitude of eyes.

Corry had been a retiring man once, uneasy with people. His life had been quiet and not very social. But this sandy asteroid had changed all that. The sun had changed it. The heat had boiled away his shyness and left a bare-bone hunger for a society to belong to. Corry looked at himself in the makeshift mirror that hung close to the window. His face had taken on a mahogany hue, but otherwise he had not changed much, except for the lightness of his hair.

About a year ago he had taken to staring at himself in the mirror, trying to force a change in the face that looked back at him. For a few days he had achieved something. He had been able to alter the appearance of the reflection. And for those few days he'd carried on long conversations with a face in a piece of glass. Until one night he started to cry and ran out into the desert night to throw himself down on the sand and sob himself to sleep under a starlit sky that was nothing more than a silence upon silence.

The face that stared back at him now was the familiar face. It was his. It belonged to him. It was a lonely face, the eyes deep-set and searching but without expectation. They looked out upon an emptiness and simply reflected it.

Corry went to the refrigerator, took out a can of beer, then reached into a plastic bag and took out two small, melting ice cubes. He opened the can, poured the beer into the glass with the ice cubes. Then he sat down in his stifling metal room and looked out the window, feeling weariness mixed with the sense of desolation. The big yellow desert stared back at him like a giant sandy face. Just as it stared back at him every waking moment of his day.

Banishment.

He had thirty more years to go and deep inside the core of

him was the knowledge that he could not live those thirty years—not with sanity. Already he felt pincer-like claws at his head. The nightmarish attack, as if by an invading army, had reached his brain, overflowed into the fortress that a man keeps behind his eyes—a screaming horde of barbaric thoughts, each drawing life blood from the remains of what had been James W. Corry's rational being.

The supply ship landed three days later. It flashed across the sky, glinting briefly from the borrowed rays of the giant white sun, then landed with a roar several thousand yards away from Corry's shack. A few moments later the crew commander followed by two other men came slowly across the sand toward the shack.

Corry stood out in front watching them, his mouth dry, his fingers unable to stop their shaking. Twice he had started an abortive, headlong leap across the desert to meet them and twice had stopped himself. He felt a sound rising in his throat, a yell, an acknowledgment of this brief respite from his torment. But he throttled himself with some hidden bands of restraint until, as they approached, he permitted himself to go slowly toward them.

Captain Walter Allenby, wading through the deep sand, looked keenly at Corry. Again he noticed how quick to age were these banishment cases. How strangely and subtly each face had changed after only three months.

Allenby had been in the space service for eighteen years, had flown everything from jet aircraft to space vehicles and, in his millions of flying hours, he had gone through everything from engine failure to meteorite storms. This, however, was something else.

This was having to spend twelve minutes four times a year with tormented, half-crazed men who would stare at him as if he were a kind of Messiah. There were four asteroids along the route and Corry's was the last. Allenby heaved a sigh of relief. Three weeks from now he would be back on Earth. Allenby felt a stab of pity, as he saw that Corry's fingers were clenched tightly in front of him.

"How are you, Allenby?" Corry asked him, his voice tight and dry from the effort of self-control.

"Just fine, Corry," Allenby answered and gestured to his two crewmen. "This is James Corry, gentlemen. And this is Adams, and this is Jensen."

The two men nodded as they stared intently at Corry. This was their first trip and Corry was the fourth banishment case they'd seen. Both noted the similarity between all four men. The hunger in the eyes, the desperate set of the faces.

Adams, a thin, wiry, dark-haired youngster in his twenties, had signed on just a week before the ship left. He was a better-than-average navigator, but eleven lonely months in space, punctuated only by the dry, hot asteroids, had taken away his appetite, stripped the protection off his nerves, and turned him into an easily combustible, foul-mouthed little malcontent who went from rage to rage, set off by everything from navigational problems to the itchy discomfort of his space suit. He associated Corry with the heat, the discomfort, with being nine million miles from home and with the last eleven months of loneliness and dislike.

"Quite a place you got here, Corry," he said.

Corry's lips trembled. "I'm so glad you like it."

"I didn't say I liked it—I think it stinks."

Corry's head shot up. "You don't have to live here," he offered quietly.

"No. But I've got to come back here four times a year, and that's eight months out of twelve, Corry, away from Earth. My wife probably won't even recognize me when I get home."

Corry's face softened. He half turned away. "I'm sorry."

Adams's mouth twisted. "I'll bet you are," he said acidly. "But you've got it made, don't you, Corry? It makes for simple living, doesn't it?" He bent down, picked up a handful of sand, and held it out toward Corry.

"This is Corry's Kingdom," Adams said. He let the sand run through his fingers. "Right here. Six thousand miles north and south. Four thousand miles east and west. And all of it's just like this."

Corry felt his fingers tremble. He wet his lips, looked briefly at Allenby who had turned away, embarrassed, and forced a smile when he spoke to Adams again. "You ought to try it three hundred and sixty-five days a year, Adams. You feel like a roast that never leaves an oven."

Adams's laughter was not related to humor. "How about it, Captain?" he said abruptly to Allenby. "We've only got a few minutes."

Allenby nodded. "Fifteen minutes this time, to be exact, Corry."

Corry tried to keep the supplication out of his voice. "Nobody's checking your schedule," he said to Allenby. "Why don't we have a game of cards or something?"

Allenby kept his voice firm, with obvious effort. "I'm sorry, Corry," he said. "This isn't an arbitrary decision. If we delay our time of departure any more than fifteen minutes, that places us in a different orbital position. We'd never make it back to Earth. We'd have to stay here at least fourteen days before this asteroid was in position again."

Corry's voice went higher. "So? Fourteen days! Why not have us a ball? I've got some beer I've saved. We could play some cards, you could tell me what's going on back there—" Words poured out of him, strung together with little gasps, and to Allenby it was like watching a full-grown man get whipped.

Allenby made a show of checking the sky. "I wish we could, Corry," he answered, "but like I said—we've only got fifteen minutes."

Corry's voice overlapped the captain's. "Well . . . well, what's a few lousy days to you? A coupla card games." He turned toward the other two men. "How 'bout you guys? You think I'll murder you or something over a bad hand?"

Jensen turned away discomfited, but Adams stared at Corry with disgust and accusation.

"I'm sorry," Allenby said quietly. Then he took Corry's arm. "Let's go to the shack—"

Corry flung the arm off, but with desperation, not anger. "All right," he shrilled. "All right, two minutes are gone now. You've got thirteen minutes left. I wouldn't want to foul up your schedule, Allenby. Not for a . . ." He looked away. "Not for a lousy game of cards. Not for a few bottles of crummy beer." He looked down at his feet in the sand and then slowly raised his eyes to face Allenby like an animal caught in a trap, pleading for release. There was a nakedness to it as if pride had been swept away. When Corry spoke again, the voice was that of a man falling down into hell and scrabbling for the last ledge which offered him salvation.

"Allenby," he said very softly. "Allenby . . . what about the pardon?"

There was a silence broken finally by Adams. His voice dripped with malice like some kind of putrefying liquid from a running sore. "A pardon, Corry," he said harshly. "You're out of luck, pal. Sentence reads thirty-five years and they're not even reviewing cases of homicide. You've been here five now, so that makes thirty to go."

Corry felt a strange, icy cold moving through his body. But still Adams did not stop.

"Thirty to go," he continued, "so get comfortable, dad, huh?" He laughed briefly, his head back, his face red and itchy from the sun, the discomfort spewing out of him in the form of an attack on another human being. The laugh stopped when he saw Allenby's face.

The tall captain shut him off with his eyes, made a brief gesture to Corry to follow him, and headed toward the shack. Corry walked beside him, the sand sending up crunchy sounds as they sank down through the crust of the top layer. At intervals Allenby glanced surreptitiously at Corry, who looked beaten and sick. They reached a small knoll close to the shack, and there Corry stopped. Both men gazed down on the metal structure and the old car that sat in a mute, ugly loneliness.

"It just crossed my mind, Captain," Corry said, "—it just crossed my mind this is ninety percent of the view I'm gonna have for the next thirty years. Just what I'm looking at right now. That shack, that car, and all that desert . . . and this is my company for the next thirty years."

Allenby touched his arm with an instinctive gentleness and compassion. His own voice was quiet. "I'm sorry, Corry," the captain said. "Unfortunately we don't make the rules. All we do is deliver your supplies and pass on information. I told you last time that there'd been a lot of pressure back home about this kind of punishment. There are a whole lot of people who think it's unnecessarily cruel." He paused for a moment. "Well, who knows what the next couple of years will bring? They may change their minds, alter the law, imprison you on Earth like in the old days."

Corry turned to stare at the captain's face. There was no emotion in his voice now. It was flat. Flat like the desert around him. Dry like the sand. Unrevealing like the vast expanse of nothingness that surrounded them.

"Allenby," Corry said. "I'll tell you something. Every morning . . . every morning when I get up, I tell myself that this is my last day of sanity." His voice broke for a moment and then he recovered. "I won't be able to live another day of loneliness. Not *another* day! And by noon I can't keep my fingers still and the inside of my mouth feels like gunpowder and burnt copper and deep inside my gut I got an ache that won't go away and seems to be crawling all over the inside of my body, pricking at me, tearing little chunks out of me—and then I think I've got to hold out for another day, just another day." He turned away from Allenby and stared down at the shack again. "But I can't keep doing that day after day," he continued, "for the next thirty years. I'll lose my mind, Allenby. I swear to Christ . . . I'll lose my mind."

Adams, coming up the knoll and only a few yards away, heard part of what Corry said. He shook his head. The heat was burning the back of his neck and he felt stifled. "Jesus," he exploded. "Honest to God, Corry, you're breaking my heart!"

Corry whirled around, his face contorted. He growled like an animal and then screamed from deep inside his chest. He lunged at Adams, catching him off balance and sending him sprawling backwards down the knoll. He was on him in an instant, hitting him in the face, crunching, desperate blows that smashed against flesh and bone, until Allenby and Jensen pulled Corry off and threw him backwards.

Allenby, standing between the prostrate man and his attacker, shouted at Corry. "Easy . . . easy, Corry. For God's sake!"

Very gradually Corry let his body relax, moving the route from a trembling, shaking ague to the tired, heavy motionlessness that served better in this heat.

Adams slowly got to his feet, feeling the tear on his cheek, the throbbing bruise on his jaw. "I wouldn't worry about going off my rocker if I were you, Corry," he said. "It's already happened. Stir-crazy they used to call it. Well that's what you are now, stir-crazy."

Allenby took a step toward him to make certain he'd stay in one place. "Back off, Adams," he ordered. "You and Jensen go back and get the supplies. Bring them over to the shack."

Adams bridled. "Mr. Corry has a broken leg or something?" He pointed to Corry.

Allenby said, "Adams, do as I tell you." He paused, looking briefly at Corry, then back toward Adams. "And the big crate," he continued, "with the red tag—handle that one gently."

Jensen looked over toward the car and grinned. "How about the use of his buggy there? Some of the stuff's heavy."

Corry answered as if shaken out of his dream. "It isn't running today," he said.

Once again Adams laughed. "It isn't running today! What's the matter, Corry—use it too much, do you?" He turned to Jensen. "You know there's so many places a guy can go out here. There's the country club over the mountains there, and the seashore over that way, and a drive-in theatre—that's some place around here, isn't it, Corry?"

Corry stood motionless, his head down.

Allenby faced the young navigator. The gentleness of his tone did not disguise the sense of absolute command that permeated the voice. "I'm going to tell you one more time, Adams. Go get the stuff or you'll wind up the rest of the trip with your hands tied behind your back, and I'll have every right to handle it that way!"

Adams opened his mouth to retort, then shut it tight. He cast a vindictive look at Corry, then turned and started back across the desert, Jensen following him. Allenby took Corry's arm and the two men walked down the knoll toward the shack, up the steps of the burning hot metal porch, and inside.

Corry sat down on his cot, staring at his folded hands. Allenby went to the refrigerator and took out a jug of water.

"Glasses?" he asked.

Corry motioned toward the shelf. "Paper cups up there."

Allenby unscrewed the jar, sniffed it, made a face. He poured some water into a cup, took it in a quick gulp.

"We've got some fresh on board," he said to Corry. "They'll be bringing it over."

Corry nodded numbly, not looking at him. Allenby took a deep breath, then pulled up a chair directly opposite Corry. He studied the man on the cot as if formulating an approach.

"I brought you some magazines, too," he said, "strictly on my own."

Corry nodded. "Thanks."

"And some microfilm. Old vintage movies. Science fiction stuff. You'll get a kick out of it."

Again Corry nodded. "I'm sure I will."

Allenby ran his tongue over his lips, stared at Corry for a long, silent moment, then rose and crossed over to the window.

"I brought you something else, Corry," Allenby said, over his shoulder. "It would be my job if they suspected." He paused. "It would be my neck if they found out for sure."

"Look, Allenby," Corry said grimly, "I don't want gifts now. I don't want tidbits. It makes me feel like an animal in a cage and there's a nice old lady out there who wants to throw peanuts at me." He was suddenly on his feet, his voice high again and shrill. "A pardon, Allenby," he shouted. "That's the only gift I want." The words tumbled out, propelled by his grief, by his urgency, by a sudden hopelessness that descended on him. "I killed an animal, Allenby. As God is my witness, I killed an animal and he had no business living anyway. All right, punish me . . . stick me in jail . . . but, Allenby . . ." his voice quivered and his eyes glistened, "Allenby . . . not this. Jesus God, Allenby . . . not this!"

Allenby nodded and said, "I know, Corry. I know all about it." He retraced his steps to the chair and sat down. "I doubt if it'll be any consolation to you, Corry, but it's not easy handling this kind of an assignment. Stopping here four times a year and having to look at a man's agony!"

Allenby spoke truth and only truth, and Corry realized it. There was compassion in Allenby and honesty, but Corry was unable to keep back the harshness.

"You're quite right, Allenby!" He spit it out. "That's precious little consolation."

Allenby rose. He walked directly over to Corry. "I can't bring you freedom, Corry. This is the one thing I can't bring. All I can do . . . all I can do is try to bring you things to help keep your sanity. Something . . . anything so you can fight loneliness."

They heard Adams and Jensen who were lugging a small metal cart down from the knoll toward the shack. Allenby could see the box of supplies on the cart and a rectangular crate that measured seven feet and had a red tag fluttering from one end.

"Captain," Jensen called out, "you want this big crate opened up?"

Allenby hurriedly answered him. "Not yet. Stay out there. I'll be right out."

Corry, looking out the window, turned to Allenby and said,

"I'll bite, Captain. What's the present?" He looked through the window. "What is it?"

Allenby turned very slowly toward Corry. "It's . . . it's something I brought you, Corry."

Corry laughed shortly. "If it's a twenty-year supply of puzzles—lots of luck—I'll have to decline with thanks. I don't need any puzzles, Allenby. If I want to try to probe any mysteries—I can look in the mirror and try to figure out my own."

Allenby went to the door and put his hand on the knob. "We've got to go now. We'll be back in three months." There was a silence. "You listening to me, Corry?" he continued. "This is important."

Corry looked up at him.

"When you open the crate," Allenby said, "there's nothing you need do. The . . . the item has been vacuum packed. It needs no activator of any kind. The air will do that. There'll be a booklet inside too that can answer any of your questions."

"You're mysterious as hell," Corry said.

"I don't mean to be," Allenby answered. "It's just like I told you, though—I'm risking a lot to have brought this here." He pointed toward the window. "*They* don't know what it is I brought. I'd appreciate your waiting till we get out of sight before you open it."

Corry was barely listening. "All right," he said flatly. "Have a good trip back. Give my regards to . . ." he wet his lips and looked down at the floor. ". . . to Broadway and every place else while you're at it."

Allenby nodded and studied the other man. "Sure, Corry," he said quietly. "I'll see you."

He opened the door and went out. Through the window Corry could see him motion to the others as they followed him across the desert back toward the ship. Corry, watching the retreating back of the captain, suddenly called out:

"Allenby!"

The three men stopped and turned toward him.

"Allenby," Corry yelled. "I don't much care *what* it is. But for the thought, Allenby. For the . . . decency of it . . . I thank you."

Allenby nodded, his mouth taut, feeling a sickness in his

stomach. "You're quite welcome, Corry," he said softly. "You're quite welcome."

Corry watched them for a long, long time until they disappeared over the line of dunes. Then aimlessly, without direction, without much thought, he went outside.

The crates were piled end on end beside the long rectangular box with the red tag. Corry studied it, throwing questions at himself in his mind as to what it might be. It was a mystery, but an insignificant mystery. What the hell difference did it make what it was. Games, cards, puzzles, books, microfilm— whatever! The newness of it would be corroded under the sun and it would change into what everything else changed into on the asteroid. A blob of weary familiarity without excitement and without challenge. He kicked at the box with his foot, then slowly turned and studied the horizon in the direction where Allenby had disappeared.

Alongside the ship, Jensen was clambering up the metal ladder to the open hatch. He disappeared inside and Allenby motioned Adams to follow. Adams went halfway up the ladder, then looked down toward Allenby, who was staring off into the distance.

"Captain," Adams said. "Just man to man, huh?"

Allenby, as if shaken from a trance, stared up at him. "What?" he asked.

"What did you bring him?" Adams asked. "What was in the box?"

Allenby smiled and then said softly, more to himself than to Adams, "I'm not sure, really. Maybe it's just an illusion. Or maybe it's salvation!"

He waved Adams up the ladder and followed him toward the open hatch. Ten and a half minutes had gone by and they'd blast off in exactly fifty-three seconds.

Moments later, as the ship raced through the sky on the long trip home, Allenby felt a pang of guilt. They were going back to Earth. The green earth. An earth full of sounds and smells. An earth that was home. He could not bring himself to look back through the rear scanner at the tiny yellow blob that floated through space carrying a man in anguish who sat in a metal shack contemplating nothing but more anguish.

* * *

Corry had opened the crate, removed what was inside and was reading a booklet.

"You are now the proud possessor," the first paragraph began, "of a robot built in the form of woman. To all intents and purposes this creature is a woman. Physiologically and psychologically she is a human being with a set of emotions, a memory track, the ability to reason, to think, and to speak. She is beyond illness and under normal circumstances should have a life span similar to that of a comparable human being. Her name is Alicia."

Very slowly Corry let the booklet slip out of his fingers. He looked across the yards of sand over to the crate and to the creature who stood alongside it.

She looked human. She had long brown hair, deep-set brown eyes, a straight, tiny nose, a firm jaw. She was dressed in a simple, loose-flowing garment that neither added to nor detracted from her femininity.

But it was her face Corry stared at. There was no expression in the eyes. There was a deadness, a lack of vitality, an almost comatose immobility of the features, the mouth, the eyes, the face muscles. It was a mask—a beautiful mask. The face of a woman . . . but nonetheless just a mask, a covering.

Corry felt a revulsion, a horror at this thing that looked at him with glassy orbs that so resembled human eyes, but were so emotionlessly unhuman in their empty stare.

"Get out of here," Corry said in a low voice as he advanced toward her. "Get out of here." His voice was louder as he glared at her, the horror he felt crawling across his skin. "Get out of here! I don't want any machine in here! Go on, get out of here!"

The robot looked back at him, then she opened her mouth and spoke. "My name is Alicia," the mouth said. The voice was that of a woman, but there was a coldness to it. "My name is Alicia. What's yours?"

It was ludicrous. It was beyond belief. This . . . this thing that spoke to him from the desert floor. This machine that mouthed proprieties as if from a book on etiquette. It spoke to him in a language of tea parties and civilization.

Corry took another step to stand near her, staring at her. He no longer shouted. He just stood there shaking his head and finally he said in a flat, even tone, "I'm going inside now. And when I come back out . . . when I come back out, I don't want to find you here. Understand?

Without waiting for a reply, he turned and walked back toward the shack, leaving this thing that looked so much like a woman standing in the sand watching him as he disappeared inside.

She had come on what Corry was certain was Thursday and now it was Saturday afternoon. He had seen little of her. During the day she would stand on the knoll close to the shack watching him and at night she was either gone or on occasion he could hear her on the metal porch, but he never spoke to her.

He was digging a hole for garbage now and, as always, had waited till the late afternoon. Not that it was much cooler or that there was any more shade, but the habit pattern of a life spent on Earth still persisted in the functions of Corry's existence. Late afternoon he'd always associated with cooling and even when it stayed breathlessly hot he did most of his physical labor then.

He leaned on his shovel, wiping a sweatless face, looking at a sun just reaching the top of the mountains. Now bright orange instead of glaring white, it nonetheless sent out its cascades of heat.

Alicia came walking down the dune toward him. She carried a bucket of water which she put down on the sand a few feet from him, her mechanical face staring at him as if sightless.

"Well?" Corry asked her.

"I brought you some water. Where shall I put it?"

"Just leave it there and get out of here."

"It'll get warm," Alicia said, "just sitting there."

Corry took the dipper from the bucket, tasted the water, spit some of it out, and then put the dipper back. He stared at her and saw how intently she seemed to stare back.

"You'd know, huh?" he asked.

"Know what?"

"You'd know that water'd get warm."

The corners of Alicia's mouth wrinkled and it was as close to a smile as he'd ever noticed from her.

"I can feel thirst," she said.

Corry wiped his mouth with the back of his hand and stared at her again. He found himself staring at her a lot lately, but it was not the inventory of interest that a man uses to look at a woman. It was a clinical examination of a foreign object. It was the reluctant stare of a man who finds himself in a freak house and yet feels the painful fascination of all that which is strange and odd and unearthly.

"What else can you feel?" Corry asked. The question was rhetorical.

"I don't understand—" Alicia began.

"I suppose you can feel heat and cold, can't you?" Corry interrupted her. "How about pain? Can you feel pain?"

Alicia nodded and the flat voice suddenly sounded strangely soft. "That, too."

Corry took a step over to her and looked at her. "How?" he asked. "How can you? You're a machine, aren't you?"

"Yes," Alicia whispered. "I am a machine."

"Of course you are," Corry said. His mouth twisted. His eyes glared at her with distaste. "Why didn't they build you to look like a machine? Why aren't you made out of metal with nuts and bolts sticking out of you? With wires and electrodes and things like that?" His voice rose.

"Why do they turn you into a lie? Why do they cover you with what looks like flesh? Why do they give you a face?" His nails dug deep into the palms of his hands and something else went into his voice at this moment. "A face," he said, his voice very low. "A face that, if I look at it long enough, makes me think . . . makes me believe that . . ." His hands grabbed her shoulders and went up past her neck to cup her face in a hard and painful grasp.

Alicia closed her eyes against the pain. "Corry," she said, her voice pleading.

"You mock me," he said to her, "you know that? When you look at me. When you talk to me—I'm being mocked."

"I'm sorry," Alicia answered. She slowly reached up and felt her neck and shoulders. "You hurt me, Corry."

Corry stared at her, repugnance in his eyes. "Hurt you?" he asked her, his hands grabbing her shoulders again. "How in the Goddamn hell could I hurt you?" His fingers dug into her flesh. "I'd like you to explain that to me. How could I possibly hurt you? This isn't flesh. There aren't any nerves under there. There aren't any tendons or muscles."

Corry felt the soft yielding stuff under his fingertips and for just an illogical moment he thought he smelled a perfume, a gentle sweetness that filled the air around her. And again the feeling rose in him that he must crush this thing in front of him. He must twist and pull it apart. He must end its standing there and mocking him from morning till night.

His fingers pressed tighter into her until, forced down by weight and pain, she was on her knees. He reluctantly pulled his hands away from her, looked at her kneeling there, her head down, her tousled brown hair hanging long in front of her.

The fury that he felt was beyond any understanding. He knew only that he must destroy. Kneeling in front of him was his loneliness. Prostrate at his feet was the heat and the discomfort. Vulnerable and weak was the massive desert. It was all in front of him now in the form of this mocking machine. This was the wildness in his mind as he picked up the shovel, lifted it high in the air. He had already begun the downward arc of the swing as he screamed at her.

"You know what you are?" The metal face of the shovel glinted in the departing sun. "Do you know what you are? You're like that broken-down heap I've got sitting in the yard. You're a hunk of metal with arms and legs instead of wheels." The shovel stopped its descent and shook in his hand. His voice took on a different tone, quieter and somehow plaintive.

"But that heap . . . that Goddamn heap doesn't mock me like you do. It doesn't look at me with make-believe eyes and talk to me with a make-believe voice. Well listen, you . . . listen, machine. I'm sick of being mocked by a ghost, by a memory of woman. And that's all you are. You're a reminder to me that I'm so lonely I'm about to lose my mind."

The woman raised her face to him and it was only then that he realized that her eyes were wet and that tears rolled down her cheeks. Very slowly his hand went loose and he was unaware of it when the shovel slipped from his fingers and dropped down to the sand. He stared at her. The face was no longer inanimate, no longer immobile. It had depth and emotion. It was filled with the nuances and the mysteries of that which is woman and there was beauty in the face, too. Corry trembled and slowly went down to his knees to kneel close to her. He extended a shaking hand that met her cheek and he felt the wetness.

"You can cry, too, can't you?"

Alicia nodded. "With reason," she looked up at him again. "And I can feel loneliness, too."

He took her arm and helped her to her feet, then stood very close to her. There was a moment's silence before he could bring himself to speak. Finally he said, "We'll go back home now. We'll eat our dinner."

She nodded again. "All right." She started to walk ahead of him.

Corry called out to her. "Alicia?"

She stopped and turned.

"Alicia," he began. There was something in his tone. Something rich. Something deep. It was man talking to woman. There was gentleness and compassion and something that went beyond both.

"Yes, Corry?"

"I don't care . . . I don't care how you were born . . . or made. You're flesh and blood to me. You're a woman." He took a step toward her and reached out for her. Her hand met his. "You're my companion. Do you understand, Alicia? You're my companion. I need you desperately."

She smiled at him. A smile of infinite warmth. A smile that lit up the face and that shone in the eyes. A smile that was yet another part of the beauty that was this woman. "And I need you, Corry."

They held hands as they walked back toward the shack. Corry would reflect later that at this moment he had felt a peace and composure almost unbearably sweet. And, walking toward the shack he was conscious of the feel of her hand. When he stole a look at her profile he felt that this was one of the most beautiful women he'd ever seen.

They went into the shack and she started to set the table. Corry's eyes never left her. This woman must never leave his sight again. He must never be without her. And though he could not articulate this because his whole being was so scarred and battered by conflicting emotions, James W. Corry had indeed found salvation. It had come in the form of a woman. James W. Corry was in love.

Eleven months had passed. They had been incredible months for Corry. Incredible in the sense that everything had changed. Loneliness had become quiet and solitude. The vast expanse of desert had taken on a strange beauty. The star-filled nights held interest and mystery. He sat on the porch at the close of a day and wrote in his diary. "Alicia has been with me now for almost a year. Twice when Allenby has brought the ship in with supplies I've hidden her so that the others wouldn't see her. I've seen the question in Allenby's eyes each time. It's a question I ask myself. It is difficult to write down what has been the sum total of this very bizarre relationship. It is man and woman, man and machine, and there are times when I know that Alicia is simply an extension of myself. I hear my words coming from her. My emotions. The things that she has learned to love are the things that I have loved."

He stopped and listened to the sound of Alicia singing from inside the shack. The voice high and clear. He smiled and continued to write again. "But I think I've reached the point now where I shall not analyze Alicia any longer. I shall accept her simply as a part of my life—an integral part."

He continued to write, silently turning the page, conscious of Alicia's voice as it drifted from inside the shack. She came to the door and smiled at him. He knew the smile as he knew the face. Each line. Each expression. Each look of the eyes. He smiled and winked at her, then threw her a kiss. She turned from the door and disappeared. He looked down at what he had been writing. "Because I'm not lonely any more, each day can now be lived with. I love Alicia. Nothing else matters."

It was night and she lay cradled in his arms as they looked up toward the stars.

"Look, Alicia," Corry said. "That's the star, Betelgeuse. It's in the constellation of Orion. And there's the Great Bear with its pointer stars in line with the Northern star. And there's the constellation Hercules. See it, Alicia?" He traced a path across the sky with a finger, then turned to look down at her face. It was in shadow, only her eyes visible in the starlight.

"God's beauty," she answered softly.

Corry nodded. "That's right, Alicia. God's beauty."

The girl suddenly stiffened. "That star," she asked. "What's that star, Corry?"

Corry studied the tiny dot that traversed the night sky. "That's not a star. That's a ship, Alicia."

"A ship?"

The tiny dot grew in brightness and dimension as they were

watching. Alicia turned to him. "There's no ship due here now, Corry. You said not for another three months. You said after the last time it wouldn't be for another—"

Corry's voice interrupted her. "It must be Allenby's ship," he said thoughtfully. "It's the only one that ever comes close. They stop at the other asteroids, then go home." He looked away pensively. "That means they'll probably be here by morning." His voice was heavy with question. "I wonder why."

Alicia rose. "Corry? What does it mean?"

He smiled at her in the darkness. "In the morning we'll find out." He held out a hand to her and she moved back down to him, clinging to him, and Corry felt again the closeness . . . almost the oneness. He put his lips to her hair then touched her cheek and then her chin. He kissed her and was no longer aware of desert or stars or of the tiny dot of light that hurtled through space toward them.

Like all dawns, it was bright and hot and the stillness was broken only by the distant voice of Allenby. His shout carried over the silence and after a moment Corry could see him running from far off beyond the first ring of dunes. Behind him were two space-suited figures trying to keep up with the commander. When Allenby reached Corry he was out of breath, his face white with exhaustion.

"Where the hell have you been?" Allenby asked.

Corry saw something special in his face, a look he had not seen before. "Right here. You have trouble?"

Allenby grinned, some of the exhaustion seeping away. "No, we didn't have any trouble." He took a side look at the other two men who also grinned—even Adams. Allenby touched Corry's shoulder. He was obviously trying to restrain himself. There was something going on that Corry couldn't guess at.

"This is a scheduled stop," Allenby said.

"We've got good news for you, Corry," said Adams.

Corry looked from face to face and he said, "That's fine, but I'm not interested."

Allenby squinted against the sun, then grinned again. "You better hear what it is."

"Allenby. I'm not interested."

"You will be. This I guarantee."

Corry again studied the faces of the space-suited men and took a step back from them. There was suspicion now, a germ of doubt and the beginning of an alarm.

"Allenby," he said. "Give me a break, will you? I don't want any trouble."

Allenby laughed. "We don't either, Corry—"

Adams turned to Jensen. "He gets worse," he said. "If we'd come a month later, he'd have been eating sand or something."

Corry suddenly felt that he had to get away from these men. He turned with a kind of enforced nonchalance and started away from them back toward the shack.

"Corry!" Allenby called out after him.

Corry walked faster and then, hearing Allenby's footsteps behind him, broke into a dead run.

"Corry!" Allenby caught up with him, grabbed him by the shoulders and whirled him around. "Listen, you Goddamn idiot. It's this way! Your sentence has been reviewed. You've been given a pardon. We're to take you back home on the ship."

Corry's eyes went wide. His mouth was open. He did not believe what he heard. Allenby saw the look and laughter came back into his voice, the laughter of relief; the laughter of the bearer of such fantastically good tidings that they could almost not be put into words.

"But I'm going to tell you something, you dumb bastard," Allenby roared at him. "We've got to take off from here in exactly twenty-one minutes. We can't wait any longer. We've been dodging meteor storms all the way out and we're almost out of fuel. Any longer than twenty-one minutes, we'll have passed the point of departure and then I don't think we'd ever make it."

Tears were in Corry's eyes as he looked at Allenby and the two men who stood on one of the dunes watching him. Corry closed his eyes, blinking back the wetness. He tried to speak and for a moment nothing came out.

"Allenby . . . Allenby, wait just a minute, will you?" He opened his eyes. "What did you just say? What did you just say about a—"

"A pardon," Allenby said, his voice rich and deep and still full of laughter. "A pardon, Corry."

"But it won't do any of us any good," Adams called out, "unless you get your stuff together and ready to move, Corry. We've picked up three other men off asteroids and we've only got room for about fifteen pounds of stuff. So you'd better pick up what you need in a hurry and leave the rest of it behind." He looked off, grinning, in the direction of the shack. "Such as it is," he added.

Corry's voice shook with excitement and he tried to throttle himself. "Stuff?" he asked. "My stuff? I don't even have fifteen pounds of stuff."

He started to laugh as he walked back toward the shack. The words came out between gusts of laughter, roaring, unquenchable, joyful laughter. Laughter of such massive relief and thanksgiving that it was unrelated to any emotion he had ever felt before.

"I've got a shirt," he said as he walked, "a pencil and a ledger book and a pair of shoes." The tears rolled down his cheeks as he laughed again. "A Goddamn pair of shoes, that's what I've got." He looked across the bare space toward the antique car. "The car you can keep here. That'll be for the next poor devil."

Allenby shook his head. "There won't be any next poor devil, Corry. There won't *be* any more exiles. This was the last time."

"Good," Corry said. "Wonderful. Thank God for that."

He talked as they walked back toward the shack, his words spewing out, propelled by his excitement and the incredible joy he felt. "We'll let it rest here then. The farthest auto-graveyard in the universe, and Alicia and I will wave to it as we leave. We'll just look out of a porthole and throw it a kiss good-by. The car, the shack, the salt flats, the range. The whole bloody works! Alicia and I will just—"

He was suddenly aware of the silence and finally he brought himself to look up at Allenby's face. It looked white and somber. Behind him Adams had stopped, puzzled.

"Who, Corry?" Adams asked. "Who?"

Allenby shut his eyes tight. "Oh my dear God," he whispered. "I forgot her."

Corry again looked from face to face and then stopped on Allenby. "Allenby . . ." It was almost an accusation. "Allenby, it's Alicia."

Jensen whispered to Adams, "He's out of his mind, isn't he?"

Adams started a slow walk toward Corry. "Who's Alicia, Corry?"

Corry smiled, shaking his head at what was obviously an

absurdity that they shouldn't know Alicia, that they shouldn't be aware of her.

"Who's Alicia?" he laughed aloud. "Adams, you idiot! Who's Alicia? You brought her! She's a woman—" Then catching Allenby's look, his voice was softer. "A robot. But closer to a woman," he added. "She's kept me alive, Allenby. I swear to God—if it weren't for her," he looked around at the circle of silent faces.

"What's the matter?" Corry asked. "You worried about Alicia?" He shook his head. "You needn't be. Alicia's harmless. She's like a woman. She *is* a woman. And she's gentle and kind and without her, Allenby, I tell you without her I'd have been finished. I'd have given up." His voice was quiet now. "You would have had to come back here only to bury me."

Adams looked at the commander. "That's what you wouldn't let us look at, huh? The crate with the red tag?"

Allenby turned away.

"I'm sorry, Captain," Corry said to him, "but I had to let it out—"

Allenby held up his hand. "That's all right, Corry. That's all over with. But unfortunately, that's not the problem—"

Again Corry laughed high and uncontrollable. "Problem? There aren't any problems. There are no more problems in Heaven or on Earth. We'll pack up fifteen pounds of stuff and we'll climb in that ship of yours and when we get back to the beautiful green Earth—"

He stopped abruptly. In some hidden portion of his mind realization had come to him. His lips formed the silent words. "Fifteen pounds." Then he whispered it, "Fifteen pounds." It came out now as a shout, *"Fifteen pounds!"* He reached out and grabbed Allenby, his face taut, his eyes pleading. "You've got to have room for more than that, Allenby. Throw out stuff. Throw out equipment. Alicia weighs more than fifteen pounds."

Allenby very slowly reached up to remove Corry's hands from his suit. His voice was heavy with misery. "That's the point," he said quietly. "We're stripped now, Corry. We've got room for you and nothing else except that ledger of yours and the pencil." He shook his head slowly back and forth. "You'll have to leave the robot behind."

Corry stared at him aghast. His voice shook. "She's not just a robot, Allenby. You don't understand. You simply don't understand. You leave her behind . . . that's . . . that's murder."

Allenby shook his head again. "I'm sorry, Corry. I don't have any choice! God, man, don't *you* understand? I simply don't have any choice!"

Corry backed away, his body suddenly feeling cold. "No, Allenby. *You* don't understand. You can't leave her behind." He suddenly turned and screamed. "Alicia! Come here!" He whirled around toward the three men. "You'll see," he shouted at them. "You'll see why you can't leave her behind. Alicia!" he shouted again.

He turned and ran toward the shack, climbing the steps in a single bound, slamming against the door and flinging himself into an empty room. Allenby was behind him. The other two stood on the porch.

"Where is she, Corry?" Allenby asked.

"I don't know. But when you see her, you'll know why you can't leave her behind."

"Look, Corry," Adams said from the porch, "we just want you to get your gear packed and get out of here." He looked at his watch nervously. "We've only got about ten minutes. How about it, Captain?"

Allenby took a deep breath. "Come on, Corry," he said gently.

Corry backed into the room. "I'm not leaving, Allenby," he said. "I told you that. I can't leave."

He stood against the far wall. It was incredible to him that they didn't understand. It was beyond belief that they didn't perceive what surely must be such an evident truth. You couldn't leave a beautiful woman alone on an asteroid. Not someone like Alicia.

Allenby read his thoughts. He gritted his teeth, his fingers clenched and unclenched. He took a step toward Corry. "Corry," he said, "this is our last trip here. This is everybody's last trip. It's off the route now. That means no supplies, no nothing. That means if you stay here—you die here. And that way, there'd be a day, Corry, when you'd pray for death to come quicker than it's bargained for."

Corry shook his head, rejecting him, rejecting his words. There was no logic. There were no answering facts. There was just this one simple truth. "I can't leave her behind, Allenby. And you won't take her. So that means I stay." His face agonized, he threw himself against the window and screamed out toward the desert beyond. "Alicia! Alicia . . . *don't come*. Stay away!"

Allenby moved across the room hurriedly. He grabbed Corry, pulled him close to him. It was now and only now. The thing had to be done now.

"Corry," he said, "I saw this . . . this *thing* get crated and shoved into a box."

"I don't care," Corry whispered.

"She's a machine, Corry. She's a motor with wires, tubes, and batteries."

"She's a woman," Corry said brokenly. "Oh God, Allenby, she's a woman. She's *my* woman."

Jensen's voice came from the porch. "Captain, we've only got four minutes, sir. We've got to leave, sir."

Adams came in, tense and frightened. "How about it, Captain Allenby? What do you say we leave him here?"

Allenby shook his head. "We can't leave him here. Sick, mad, or half-alive, we've got to bring him back. Those are the orders." He turned again toward Corry. "It isn't just you now, Corry," he said evenly. "Now it's all of us. So that means we can't talk any more and we can't argue with you. We simply have to take you with us."

Allenby felt a shock of pain in his stomach as Corry lunged against him, flailing with an elbow and pushing him aside. Adams toppled sideways as Corry backhanded him away. They could hear him shouting as he raced across the desert away from the shack.

"Alicia! Alicia!"

Allenby was on his feet and out the door in a moment, Adams and Jensen following. It was as if the whole purpose of Allenby's life was funneled into this pursuit. He had to take this man back. He had to save him.

A hundred yards ahead he saw Corry stop and then disappear in a gully. When he reached the spot he was almost afraid to look. Adams and Jensen caught up with him and he heard them gasp.

Corry was kneeling beside the figure of a woman. She looked up at them with eyes like a frightened child's. Corry saw the three space-suited figures. Desperation clawed at his voice.

"Alicia, talk to them," he begged. "Tell them you're a woman. Explain to them."

Allenby walked slowly down the dune toward the gully. He had a rocket pistol in a holster on his belt. He unbuckled it as he walked. "Corry," he pleaded, "you've got to understand this." He stopped a few feet from them. His voice was an agonized whisper. "I don't have any choice. God help me, I just don't have any choice."

He took the gun out of the holster and held it up. Corry turned to him, still on his knees.

"Allenby, she's a human being. Don't you understand, Allenby? Alicia's a human being." He started to crawl toward Allenby, sobbing. "Allenby, Allenby, she's a human being. She's a human being, Allenby. She's a human being—"

His voice was drowned out by the shrieking whine of the rocket pistol as it blasted the hot stillness of the morning. Corry felt his blood congeal and something, he didn't know what, forced him to turn and look at the woman behind him.

She had been hit in the face and the force of the blast had lifted her off the ground and flung her aside. She lay against the side of the dune, propped up like a puppet. The big hole where had been the face ringed by brown curls was a horror of twisted wires, smashed tubes, and a thin spiral of smoke. The remnant of an eye hung down in front and incredibly a voice yet came from this.

"Corry," it said. "Corry . . . Corry . . ." It made other sounds like a record running down on a turntable and then it was quiet.

"Captain," Adams said, *"it's got to be now."*

Allenby, staring down at the gun in his hand, nodded. "It will be now," he said softly. Then he looked at Corry. "Let's go, Corry. It's time to go home."

The four men walked across the desert toward the spaceship that awaited them. Corry moved like an automaton.

"It's all behind you now, Corry," Allenby said to him as they approached the ship. "It's all behind you. Like a bad dream. A nightmare. And when you wake up, you'll be on Earth. You'll be home."

"Home?" Corry's voice sounded hollow and strange.

"That's right," Allenby said. He touched the other man's arm. "All you're leaving behind you, Corry, is loneliness."

Corry stopped, then slowly turned to stare back toward the glinting metal thing that was the shack and beyond it, to the right, a tiny blob of color that was a woman's dress, lying in the sand. He could not cry now except those silent tears that come from deep within.

"I must remember," he said. "I must remember to keep that in mind."

He let Allenby take his elbow, turn him around and lead him to the giant metal cylindrical thing that stood poised pointing impatiently toward the sky. Moments later there was a roar, and the ship headed upward.

Down below on a microscopic piece of sand that floated through space was a fragment of a man's life. Left to rust were the place he'd lived in and the machines he'd used. Without use they would disintegrate from the wind and the sand and the years that acted upon them. All of Mr. Corry's machines . . . including the one made in his image and kept alive by love. It lay mutilated in the sand. It had become obsolete.

MR. DINGLE, THE STRONG

It was that uniquely American institution known as the neighborhood bar, small, softly lit and at this moment catering to that unsophisticated pre-cocktail group whose drinking was a serious business undisturbed and uncomplicated by the social frivolities of the five-thirty crowd. The latter group were the cocktail folks whose alcohol was part of a master plan of either business contacts or logistically planned seduction.

Reading left to right in the small, dark room were first, Mr. Anthony O'Toole the proprietor, who watered his drinks like geraniums, but who stood foursquare for peace and quiet and booths for ladies.

A scrawny, tired-faced, hollow-cheeked customer sat across from him and this man's name was Joseph J. Callahan. He was an unregistered bookie whose entire life was any sporting event with two sides and a set of odds. His concept of a "meeting at the summit" was the dialogue between a catcher and a pitcher with more than one man on base.

Sitting next to him, with his nose a quarter of an inch away from Mr. Callahan's, was Mr. Hubert Kransky, whose two hundred and fifty-eight pounds were packed into a five-foot-eight frame the way onions are crowded into pickled herring jars. Mr. Kransky had a voice like a French horn and perpetually florid cheeks that burned crimson whenever his dander went up, an occasion which was both frequent and regular.

In a sense Mr. Kransky was the spokesman for every anonymous bettor who had ever dropped rent money on a horse race, a prize fight, or a floating crap game. It was his custom during these Indian summer afternoons to take out his frustrations, not to mention his insolvency, on any vulnerable fellow bar-stool companion within arm's and fist's reach.

And sitting across the room was a spindle-framed, gentle-faced little man in glasses, drinking a beer and listening to the conversation. On the table beside him was a vacuum cleaner, resplendent with attachments and odd impedimenta that made it look like a cross between a sickly octopus and a surplus bagpipe.

This man was Mr. Luther Dingle who sold the aforementioned vacuum cleaner, or at least went through the motions. His volume of business was roughly that of a valet at a hobos' convention. And while he was a consummate failure in almost everything else, he was an exceptionally good listener and, whenever Mr. Kransky had a mad on, Mr. Dingle proved a most accessible, vulnerable, prominent-jawed scapegoat.

Kransky's voice blasted through the room like a bugle call at Hialeah. "Don't gimme that, Callahan," he roared, pushing the bookie's forefinger out of the way. "I told yuh before—I don't pay off on a bum call!"

Callahan opened a toothless mouth and slammed his beer glass on the bar. "T'ree umpires called him out," the bookie said positively. "I called him out. Eleven thousand fans called him out. Final score, Pittsburgh three, Dodgers nothin'. You and me got an even bet. I got the Pirates—hence you owe me five bucks."

Hubert Kransky left his stool like Discoverer II off a launching pad at Canaveral. He stuck a gnarled fist in front of Callahan's face. "I know a bum call when I see one," he announced. "That ball was foul when it hit him. So instead of an out, it was a foul ball. So who's to say he wouldn't've got on base so that when Pignatano hit the single, a run would have scored, and like that! And furthermore, Callahan"—Kransky's voice shook with rage—"you're a cheatin' insult to the American bookie."

Callahan too rose from his stool and put two hands on his breast like Sarah Bernhardt, his toothless mouth working furiously as injured innocence rose up from deep within. This was shortly replaced by a pugnacity that made O'Toole the bartender reach down to a shelf under the bar where he kept odd and assorted items like blackjacks, a World War I revolver, and one half of a broken bottle. He pointed the bottle menacingly at Callahan.

"I told you once before awready, Callahan! You start a brawl in here again and I'll fix that mouth of yours so that you'll be doin' your drinkin' through a tube stuck in a vein."

The bookie's hands stroked his breast and he looked positively outraged. "Me?" he asked. "Me? I give you trouble?" He pointed to Mr. Kransky. "Tell that to the number one welsher of all the western states over there! This guy still owes me money on the second Dempsey-Tunney fight."

Kransky's answering shout had the volume and carry of the brass section of the Boston Pops. "Yeah, yeah, yeah! Mainly on account of that was a bum call! And I don't pay off on bum calls."

His bullet head slowly revolved atop the bull-like shoulders uninterrupted by anything remotely resembling a neck. His eyes fixed finally on Mr. Luther Dingle who sat smiling happily over his beer.

"You remember that fight, Dingle?" Kransky shouted as if the vacuum cleaner salesman were five blocks away. "Tunney's out of the ring and the ref gives him a long count like everybody in the room coulda gone out for a beer, engaged in some small talk, and then come back and still sit down before the ref is finished counting. Now how about that? I'm askin' you—*you*—how about that?"

Dingle pointed to himself. "Me?" he asked.

Kransky walked over to him. "You. Yeah, you. You talk about bum calls. You see the game on television last night? Ninth inning? Snider's up with two down and we got Howard and Moon on first and second and this umpire with no pupils in his eyes calls a foul ball an out! You see that?"

Dingle nodded happily. "As a matter of fact, I did watch the game on television," he said, sipping the head off his beer. "Exceptional defensive play, exceptional. Abner Doubleday would have been proud."

"Never mind Abner Doubleday," Kransky said, poking a finger against Dingle's chest. "I leave it up to you. Was that a foul ball or was that an out?"

Dingle thoughtfully wiped the foam from his mouth. "Well, it appeared to me," he said, "that the ball was hit in fair territory. Consequently, upon its striking the ground and then hitting the batter, the rules would very plainly indicate that the batter was out."

He sat back contentedly and smiled up at the chunk of concrete that glared back at him.

"You realize, of course, pal," Kransky said softly, "that you're calling me a liar! Now I ain't an unreasonable man, so I'll give you one more chance." He put his face an inch away from Dingle's. "Was that a foul ball or was it an out?"

Luther Dingle stared intently into the red-hazed retinas, smiled again, and began, "Well, it's my considered opinion—"

The sentence was fractured by a looping right hand that Mr. Kransky threw with great precision and considerable verve. It landed with impact somewhere between the bridge of Mr. Dingle's nose and his right cheekbone. It catapulted his one-hundred-and-eighteen-pound frame over the back of the chair and propelled him through the air to land within spitting distance of the brass bowl close to the bar.

Mr. Anthony O'Toole lifted Dingle easily to his feet, dusted him off and patted him back into consciousness. With equal finesse, he placed Mr. Dingle on the bar stool where the salesman wafted gently to and fro like a willow stalk in a north wind. (Mr. O'Toole felt very strongly that a reputable place of business simply could not have unconscious customers on the floor.) He waited a moment for the color to come back into Dingle's face, then turned accusingly toward Kransky.

"How come you always gotta hit Dingle, Kransky? You hit him last week, you hit him the week before."

"A man can only stand so much," Kransky said, as he marched back to his stool at the bar. "I'm tired of this guy contradictin' me! And when somebody calls me a liar—there's my honor to consider." He drained the beer from his glass and looked threateningly into the glazed eyes of Luther Dingle.

"Your honor?" Callahan, the bookie, snorted deprecatingly. "Why you've got nothin' but larceny in you all the way from your crotch to where you part your hair. When you die, Kransky, they're gonna have to screw you into the ground."

Once again Kransky leaped to his feet. A thick left arm shot out to grab the gently oscillating Dingle by his coat front.

"How about *that*?" he roared. "Is that true? I'm crooked? I leave it to you, Dingle. Am I crooked?"

Dingle was having a dream. He was standing in the wings of Minsky's burlesque on 46th Street. A tall, statuesque blonde had just beckoned to him from the other side of the stage. Dingle nodded happily his absolute, unequivocal acceptance of whatever the young lady had in mind. The affair was ended by Mr. Kransky's right hand, which landed on the side of Dingle's face and sent him sprawling head first off the stool.

Once again O'Toole ministered to him with at least a perfunctory professionalism if not tender loving care.

Mr. Kransky began another battle with Mr. Callahan on the kind of odds any decent and legitimate bookie would give on Saturday's St. Louis-Cincinnati double-header and Mr. Dingle lapsed into another dream.

And, though none of the aforementioned gentlemen knew it, they were being observed very closely and with great attention by a large, two-headed figure, complete with antennae and a radar-like, protuberant wand that undulated, revolved, and let out small metallic bleeps at regular intervals.

To the human eye this figure was quite invisible and the voices of the two heads were inaudible to the human ear. This figure was in fact a visitor from the planet Mars and of sufficiently advanced intelligence to know beyond any doubt that no leaders were to be found in this nondescript Earth bar.

One waxen, slightly greenish face nodded toward the other, as Kransky's voice traveled through their hearing apparatus and was automatically translated into a Martian tongue. ". . . and I say that anybody who tells me that the Philadelphia Phillies had any right winning the pennant that year is out of their green grass mind! And furthermore if you're going to sit there and tell me—"

Kransky's voice continued its strident blare as Head One of the Martian creature said to Head Two, "Are you sure we're invisible?"

The second head nodded and answered, "Beyond any

doubt." Its slightly orangish eyes stared toward the group of men. "I wish *they* were!" Then with a shudder, "Did you ever see such jerky-looking creatures?"

The other nodded in agreement. "Typical Earth men." The antenna atop his head vibrated slightly. "Not all of them, though," the head continued. "The one in the middle. The one who's just suffered the physical damage. Now this might be the very one we're looking for. Sssh," he added hurriedly after a pause. "I'm receiving his waves now."

The two heads remained motionless for a moment as the "waves" left Mr. Dingle's battered little frame.

"He's referred to as a Dingle," Head Two announced. "He's an abject coward. He doesn't even possess what the Earth creatures call 'minimum muscles.' He's a decidedly subphysical type." He turned to his companion head and announced positively, "I believe we have found our subject!"

"You intend to give him the additional strength?"

"We haven't found anyone weaker, have we? Yes, this one will make an exceptional subject. I would think . . . oh, about eleven secograms, atomic weight. That should make him roughly three hundred times as strong as the average man." He paused, staring across the room at "the Dingle." "Yes," he continued with a nod, "I believe that ought to do it. We'd better check with central laboratories. Tell them we've picked a subject and they can start observing him now." He turned to the other head. "You may proceed."

At this moment the bartender was patting Luther Dingle's face, mumbling something about just why the hell Dingle couldn't learn to be neutral. "Luther," he said into the blinking eyes of the vacuum cleaner salesman, "you don't got to answer this guy at all. Just because he didn't happen to like the Phillies—"

"Let him tell me," Kransky interrupted. "You got a brain, don't you, Dingle? You got a point of view? All right, what did you think of the Phillies in 1953?"

Dingle looked from one to the other. "The Phillies in 1953," he repeated dully.

"That's right," Kransky prodded him. "You tell me for example if you think Robin Roberts was one half the pitcher that Clem Labine was that year."

The bartender closed his eyes and shook his head, waiting for the sound of Dingle's voice and then the inevitable crack of knuckle against face.

"Well," Dingle began, clearing his throat. "Of the two . . . I'd be inclined to take . . ." He looked up wistfully. "Roberts," he whispered.

Kransky's bloodshot eyes narrowed. "Buddy," he said softly, "why alla time you got to fight me? Now let's run through it one more time. You say that Robin Roberts had more stuff than Clem Labine?"

Dingle's smile was a pathetic grimace. "To be perfectly honest," Dingle said, simply because he could be nothing else, "as to the two men, as good as they both are, all things being equal—"

"So c'mon awready," Kransky interrupted. "Who do you pick?"

Dingle's voice was a frail murmur. "Roberts?"

The bartender flinched and looked away as once again Mr. Dingle landed spread-eagle on the floor, a small, dark mouse appearing under his right eye. And while O'Toole helped Dingle to his feet he informed Kransky, "I'm tellin' you for the last time, you pull any more rough stuff around here and I ain't gonna let you in that front door." He slapped Dingle's cheeks. "How do you feel, Dingle?" he asked with concern.

"Clem Labine was definitely superior," Luther Dingle announced, though his eyes were atilt and it was quite obvious he had no idea where he was.

"You see," Kransky shouted triumphantly, "all I'm doin' is makin' him see things clearer!"

As Dingle felt consciousness slowly stream back into him he became aware of yet another odd and indefinable sensation. It was a warm tingle that ran through and through him and it lasted for perhaps three or four glowing minutes. The ray of light that shot across the room from the invisible two-headed creature could not be seen by any of the sports enthusiasts, but it had landed directly on Dingle's face and remained on him for several minutes.

"How do you feel, Dingle," O'Toole asked again, patting his cheeks. "You doin' O.K. now?"

Dingle blinked his eyes and looked across at Kransky. "Definitely Clem Labine!"

Kransky looked satisfied and Dingle allowed himself to be helped to his feet once more by the bartender, who picked up the vacuum cleaner and the accessories and crammed them into Dingle's arms. At the same time he gently urged the little man toward the door.

"Dingle," the bartender said to him confidentially as they walked, "you mind a word of advice? There's some guys in this world that are gonna get punched in the nose no matter who they pick in a ball game, who they vote for, or the color of the tie they put on in the morning."

At the door the bartender patted Dingle's arm. "You're one of those guys, Luther," he said sadly. "So do you know what I think you ought to do from now on? Don't talk. Just nod. If a guy asks you who you like in the third, you just smile at him. If somebody asks you who you're votin' for—you just nod. And if you're sittin' in the ballpark at some double-header and you hear some guy yellin' for the Dodgers—you don't go yellin' for the Pirates. You just leave your seat and go buy a hot dog. Understand, Dingle?"

Dingle nodded and then suddenly looked surprised. He put down the vacuum cleaner, then held up his hands in front of him and studied his fingers.

"Whatsa matter?" the bartender asked.

"That's odd."

"What's odd?"

"I feel . . . I feel so funny," Dingle said in a strained voice.

Then he shook his head as if shrugging off the whole thing and bent over to pick up the vacuum cleaner. He did indeed lift it off the floor. As a matter of fact he lifted it high over his head, then—with the same look of surprise—juggled it in his arms.

"Now what do you suppose caused that?" he said.

"Caused what?" the bartender asked him.

"The vacuum cleaner," Dingle explained. "It feels as light as a feather." With a hasty, apologetic smile he added, "Not that the machine *isn't* light. It happens to be one of the lightest on the market. It's a handy-dandy, jim-cracker, A-one piece of merchandise, guaranteed to lighten the labor and lengthen the life of the wonderful partner in the American home—the housewife!" He lifted the vacuum cleaner above his head several times. "But . . ." he stammered, "but I never thought it was *this* light!"

He looked at the vacuum cleaner, bewildered, then reached for the doorknob. A moment later he stood gaping at O'Toole. The doorknob was still in his hand, but the door was completely ripped off three metal hinges. Both Callahan and Kransky at the bar gulped their beers and examined the insides of the glasses. The door weighed a good eighty-five pounds and there stood Dingle holding it aloft as if it were a single sheet of balsa.

Dingle slowly put down the door and leaned it against the wall. He looked at Mr. Anthony O'Toole who quite obviously took a dim view of small vacuum cleaner salesmen pulling doors from their hinges.

"Dingle," O'Toole said with vast hurt, "with all your faults—despite the fact that you cost me in iodine what I normally have to put out for the water bill—you've always been a nice type fellah who never gave me no trouble. Now why all of a sudden you got to wreck my front door?"

"Believe me, Mr. O'Toole," Dingle said in a tone that would have convinced the most hardened skeptic, "I am mystified. I am absolutely mystified. The door just seemed to—to come off in my hand." He reached over to touch the knob by way of illustration and then gasped as he heard the sound of wrenching wood. The doorknob was now in his hand and a large, gaping hole was in the door where it had been.

Kransky and Callahan goggled at one another and reached for a bottle of house whiskey from which they each gulped in turn. Dingle hurriedly went out through the opening where formerly had hung the heavy door, leaving behind him the incredulous Anthony O'Toole, his bar companions who kept on drinking and shaking their heads, and a two-headed Martian whose name was roughly translated as "Xurthya."

A little later Mr. Dingle was walking briskly along an attractive tree-lined residential street, feeling younger and more exuberant than he could ever remember feeling before. He carried the vacuum cleaner and the attachments under his left arm and had almost forgotten their existence. Two small boys were playing catch with a football in front of one of the white picket-fenced yards. The smaller of the two boys, whose freckled face bore just a passing resemblance to that of John J. Dillinger, held the ball and turned to Dingle as he approached.

"You here again?" the boy asked. "Didn't my old man say he was gonna punch you in the jaw if you came around here botherin' us again?"

Dingle checked the jut of the little boy's jaw, looked down at his notebook, then up at the numbered address on the house.

Somewhat relieved, he nodded. "You're quite right, little man," he said, smiling. "Wrong address. I was heading next door."

He continued to walk down the sidewalk past the picket fence. The freckled little gargoyle threw the football straight and unerringly at the back of Dingle's head, knocking off his hat. Dingle smiled a little wanly, waggled a finger, retrieved his hat, then awkwardly picked up the ball.

"Now that's not the best of all possible manners, is it?" he said gently.

The little boy leered at him and made some kind of indefinable sound with a tongue sticking out. "Aww, go peddle your vacuum cleaners, ya little creep! And throw my ball back."

Dingle again moved his mouth around in the shape of a smile and, as pleasantly as he knew how, said, "Go out for a pass. Isn't that what they say? Go out for a pass?"

He daintily, albeit inexpertly, hauled back and threw the ball toward the boy. It soared up into the air as if filled with helium and disappeared over a church steeple several blocks away. The tan underneath the boy's freckles paled as he gaped toward the disappearing ball. His companion simply sat on the porch steps and closed his eyes. Three doors down the street a painter on a ladder looked up toward the sky, dropped his bucket, and slid halfway down the ladder before he could collect himself.

And some nine blocks away a man sat at a breakfast table eating grapefruit, feeling the desperate aftereffects of a sizable lodge meeting the night before. A football entered the open window, whizzed past his face, and plowed a hole through the kitchen wall, to go through a bathroom, a bedroom, and finally into a hall beyond.

Small Dillinger walked slowly up to Dingle, his voice softened by a sudden reverence. "Hey, mister," he asked raptly, "where'd you learn to fling a ball like that?"

Dingle gulped, squirmed, and then stammered, "I . . . I really don't know." He looked up toward the sky and directed the question to nobody in particular. "What's happening to me?" he asked. *"What in the world is happening to me?"*

He looked down at his undersized right hand. It was as small and weak-looking as it had ever been. He decided that he had better stop work for the day. A sufficient number of odd occurrences had happened to warrant his knocking off at least until the next morning.

A taxicab was just pulling away from the curb half a block away and Dingle waved his hand and shouted to it. "Taxi! Cab!"

The cab pulled to a stop across the way and Dingle hurriedly rushed over to it. He reached for the handle of the rear door and it was a moment before he realized that the door had suddenly become unattached from the cab. He was holding it out in mid-air. The cab driver stared at him, formulating in his mind a rather long and comprehensive speech, but quite incapable of saying anything.

"Believe me," Dingle said in a whisper, "this is as much a mystery to me as it is to you."

He scratched his jaw pensively, shook his head, looked around with a vast perplexity, then leaned against the cab. There was a wheezing, grinding, groaning noise, a wail of consternation from the driver, and suddenly the cab was lying on its side. The painter on the ladder three doors down dropped his bucket again and this time followed it to the ground.

At six-thirty in the evening, Mr. Dingle sat on a park bench, his vacuum cleaner at his feet like a faithful dog, as he stared across the park, past the thirty-foot statue of General Belvedere Washington Hennicutt, the hero of some obscure whiskey rebellion, and said nothing. A pretty nursemaid passed, wheeling a baby carriage. She looked at Dingle briefly and then, smiling, sat on the opposite end of the bench, gently rocking the carriage with a foot. After a suitable pause Dingle turned to her.

"Excuse me, miss," he said diffidently.

"Yes?"

"I don't want you to think that I'm a masher or anything like that. I'm certainly not a masher, but I wonder if you'd mind . . . I wonder if you'd mind answering a question?"

The nurse smiled. He was obviously harmless. "That depends."

"What I mean is," Dingle said, wetting his lips, "looking at me, would you say that at least upon a perfunctory, cursory, very initial surveyal . . . that I appear to be abnormal in any way?"

The nurse laughed. "Not at all." She pointed to the vacuum cleaner. "Unless you plan to use that in the park."

Dingle dismissed the handy-dandy, jim-cracker, A-one piece of merchandise with a perfunctory wave. "Oh *that!*" he said deprecatingly. "Up to a few hours ago I sold those things. Or at least I went through the motions." He shook his head in dismal recollection of his lack of prowess as a salesman. "I was a miserably bad salesman. Just miserable.

"Would you believe it?" he continued intently. "Last month I made exactly eighty-nine cents in commission. And that was for an attachment. An upholstery nozzle. And I sold it to a drunk who kept insisting it was a divining rod for alcohol." He leaned forward wistfully. "I actually expected to be fired today. But that's the least of my worries." He cocked his head a little quizzically. "Would you be interested in listening to what are the *most* of my worries?"

"Go ahead."

"Watch," Dingle announced, as he left the bench and walked around behind it.

The nurse screamed as she felt the earth leaving her feet. Dingle, with one hand, had reached under the bench and lifted it eight feet into the air, then carefully set it down again as the nurse, eyes starting, stared at him in abject fear and utter amazement.

Dingle shrugged. "Now watch this."

He walked over to a large boulder, picked it up and, with minimal effort, broke it in half, then threw the two pieces away. They landed with a thud, plowing two deep holes in the earth. Several yards away a photographer was taking shots of two attractive models. Through the corner of his eye he had seen Dingle perform the rock bit. He turned and walked hurriedly over to the little man.

"Say, buddy," he said a little tentatively. "I'm a photographer with the *Bulletin*." He waggled a finger toward the rocks. "What's with the rock? I mean . . . what's the gag?"

Dingle said, "No gag. Oh, there isn't any gag. Watch." He scanned the immediate area and then his eye lit on the statue of General Belvedere Washington Hennicutt. He went over to it, leaned down to the base of the statue and, without so much as the suggestion of a grunt, lifted the thirty-foot bronze figure high into the air. It took the photographer an instant to recover before he could attach the flash bulb and snap the picture.

Several hours later he'd had the picture developed, had an

argument with the city editor over what the latter claimed were wires obviously showing on the glossy print, persuaded the same gentleman that there were no wires and it was no gag, and then had gone out and gotten drunk.

The following morning the picture was on the front page of the *Los Angeles Bulletin*. The caption underneath it read, "Hercules? No, Luther Dingle, the Twentieth-Century Samson." And there was Luther holding the statue aloft, smiling angelically and with vast satisfaction, like some overgrown boy who had stolen his dad's car and then gone on to win the Indianapolis Five Hundred.

Mr. Dingle himself did not see the paper until some hours later. He was sleeping soundly in his bed when the alarm rang. He reached over sleepily to push the button. He did indeed push the button and in the process flattened the alarm clock into a thin metal pancake so that the numbers, the face, and the works all fused together like a Dali painting.

Realization and remembrance flooded back into Mr. Dingle's mind and he got out of bed hurriedly. He looked at the flattened clock, then stared at himself in the dresser mirror across the room. He walked over to it, examined his face and was satisfied that it was the same face which had been staring back at him for many, many years. Then, with a kind of self-conscious ritual, he picked up the Los Angeles telephone book and tore it apart with two fingers. He dressed, shaved, mentally thumbed his nose at the vacuum cleaner which rested on the one chair in the room, and then took a walk over to O'Toole's bar.

By noontime that day Mr. O'Toole's bar was as crowded as a subway car and the table at which Mr. Dingle sat by himself was circled and re-circled by a mob of con men, public relations representatives, fight managers, talent agents, television executives, carnival advance men, theatre managers, Hollywood scouts, baseball scouts, football scouts, and a Boy Scout with an autograph pad.

"Mr. Dingle . . . you realize how much money can be made on a tour with our carnival?"

"Mr. Dingle . . . your future lies in television. You're the walking, talking embodiment of every American male's wish fulfillment. You're John Q. Citizen, you're Babbitt, you're Tom, Dick and Harry. Now here's our idea for the series. A simple fifteen-minute, across-the-board address by you with little examples of your physical prowess! A natural for breakfast cereals, tonics, vitamin pills, anything!"

"And I keep telling you, Dingle, Patterson is nothin'! You line up with me, I'll get you a coupla real easy setups and inside eight months I'll have you fightin' for the world championship!"

The voices, the offers, the suggestions, the invitations flooded the air, came from all directions, and went past Mr. Dingle's beaming face to mingle in a welter of jabbering talk somewhere behind it. His smile was constant and beatific and he was the happiest of all men. The only untoward reaction elicited from Mr. Dingle was when a high-voiced and quite subdued Mr. Kransky announced that the sales manager of the vacuum cleaner company was on the phone and wanted to talk to him.

Dingle snapped his fingers and airily waved Kransky back to the phone, with a very specific suggestion as to where the sales manager could place all his unsold vacuum cleaners.

Twenty minutes later someone had moved in a television camera and special lights had been strung up across the room. One Jason Abernathy, a thin, flannel-suited little man with squirrel-bright eyes, pushed his way importantly through the crowd of people, carrying a hand mike. He stood over Dingle, then looked at the camera.

"Fine here?" he inquired professionally, pointing first to Dingle, then to the lights overhead. "Getting a picture, are we?"

He acknowledged the nods of the cameraman, the floor director, and the director, who had been pulled aside by Mr. Kransky and was being given a rundown on what cost the Dodgers the pennant in 1960. A red light shone on the camera and Mr. Abernathy's face was suddenly suffused in a hundred-watt smile.

"Hello there, everyone," Mr. Abernathy gushed. "This is Jason Abernathy here with your show—'TV Probes The Unusual.' And our unusual subject today . . ."

He moved aside and pointed to where Luther Dingle sat proudly like an underfed Cheshire cat who really didn't care that he suffered from malnutrition.

"Mr. Luther Dingle," Abernathy continued, "who, if what actual onlookers say is true, is the world's strongest man." He carried the hand mike over to the table and thrust it in front of Dingle's contented face. "Mr. Dingle," he asked, "would you give us an example of this fantastic—" he cleared his throat "—*alleged* . . . strength of yours?"

"I'd be happy to," Dingle answered. He stood up, and wiggled a couple of fingers in the direction of Anthony O'Toole who was behind the bar, furiously pouring drinks and depositing fistfuls of money in the cash register.

"Mr. O'Toole," Dingle called across the room. "Is it all right? You know, the thing we discussed?"

O'Toole grinned happily. "Are you kiddin'? I ain't done business like this since the night they repealed the Eighteenth Amendment! Be my guest, Dingle."

The ex-vacuum cleaner salesman smiled, winked at the camera, and announced in a quietly prideful voice, "Well, I'll start off with the simple things!"

He turned to the wall, chuckled a secret chuckle, and then plowed his right hand directly through it, creating a three-foot hole in the plaster. Then, still smiling, he winked broadly, walked around the table, patted the top of it as if testing it and then splintered it by simply slamming the palm of his hand on it. The table parted in the middle and collapsed on the floor. The crowd cheered and applauded. Jason W. Abernathy smiled happily and threw an "I-told-you-so" look at the camera. He then watched as Mr. Dingle went to the bar, took hold of the bottom section of one of the stool supports, and ripped it out of the floor. Dingle dusted his hands meticulously and walked past the gaping, ogling watchers toward the now white and stricken face of one Hubert Kransky.

Mr. Kransky rose, his hands held out defensively in front of him. "Now, wait a minute, Dingle," he gurgled in a voice that sounded quite unlike his own. "Please, Dingle, wait a minute. Ain't you ever heard of bygones being bygones?"

Mr. Luther Dingle, who obviously had forgotten all about bygones being bygones, if indeed, he had ever embraced the concept, lifted Mr. Kransky by the shirt, held him out at arm's length and twirled him around in one hand like a baton. This went on for roughly a minute and a half. Finally Mr. Kransky was gently re-deposited on the bar stool. There he wavered back and forth as the room spun around in front of him, a mélange of faces, walls, television camera and—shooting by at intervals like telegraph poles outside a speeding train window—the smiling and satisfied face of Luther Dingle, who had at this moment reinstated himself in the company of men by paying back a debt of long, long standing.

Mr. Kransky, it was quite obvious, would never again extrapolate his innermost thoughts against Mr. Luther Dingle's face, nose, and cheekbone. From this moment on he would be a good boy—not to say a deferential, fawning, desperately frightened drinking companion.

Once again the assemblage cheered and roared its delight as Mr. Dingle, with just the trace of a smirk, retraced his steps to what was left of his table. The cheering, however, was confined to that species of being known as "homo sapiens." The other specimen in the room—one double-headed Martian whose family name was "Xurthya"—was somewhat less impressed. The two slightly green-tinged faces looked glumly at one another, disgust showing in all four orangish eyes.

Head One finally announced, his voice dripping with boredom, "Had enough?"

Head Two nodded. "Positively. Most inferior. We give him the strength of three hundred men . . . and he uses it for petty exhibition. Let him have about twenty or thirty more seconds and then remove the power!"

Head One looked over toward Dingle and nodded in return. "Excellent idea. And then I think we'd best be off. Three planets on the itinerary for tomorrow. One is particularly interesting." The orange eyes leered ever so slightly. "Contains only females!"

There was another burst of applause as Mr. Dingle held up his hands and announced with an almost pious humility, "And now, ladies and gentlemen, I believe—the most unique feat of all. I will lift up this entire building with my bare hands!"

There was a murmur of stunned amazement. All eyes fastened on Dingle as he looked quickly around the room, then walked to a corner of the bar and stood under one of the rafters. He looked up at the giant wooden beam as if mathematically gauging it, then very carefully removed his coat, hung it over one of the chairs, and rolled up his sleeves. He then cracked his knuckles and flexed the two small, knobby nodules that showed indistinctly under the surface of the flesh somewhere between the clavicle and elbow of each arm, and could most nearly be described as "muscles."

This did not keep the crowd from taking a deep collective breath as the little man slowly stretched on tiptoe, felt the rafters and, with a great show of exertion, started to push. There was a loud crack that sounded all over the room and all eyes went to the ceiling where a long, irregular crevice began to appear in the plaster. It was a fact! Luther Dingle was beginning to lift up the entire building.

He was beginning to, that is, but did not continue the process for very long. Invisible to all assembled was a ray of light that emanated from an equally invisible two-headed thing. The light played on Dingle's face for a few moments and then was shut off. Mr. Dingle, meantime, struggled, groaned, rolled his eyes, felt the sweat pouring down his face, shoved, squeezed, hefted, thrust, and after a while collapsed in a spent heap on the floor.

He rose somewhat shakily, went to one of the tables, and slammed his fist down on it. There was a gasp as the table remained intact and Mr. Dingle's knuckles swelled up like a tired rubber balloon. He swung with his uninjured left hand into the wall. There was a loud crack as the wall remained unchanged and Mr. Dingle's hand grew painfully red.

The audience's reaction to all this was an amazed silence. But gradually the silence gave way to sporadic laughter and then the sporadic laughter in turn was supplanted by derisive catcalls, hooting, and generally unkind and uncomplimentary remarks about the charlatan in their midst.

Mr. Kransky, sitting at the bar, was the first to give vent to the editorial judgment of the crowd. He arose, walked over to Dingle, lifted him up by his collar, and threw him across the room.

There was a continued tumult of voices that turned the room into a bedlam, and it was with great difficulty that Jason W. Abernathy signed off the program with considerable apologies and a halting, red-faced reminder that on the following day the audience would be privileged to watch one Zelda Agranavitch, a former Bulgarian woman naval lieutenant who had actually fought in the Battle of Jutland in World War I, disguised as a boy. This was imparted to the audience over the shrieked catcalls that shook Mr. O'Toole's bar.

Mr. Xurthya wafted slowly across the room toward the rear door at precisely that moment when two three-foot-tall purple men entered the room by walking through the wall. They were tiny, roly-poly figures with gigantic heads and extremely high foreheads. They waved at the two-headed Martian as he was going out.

Head One and Head Two said, "How are you fellahs?"

"Nice seeing you," the Venusians answered.

"Where you from?" Head One from Mars inquired.

"Venus," was the answer. "How about you?"

"Mars. Conducting experiments?"

"Yeah. And you?"

"Sudden introduction of strength to subnormal Earthmen. What about you?"

The two little Venusians scanned the room. "Sudden introduction of extreme intelligence. Find any interesting subjects?"

"That one over there," Head One said. "He's referred to as a Dingle. He certainly is subphysical. I wouldn't be a bit surprised if he weren't submental too."

The Venusians nodded and the first one said, "Looks likely enough. We'll give him the intelligence quota ray."

"How strong?" his partner asked, as the two-headed Martian disappeared.

"Oh," his partner answered, "make him about . . . let's see . . . perhaps five hundred times more intelligent than the average human."

Neither Mr. Luther Dingle, nor anyone else in the room, saw the beam of light come out of the small glass aperture set in the middle of the Venusian's belt. It stayed on for just a fraction of a second and then was turned off. The Venusians sat in mid-air, opened a small magnesium box and began to eat their lunch.

Much later on, several hours later as a matter of fact, the people had left and the noise had totally subsided. At the bar sat Mr. Kransky and Mr. Callahan watching intently the baseball game that was in progress on the television screen over the bar. Sitting forlornly across the room alone in a booth was Luther Dingle. He had had six beers, which were quite sufficient to put Mr. Dingle in a near comatose state. He looked neither left nor right, but sat dejectedly with his chin in one hand staring at the last of his sixth beer and wondering in a vague, dreamy way exactly what had happened.

On the screen the television announcer's voice bleated excitedly about it being the bottom of the ninth inning, two Dodgers on base, and Frank Howard coming to bat.

"Go, go, go, go, go, boy," Mr. Kransky screeched, drowning out the noise of the paid customers at the Coliseum, who numbered forty-three thousand, but even in unison had their voices muffled by Mr. Kransky's booming lungs.

Mr. Callahan, the bookie, leered sardonically up to the set then turned toward Kransky and said, "Three to one he don't get onto base. Five to one he don't drive a run in. Ten to one the Dodgers lose."

Kransky's face turned white. He looked first at O'Toole behind the bar, past Callahan and then across the room toward the forlorn Dingle.

"Hey, Dingle," he shouted suddenly. "What about that? This clod's givin' odds Howard don't even get on base let alone drive in the winning run. Now, how about *that?*"

Mr. Dingle looked up across the room, frowning as he suddenly felt a strange heaviness descend on his shoulder blades. He looked up toward the screen of the television set, then down to Kransky.

"Well," he announced, in a voice that did not sound altogether like his own, "in this case the laws of probability are interspersed with the finaglion laws of chance. So through a process of calculus and a subdivision of Greppel based on physical motivating ante divisional annotating . . . in this case, of course, using the two X factors as represented by the teams . . . the gentleman at bat must of necessity hit a home run, driving in the winning run and leading the Dodgers to a five to three victory!"

"There," Kransky announced triumphantly, turning toward Callahan.

On the screen there was the sound and picture of a tall, lanky center fielder suddenly connecting with a curve ball that hung too high. He hit it hard, straight and directly, and the ball sailed out to the vicinity of the center field fence some four hundred and fifty feet from the point where it had been hit. There was a roar from the crowd and then the camera picked up a shot of three men crossing the base paths.

"It's a home run," the announcer screamed. "A game-winning home run as Frank Howard comes through for the Dodgers and they win in the bottom of the ninth, five to three."

Kransky roared his delight, pounded one fist on the bar and the other on Callahan's back as the latter glumly reached for his wallet. But suddenly both activities stopped as the two men did a double take and stared across at Dingle. Dingle had called it! The scrawny little scapegoat with the prominent jaw had announced quite clearly and precisely exactly what would happen!

And it *had* happened! Howard had hit the home run and the Dodgers had carried it away five to three.

Kransky walked to the center of the room staring at Dingle with just a shade of his former, short-lived respect. "Dingle," he said somewhat breathlessly, "how'd you know?"

Mr. Dingle smiled a little vaguely and then rose from the booth. "It was apparent," he said, as he moved toward the door, "on an advanced mathematical plane that what was operating here was the entire quantum theory of space and time relativity." He tilted his head a bit and looked up at the ceiling. "It occurs to me," he said matter-of-factly, "that there is a definite necessity of an equation between the parallellion law of definitive numerical dialectic algebraic with a further notation . . ." He went out the door still talking and his voice could be heard still as he walked down the street.

Exactly what Mr. Dingle was talking about as he walked was an academic point since there were no knowledgeable on-lookers or bystanders to overhear his remarks. (Most of those seeing the thin little man spew out gusts of quite unintelligible jargon thought he was either drunk or batty.)

Actually, in the first three blocks, Mr. Dingle had solved twelve of the most complex mathematical problems known to science, invented a perpetual motion machine, supplied the equation for a principle to govern gasoline engines that could run a year and a half on a cup full of gas, along with several minor chemical analyses that would in the long run destroy smog, take nicotine safely out of tobacco, and provide an electric light that could burn for a hundred and five years at the cost of thirteen cents. Twenty minutes later Mr. Dingle was swallowed up by the evening traffic and no one in those environs saw him again.

Mr. O'Toole's drinking establishment is quiet these days. It is only on the rarest of occasions that he is forced to brandish either the World War I revolver or the broken bottle. Mr. Callahan still occupies his favorite stool, but his bookmaking is a desultory side-line and his principal customer, Mr. Hubert Kransky, is a blunted and subdued imitation of his former glorious, raucous, quick-to-come-out-swinging self. What few bets he makes with Mr. Calla-han are colorless and without excitement, with the winning or losing of little consequence to either—a sort of dull ritual per-formed by rote.

On the one occasion when Mr. Kransky took issue with a customer's opinion of the Los Angeles Rams and stalked across the room with at least a semblance of his former grandeur, he had his jaw summarily fractured. His deceitful opponent turned out to be a former middleweight champion of the United States Navy.

The whole ugly affair accomplished only a further entrenchment of the conservatism of Mr. Kransky and he would spend long hours wistfully staring at the booth where Luther Dingle used to sit, while he himself heaved deep sighs and thought longingly of bygone days and bygone little men with prominent jaws. Little did he or his two companions realize that Mr. Luther Dingle had a great appeal to extra-terrestrial note takers and that from then on it was altogether possible that the ex-vacuum cleaner salesman would scale Mt. Everest, take off in a spaceship, prove himself the world's greatest, most effective lover, or take a position on the faculty at the Massachusetts Institute of Technology. It all could very well happen.

And it probably did.

A THING ABOUT MACHINES

Mr. Bartlett Finchley, tall, tart, and fortyish, looked across his ornate living room to where the television repairman was working behind his set and felt an inner twist of displeasure that the mood of the tastefully decorated room should be so damaged by the T-shirted, dungareed service-man whose presence was such a foreign element in the room. He looked, gimlet-eyed, at the man's tool box lying on the soft pile of the expensive carpet like a blot on Mr. Finchley's escutcheon, which emphasized symmetry above all! Mr. Finchley, among other things, was both a snob and fastidious. And snobbery and fastidiousness were not simply character traits with him; they were banners that he flaunted with pride. He rose from the chair and walked over to within a few feet of the television set. The repairman looked up at him, smiling, and wiped his forehead.

"How are you today, Mr. Finchley?"

Mr. Finchley's left eyebrow shot up. "I'll answer *that* burning question after you tell me what's wrong with that electronic boo-boo, and also acquaint me with how much this current larceny is going to cost me."

The repairman rose and wiped his hands with a rag. He looked down at the set, then up to Mr. Finchley. "Two hours' labor," he said, "a broken set of tubes, new oscillator, new filter."

Mr. Finchley's face froze, his thin lips forming a taut line.

"How very technical," he announced. "How very nice! And I presume I'm to be dunned once again for three times the worth of the bloody thing?"

The repairman smiled gently and studied Mr. Finchley. "Last time I was here, Mr. Finchley," he said, "you'd kicked your foot through the screen. Remember?"

Mr. Finchley turned away and put a cigarette in a holder. "I have a vivid recollection," he announced. "It was not working properly." He shrugged. "I tried to get it to do so in a normal fashion!"

"By kicking your foot through the screen?" the repairman shook his head. "Why didn't you just horsewhip it, Mr. Finchley? That'd show it who's boss."

He started to collect his tools and put them into the box. Mr. Finchley lit the cigarette in the holder, took a deep drag, and examined his nails.

"What do you say we cease this small talk and get down to some serious larceny? You can read me off the damages . . . though I sometimes wonder exactly what is the purpose of the Better Business Bureau when they allow you itinerant extortionists to come back week after week, move wires around, busily probe with ham-like hands, and accomplish nothing but the financial ruin of every customer on your route!"

The repairman looked up from the tool box, his smile fading. "We're not a gyp outfit, Mr. Finchley. We're legitimate repairmen. But I'll tell you something about *yourself*—"

"Spare me, please," Mr. Finchley interrupted him. "I'm sure there must be some undernourished analyst with an aging mother to care for whom I can contact for that purpose."

The repairman closed the box and stood up. "Why don't you hear me out, Mr. Finchley? That set doesn't work because obviously you got back there and yanked out wires and God knows what else! You had me over here last month to fix your portable radio—because you'd thrown it down the steps."

"It did not work properly," Finchley said icily.

"That's the point, Mr. Finchley. Why *don't* they work properly? Offhand I'd say it's because you don't *treat* them properly."

Mr. Finchley let the cigarette holder dangle from his mouth as he surveyed the repairman much as a scientist would look at a bug through a microscope. "I assume there's no charge for that analysis?" he inquired.

The repairman shook his head. "What does go wrong with these things, Mr. Finchley? Have you any idea?"

Mr. Finchley let out a short, frozen chortle. "Have I any idea? Now that's worth a scholarly ten lines in your *Repairman's Journal*! Bilk the customer, but let him do the repairing!"

"The reason I asked that," the repairman persisted, "is because whatever it is that really bothers you about that television set *and* the radio . . . you're not telling me."

He waited for a response. Mr. Finchley turned his back.

"Well?" the repairman asked.

Finchley drew a deep breath as if the last resisting pocket of his patience had been overrun and was being forced to capitulate. "Aside from being rather an incompetent clod," Finchley announced, turning back toward the repairman, "you're a most insensitive man. I've explained to you already. The television set simply did not work properly. And that rinky-dink original Marconi operating under the guise of a legitimate radio gave me nothing but static."

The TV repairman flicked the set on, watched the picture, raised and lowered the volume, then shut it off. He turned toward Finchley.

"You're sure that's all that was wrong with it?"

Finchley made a gesture and started out of the room. The repairman, with a smile, followed him.

"I'll send you a bill, Mr. Finchley," he said as they walked toward the front hall.

"Of this I have no doubt," Finchley responded.

At the front door, the repairman turned to look once again at Finchley, who stood on the first step of the long sweeping stairway which led to the second floor.

"Mr. Finchley . . . what is it with you and machines?"

Finchley's eyes sought the ceiling as if this latest idiocy was more than he could bear. "I will file *that* idiotic question in my memorabilia to be referred to at some future date when I write my memoirs. You will fill one entire chapter on The Most Forgettable Person I Have Ever Met!"

The repairman shook his head and left. Mr. Finchley stood stock-still, his features working. For just one, single, fleeting moment, his hauteur, his pre-emptive mastery of all situations, his snobbery seemed to desert his face, leaving behind a mask of absolute, undiluted terror.

"It just so happens, you boob," Finchley called out into the empty hall, his voice shaking, "it just so happens that every machine in my house is—"

He cut himself off abruptly, closed his eyes, shook his head, looked down at his hands, which were shaking, grabbed them together, then turned and walked unsteadily into the living room. A clock on the mantelpiece chimed deep, resonant notes that filled the room.

"All right," Finchley said, holding his voice down, "that'll be about enough of that! Hear me?"

The clock continued to chime. Finchley walked over toward the mantel and shouted.

"I said that'll be just about enough of that!"

He reached up, grabbed the clock in both hands, ripped the plug out of the wall, and slammed the clock down on the floor, stamping on it with his foot while the chimes continued to blare at him like the death rattle of some dying beast. It took several moments for the chimes to die out. Finchley stood over the wreckage of broken glass and dismembered fly wheels and springs, sweat pouring down his face, his whole body shaking as if with an ague. Then very slowly he recovered composure. The shaking stopped, and he went upstairs to his bedroom.

He closed the door and lay down on the bed, feeling limp, washed out and desperately vulnerable. Soon he fell into an uneasy, twisting and turning, dream-filled sleep, full of all the nightmares that he lived with during the day and that were kept hidden underneath the icy façade of superiority which insulated him from the world.

Mr. Bartlett Finchley at age forty-two was a practicing sophisticate who wrote very special and very precious things for gourmet magazines and the like. He was a bachelor and a recluse. He had few friends—only devotees and adherents to the cause of tart sophistry. He had no interests—save whatever current annoyance he could put his mind to. He had no purpose to his life—except the formulation of day-to-day opportunities to vent his wrath on mechanical contrivances of an age he abhorred.

In short, Mr. Bartlett Finchley was a malcontent, born either too late or too early in the century—he was unsure which. The only thing he was certain of as he awoke, drenched with perspiration, from his nap, was that the secret could not be held much longer. The sleepless nights and fear-filled days were telling on him, and this man with no friends and no confidants realized in a hidden portion of his mind that he urgently required both.

Late that afternoon he walked down the sweeping staircase from his sumptuous bedroom, attired in a smoking jacket, and directed himself to the small study off the living room where he could hear the sound of the electric typewriter. His secretary had come in a few hours before and was sitting at the desk typing from Finchley's notes.

Edith Rogers was an attractive thirty-year-old who had been with Finchley for over a year. In a history of some two dozen-odd secretaries, Miss Rogers held the record for tenure. It was rare that anyone stayed with Mr. Finchley for over a month. She looked up as the master entered the room, cigarette in holder, holder dangling from mouth. He looked back insouciantly and walked behind her to stare over her shoulder at the page in the typewriter. He then picked up a stack of papers from the desk.

"This is all you've done?" he inquired coldly.

She met his stare, unyielding. "That's all I've done," she announced. "That's forty pages in three and a half hours. That's the best *I* can do, Mr. Finchley."

He waggled a finger at the typewriter. "It's that . . . that idiotic gadget of yours. Thomas Jefferson wrote out the preamble to the Constitution with a feather quill and it took him half a day."

The secretary turned in her chair and looked directly up into his face. "Why don't you hire Mr. Jefferson?" she said quietly.

Finchley's eyebrow, which was one of the most mobile features in a mobile face, shot up alarmingly. "Did I ever tell you," he asked, "with what degree of distaste I view insubordination?"

Edith Rogers bent over the typewriter. "Often and endlessly," she said. Then she straightened up. "I'll tell you what, Mr. Finchley," she said, rising and reaching for her bag, "you get yourself another girl, somebody with three arms and with roughly the sensitivity of an alligator. Then you can work together till death do you part. As for me—" she shut her pocketbook "—I've had it!"

"And you are going where?" Finchley asked her as she started into the living room.

"Where?" the girl answered, turning toward him. "I think I might take in Bermuda for a couple of weeks. Or Mexico City. Or perhaps a quiet sanitarium on the banks of the Hudson. Any place," she continued, as she walked across the room toward the hall, "where I can be away from the highly articulate, oh so sophisticated, *bon vivant* of America's winers and diners—Mr. Bartlett Finchley."

She paused for breath in the hall and found him staring at her from the living room.

"You've even got me talking like you," she said angrily. "But I'll tell you what you *won't* get me to do. You won't turn me into a female Finchley with a pinched little acorn for a heart and a mean, petty, jaundiced view of everybody else in the world!"

Finchley's instinct conjured up a tart, biting, cutting, and irreproachable reply, but something else deep inside shut it off. He stood for a moment with his mouth open, then he bit his lip and said very quietly in a tone she was quite unfamiliar with, "Miss Rogers . . . please don't leave."

She noticed something in his face that she had never seen before. It was an unfrocked, naked fear so unlike him as to be unbelievable. "I beg your pardon?" she asked very softly.

Finchley turned away, embarrassed. "I do wish you'd . . . you'd stay for a little bit." He waved an arm in the general direction of the study. "I don't mean for work. All that can wait. I was just thinking . . . well . . . we could have dinner or something, or perhaps a cocktail." He turned to her expectantly.

"I'm not very hungry," she said after a pause. "And it's too early for cocktails." She saw the disappointment cross his face. "What's your trouble, Mr. Finchley?" she asked pointedly but not without sympathy.

Finchley's smile was a ghostly and wan attempt at recovery of aplomb, but his voice quickly took on the sharp, slicing overtones that were so much a part of him. "Miss Rogers, my dear, you sound like a cave-dwelling orphan whose idea of a gigantic lark is a square dance at the local grange. I was merely suggesting to you that we observe the simple social amenities between an employer and a secretary. I thought we'd go out . . . take in a show or something."

She studied him for a long moment, not really liking the man either at this moment or any other moment, but vaguely aware of something that was eating at him and forcing this momentary lapse into at least a semblance of courtesy.

"How very sweet, Mr. Finchley," she said. "Thank you, but no thank you."

Finchley half snorted as he turned his back to her and once again she felt the snobbery of the man, the insufferable ego, the unbearable superiority that he threw around to hurt and humiliate.

"Tonight," she said, feeling no more pity or fascination, "tonight I'm taking a hog-calling lesson. You know what a hog is, don't you, Mr. Finchley? He's a terribly bright fathead who writes for gourmet magazines and condescends to let a few other slobs exist in the world for the purpose of taking his rudeness and running back and forth at his beck and call! Good night, Mr. Finchley."

She saw his shoulders slump and he was silent. Again she felt compelled to remain because this was so unlike him, so foreign to him not to top her, not to meet her barb head on, divert it, and send one of his own back at her, stronger, faster, and much more damaging. When he finally turned she saw again that his face had an odd look and there was something supplicating, something frightening and something, inconceivable though it was, lonely.

"Miss Rogers," he said, his voice gentler than she'd ever heard it, "before you do . . . before you go—" he made a kind of halfhearted gesture, "—have a cup of coffee or something." He turned away so that she would be unable to see his face. "I'd like very much," he continued, "I'd like very much not to be alone for a while."

Edith Rogers came back into the living room and stood close to him. "Are you ill?" she asked.

He shook his head.

"Bad news or something?"

"No."

There was a silence.

"What's your trouble?" she asked.

He whirled on her, his thin lips twisted. "Does there have to be trouble just because I—"

He stopped, ran a hand over his face, and half fell into a chair. For the first time she observed the circles under his eyes, the pinched look of the mouth, the strangely haunted look.

"I'm desperately tired," he said abruptly. "I haven't slept for four nights and the very thought of being alone now—" He grimaced, obviously hating this, feeling the reluctance of the strong man having to admit a weakness. "Frankly," he said, looking away, "it's intolerable. Things have been happening, Miss Rogers, very odd things."

"Go on."

He pointed toward the TV set. "That . . . that thing over there. It goes on late at night and wakes me up. It goes on all by itself." His eyes swept across the room toward the hall. "And that portable radio I used to keep in my bedroom. It went on and off, just as I was going to sleep."

His head went down and when he looked up his eyes darted around paranoically. "There's a conspiracy in this house, Miss Rogers." Seeing her expression, he raised his voice in rebuttal. "That's exactly what it is—a conspiracy! The television set, the radio, lighters, electric clocks, that . . . that miserable car I drive."

He rose from the chair, his face white and intense. "Last night I drove it into the driveway. Just drove it into the driveway, mind you. Very slowly. Very carefully." He took a step toward her, his fingers clenching and unclenching at his sides. "The wheel turned in my hands. Hear me? *The wheel turned in my hand!* The car deliberately hit the side of the garage. Broke a headlight. —That clock up there on the mantelpiece!"

Edith looked at the mantelpiece. There was no clock there. She turned to him questioningly.

"I . . . I threw it away," Finchley announced lamely. Then, pointedly and forcefully he said, "What I'm getting at, Miss Rogers, is that for as long as I've lived . . . I've never been able to operate *machines*." He spit out the last word as if it were some kind of epithet.

Edith Rogers stared at him, for the first time seeing a part of the man that had been kept hidden beneath a veneer and a smoking jacket.

"Mr. Finchley," she said very softly, "I think you ought to see a doctor."

Finchley's eyes went wide and the face and the voice were the Finchley of old. "A *doctor*," he shrieked at her. "The universal panacea of the dreamless twentieth-century idiot! If you're depressed—see a doctor. If you're happy—see a doctor. If the mortgage is too high and the salary too low—see a doctor. You," he screamed at her, "Miss Rogers, *you* see a doctor." Fury plugged up his voice for a moment and then he screamed at her again. "I'm a logical, rational, intelligent man. I know what I see. I know what I hear. For the past three months I've been seeing and hearing a collection of wheezy Frankensteins whose whole purpose is to destroy me! Now what do you think about *that*, Miss Rogers?"

The girl studied him for a moment. "I think you're terribly ill, Mr. Finchley. I think you need medical attention." She shook her head. "I think you've got a very bad case of nerves from lack of sleep and I think that way down deep you yourself realize that these are nothing more than delusions."

She looked down at the floor for a moment, then turned and started out of the room.

"Now where are you going?" he shouted at her.

"You don't need company, Mr. Finchley," she said from the hall. "You need analysis."

He half ran over to her, grabbed her arm, whirled her around.

"You're no different from a cog-wheeled, electrically generated metal machine yourself. You haven't an iota of compassion or sympathy."

She struggled to free her arm. "Mr. Finchley, please let me go."

"I'll let you go," he yelled, "when I get good and ready to let you go!"

Edith continued to struggle, hating the scene, desperately wanting to end it, and yet not knowing how.

"Mr. Finchley," she said to him, trying to push him off, "this is ugly. Now please let me go." She was growing frightened. "*Let go of me!*"

Suddenly, instinctively, she slapped him across the face. He dropped her arm abruptly and stared at her as if disbelieving that anything of this sort could happen to him. That he, Bartlett

Finchley, could be struck by a woman. Again his lips trembled and his features worked. A burning fury took possession of him.

"Get out of here," he said in a low, menacing voice, "and don't come back!"

"With distinct pleasure," Edith said, breathing heavily, "and with manifest relief." She whirled around and went to the door.

"Remember," he shouted at her, "don't come back. I'll send you a check. I will not be intimidated by machines, so it follows that no empty-headed little broad with a mechanical face can do anything to me either."

She paused at the door, wanting air and freedom and most of all to get out of there. "Mr. Finchley," she said softly, "in this conspiracy you're suffering . . . this mortal combat between you and the appliances—*I hope you get licked!*"

She went out and slammed the door behind her. He stood there motionless, conjuring up some line of dialogue he could fling at her, some final cutting witticism that could leave him the winner. But no inspiration came and it was in the midst of this that he suddenly heard the electric typewriter keys.

He listened for a horrified moment until the sound stopped. Then he went to his study. There was paper in the typewriter. Finchley turned the roller so that he could read the words on it. There were three lines of type and each one read, "Get out of here, Finchley."

That was what the typewriter had written all by itself. "Get out of here, Finchley." He ripped the paper from the machine, crumpled it, and flung it on the floor.

"Get out of here, Finchley," he said aloud. "Goddamn you. Who are you, to tell me to get out of here?" He shut his eyes tightly and ran a fluttery hand over a perspiring face. "Why this is . . . this is absurd. It's a typewriter. It's a machine. It's a silly, Goddamn machine—"

He froze again as a voice came from the television set in the living room.

"Get out of here, Finchley," the voice said.

He felt his heart pounding inside him as he turned and raced into the living room. There was a little Mexican girl on the screen doing a dance with a tambourine. He could have sworn that each time she clicked her heels past the camera she stared pointedly at him. But as the music continued and the girl kept on dancing, Finchley reached a point where he was almost certain that the whole thing was a product of his sleeplessness, his imagination, and perhaps just a remnant of the emotional scene he had just gone through with Edith Rogers.

But then the music stopped. The girl bowed to the applause of an unseen audience and, when she had taken her bows, looked directly out of the screen into Finchley's face.

She smiled at him and said very clearly, "You'd better get out of here, Finchley!"

Finchley screamed, picked up a vase, and threw it across the room. He did not think or aim, but the piece of ceramic smashed into the television set, splintering the glass in front to be followed by a loud noise and a puff of smoke. But clearly—ever so clearly from the smoking shambles of its interior—came the girl's voice again.

"You'd better get out of here, Finchley," the voice said, and Finchley screamed again as he raced out of the room, into the hall and up the stairs.

On the top landing he turned and shouted down the stairs. "All right! All right, you machines! You're not going to intimidate *me*! Do you hear me? You are not going to intimidate me! You . . . you machines!"

And from down below in the study—dull, methodical, but distinctly audible—came the sound of typewriter keys and Finchley knew what they were writing. He started to cry, the deep, harsh sobs of a man who has gone without sleep, and who has closeted his fears deep inside.

He went blindly into his bedroom and shut the door, tears rolling down his face, making the room into a shimmering, indistinct pattern of satin drapes, pink walls, and fragile Louis XIV furniture, all blurred together in the giant mirror that covered one side of the room.

He flung himself on the bed and buried his face against the pillow. Through the closed door he continued to hear the sound of the typewriter keys as they typed out their message over and over again. Finally they stopped and there was silence in the house.

At seven o'clock that evening, Mr. Finchley, dressed in a silk bathrobe and a white silk ascot, perched near the pillow of his bed and dialed a number on the ivory-colored, bejeweled telephone.

"Yes," he said into the phone. "Yes. Miss Moore please. Agatha? Bartlett Finchley here. Yes, my dear, it has been a long time." He smiled, remembering Miss Moore's former attachment to him. "Which indeed prompts this call," he explained. "How about dinner this evening?" His face fell as the words came to him from the other end of the line. "I see. Well, of course, it *is* short notice. But . . . yes . . . yes, I see. Yes, I'll call you again, my dear."

He put the phone down, stared at it for a moment, then picked it up and dialed another number.

"Miss Donley, please," he said, as if he were announcing a princess entering a state ball. "Pauline, is this you?" He was aware that his voice had taken on a false, bantering tone he was unaccustomed to and hated even as he used it. "And how's my favorite attractive young widow this evening?" He felt his hand shake. "Bartlett," he said. "Bartlett Finchley. I was wondering if—Oh. I see. I see. Well I'm delighted. I'm simply delighted. I'll send you a wedding gift. Of course. Good night."

He slammed the telephone down angrily. God, what could be more stupid than a conniving female hell-bent for marriage. He had a dim awareness of the total lack of logic for his anger. But disappointment and the prospect of a lonely evening made him quite unconcerned with logic. He stared at the phone, equating it with his disappointment, choosing to believe at this moment that in the cause and effect of things, this phone had somehow destroyed his plans. He suddenly yanked it out of the wall, flinging it across the room. His voice was tremulous.

"Telephones. Just like all the rest of them. Exactly like all the rest. A whole existence dedicated to embarrassing me or inconveniencing me or making my life miserable."

He gave the phone a kick and turned his back to it. Bravado crept backwards into his voice.

"Well, who needs you?" he asked rhetorically. "Who needs any of you? Bartlett Finchley is going out this evening. He's going out to have a wonderful dinner with some good wine and who knows what attractive young lady he may meet during his meanderings. Who knows indeed!"

He went into the bathroom. He studied the thin, aristocratic face that looked back at him from the mirror. Gray, perceptive eyes; thinning but still wavy brown hair; thin expressive lips. If not a strong face, at least an intelligent one. The face of a man who knew what he was about. The face of a thoughtful man of values and awareness.

He opened the medicine cabinet and took out an electric razor. Humming to himself, he plugged it into the wall, adjusted its head, then laid it aside while he put powder on his face. He was dusting off his chin when something made him look down at the electric razor. Its head was staring up at him for all the world like a kind of reptilian beast, gaping at him through a barbed, baleful opening in a grimacing face.

Finchley felt a fear clutch at his insides as he picked up the razor and held it half an arm's length away, studying it thoughtfully and with just a hint of a slowly building tension. This had to stop, he thought. This most definitely and assuredly had to stop.

That idiotic girl was brainless, stupid, and blind—but she had a point. It *was* his imagination. The TV set, the radio, and that damned phone in the other room. It was all part of his imagination. They *were* just machines. They had no entities or purpose or will. He grasped the razor more firmly and started to bring it toward his face. In a brief, fleeting, nightmarish instant the razor seemed to jump out of his hand and attack his face, biting, clawing, ripping at him.

Finchley screamed and flung it away from him, then stumbled backwards against the bathroom door. He scrabbled for the ornate gold doorknob, pulled it open and ran stumbling into the bedroom. He tripped over the telephone cord, knocking the receiver off the cradle, and then gasped as a filtered voice came out of the phone.

"Get out of here, Finchley," it trilled at him. "Get out of here."

Down below the typewriter started up again and from the destroyed television set the little Mexican dancer's voice joined the chorus. "Get out of here, Finchley. Get out of here."

His hands went to his head, pulling spasmodically at his hair, feeling his heart grow huge inside of him as if he were ready to explode and then, joining the rest of the chorus, came the sound of the front-door chimes. They rang several times and after a moment they were the only noises in the house. All the other voices and sounds had stopped.

Finchley tightened his bathrobe strap, went out of the room, and walked slowly down the stairs, letting bravado and aplomb surge back into him until by the time he reached the front door, his face wore the easy smirk of an animal trainer who has just completed placing thousand-pound lions on tiny stools. He adjusted his bathrobe, fluffed out the ascot, raised an eyebrow, then opened the door.

On the porch stood a policeman and, clustered behind him in a semicircle, a group of neighbors. Over their shoulder Finchley could see his car, hanging half over the curb, two deep furrows indicating its passage across the lawn.

"That your car?" the policeman asked him.

Finchley went outside. "That's correct," he said coldly. "It's my car."

"Rolled down the driveway," the policeman said accusingly. "Then across your lawn and almost hit a kid on a bike. You ought to check your emergency brake, mister."

Finchley looked bored. "The emergency brake *was* on."

"I'm afraid it wasn't," the policeman said, shaking his head. "Or if it was—it's not working properly. Car rolled right into the street. You're lucky it didn't hit anyone."

The neighbors made way for Finchley, knowing him to be a man of mercurial moods and an acid, destructive tongue. As he crossed the lawn toward his car, he gazed at a small boy with an all-day sucker in his mouth.

"And how are you this evening, Monstrous?" Mr. Finchley said under his breath. He looked his car up and down, back and forth, and felt a cold spasm of fear as the thought came to him that, of all the machines, this was the biggest and the least controllable. Also, wasn't there an odd look about the front end of the thing? The headlights and grill, the bumper. Didn't it resemble a face? Again from deep inside Finchley there blossomed the beginning of hysteria, which he had to choke down and hide from the people who were staring at him.

The policeman came up behind him. "You got the keys?"

"They're in the house," Finchley said.

"All right then, mister. You'd better pull her back into the garage and then you'd better have those brakes checked first chance you get. Understand?"

There was a pause as Finchley turned his back to him.

"Understand, mister?"

Finchley nodded perfunctorily, then turned and gazed at the circle of faces, his eyes slitted and suspicious. "All right, dear friends," he announced. "You may remain on my property for another three and a half minutes goggling at this amazing sight. I shall then return with my automobile keys. At that time I should like all of you to be off my property or else I shall solicit the aid of this underpaid gendarme to forcibly evict you." He looked along the line of people, raised an eyebrow and said, "Understand, clods?"

He very carefully picked his way through the group and headed back toward the house, fastidiously avoiding any contact like a medieval baron fresh from a visit to an area of the black plague. Not really frightened of catching it, you understand, but playing it safe, just the same. When he reached his house and left the gaping neighbors behind, his shoulders slumped, the eyebrow went back to normal and his cold, rigidly controlled features suddenly became loose and pliable, the flesh white, the eyes nervous and haunted.

At nine o'clock in the evening, Bartlett Finchley had consumed three quarters of a bottle of excellent bourbon and had forgotten all about going out for the evening. He lay half-dozing on the couch, his well-tailored tuxedo crumpled and unkempt. There was a noise on the stairs and Finchley opened his eyes and turned his head so that he could stare across the room toward the hall. The telephone repairman was just coming down the steps. He paused at the entrance to the living room, looked in.

"She's operating all right now, Mr. Finchley," the repairman said.

"I'm deeply indebted," Finchley answered acidly. "Convey my best to Alexander Graham Bell."

The telephone repairman lingered at the entrance. "You tripped over the cord—is that what you said?"

"If that's what I said," Finchley barked at him, "that's precisely what happened."

The repairman shrugged. "Well, you're the boss, Mr. Finchley. But those wires sure look as though they'd been yanked out."

Finchley rose to a sitting position on the couch and carefully smoothed back his hair. He took a cigarette from a hand-carved teakwood box on the coffee table, careful that the repairman should not see how his fingers shook as he fitted the cigarette in the holder.

"Do they indeed?" Finchley said, concentrating on the cigarette. "Proving what a vast storehouse of knowledge you've yet to acquire." Then, looking up with disdain, he said, "Good night!"

The repairman went out the front door and Finchley rose from the couch. He hesitated, then went to the television set. Its broken screen was a yawning abyss into the darkness beyond and Finchley hurriedly backed away from it.

At the bar in the corner of the room, he poured himself a large drink, downed half of it in a gulp, then stared almost challengingly at the television set. It stood in silent defeat, this time shattered beyond any repair and Finchley felt satisfaction. He was about to take another drink when the sound of the clock chimes suddenly clanged into the room. Finchley's glass dropped and broke on the bartop. Again the cold, clammy, impossible fear seized him as he looked toward the empty mantel where the clock had been and then down to the floor where he himself had smashed it into nothingness.

And yet there was the sound of the chimes, loud, deep, resonant and enveloping the room. He ran toward the hall and then stopped. From the study came the sound of the electric typewriter, the keys, then the carriage, then the keys again. And still the chimes of the clock joining as an obbligato. Finchley felt a scream building up in his throat.

He ran into the study in time to see the typewriter finishing a final line. He took a stumbling step and ripped the paper out of the carriage. "Get out of here, Finchley." It covered the page, line after line after line. And then suddenly came another horror from the living room. The little dancer's voice that he'd heard on the television set that afternoon.

"Get out of here, Finchley," it called sweetly. "Get out of here, Finchley."

The chimes continued to ring and then, inexplicably, another chorus of voices joined the girl's.

"Get out of here, Finchley," it said, like some kind of vast *a cappella* choir. "Get out of here, Finchley." Over and over again. "Get out of here, Finchley. Get out of here, Finchley. GET OUT OF HERE, FINCHLEY!"

Finchley let out one gasping, agonizing sob and thrust his knuckles into his mouth as once again he ran into the living room and stared wildly around. He picked up a chair and threw it at the television set. It missed and shot past to smash against a fragile antique table holding an expensive lamp, both of which went to the floor with a loud clatter of broken wood and glass. And still the voices, the typewriter, the chimes.

And when Finchley, a steady, constant scream coming from his throat like a grotesque human siren, raced back into the hall and started upstairs, another nightmare was heading toward him from the top. There was the electric razor slithering down, step by step, like a snake with an oversized head.

Finchley's scream stopped and he was unable to conjure up another one, though his mouth was open and his eyes popped and he felt pain clawing the inside of his chest. He tripped and landed on his knees as he tried to reach the door. He yanked at it and finally got it open as the electric razor came unerringly after him.

He tore out into the night, the sounds of his house following him, a deafening chorus of, "Get out of here, Finchley," orchestrated for typewriter keys, clock chimes, and the hum of an electric razor.

He tripped again and landed in a heap on the sidewalk. He felt the needle of a rose bush through his trousers as he ran toward the garage and was able to scream once again, as the garage doors creaked open and the headlights of the car inside went on and bathed him in hot, white light.

The engine growled like a jungle beast as the car started to roll slowly out toward him. Finchley yelled for help, ran out to the street, tripped and fell, feeling the shock of protesting nerves as the curb tore a bleeding gash down the side of his face to his jaw.

But he had no time for concern because the car was pursuing him. He ran down the street and back and forth across it, and the car, all by itself, followed the contour of the street and refused to allow Finchley out of its sight. When he went on the sidewalk, the car jumped the curb and followed him. When he went back in the street, the car did likewise. It was unhurried, calculating, and patient.

When Finchley reached the corner the car seemed to hesitate for a moment, but then it turned and followed him down the next block. Finchley knew his legs were beginning to give out and he could scarcely breathe. Calling on some hidden resource of logic and calculation to overcome his blinding, numbing fear, Finchley jumped over the white picket fence of one of the houses flanking the road and hid behind its front porch.

The car moved slowly past, stopped after a few yards, shifted itself into reverse and backed to a stop directly in front of the house where Finchley was hiding. It idled there at the curb, engine purring, a patient, unhurried stalker menacingly secure in the knowledge of its own superiority.

Finchley ran diagonally across the lawn back toward his own block. The car shifted its gears, made a U-turn in a wide arc, and again bore down on him. Bartlett Finchley made his legs move back and forth, but they grew heavier and heavier and became harder and harder to lift. His heart beat in spasmodic, agonizing thumps and his lungs were torn bellows wheezing hollowly with overexertion and fast reaching that moment when they would collapse. Pain coursed through Finchley's body with every breath he took.

As he ran through the night it seemed to Finchley that he'd never done anything else all his life. He tried to prod his panicked mind into some kind of thought, rather than to succumb to the enveloping disaster that followed him with such precision and patience, as if never doubting for one moment that this was simply a cat-and-mouse game and that Finchley was the mouse.

He tripped over his feet and again plowed head first into the street, causing the blood to run afresh down the side of his face. He lay there for a moment, sobbing and moaning.

But again there was the sound of the engine and again the bright lights played on him. He rose to his hands and knees and looked over his shoulder. The car was not a hundred feet away, moving slowly toward him, its headlights two unblinking eyes, the grill a metal mouth that leered at him.

Finchley got up again and ran, up one street and down another, across a lawn and then back onto the sidewalk, down another street, down another, then back to his own block.

How he kept going and moving and breathing, Finchley could not understand. Each breath seemed his last, each movement the final exertion, but he kept running.

Suddenly he realized he was once more in front of his own house. He turned sharply to run into the driveway, past the side of the house to the back yard. Its tires shrieked as the car followed him up the driveway, picked up speed as it went into the garage, smashed through the opposite wall and into the back yard to meet Finchley just as he came around the corner.

All of the insides of Bartlett Finchley's body constricted at that moment. His throat, his lungs, his heart, the linings of his stomach. He fell once again to his hands and knees and began to crawl across a rock garden, tasting dirt and salty sweat, an hysterical animal, pleading over and over again to be left alone.

His voice was an insane, gurgling chant as he crawled across his patio, toppled sideways over a flight of concrete steps, and wound up on the edge of his swimming pool. The lights went on and the pool appeared a blue, shimmering square carved out of a piece of darkness.

Finchley's head slowly rose. The car slowly rolled down the small hill toward him, plowing up the earth, the garden, pushing aside the patio furniture in its slow, steady, inexorable pursuit. And Finchley, on all fours, his face streaked with mud and torn flesh, his eyes glazed, his hair lying over his forehead in damp masses, his clothing flapping in torn fragments around him, had now reached the pinnacle of his fear. This was the climax of the nightmare. It was the ultimate fear barrier and he smashed through it with one final, piercing, inhuman scream.

He flung up his hands in front of his face, rose to his shaking feet as the car bore down on him. Then he felt himself falling through space. The wet surface of the pool touched him, gathered him in and sucked him down.

In that one brief, fragmentary moment that lay between life and death he saw the headlights of the car blinking down at him through the water and he heard the engine let out a deep roar like some triumphant shout.

Then he could see nothing more because he had reached the bottom of the pool and his eyes had become simply unfunctioning, useless orbs that stared out of a dead face.

A narrow, irregular line of water drops led from the pool to the ambulance where the body of Bartlett Finchley lay on a stretcher. A policeman with a notebook scratched his head and looked from the pool over to an intern who walked around the ambulance, past the fascinated faces of neighbors and then closed the two rear doors.

"Heart attack, Doc?" the policeman asked him. "Is that what you think?"

The intern looked up from his examination papers and nodded. "That's what it appears."

The policeman looked over toward the pool again, then up

past the crushed garden and overturned patio chairs, to the big, gaping hole in the rear end of the garage where an automobile sat, mute and unrevealing.

"Neighbors said they heard him shouting about something during the night," the policeman said. "Sounded scared." He scratched his head again. "Whole Goddamn thing doesn't make much sense. The busted garage wall, those tire tracks leading to the pool." He shook his head. "The whole Goddamned thing doesn't make any sense at all."

The intern leaned against the ambulance doors, then looked down at the water drops that led to the pool's edge. "Funny thing," the intern said softly.

"What is?" asked the policeman.

"A body will float for a while after a drowning."

"So?" the policeman inquired.

The intern jerked a thumb in the direction of the ambulance. "This one wasn't floating. It was down at the bottom of the pool just as if it had been weighted or something. But that's the thing. It hadn't been weighted. It was just lying there down at the bottom. That'll happen, you know, after a couple of weeks when the body gets bloated and water logged." The intern pointed toward the pool. "He hadn't been there but a few hours."

"It was his face," the policeman said with a shudder in his voice. "Did you look closely at his face, Doc? He looked so scared. He looked so God-awful scared. What do you suppose scared him?"

The intern shook his head. "Whatever it was," he said, "it's a little item that he's taken with him!"

He folded the examination papers, went around to the passenger's seat of the ambulance and opened the door, motioning the driver to move out. The policeman folded up his notebook. He was suddenly conscious of all the neighbors.

"All right, everybody," he said, putting firmness and authority into his voice, "the show's over. Come on now . . . everybody get out of here and go home!"

The crowd slowly dispersed in soft, whispering groups, voices muted by the fascination of death that all men carry with them in small pockets deep inside them. The policeman followed them toward the front yard, running over in his mind the nature of the report he'd have to write and wondering how in God's name he could submit such an oddball story to the powers that be and have it make any sense. A press photographer was the last man on the scene. He took pictures of the pool, the departing ambulance, a few of the neighbors. He asked a few questions of the latter, jotted them down hurriedly and, as an afterthought, took a picture of the car that was sitting in the garage. Then he got in his own car and drove away.

The following afternoon there was a funeral and only about nine people came because Bartlett Finchley had so few friends. It was a somber but business-like affair with a very brief eulogy and a dry-eyed response. Bartlett Finchley was laid to rest, a lightly lamented minor character, who would be remembered more for his final torment than for his lifelong tartness. The conglomeration of odd and unrelated circumstances surrounding his death— the demolished garage, the destroyed garden, the wrecked patio—were grist for some gossip and conjecture. But they soon palled and were forgotten.

About a year later, the caretaker of the cemetery where Mr. Finchley was interred, a taciturn, grim man, did tell an odd story to his wife one night at the dinner table. He had been using a power mower on the cemetery lawn, and two or three times it had shown a disconcerting tendency to veer off to the right and smash against Bartlett Finchley's tombstone.

It had elicited little concern on the part of the caretaker and he brought it up only as an additional support for a rather long-standing contention, oft stated to his wife, that those God-damned power mowers weren't worth their salt and a good old reliable hand mower was really a far better item, albeit slower. And after this briefest of colloquies with his wife, the caretaker had eaten a Brown Betty for dessert, watched television, and gone to bed.

Nothing more was said.

Nothing more needed to be said.

THE BIG, TALL WISH

In this corner of the universe, in a shabby, sparsely furnished bedroom inside an aging and decrepit brownstone tenement, stood a prize fighter named Bolie Jackson, staring at himself in the dresser mirror. He weighed a hundred and sixty-three pounds and was an hour and a half away from a comeback at St. Nick's.

Mr. Bolie Jackson, at thirty-three, was, by the standards of his profession, an aging, over-the-hill relic. At this moment he was looking at the reflection of a man who had left too many pieces of his youth in too many stadiums for too many years before too many screaming people.

He regarded the ebony face, crisscrossed with thin, irregular white scars, and the battered nose that had been smashed this way and that way and finally settled into a shapeless lump, flattened down so that the nostrils were only a fraction of an inch away from an equally scarred upper lip. But, with it all, it was a good face and a gentle face. The eyes were clear, the features expressive, the mouth determined, but not without humor. Nor was the face without character.

In the right-hand corner of the mirror was the reflection of Henry Temple who sat on Bolie Jackson's bed across the room and stared with undisguised hero worship at the lithe black man who stood in front of him buttoning his shirt. Little Henry Temple, a nine-year-old colored boy, had a personal God named Bolie Jackson and a personal shrine that was this nondescript bedroom on the floor above his own.

Henry looked happily at the fighter's shoulder muscles, which rippled underneath the shirt. He noted with an adult satisfaction Bolie Jackson's poise, the way he stood flat-footed, the grace of the man. He was a fighter, a *professional* fighter, and he was an expert at his craft.

"You feelin' good, Bolie?" Henry held out his little fists. "Feelin' sharp? Take a tiger tonight, huh, Bolie?"

Bolie smiled gently at the little boy's reflection in the mirror. He winked and held out his fists, aping Henry's gesture. "Take a tiger, Henry," Bolie announced. "Gonna take me a tiger. Hard left, then a right. One in the stomach and then lift him up by the tail and throw 'im out to the ninth row."

Henry's intent, serious face in the mirror showed a big, even, white-toothed smile. God, but he loved this kid. He watched the boy get up and come over to him.

"You're lookin' good, Bolie." It was a final judgment. It was an absolute, irrevocable analysis from an expert, albeit a nine-year-old worshiper. "You're lookin' sharp, Bolie. Oh, boy, you're lookin' sharp."

Bolie's smile faded as he bent down to look at the little face and then cupped the small chin, pressing it gently. "You gonna watch it on television?"

"You foolin'?" Henry laughed. "I'll yell so loud you'll hear me all the way to St. Nick's."

They stood and laughed together, then Bolie finished buttoning his shirt. He leaned toward the mirror studying the scars on his face. He touched the biggest one, the ugliest, the one that had taken three months to heal and now stood out in sharp, dead-white, unpleasant relief over the right eyebrow.

"A fighter don't need a scrapbook, Henry," Bolie said softly and reflectively. "Want to know about what he's done? Where he's fought? Read it on his face. He's got the whole story cut into his flesh." He tapped the scar over the right eye. "St. Louis, 1949. Guy named Sailor Levitt. Real fast boy. Saw me start to bleed up there that night and it was like it was painted red, white, and blue with a big dot in the center. Never let up off of it. Just kep givin' it to me in that same spot. I bet that hole was an inch and a half deep by the time he finished."

He touched the bridge of the battered nose. "That was Memorial Stadium, Syracuse, New York. Italian boy. Fought like Henry Armstrong. All hands and arms, just like a windmill all over you. First time I ever had my nose broken twice in one fight." He touched the thin scar and the pouched flesh near his ear. "Move south, Henry. Miami, Florida. Boy got me up against a ring post. Did this with his laces."

Once again he was aware of the little boy's reflection in the mirror. Henry's eyes were grim and concerned and it was like a face of a little gnome grown old before his time. Bolie noticed the look, smiled and tried to make his voice lighter.

"On the face, Henry," he continued. "That's where you read it. Start in 1947 and then move across. Pittsburgh, Boston, Syracuse . . ." He touched the scars and then closed his eyes, pressing two fingers against them. His voice was soft and now sounded tired. "Old man, Henry. Tired old man tryin' to catch a bus. But the bus already gone. Left a coupla years ago." He opened his eyes, turned and looked down at the boy. "Hands all heavy. Legs all rubbery. Breath short. One eye not so good. And there I go, runnin' down the street tryin' to catch this bus to glory."

Henry compulsively gripped Bolie's arm, his voice intense. "Bolie," Henry said, "you gonna catch a tiger tonight. I'm gonna make a wish. I'm gonna make a big, tall wish. And you ain't gonna get hurt none either. I'm gonna make a wish you don't get hurt none. You hear, Bolie? I don't want you gettin' hurt none. You've been hurt enough already. And you're my friend, Bolie. You're my good and close friend."

Bolie stared into the little face and felt an access of tenderness and affection of man for boy that did tight things to his throat. He knelt down in front of Henry and held him by the shoulders, then very gently he kissed him on the cheek, rose, went over to the bed, and took an overnight bag from it.

He left the little boy standing there as he went out the door and down the steps, conscious of the hundreds of nights he'd walked down these steps on his way to this stadium or that stadium. Sometimes to win and come back in a glorious homecoming to back-slapping neighbors. Other times to lose and to sneak skulking back in the dead of night, not wanting to see anyone, hating the pitying look of friends and hating more the accusing looks of people who had bet on him and lost.

It was almost as if he could funnel all the fights into a giant, vast moment of recollection and the result was one mass of remembered pain. The shocking, incredible, blinding agony of the broken nose; the dull throbbing ache of the kidney, the rib cage, the stomach that went on for weeks after a bad one. It all went through his mind as he walked slowly down the steps.

Standing near the front door was Henry Temple's mother, an attractive widow in her thirties. She had just come out of her apartment and she smiled at Bolie. He stopped and smiled at her, then jerked his thumb in the direction of the stairs.

"You got quite a boy there, Frances," Bolie grinned. "You got quite a boy. Talks like a little old man, you know? I'm his 'good and close friend.' That's what he says. Real intense like. I'm his good and close friend." He laughed softly and shook his head.

"You're good to him," Frances said. "You're real good to him, Bolie. Takin' him to ball games all the time. Takin' him out for walks." She looked up toward the steps and said simply, "Hard for a boy not to have a father. He never did know his." She looked closely at Bolie and touched his arm. "He won't be going to bed tonight till you get back. Take care of yourself, Bolie. Don't get hurt none."

Bolie's smile was slight and crooked. "I'll work hard on it."

They both turned at the sound of footsteps coming down the stairs. Henry walked past his mother directly over to Bolie. He reached up and took the fighter's hand and then stared up intensely into his face.

"I'm gonna make a wish, Bolie," he announced. "I'm gonna make a wish nothin' happens to you. So don't you be afraid, Bolie. Understand? Don't you be afraid."

He let go of Bolie's hand, and went into his apartment. Bolie looked down at the floor.

"You're his friend, Bolie," Frances said softly. "He's got you in a shrine."

Bolie's head jerked up and he laughed without humor. "Scared old man who don't remember nothin' except how to bleed." He shook his head. "I don't fit in no shrine, Frances." He studied the closed door of the apartment and then smiled. "But you tell him, Frances . . ." his voice was softer. "You tell him how

I'm obliged for his wish. That's what I need right now." He looked down at his big-knuckled hands, crisscrossed with bulging tendons and muscles and scarred like his face.

"That's what I need," he whispered. "A little magic." He ran his hand over the line of mailboxes along the wall and he felt afraid. He felt desperately afraid.

"He's been talking about makin' a wish all night," Frances said. "All the time makin' wishes, Bolie. I see him standin' there in his bedroom in the dark, lookin' out the window. I come in real quiet and I say, 'Henry, boy, why don't you go to sleep?', and he turns to me with that serious little face of his and he says, 'Makin' a wish, Mama.' Makin' a wish for this. Makin' a wish for that. Oh, he's all the time wishin'. Why just the other night—" She stopped abruptly and looked away. There was a puzzled look on her face and her eyes narrowed as she remembered something.

"What, Frances? What happened?"

Frances smiled at him then looked away. She laughed softly as if scoffing at herself. "I needed fifteen dollars for the rent," she said. "Henry said he was gonna make the big, tall wish. That's his biggest kind, the big, tall wish." She laughed lightly again. "He don't waste that wish on just anything. That's what he calls the important one." She was silent for a moment and again her voice was thoughtful. "That was last Friday and a woman I done some nursing for out on the Island sent me a check." She looked at Bolie closely. "A check for fifteen dollars."

Bolie smiled and shook his head. "Little boys," he said. "Little boys with their heads full up with dreams. And when does it happen, Frances? When do they suddenly know there ain't any magic?" He fiddled with one of the open mailboxes and then suddenly, impulsively, slammed it shut.

"When does somebody push their face down on the sidewalk and say to 'em—'Hey, little boy—it's concrete. That's what the world is made out of. Concrete and gutters and dirty old buildings and tears for every minute you're alive.'" The black, scarred face was contorted and bitterness showed in the eyes as he turned to the woman. "When do they find out that you can wish your life away, Frances?"

"Good luck tonight, Bolie," she said gently. "We'll be waiting for you."

"Sure, Frances, sure," Bolie nodded. He pointed toward the closed door. "Kiss him good night for me."

Then he went out the front door and down the steps of the brownstone toward the sidewalk. People lounged on the steps and curbs, fanning the sultry air with the sports pages of the evening newspaper.

"Give 'im hell, Bolie," screeched a scrawny little old man from the top steps.

"The old one, two, Bolie," a fat woman said, going through a complicated motion with arms and trunk.

Somebody slapped him on the back and a newsboy asked for his autograph, but in a moment he was alone walking down the sidewalk toward the bus stop. In a few minutes he'd be in his dressing room at St. Nick's Arena. In a strange way he felt at home there. The very ugliness of the place and everything connected with it were well-remembered adjuncts to his life. The smell of sweat that stayed on towels even after a washing. The odor of cheap liniment. The collective smell of people that permeated the walls. The cigar and cigarette smoke and the noises from up above. The stamping and whistling and shouting of the hard-to-please coterie of fight followers who wanted at least one bleeding, cut eye for every twenty-cent fraction of their admission ticket.

Riding on the bus down toward Sixty-sixth Street, Bolie thought about the thousands of hours he'd spent in dressing rooms and how the faces of the people dimly visible beyond the ring lights in the fourth and fifth rows always looked the same, as if the identical men had followed him over the years and across the country—always to show up booing and stamping while the pain came to him.

He looked out the window at the passing neon lights and knew that this would be the last bus ride to St. Nick's Arena or any arena and this would be the last night spent in a dressing room and then in a ring. It would be the last of everything if he didn't win. This was the comeback. This was the single and solitary last chance to prove he could still be reckoned with as a fighting entity.

And even as he pondered, he realized he was tired and old, and this whole thing was just a gesture, a ritual to deny all the opponents and all the years when in truth opponents and years had long ago cost him this fight as well as so many earlier ones.

He pushed this thought out of his mind, shaking his head

and mumbling to himself, as if by the very act of rejection he might yet salvage a victory from a set of impossible odds.

Joe Mizell was what was called in the trade a "cut man." This term covered a multitude of services but, boiled down, it meant he was a fighter's handler, preparing him for the fight and "servicing" him between rounds. In some thirty-one years in the business, this little, partially hunchbacked, bald gnome of a man had deftly stopped the blood flow of fifty thousand cuts; pulled out the trunks of perhaps five hundred fighters as they tried torturously to breathe inside a body that had been punished beyond reason; and had, like a laboratory technician, opened up a comparable army of jaws to supply just the right amount of water to wet the insides of swollen mouths without allowing their owners to swallow any of it.

In short, Joe Mizell was an expert ringside functionary who had probably kept too many fighters on their feet when by all physical laws they should have been back in dressing rooms or in ambulances. Sometime back over the years he had trained himself never to look at fighters' faces. He had assumed a kind of numb professionalism, allowing no emotion to enter his ministrations of aid. A fighter was just an evening's job. But on occasion, rare occasion, Mizell couldn't help but feel a sharp tug inside as he prepared an old-timer like the soft-voiced colored boy he was handling tonight.

He had seen Bolie Jackson fifteen years ago when he was a clear-faced, ebony young destroyer who had strength, resilience, and more brains than most. He'd handled Bolie for a four-year period when he was heading up for the championship and had been around in his corner the night Bolie's right eye had been cut to ribbons and the fight had been called in the eleventh round.

That had been the pinnacle. From that moment on Bolie Jackson had gone downhill and Joe Mizell had been around for the downward trip as well. There were the close fights, the good fights with the rising newcomers who fought Bolie Jackson for his name value. And then there was the long line of over-matched evenings when Bolie had had no right even to enter a ring.

Now Mizell carefully finished taping the fighter's hands and forced himself to look up into the scarred face, making an unconscious comparison between this hopelessly damaged countenance and the smooth, handsome face of Bolie Jackson at eighteen.

Mizell felt the little twinge of ache that came deep inside whenever he worked on over-the-hill fighters who stayed in a profession that sucked its warriors dry, held out a teasing promise of comeback, but in every case left them torn and scrambled and unfit for anything else. He finished the taping, then stepped back and held up the palms of his hands.

"Try it, Bolie," he said.

Bolie flexed his hands and then cracked Mizell's palms several times with his bandaged fists. "Feels okay, Joe," Bolie said. "Feels good. Thanks."

Mizell grunted an acknowledgment, then with strangely graceful fingers, began to knead Bolie's back muscles, rippling his hands over the fighter's shoulders and arms, first digging, then gouging, then gently massaging. Once when Bolie flinched, Mizell winked at him and the wink reminded Bolie of all the hours this small, misshapen man had worked on him. What decency, honesty, what precious little compassion there was to be found in the legal slaughterhouse known as professional prize fighting, was limited to men like Joe Mizell.

"You ain't lost your touch, Joe," Bolie grinned at him.

Mizell half smiled and continued the massage. Very gradually the taut, tense muscles, the bunched-up tendons loosened and became more pliable, and the fear that Bolie had carried into the room with him, though not dissipated, had been pushed into a corner.

Harvey Thomas came in. He was Bolie's manager for the night—an obese, greasy-looking man who chewed wetly on the stub of a cigar. Bolie couldn't afford a regular manager. There were transient managers who would handle a fighter on a one-fight basis. Thomas was one of these. He blew a cloud of dirty smoke into the air and Bolie noticed the spittle on the corners of Thomas's mouth. Bolie turned away, rubbing his jaw with the back of a bandaged hand.

"He's all ready," Mizell announced shortly.

Thomas nodded without interest, formed his mouth into an "O" and blew out another stream of smoke. Bolie looked up at the clock. It was almost ten and he was beginning to feel that wet tension he always knew before a tough one. The room was small and the smoke from the cigar seemed to envelop him. He was frightened and angry. He had to strike out at someone. Thomas stood there, fat and ugly, and Bolie hated him.

"Butt it out, will you, Thomas?" Bolie barked. "I want to breathe."

Thomas smiled and revealed a set of broken black and yellow teeth. He deliberately took another drag on the cigar. "You hired me for the fight, Bolie. It's a package deal—me and the cigar."

A thousand needles tore holes in Bolie's mind and body. He could feel sweat under the bandages. He bolted up from the table.

"I told you to butt it out, Thomas."

The two men stared at one another. Mizell turned away, busying himself collecting dirty towels that were strewn on the floor. Finally, Thomas, chuckling softly, held up the cigar and let the soggy thing drop from his hands.

"Feisty little old man," he said softly. "Older they get—the louder they talk. The more they want—" he stared coldly at Bolie "—and the less chance they got to get it!"

Bolie looked at the fat man's greasy, big-pored face, hating the sight of it. "How'd I get *you* tonight?" he asked.

Thomas feigned surprise. "Me, Bolie? Why I'm a bargain. I'm an expert on has-beens."

Bolie nodded. "I've seen the boys you usually handle," he said to the fat man. "Catchers, aren't they? Guaranteed two rounds each. Shovel them in, shovel them out, then sew them together for the next time."

Thomas laughed. "That's the only way to do it," he said. "Month or so from now maybe I'll find *you* at the back door. Why not, Bolie? You're long gone. You've had it. Wait'll after tonight. You'll want to get in the stable too. All you have to do is guarantee two rounds. Three, four prelims every month. Do that standing on your head, can't you?"

Mizell stood up, touched Bolie's arm, and felt the fighter's whole body quivering. Bolie took a step toward the manager, shrugging off Mizell's restraining hand.

"I thought the smell came with the cigar," Bolie said. He shook his head. "You wear it all over you. You stink, Thomas."

Thomas laughed aloud as if Bolie had just cracked a joke. "You tell 'em, champ," he said. "You tell 'em."

There was a knock on the door and a muffled voice called out, "Five minutes, Jackson."

"He'll be there," Mizell said, though it was Thomas's job to reply.

Bolie sat on the rubbing table and Mizell began to massage his back again. Thomas leaned against the wall near the door and looked a little longingly at the cigar butt on the floor. He ran his tongue across his teeth, probing and darting around inside for food particles or whatever other treasures he might find. His fingers drummed on the wall. He looked up toward the ceiling. He was very bored.

Finally Bolie said, "What about tonight? What should I look out for? I only seen this boy fight once. That was a coupla years ago . . ."

Thomas shrugged. "I ain't never seen him."

Mizell's fingers stopped abruptly and he froze. This was a sellout. He wondered if Bolie recognized it as such, and then, looking up very slowly toward the fighter, he realized that Bolie understood it only too well. The colored fighter looked from Mizell to Thomas. He slid off the rubbing table.

"Bolie," Mizell began placatingly.

Bolie shook his head, motioning Mizell out of the way. He walked across the room to where Thomas stood, his face a shade more pale. Bolie's bandaged hands shot out, connected with the grease-stained checked sport coat of the manager and almost yanked him off his feet.

"You've watched him fight," Bolie said in a low voice, trying to keep the tremor out of it. "You've seen him six times the past year. You piece of garbage, you, Thomas! You're bettin' on him, aren't you?" He pushed Thomas backwards then cocked his right fist.

"Bolie," Mizell screamed, running over to him and trying to get between the fighter and the fat man.

Sweat poured down Bolie's face and his lips quivered. "It ain't enough he sells wrecks by the pound. He comes in here for a dirty twenty bucks, supposed to help me and *then bets on the other guy!*"

He moved toward Thomas again, Mizell hanging on him trying to whisper, cajole, placate, anything to prevent Bolie from letting himself out. Bolie's voice drowned him out.

"Thomas," Bolie said, "I may be a bum upstairs in another

ten minutes . . . but I'm gonna fight a beautiful first round right here."

Thomas squirmed against the wall. He raised a shaking finger, pointing it at Bolie. "Bolie," he squealed, "you touch me and I'll have you up for ten years. I swear to you, Bolie—I'll fix your wagon good—"

He felt himself lifted up by Bolie's bandaged hands and flung against the wall. His body crawled with sweat and he couldn't bring himself to look into the deep-set eyes, so full of hatred, in the black, scarred face before him.

Again Mizell stepped between them. "Bolie," he urged gently. "He's right. He's a dirty blood sucker and he's a sonofabitch, but if you touch him, Bolie—you've had it."

"Listen to him, Bolie," Thomas screeched. "You listen to him, you crummy tanker you—"

Bolie saw only the fat sweating face, the piggish eyes, the creature who jobbed off flesh by the pound. Bolie didn't care about consequences. He swung from the floor and it was only when he felt the agonizing bolt of pain shoot up his right arm that he realized he had hit something stronger and much more unyielding than bone or flesh. Thomas had moved aside and Bolie Jackson's right fist had connected with the concrete wall.

Thomas scrambled for the doorknob and rushed out. Mizell grabbed Bolie's bandaged right hand and studied it. He felt it in a few places, and Bolie winced at the touch. He looked up with wise, old eyes, the eyes of the expert on pain and human damage, and shook his head slowly.

"It wasn't enough you had to spot him all those years," he said. "It wasn't enough was it, Bolie? Now you've got to walk upstairs with four busted knuckles."

There was another knock on the door. "Okay, Jackson," the voice said from the corridor. "You're on."

Mizell let Bolie's hand drop. "Well?" he asked.

Bolie took a deep breath, held up his right hand and looked over toward Mizell. "Well, nothing," he said. "Let's do it."

Mizell's lips were a thin line. He took the gloves hanging on the end of the rubbing table and very carefully started to put them on Bolie's hands. The knuckles under the bandage were beginning to swell and it was only with effort that he could even get the glove laced on that hand. He said softly, "You know what I'd do if I was you? I'd rent me a bicycle and I'd pedal the hell out of here." He pointed to the right glove. "That ain't gonna do a Goddamn thing for you up there. Not a Goddamn thing."

Bolie smiled and felt the tension ease off. He was dead and he knew it and with that knowledge came a resignation. "Poor little Henry Temple," Bolie said as he suddenly remembered. "Poor little old Henry Temple. I'm putting two strikes on all his magic. Two strikes."

"Who?" Mizell asked as he draped Bolie's bathrobe over his shoulder. "What are you talking about, Bolie?"

"Nothin'," Bolie answered softly. "Nothin' at all, Joe. There ain't no such thing as magic."

Mizell opened the door for him. They went into the corridor, going toward the ramp that led to the arena above. A hunchbacked little handler, who felt like crying, and a man of thirty-three, who was the oldest of the old and who let his steps take him toward the sound of the stomping feet and the catcalls, to the big, smelly, smoke-filled room where men had paid on the average two dollars and eighty-five cents to see more scars get cut into his face for this, the last time.

Frances Temple made a pretense of sewing on buttons as she sat across the room from the television set. Her little son's face was pressed against the screen, his eyes tightly closed, his fists clenched, half obliterating the picture of carnage. The tired voice of a bored announcer feigned excitement and rattled inanely the clichés of fifty years of fighting.

"Another left and right. *Another* left and right. A smashing right to Jackson's head. Then a left that catches him high above the cheek and we see the blood again. But he's a gamester, this boy. He's a real gamester. Yes siree, this Bolie Jackson is a real gamester. Three rounds it is and he's still on his feet. Yes sir, this Bolie Jackson is a real gamester. Now Corrigan comes in stalking, flat-footed. He comes in stalking. He leads with a left. Another left. A smashing right that crosses over and connects with Bolie Jackson's nose. Jackson folds into a clinch . . ." The voice went on, the drumfire of an antique machine gun, firing dud ammunition.

And in the ring Bolie Jackson had long ago stopped feeling fear. Through the red gauze of pain that surrounded him, he would see the fists of the other fighter probing at him and then landing. A left to the side of his head shook him down to his arches and he felt his knees go wobbly. He partially blocked a right and tried to get inside, but the other fighter, smart and ring-wise, stepped back and kept measuring him.

Bolie lumbered in, head down, both hands up in front of his face and then felt the raw, slicing agony of a six-ounce glove buried to the wrist in his stomach.

His breath went out of him, he choked, and then, from nowhere, lightning hit him between the eyes and he met the bruising shock of the canvas against his face. He was dimly aware that he was down. He heard the crowd roar and scream. The giant ring light beat down on him, revealing his agony in sharp relief.

"Please, Bolie . . . please, Bolie," Henry Temple whispered into the television screen. "Please. Bolie, Bolie, Bolie . . . I wish you wouldn't be hurt . . . I wish, Bolie, I wish."

The tiny voice was an obbligato to the crowd roar that came from the set. It was a tiny, frail oboe set against the enormous brass section of human voices that cried out for murder and bloodshed.

"Bolie, I wish . . . Bolie, I wish . . ."

It was a chant. It was the beckoning to magic that was nothing more than the anguish of a little boy.

But suddenly something happened. The referee, swinging his arm down in measured arcs, froze, his face static, his right hand pointed toward the canvas and the sprawled figure of the fighter.

The crowd of people became mannequins. There was no motion, no sound. Everything had stopped as if captured on a photograph. Clapping hands were suspended in air. Jaws chewing popcorn were wide open. Beer cans stopped on the way to stationary mouths. Time had stopped moving. And then there was noise again. There were screams and shouts and catcalls and stamping feet. Smoke, that in that brief fragment of an instant had floated like a motionless cloud, again began to drift through the arena. In the ring the referee resumed counting.

"Seven," he shouted. "Eight. Nine. Ten."

His flat palms crossed one another in the traditional signal of the knockout.

Then he pointed toward Bolie Jackson who danced in a neutral corner, reached for the right arm and held it aloft as the crowd screamed its approval.

On the canvas a youngster named Corrigan, with a split jaw, a closed right eye, lay like the dead, as if his brains had departed without leaving a message. His somber-faced manager and handler scrambled through the ring ropes to lift him and drag him back to his corner. Little Joe Mizell hugged Bolie and kissed him on the cheek, as Bolie smiled happily and waved his right arm. No one noticed the look of absolute bewilderment in Bolie's eyes.

Mizell put the bathrobe over Bolie's shoulders and led him out of the ring. People slapped his back and cheered him again, then turned toward the ring, checking their program for what would be the next sacrifice!

In the dressing room Bolie was putting on his clothes. Occasionally he would look down at his right hand, flexing the fingers, folding it into a fist and striking his other hand. Mizell was cleaning up the room.

"Joe," Bolie said. He held up his right hand. "You were wrong. Just bruised, I guess, huh? Hurt like anything, but somebody said I got him with it. Couldn't have been broken after all."

"Who said it was?"

Bolie gave him an odd look. "*You* said. It felt like it, too. I could feel the knuckles coming up through the bandages. I could have sworn it was busted. And when he knocked me down—"

There was a silence. "What?" Mizell asked. "He did what?"

Bolie pushed his shirt into his trousers. "Knocked me down, Joe. When he knocked me down. I don't even remember getting up. Next thing I knew, there he was at my feet."

Bolie was waiting, his eyes asking questions. Mizell grinned and shook his head.

"We was in different arenas tonight," he said, with a soft chuckle. "You didn't get knocked down, Bolie. You was never off your feet."

Bolie's head cocked to one side. "I *wasn't*?"

Mizell said, "No. You sure wasn't. This one you carried all the way, baby."

Bolie put his coat on, stared at the floor for a long moment, then looked up at Mizell. "I wasn't off my feet?" he asked intensely. "I didn't go down?"

"Not once," Mizell answered. "Good night," he said softly. "Good night, old timer. I'm proud of you!"

He shuffled out. Bolie Jackson stood looking at his hands and then, with wonderment, at his reflection in the cracked, dirty mirror. Exultation surged through him and he wanted to shout and jump around and sing. He'd won!

A crazy conglomeration of half-remembered, disjointed, kaleidoscope visions ended on a giant question mark. But he had won. The smile stayed on his face as he walked out into the corridor and happy excitement cloaked him in goose pimples as he headed toward the exit. Bolie Jackson had won. He'd made his comeback. Everything might change now. Everything. This was the road back and tonight he had taken a giant step along it.

He went out into the summer darkness and the night smelled sweet to him. He didn't even feel tired. He didn't feel old. All he wanted now was to see the little boy. Because this night had to be shared.

The neighbors were waiting for him on the steps even though it was one in the morning. He walked among them responding to the back slaps and handshakes with a kind of joyous numbness. When he got inside, Frances was waiting for him at the apartment door. She hugged him.

"You should have seen him, Bolie. He'd like to go out of his mind, he was so happy! Whole building was shaking—you'd never believe it!"

Bolie looked questioningly over her shoulder into the living room.

"He's up on the roof," Frances said, "waiting for you."

Bolie nodded and started to take the steps two at a time.

"Bolie," Frances called up to him.

Bolie stopped.

"Send him down real soon. It's real late."

Bolie winked, grinned agreement, and continued up the steps. Henry Temple stood at the edge of the roof. The last neon of the late night, flashing on and off, sent sporadic light against the little boy's profile. Bolie hurried over to the boy, knelt by him and grabbed his little shoulders.

"What do you say, Henry Temple?"

"You were a tiger, Bolie. You were a real tiger."

Bolie grinned. "Look okay?"

"Sharp," Henry answered in a serious little voice. "Sharp like a champ. You was Louis and Armstrong and everybody all wrapped up into one."

Bolie laughed, warm, rich laughter that rolled out of him in waves, so filled up was he with the joy of it and the wonder of it. It had been so long, so very long. He pounded a fist into his palm.

"Hey," he said, "you know something? That boy musta hit me so hard he knocked the hurt right outa me." He laughed again, then shook his head with bewilderment. "I don't remember a doggone thing, Henry. I must have really been punchy for a second, because I thought he had me down and there I was with the old ref wavin' his arm down on me. It must have been some kind of dream or somethin'."

A strange look passed fleetingly across Henry's face. The little boy turned away. Bolie followed him.

"Henry," Bolie asked in a different voice. "I was never off my feet. I never got knocked down."

The little boy didn't answer. Bolie grabbed him firmly, turned him around and stared intently into his face.

"Henry!" Bolie gripped him hard. "Henry, I was never off my feet." It was a pronouncement. It was a final judgment designed to end the gnawing disquiet that Bolie had felt deep down since he found himself standing in the wing with his arm raised. He saw the little boy's lips quiver.

Bolie's voice was still. "Henry, was I? Was I lying on my back and on the way out?"

Henry nodded very slowly. Bolie stood up and looked off toward the darkened city.

"But nobody remembers it," he whispered. "Nobody at all. 'Cept me. I thought it happened . . . but it didn't. I thought I was lying there on my back gettin' counted out, but everybody tells me—"

Henry Temple moved very close to the fighter and stared up at him. "Bolie," he said simply, "I made a wish then. I made the *big* wish. I had to. I wished you was never knocked down. I just shut my eyes and I . . . I wished real hard. It was magic, Bolie. We had to have magic then."

Bolie shook his head, his voice whispering, "No, no, no," his eyes closing tight against the words, against the intensity, against the belief of the little boy in front of him.

"Had to, Bolie," Henry said. "*Had* to. Nothing left for us then. Had to make a wish. Had to . . ."

Bolie's head kept going back and forth in disbelief, in rejection, in denial.

The little boy's words kept coming out like a chant. "Had to, Bolie. Had to. Had to."

Then Bolie grabbed the boy. His voice was cold fury, "You crazy kid. You crazy, kookie kid." He shook him. "Don't you know there ain't no magic? There ain't no magic or wishing or nothin' like that. You're too big to have nutsy thoughts like that. You're too big to believe in fairy tales."

Tears rolled down Henry Temple's face. "If you wish hard enough, Bolie," he said, "it'll come true. If you wish hard enough . . ."

Bolie had stood up and moved across the roof. Henry held out his hands to him.

"Bolie, if you wish and then believe. The whole thing is believing because if you believe it'll stay that way."

Bolie stood with his back to the boy and shook his head again. "Somebody got to knock it out of you, don't they? Somebody got to take you by the hair and rub your face in the world and give you a taste and a smell of the way things are, don't they?" He turned toward Henry. "Listen, boy," he said, his voice crusted with misery. "I've been wishing all my life. You understand, Henry? All my life. I got a gut ache from wishing. And all I got to show for it is a faceful of scars and a headful of memories of the hurt and the misery I've had to eat with and sleep with all my miserable life."

His voice broke as he heard the sobbing intake of Henry's breath. "You crazy kid, you," Bolie said, his voice breaking. "Crazy, crazy, kookie kid. You tellin' me you wished me into a knockout? You tellin' me it was magic that got me off my back?" He took a step toward Henry. "Well now you listen, boy. There ain't no magic. No magic, Henry. I had that fight coming and going. I had it in my pocket. I was the number one out there and there ain't no such thing as magic."

"Bolie," the little boy sobbed, "Bolie, if you believe, understand? You've got to believe. If you don't believe, Bolie, it won't be true. That's the way magic works." He took a stumbling run over to the fighter and grabbed him around the waist, burying his face against him. "Bolie, you got to believe. Please, please believe."

"Little kook," Bolie said to the tiny, kinky head. "Little

kook, that's what you are. How come I got mixed up with you? Ain't I got enough trouble without getting mixed up with some dopey kid who—"

He stopped and looked down at the little boy and then he was on his knees and had suddenly swept the boy into his arms, holding him tightly, pressing his cheek against his.

"Henry," he said softly, "I can't believe. I'm too old and I'm too hurt to believe. I can't, boy. I just can't!" He held the little boy's face in both hands and wiped away the tears with his thumbs. "Henry, there ain't no such thing as magic. God help us both, I wish there was."

"Bolie, you *got* to believe."

"I can't."

"You got to, Bolie. You got to believe, or else—"

"I can't."

They stood there close together. Henry's voice, a plaintive, hopeful prayer; the fighter's, a hollow, empty rejection. The sick, thin yellow light from the bulb over the roof door held them briefly in a weak illumination and then time froze again. The light gradually changed until it was no longer on the roof. It was the white-hot orb of the ring light bathing the canvas of the roped-off area of a fight arena where a dark and bleeding fighter lay on his stomach, his face against the canvas and rosin of the ring floor. Above him a referee brought down his arm in measured sweeps.

"Eight, nine, ten."

He swiped his hands out in opposite directions like a baseball umpire judging someone safe, then pointed to the stocky white man in purple trunks, who stood nonchalantly in the neutral corner, waiting for the victory that he knew was his to be made official. The referee came to him, raised his right arm, and he was then engulfed by handlers, his manager, and other people who swarmed in over the ropes.

Mizell walked tiredly to Bolie, who had just risen to his hands and knees like a blind, groping animal. Bolie allowed Mizell to help him to his feet and took the traditional, beaten, stiff-legged walk back to his corner.

He did not hear the crowd nor see the light. He did not hear the voice on the loudspeaker announce, "The winner by a knock-out, one minute, thirteen seconds of the fourth round, Jerry Corrigan."

Another cascade of cheers rippled over the room and the

next thing Bolie knew he was standing on his feet in street clothes with Joe Mizell opening the door for him. He looked down at the misshapen little handler and forced a grin.

"How many of them was there?" he said, with a crooked smile.

"Just the one boy," Mizell answered softly. "Nine years your junior and with *two* good hands." He pointed to Bolie's bandaged right hand. "But I'll tell you something, Bolie," he continued softly. "You took it good. You took it like a man. They're jackals up there," he jerked his head toward the ceiling. "Jackals. They don't know what's what, but I know. You showed them the kind of guts they don't get too often. I'm proud of you, old timer. I really am."

He patted Bolie on the back and held the door open a little wider. Bolie walked slowly out of the room and then down the corridor toward the exit.

He walked through the still stifling heat along the sidewalk heading toward his brownstone. Just three people sat on the steps. The scrawny little old man looked up at him through slitted eyes then spat through the railing.

"You should have stood in bed," he announced coldly. "Why the hell didn't you use your right hand?"

The other two people just looked away. Bolie looked briefly at his swollen, bandaged right hand, then walked up the steps and inside. He knocked at Frances's door and heard her footsteps approaching from inside. She opened the door a few inches then, seeing Bolie, swung it open completely to let him enter.

"He's in bed," she said quietly. "That's a sad little boy in there."

"Can I see him?" Bolie asked.

"Sure. I expect he's waiting for you."

Bolie went to the bedroom door.

"Bolie?"

He stopped at the door and turned to her.

"I'm real sorry," Frances said.

Bolie smiled, nodded.

Henry lay in bed, his eyes wide open, staring up at the ceiling. He half rose as Bolie came in. Bolie stopped halfway to the bed, suddenly, inexplicably, ill at ease. He cleared his throat.

"Pulled a rock, Henry," he said, grinning. "Threw a punch

before I should have. Hit the wall. Busted my knuckles. I went in with half my artillery gone."

The little boy smiled at him through the darkness and held out his hand. Bolie went to the bed, took Henry's hand and held it.

"You looked like a tiger, even so," Henry said. "You looked like a real tiger. I was proud of you. I was real proud."

Bolie leaned over and kissed the boy on the cheek, then stood up and started toward the door.

"Bolie?" Henry's voice was heavy with sleep.

"You go to sleep, Henry Temple. Tomorrow we'll go to the baseball game. We'll get some hot dogs in the park, you and me."

"Sure thing, Bolie. That'll be nice." Then he called softly, "Bolie."

"What, boy?"

"I ain't gonna make no more wishes," Henry said. "I'm too old for wishes. There ain't no such thing as magic, is there?"

Outside the neon lights blinked on and off and distant traffic was a light hum. Bolie thought for a while and then said gently, "I guess not, Henry. Or maybe . . . maybe there *is* magic. Maybe there's wishes, too. I guess the trouble is . . . I guess the trouble is, there's not enough people around to believe." He looked at the tiny huddled figure on the bed. "Good night, boy."

"Good night, Bolie," Henry's voice was a barely discernible whisper as the gates of sleep closed him off.

Bolie said good night to Frances and went up to his room. He thought about what he would have to do next. There would be no more fighting, no more comeback. Fifteen years of his life had been bound up in fight arenas, irretrievable years that could supply him nothing in the future but memories. He was tired and his hand hurt and there was an ache to his body like all the other aches he collected. And he was much too tired to think any further.

Mr. Bolie Jackson, a hundred and sixty-three pounds, had on that night left a second chance lying in a heap on a rosin-spattered canvas at St. Nick's. And Mr. Bolie Jackson shared the common ailment of all men . . . the strange and perverse disinclination to believe in a miracle. He went into his room and lay down on the bed and closed his eyes and let the pain drain from him. Tomorrow the sun would come up and it would be morning. He had plans to make . . . but they would have to wait until morning.

A STOP AT WILLOUGHBY

Mr. Oliver Misrell sat at the end of the conference table, his piggish eyes half-buried in his fat, jowly face, blinking like a shaven owl. He looked dourly past the eight men who sat four on each side of the table until his gaze stopped and focused on the tall, thin man at the opposite end, his chair pulled away so that he half-faced the big double doors.

This was Gart Williams who was suffering from a stifling heat brought on by his own fears. They'd been there almost two hours and Jake Ross, the young man they were waiting for, had sent no message explaining his delay. Williams stared at the double doors, poised and tense, imagining footsteps, playing secret mental games with himself. He would wait five more minutes, or he would count to two hundred, or he would wind his watch—each time setting the deadline for some comment he would make, or some resolve he would announce. But when the deadline came and went he could do no more than sit staring at the doors.

The other men in the room felt his discomfort and knew what was happening. Jake Ross was Gart Williams's personal recommendation to take over a major automobile account. This meeting had been called to discuss its advertising campaign. Mr. Misrell, head of the firm, had been violently opposed to Ross, but had agreed to Williams's recommendation with a grudging "it's your funeral" kind of acquiescence.

The account execs were secretly reveling in their roles as dispassionate onlookers, while Mr. Misrell's looks spelled out precisely the guilt of the single party whose brand of vulnerability shone on his pale, perspiring face. For Gart Williams was a frightened man. The thought came to him that this was like a funeral. He was the corpse and the other men were mourners who were waiting impatiently for him to assume the position.

Gart Williams hated his job, hated ad agencies and hated Mr. Misrell. It was an extension of the utter dislike he felt for himself and for the things he had to do for his twenty thousand a year. He glanced at Mr. Misrell with revulsion. How deep a man could dive, to seek that small nugget of security that sometimes could be found only several fathoms below a man's self-respect.

He'd been with the agency for fifteen years and each day it had become easier to say "sir" to Mr. Misrell, to laugh at his jokes, to deferentially praise him and to deny to himself that this man was a walking, belching symbol of the twentieth-century huckster. That's what they all were in a sense, Williams knew this. They wore expensive silk suits, but they were carnival men. They had deftly draped themselves with the trappings of respectability, but they were barkers and pitchmen.

They could, Gart reflected, dress up their jobs with the terminology of Madison Avenue—"statistics"; "interviews in depth"; "research"; and all the rest of the pseudo-scientific jargon. They could house it all in sumptuous offices like this one, but down deep and close to the nerve of it was the ugly truth of their whole function.

They were con men as crooked and devious as any nineteenth-century snake oil vendor. Fragments of all this crossed Gart Williams's mind as he stared at the door, listened to the creak of chairs as men fidgeted around him, and felt the glare of Mr. Misrell's coldly accusing eyes. While somewhere outside, in the early Manhattan winter, catastrophe, like a dark and billowing cloud, was forming. Williams rose from his seat, palms perspiring. He wet his lips and, for want of something else to do, picked up the telephone for the fourth time in half an hour.

"I want Jake Ross's secretary," he said into the phone.

"Williams," Misrell said softly, "we're still waiting for your Mr. Ross."

Williams threw a brief, sick smile over his shoulder and said, "I'm trying to get him now, sir."

A girl answered the phone.

"Is this Jake Ross's secretary?" Williams said, trying to keep the tremor out of his voice. "Is this Joannie? *Joannie, where is he?* . . . I know he's out to lunch, but there was a conference called here at one-thirty. It's twenty-five minutes to four. Now where the hell is he?" He forced his voice down an octave. "All right, Joannie. Check around. Call Sardi's East, or The Colony, and tell him to get his kiester back here in a hurry!"

He slammed down the receiver and kept his back to the men until he could fix his face into a smiling nonchalant mask.

Misrell's fat fingers drummed on the table top. "Well, Williams? Where's your protégé with the three-million-dollar automobile account?"

The perspiration was now rolling in rivulets down Williams's back. "He's due at any moment, sir. Probably a big lunch crowd or something—"

"Don't be an idiot," Misrell's graveled voice interrupted him. "More likely a big martini, or three or four of 'em." He leaned over the table, his big paunch folding and unfolding in front of him, picked up a pencil and pointed it at Williams. "He is too young to put on this account. I told you that, Williams. I kept telling you that. He is much too young to put on so large and important an account!"

There was a knock. Williams bolted out of his seat as the double doors opened and a young woman entered carrying an envelope. He literally yanked it out of her hand and ignored her stricken expression as she backed out. He kicked the door shut and ripped open the envelope.

The men watched him carefully, seeing him turn white. Misrell's piggish little eyes narrowed. The flappy "O" of his mouth remained open and poised like some kind of man-eating plant ready to pounce on a victim. Gart Williams crumpled the note in his hand.

"Well?" Misrell's voice grated against the silence. "We have now been here a little over two hours, Mr. Williams."

Williams nodded, not looking up, then he took a deep breath. "This is a communication from Jake Ross."

Misrell looked around with a half-smile. "Would you be so kind as to share its contents with us?" he invited and commanded at the same time.

Williams took another deep breath. He was at the precipice and he knew there was no sense in delaying the jump any longer. He threw the crumpled paper on the table, squared his shoulders and said quietly, "I can give you the sense of it very quickly, Mr. Misrell. This is Ross's resignation. He's moving over to another agency."

There was an intake of breath all over the room. Each man sat transfixed. Only Misrell moved slightly. His jowls twitched and again his fingers began to drum.

"And?" Misrell asked.

Williams's voice was almost a whisper. "And he's taking the automobile account with him."

Again the intake of breath. Again the frozen suspension of each man at his place. This was the catastrophe that had been building up through the afternoon like a hurricane off shore, ready to move in with crushing destructive force.

A billing like this represented a quarter of an agency's take during a given year. Its loss was a back-breaking, irreparable wound to an organization and each man in the room knew it. They kept their eyes averted, but listened to the squeak of Misrell's chair as the president ponderously rose. They heard the flats of his hands slam down on the table top. They heard his short, wheezing breath and then his voice, icy and outraged.

"That account represented a gross billing of something in the neighborhood of three million dollars a year."

Nausea rose up in Gart Williams. He had to hold on to the table. "This is as much a shock to me as it is to you, Mr. Misrell."

"Is that an honest-to-God fact?" roared Misrell. "It's as much a shock to you as it is to me, huh? You stupid bastard— don't con me! It was your pet project! *Your pet project.*" The fat man's face quivered and rolled and undulated. His eyes blazed as he fed rage into himself and roared like a furnace.

"It was your idea to give it to that little college greeny," he shouted. "Now get with it, Williams! Get with it, boy." He kicked his chair aside and screwed up his face like a little baby about to cry. He pointed a finger at Williams. "So what's left, Williams? Not only has your pet project backfired, but it's sprouted wings and left the premises." Grandly, emotionally, and with great theatricality, he spread his fat hands. "I'll tell you what's left to us, in my view. Nothing but a deep and abiding concern about your judgment in men."

The various executives sat with their heads down, in the vast embarrassment that permeated the room. Williams continued to gaze at the table, wondering how long it would last. He felt like a man in a rack, the screws being turned tighter and tighter, the pain going higher and higher, thinking all the while it couldn't get worse, while all the time it did get worse.

Misrell pounded the flats of his hands on the table again. "This is a push business, Williams," he said.

(God, how many times Williams had heard him use that phrase.)

"Push, push, push business! Push and drive! But *personally* push and drive! You don't delegate responsibility to little boys, Williams!" he screamed, making Williams look up to face the punishment. "You should know better than anyone else."

A thought crossed Gart Williams's mind. Misrell was enjoying this. He was taking pleasure in it. It was a twisted, perverse, ugly enjoyment, but enjoyment it was, and something deep inside the thin, sick man revolted in disgust. He stared, fascinated, at the big mouth that jabbered at him and screamed and wiggled and twisted and spewed out phrases that were so repetitious, so familiar and so impossible to listen to again.

"It's a push, push, push business, Williams," the fat mouth railed at him. "It's a push, push, push business all the way, all the time, right on down the line—"

Williams knew the words were coming up. He didn't think he would let them out, but they came out. Like screaming shrapnel, they exploded into the room and smashed against the walls.

"Why don't you shut your mouth, fat boy?"

The executives stared at Williams, openmouthed, aghast. Misrell's jaw hung down in almost comic fashion as he gaped at the insane man at the other end of the table.

There was no retreat for Williams now. There was no evading, no covering up. "Why don't you shut your mouth, fat boy?" It had been said. The outrage had been committed. It was now a matter of record and could not be obliterated. Gart Williams knew all this. So he leaned forward in his chair and pointed a finger at Oliver Misrell.

"God, but I can't stand the sight of you," he said. "You're about as palatable as a Crisco sandwich. In addition, you're the most predatory, thoughtless, unfeeling animal of a man I've ever met, let alone worked for." He looked around the table, his face white and glistening with sweat. "God, how do you stand it, all of you? How *do* you?"

Again the wave of nausea rose up in him. He lowered his head, spent a moment recovering. Then he took a deep breath and walked out of the room. Sick and frightened, he still could find a tiny fragment of perverse pleasure at the problem in conversation he had left behind. Who says what and how do they start? Perhaps that fat bastard would have a coronary and there would be no need for conversation.

In his own office, his secretary smiled up at him.

"Messages on the desk," the attractive girl said, "and hot coffee out here. Can I bring you some?" Her smile faded as she saw the look on Gart's face. "Do you want anything at all?" she asked in a whisper.

Williams leaned against the door and shut his eyes. "Yeah. A sharp razor and a chart of the human anatomy showing where all the arteries are!"

He went into his office and closed the door behind him. He flicked off the fluorescent lighting, and sat down at his desk in the semidarkness. On the desk was a picture of the beautiful woman who was Jane, his wife. And she was beautiful. Beautiful and cold as a glacier.

He put two fingers to his eyes and closed them. He knew what he was. He was a forty-one-year-old man, protected by a suit of armor all held together by one bolt. A moment ago the bolt had been removed and his protection had fallen away from him and left him a naked target.

He had been cannonaded this afternoon by all the enemies of his life. His insecurity had shelled him; his oversensitivity had straddled him with humiliation; his deep-rooted disquiet about his own worth had zeroed in on him, landed on target and blown him apart. He had the ridiculous feeling that he must suddenly burst into tears and it was only with effort that he kept himself from doing so.

After a while he began to hear the whisperings from outside. Secretaries' voices, the buzzing of interoffice phones. He smiled slightly to himself. The news was getting around. "Did you hear what Williams said to the old man in the conference room? . . . *Did you hear? . . .*"

He got his topcoat from the closet, told his secretary that he was going home for the day and went down in the elevator, leaving the shambles behind him.

The New Haven Railroad ran northeast from New York, close to the coast, stopping every twenty-odd minutes to unload tired-eyed men in wrinkled suits. It was on the stretch between Stamford and Westport, where Gart lived, that the conductor paused to take his seat tab and then lingered, smiling.

"How are you tonight, Mr. Williams?"

Williams, aware that his face was gray, nodded. "In the absolute pink."

"Cold winter this year," the conductor said conversationally. "It seems to get dark earlier than it ever has."

"That's the way of the world," Williams answered. "The rich get richer and the days get shorter."

He vaguely heard the conductor chuckle as he moved down the car, then closed his eyes and leaned back in the uncomfortable seat. Over and over inside his mind he played the scene that had occurred that afternoon. Misrell's voice kept pushing around deep inside his mind. "It's a push, push, push business," the voice said as it tore into him. "It's an absolutely push, push, push business. You've got to stick with it, boy. You absolutely have to stick with it. It's a push, push, push business. It's a push, push, push business."

Over and over the raspy, grating voice tore at his nerve endings until finally he opened his eyes and shouted out into the car, *"That's enough!"*

A surprised and frightened woman turned around to gape at him from the seat in front. Williams looked away, pretending not to notice her, and watched the bare, lifeless trees shoot by the window, the patches of dirty, early snow, the dull gray-black of rolling hillocks, stripped of color. It was a naked winter twilight that stared back at him. After a while the humming clickety-click of the train softened and then blunted Williams's consciousness and he fell asleep.

He didn't know how long he dozed, but he was awakened by

the noise of the train coming to a stop. A voice called out, "Willoughby! This is Willoughby."

Williams opened his eyes, rubbed the sleep out of them, and looked out the window. He stared, first with incredulous amazement and then with fear, because outside was a summer afternoon.

The train had stopped at a small station with a sign that read, "Willoughby." On the platform of the station were women with parasols and long dresses. Boys in knickers ran back and forth. One carried a fishing pole. Beyond the station was a small village square with a bandstand. Williams could hear the strains of the Sousa music, happily discordant and marvelously reminiscent. The whole scene was bathed in a hot summer sun. Williams tried to digest it, knowing it was a dream, but confused by the absolute reality.

Then he became aware of the railroad car he was sitting in. It was no longer the ugly chrome and green plastic of the car he'd entered in Grand Central Station. It was now the ornate nineteenth-century wood and velvet of trains he'd seen only in pictures or in Western movies on television. Gas lamps hung from the ceiling and soon a little, white-haired conductor appeared at the opposite end of the car dressed in a tight, brass-buttoned suit with an old-fashioned trainman's cap. He sauntered slowly down the car, smiled at Williams and winked at him.

"This stop is Willoughby," he announced again.

He started to walk past Williams, who grabbed him.

"What do you mean Willoughby? What's Willoughby?"

The conductor smiled and nodded toward the window, "That's Willoughby, sir. Right outside."

"Wait a minute," Williams said, his voice tight and unbelieving. "Wait just a minute. What's going on? There's no place called Willoughby on this line. And look at it outside. The sun is out. It's . . . it's summer."

The conductor smiled and winked. "That's what she is, mid-July and a real warm one, too."

"But listen," Williams said, "it's November. What's going on, anyway?" Williams shut his eyes tightly, then opened them again. "It's November," he repeated. "What is this place? Where are we? What's happened?"

The conductor gently removed Gart's hand from his sleeve.

"Please," Williams said, lowering his voice, "please, what's going on? *Where is Willoughby?*"

"Willoughby, sir," the conductor answered. "That's Willoughby right outside. Willoughby. July. Summer. It's 1880. It's a lovely little village." His smile faded and something intense crept into his voice. "You ought to try it sometime. Peaceful, restful, where a man can slow down to a walk and live his life full measure."

He walked down the car toward the opposite entrance. "Willoughby," he announced as he walked. "This stop is Willoughby."

Williams bolted from his seat. He raced down the car to the door that the conductor had closed behind him and out onto the train platform. The next car was completely empty. The conductor had disappeared. Williams stopped, his face twisted with pain and bewilderment. His mouth opened to protest or question or plead for someone to give him understanding.

The train lurched, throwing him against the side of the car. He grabbed at the door for support. In that brief moment it had become dark outside and the train car that he walked through, going back to his seat, was once again full of fluorescent lights, reclining seats and ashtrays, with a sprinkling of tired-faced commuters. Williams sat down and gave a quick look out the window at the winter landscape.

"Westport-Saugatuck, next stop," a man's voice said.

Williams looked up to see the conductor he was familiar with.

"Have a good sleep, Mr. Williams?" he asked.

"Yeah," Williams said. "I had a good sleep. A good sleep with an idiotic dream. Idiotic . . . At least . . . at least I guess it's idiotic." He looked up at the conductor. "Ever hear of a town named Willoughby?"

The conductor screwed up his face thoughtfully. "Willoughby? Willoughby where?"

"Willoughby, Connecticut, I guess, or Willoughby, New York."

The conductor shook his head. "No, not on this run. There's no Willoughby on the line. No town named Willoughby."

"You sure?"

"No Willoughby that I've ever heard of." He continued

down the aisle. "Westport-Saugatuck, next stop. Westport-Saugatuck."

Gart Williams picked up his briefcase and, very slowly, questions pressing down on him, he walked to the end of the car and out into the winter night.

Gart stood at the bar in the ornate den adjoining the living room of his ranch-house home. He sipped slowly on a long bourbon, relishing the heat of it and the soothingness. It was dulling some of the sharp and ugly recollections of the afternoon and making even more dream-like his experience on the train.

He'd been on the phone to the office and received a complete report on everything that went on after he left. Misrell, it seemed, had shut himself up in his office, incommunicado, for at least two hours after the scene. Then, however, he had sent a memo to Gart's secretary, announcing yet another meeting for the following day. So, it seemed, the wound had been deep and tearing, but not fatal.

His wife, Jane, came in. She was a striking blonde, with small, perfect features, large, wonderfully deep brown eyes. But her face was without laughter. He had discovered this twenty-four hours after their marriage ten years ago. This was a woman of plans and campaigns, but of little emotion. Life to her was something to be mapped out, not simply lived. She surveyed him analytically as she crossed the room and sat down facing the bar.

"And what are your plans this evening?" she inquired. "To get quietly plastered and then sing old college songs?"

Williams's smile was wan. "It's been one of those days—"

"I know all about it," she interrupted him. "Bob Blair's wife called me. Said he'd been in the meeting with you. You got—you got hysterical or something. She called to find out how you were."

"They were all very solicitous," Williams said wryly. "All the boys at the meeting." He jiggled the ice in his glass. "That free-flowing compassion which is actually relief because I'm the victim—not they! They've mistaken an intake of breath for an outpouring of sympathy!"

He started to pour himself another drink, but his wife's voice stopped him. It cut across the room like a lance.

"Would you spare me your little homilies now," she said, "and just give me a simple, frank, and honest answer? Did you wreck a career this afternoon? Did you throw away a job?"

Williams grinned again. "It appears not. Mr. Misrell sent a message to my secretary after I left the office. He has found it in that giant, oversized heart of his to forgive. This somewhat obese but gracious gentleman will allow me to continue in his employ simply because he's such a human-type fellah." He grinned knowingly into his glass. "With a small, insignificant, parenthetical, additional reason that if I were to go to a competitive agency, I might possibly take a lot of business with me!"

"Go on," Jane ordered.

Williams shrugged. "That's it. That's all of it." He carried his drink across the room and sat down in a chair next to her. "I'm tired, Janie. I'm tired and I'm sick."

Jane got up and walked away. "Then you're in the right ward. We specialize in people who are sick and tired, Gart. I'm sick and tired of a husband who lives in a kind of permanent self-pity! A husband with a heart-bleeding sensitivity he unfurls like a flag whenever he decides that the competition is too rough for him."

Williams's head shot up. He was surprised, even after ten years, that so much coldness could come out in language; that so much utter distaste and dislike could be unmasked by a few sentences.

"Some people aren't built for competition, Janie," he said. He rose and carried his glass across the room to stand near her. "Or big pretentious houses that they can't afford. Or rich communities they don't feel comfortable in. Or country clubs that they wear around their necks like a badge of status—"

"And what would you prefer?" Jane shouted at him.

His control snapped and he shouted back at her. "I would prefer, though never asked before, a job! Any job . . . any job at all where I could be myself! Where I wouldn't have to climb on a stage and go through a masquerade each morning at nine and mouth all the dialogue and play the executive and make believe I'm a bright young man on his way up." The glass shook in his hand and he put it down on an end table. "Janie . . . I'm not that person," he said, his voice quieter. "You tried to *make* me that person, but that isn't me. That isn't me at all. I'm . . . I'm a not very young, soon to be old, very uncompetitive, rather dull, quite uninspired, average-type guy." His mouth twisted. "With a wife who has an appetite."

"And where would you be if it weren't for my appetite?"

Williams sat down on the steps that led to the living room. "I know where I'd like to be," he said.

"And where would that be?" Jane challenged him, her voice brittle and shrill.

"A place called Willoughby," Gart said. "A little town that I charted inside my head. A place I manufactured in a dream." His voice was low and reflective and he spoke almost as if to himself. "An odd dream. A very odd dream. Willoughby. It was summer. Very warm. The kids were barefooted. One of them carried a fishing pole. And the main street looked like . . . like a Currier and Ives illustration. Bandstand, old-fashioned stores, bicycles, wagons." He looked toward his wife. "I've never seen such a . . . such a serenity. It was the way people must have lived a hundred years ago." He looked down toward the floor again. "Crazy dream."

Jane walked across the room to stand over him. The perfect face was lined with impatience and frustration; she had a deep-rooted and abiding lack of respect for this man, in addition to a sense of impotence. Her campaign, so perfectly planned, timed, and executed was turning into a miserable failure.

"My mistake, pal," she said. "My error. My wretched, tragic error to get married to a man whose big dream in life is to be Huckleberry Finn!" She walked away.

"Janie," Gart called after her.

She stopped at the door, her back to him.

"Janie." His voice was yearning. "You should have seen this place. This . . . this Willoughby. It wasn't just a place or a time. It was like—it was like a doorway that leads to sanity. A sound-proof world where shouts and cries can't be heard."

She whirled around. Her words were thin, feminine daggers, jewel-encrusted and poison-tipped. "Nothing serious, Gart," she said. "It's just that you were born too late. That's the problem. You were born too late, and your taste is a little cheap. You're the kind of man who could be satisfied with a summer afternoon and an ice wagon pulled by a horse. That's all it takes for you, isn't it?"

"Something like that," he answered her. "A place . . . a time . . . where a man can live his life full measure." He frowned thoughtfully. "That's what *he* said. That's what that . . . that conductor said. A place where a man can live his life full measure!"

He picked up his glass again and drained it, unaware that he was now alone in the room, conscious only of a persistent little memory of a warm summer afternoon that was simply part of a fabric of a dream. A summer afternoon and a small town with a village square and a bandstand and people in old-fashioned dress. In his whole life, he thought, his whole forty-one years, he had never felt such a stirring deep inside, such a hunger to see a place again, such a yearning to recapture a moment that had slipped by too fast. Much too fast.

"Willoughby?" the conductor asked.

Gart Williams, half-dozing in his seat, sat bolt upright, his eyes wide and gaping. Then he saw the conductor smiling down at him. "What?"

"A while back you asked me about a town called Willoughby," the conductor said. He scratched his jaw. "I looked it up in every old timetable I could find. No such place as far as I could see."

Williams relaxed against the back of his seat. "Thanks. It was a dream, that's all."

The conductor continued on down the car. "Probably was." And then shouting out to the half-empty car, "Stamford next stop. Next stop Stamford!"

Williams put his head back and sighed deeply. Outside he could see nothing but an occasional gust of snow, the rest blackness. He could hear the conductor's voice far off shouting "Stamford. Next stop Stamford." He closed his eyes, felt the tiredness, the weakness, the resignation of the past few weeks. Almost a month had passed since the affair in the conference room, Jake Ross's departure, and his own detonation. But nothing had changed really. He had gone back into a mold, acting and reacting much as he always had. Misrell had not changed. The company had not changed. The jingles and the overnight ratings and the product-pushing—they were as constant as weather.

"Stamford," the conductor's voice called out, faintly now, and Williams leaned his head against the cold window, wishing in a portion of his mind that it was a longer trip; that he could sit there for a parcel of hours and sleep deep and undisturbed. He didn't want to get home. He didn't want to see Jane. He would never put this feeling into words, but he felt it and he knew he felt it.

"Willoughby," a voice said, "next stop, Willoughby."

Gart Williams opened his eyes and felt the train pull slowly to a stop. The car seemed suddenly very warm and light played on his face. He stared out the window and there it was, the little station with the village behind it, the town square, the women in long dresses, carrying parasols. The men in tight pants and derbies. A teenager rode by on a bicycle with a huge front wheel and a tiny rear one. The musicians on the bandstand had paused for a break and were laughing and talking with the townspeople as they walked by. A bed of flowers went halfway around the square and added reds and whites and blues to the deep green of the lawn. An organ-grinder with a uniformed monkey came toward the train, followed by a troop of laughing kids. And there were two boys with fishing poles, barefoot like Tom Sawyer and Huck.

And then Williams realized that once again he stood in the middle of an old-fashioned train car and, approaching him from the opposite end, was the old conductor with the brass buttons and the old-fashioned cap.

"Willoughby," the conductor smiled at him. "All out for Willoughby."

Williams stood transfixed, torn between reluctance and a strange resolve. He made a move as if to run, then was thrown off balance by the jerk of the train as it started. He walked, lurching, to the platform at the end of the car.

The train was moving and the town was being left behind. Williams stood poised on the steps, fighting a battle whose rules and terms he didn't understand. But after a moment it was too late. The decision had been made for him. The little station faded into the distance and it was night again, a night filled with snow; a railroad car filled with people in topcoats, carrying briefcases and waiting for Westport and points beyond.

He went back to his seat and sat down. He looked at his reflection in the window. He saw the pouched eyes, set deep in the tired face. He saw the age that was somehow deeper than years. He saw a Gart Williams who was like a small boy in a marbles trade. Only in his case, he had given away his freedom, his prerogatives and his self-reliance in exchange for a menu-planned life and a paycheck, and he'd been taken!

"Willoughby," he said softly to himself. "Next time . . . next time I'm going to get off!"

His face was grim and determined. *"I'm going to get off at Willoughby!"*

It was a January full of cold and dirty slush and a running battle each evening with Jane at home. And a running battle with everyone at the office. He sat at his desk talking on the phone with Oliver Misrell and the harsh voice of the fat man grated out of the receiver.

"What we need here, Williams," the voice said, "is a show with *zazz*! An entertainer with moxie! We've got to take the audience by the ears and give 'em a yank! Jar 'em! Rock 'em! Give them the old push, push, push!"

"I understand, Mr. Misrell," Williams said into the phone, closing his eyes. He felt the pain in his stomach again and reached inside his shirt to massage the taut flesh.

"It's got to be bright, though, Williams," the voice persisted. "Bright with patter. Dancing, comedy, and everything push, push, push. That's the kind of show the client'll like."

"I understand, Mr. Misrell. I understand—"

"Tomorrow morning, Williams! Understand? I want at least a preliminary idea for the show. You know what I want—a rough format with some specifics as to how we integrate commercials within the body of the show."

"I'll do what I can," Williams said.

"Do *more* than you can. With me, Williams? Aspire! Dream big and then get behind it. Push, push, push."

Williams moved the phone away from him, listening to the "push, push, push" as it barked at him. He slowly hung the receiver up, feeling weak and inundated by pain. The phone rang again. This time a filtered voice blabbed at him at first unintelligibly, then with an urgent clarity.

"Well, I haven't seen the ratings," Williams tried to interject. "No. No, well it was the time slot the sponsor wanted—"

Another phone rang. "Hold on for just a second, will you?" he said into the first phone. He pushed the button and talked on the other line. "Yes? They were what? Wait a second." He called out toward the half-open door, "Helen?"

His secretary appeared.

"What film outfit did the commercials on the Bradbury account?" he asked her. "The negatives were all scratched. They're screaming bloody murder at me."

"I'll have to check it, sir," his secretary said. "Mr. Misrell would like to see you."

The voice on the phone came out loud and strident. Williams uncovered the mouthpiece. "I'm going to have to check it out for you here—" he began.

"Mr. Misrell, sir." His secretary showed alarm.

The voice continued its drumfire at the other end of the phone.

"Mr. Williams," his secretary said. "Mr. Misrell seemed rather insistent—"

Williams sat there with his pain, and with the demands continuing to probe at him—the voice jabbering on the phone, his worried secretary, and the two lights on the little panel near the phone giving promise of crises yet unfaced. Once again the secretary tried to get through to him.

"Mr. Misrell, sir," she said.

Williams slowly rose and like an automaton went into the small private bathroom adjoining the office. He looked at himself in the mirror and was shocked. The dead white of the skin, the haunted look in the eyes. Behind him he could still hear the jabbering of the phone, and the buzzing of the intercom. In the mirror suddenly appeared Misrell's face, the fleshy jowls, piggish eyes and the lips that moved up and down, up and down.

"It's a push, push, push business," the fat face said to him. "Push, push, Williams. Push, push, push. Always push, push, push. Constantly push, push, push."

Gart Williams sent his right fist smashing into the mirror, breaking it into a hundred pieces and obliterating the mirage his mind had planted there. He had taken all he could. He had talked on the phone for the last time. He had plugged up, sifted, juxtaposed, switched around, endured all the crises he could stand, and felt all the cold fear he would ever be able to feel.

"No more," he said, his face gray, his mouth twitching. "No more in the name of God . . . no more!"

He went back to his office, leaned against the wall for a moment, then picked up the phone and dialed.

"I'd like Westport, Connecticut, please," he said. "Capital 7–9899. Yes, please." In a moment he heard the voice of his wife. "Janie," he said, "this is Gart, honey. Stay there, will you please?

I just want you to stay there. I'm coming home." He barely heard the cold, argumentative logic that was thrust back at him over the wire. "Janie . . . Janie, please listen."

He began to shout. "Janie! I've had it. Understand? I've had it. I can't go on for another day. I can't go on for another hour. This is it, right now. I've got to get out of here." There was a pause. "Janie?" He felt tears rolling down his face. "Janie, help me, will you? Please . . . please help me. Janie?" There was a silence at the other end. "Janie?"

He clicked the receiver a few times and listened to what he knew was a dead line. Then he slowly replaced the phone and massaged his stomach as he stared at the picture of his wife on the desk. The cold, alabaster beauty of the woman. The perfection that had no warmth whatsoever. He put on his overcoat and headed out of the office. The pain deep inside was clutching, pulling, biting at him. He didn't bother to tell his secretary where he was going and when she saw his face, she didn't ask.

He took a cab to Grand Central, and waited forty minutes for the train to Westport. There would be a scene with Jane, but he had to suffer this. He could handle it best by silence. She would scream at him, but he'd take a drink and go to bed. . . .

The conductor grinned at him as he went down the aisle collecting tickets. "You're going home early tonight, huh, Mr. Williams?"

Williams nodded, then closed his eyes tiredly.

"Feelin' okay?" the conductor asked.

"Yeah," Williams said. "Feeling fine."

The conductor announced, "Stamford, next stop. Stamford," as he disappeared into the other car. Williams pulled down the window shade, let the seat recline a notch and closed his eyes again. "Stamford, next stop." The voice was growing faint and indistinct. "Stamford." And then another voice fused with it.

"Willoughby," the other voice said. "Willoughby, next stop."

Williams felt a warmth on his face as if the sun were trying to get through to him. He released the blind and guided it slowly up toward the top of the window. There was the town outside. There was the summer afternoon. The band, the children, the laughing men and women, the organ-grinder, the village square, the whole thing. It lay there like a beautiful tableau.

"Willoughby," the old conductor said, coming into the car.

Williams jumped to his feet. "Willoughby?" he asked excitedly.

"That's right," the conductor said.

"Then that's where I get off. Willoughby. That's my station."

"Yes, sir. That's your station. Willoughby."

Williams walked through the old wood and velvet car to the platform and down the steps to the summer afternoon that waited for him outside.

"Hi, Mr. Williams," a boy said, carrying a fishing pole.

"Hi, Mr. Williams," another freckle-faced kid called, as he rode past on a bicycle.

Williams looked from one to the other. "Hi, boys," he said. "Catch some big ones today, huh? I think tomorrow I may join you."

The first boy laughed. "Plenty of room and lots of fish." He continued on, waving as he went.

A man on a wagon waved. "Hi, Mr. Williams. Welcome."

"Thank you," Gart answered. "Thank you. I'm . . . I'm glad to be here."

He headed toward the bandstand and the village square. People greeted him and welcomed him. The organ-grinder wiggled a finger at him and made the monkey bow and take off his cap. Williams laughed, feeling a repose, a peace, a serenity he could never remember before. He paused in front of a store window and looked at the huge grandfather clock that was on display. Its pendulum went back and forth and the clock was like everything else around him. It was solid and had meaning and a function and it was unhurried, and steady. Williams slowly loosened his tie and felt good about everything. The pendulum continued to swing back and forth, back and forth.

The trainman's lamp swung back and forth in an orange arc, casting light and shadow on the snow underfoot and illuminating the overcoated body of Gart Williams who lay face up, snow on his rumpled clothes, on lips, eyebrows, and hair. A sheriff's deputy motioned with his lantern for the ambulance to pull up closer.

"Just jumped off the train, did he?" the trainman asked.

The conductor nodded. "Shouted something about Willoughby, ran out to the platform and that's the last I seen him."

He looked questioningly at the deputy. "Died instantly did he? That what I heard you say?"

The deputy nodded. The ambulance backed slowly through the snow toward where Gart Williams's body was being placed on a stretcher. "It appears so," the deputy said. "We'll take him into town for an autopsy. Funeral parlor there sent the ambulance."

"Poor fellah," the trainman clucked. "Poor, poor fellah."

The ambulance stopped, its rear doors wide open. Four men carefully lifted Gart Williams's body and put it into the rear of the ornately scrolled black vehicle. The driver gunned the engine very slowly and moved the ambulance gingerly through the snow toward the highway. The trainman's lantern briefly illuminated the lettering on the rear doors.

"Willoughby and Son, Funeral Home" the lettering read. And then the ambulance disappeared into the night and, for a brief moment, its headlights could be seen probing the snow-filled darkness, as it reached the highway and turned toward town. The train started up again. Twenty-one minutes behind schedule, it headed toward Westport, Connecticut, its next stop.

Mr. Gart Williams had climbed on a world that went by too fast and then had reached out trying to grasp at a respite from torment. In a sense he had merely jumped off this world. He did not feel the snow melting over his dead flesh as the ambulance sped through the night. Quite the contrary, the sun was very warm in the little village and he'd taken off his coat and tie. He was with a group of boys heading toward a stream where the trout were and he was laughing because it was summer and there was peace. And this was a place where a man could live his life full measure. This was Willoughby.

THE ODYSSEY OF FLIGHT 33

They don't talk about the flight much anymore—at least the pros don't. On occasion a vastly theoretical article will appear in a Sunday supplement or mention will be made in a book on air disasters but, by and large, the world's day-to-day catastrophes are sufficient in scope and number to take even the loss of a giant airliner off the agenda.

But with the pros it's different. It isn't that other flight talk takes precedence. It's simply that Flight 33, and what did or didn't happen to it, carries a chill. Even now, just eleven months later, you never hear it mentioned in the Ops Rooms, where the pilots chain-smoke and watch the weather reports, nor in the control towers, when the tense and tired men who talk the planes down get a respite for a quick cup of coffee and a smoke.

There are other cases of disappearing aircraft on record, of course. There was Amelia Earhart, who took off from New Guinea for the mid-Pacific island of Howland, and was never heard from again. There was the less well-known, but equally tragic case of the two U.S. Navy AD6 Sky Raiders, on a flight for Fallon, Nevada, who neither arrived nor left a clue as to what happened to them. There was the mysterious case of the two British airliners, the Star Ariel and a sister ship the Star Tiger. Tiger vanished over that sea of weeds called Sargasso which lies in the Atlantic off the Bahamas. Thirteen days later Ariel followed her into oblivion. No trace of either plane was ever found.

But Flight 33 was different. It was a jet airliner. Beautiful, graceful, full of incredible power, as safe as any plane could be. And it simply had no business disappearing. It was too fine an aircraft. And whatever yanked it out of the skies was a power that couldn't be reckoned with on a design board or in an engineer's manual. That's why you rarely hear of it where pilots and crews congregate.

Call it superstition, vestiges of black magic. Call it that strange and unspoken mysticism that somehow, incongruously, is to be found among the highly scientific body of men who fight gravity for a living. But whatever you call it, don't ever ask a captain, a first officer or any crew member to talk about the Trans-Ocean flight that disappeared between London and New York on a quiet, otherwise uneventful June afternoon. They'll pretend they didn't hear you.

Trans-Ocean 33 was airborne at eight-thirty A.M. and left a fog-shrouded London International Airport under normal and routine circumstances. It was marshmallow and drifting whip cream until the 707 reached 21,000 feet and broke into that incredibly clear blue sky, the vast universe that hangs perpetually and majestically above the crowded, dingy world.

Three hours later the aircraft was a thousand miles from the Atlantic seaboard. The crew and the one hundred and three passengers aboard had enjoyed a pleasant, unruffled flight. They were on course and on time and estimated arrival at Idlewild, New York, within a couple of hours.

Inside the cockpit Captain William Farver, a ruddy-faced, forty-five-year-old pilot with several hundred thousand hours of flying time, made a visual sweep of the instrument panel, a ritual he performed every thirty or forty minutes. His practiced glance took in the altimeter, the Mach meter, the rate-of-climb indicator, the Ram air indicator, and two dozen other instruments whose dials, levers, and tabs were as familiar to him as shirt buttons to the average male. At his right side sat the first officer, Joe Craig, tall, youngish, blond. Craig had a tendency to quick anger, but he was a good pilot with know-how and a mind not a half a beat from that of the captain. Farver looked over his shoulder toward the navigator.

"Hey, Magellan," he said, using the sobriquet common to navigators, "how about a flight progress report?"

"Coming up, Skipper," Hatch, the navigator, answered him. "We'll be about four minutes behind flight plan at thirty degrees west."

Second Officer Wyatt, who sat at the captain's left, removed his earphones. "Captain," Wyatt said. "Gander wants to know if you intend an altitude change after we pass thirty west?"

"Advise Gander negative," Farver responded.

Hatch took a sheet of paper off a clipboard and handed it across to Purcell, the Flight Engineer, who scanned it briefly and gave it to Farver. Farver checked it, then grinned around the tiny, instrument-packed cubbyhole.

"Gentlemen," he said happily, "you'll be pleased to know that thanks to the quality of this aircraft, the fine weather and my brilliant flying, we'll hit Idlewild on schedule if our speed holds up." He handed the report over his shoulder to Wyatt, the second officer. "Send it in, Wyatt," he ordered.

Wyatt put on his earphones, flicked a switch on the complex radio equipment and spoke into the mike. "Shannon, Shannon," he said over the whistling jet engines, "Copy Gander . . . Trans-Ocean Flight 33, position 50 north, 30 west, time 14–OH–3 . . . flight level 35,000. Estimating 52 north, 40 west at 14–31. Estimating Idlewild 18–30. Endurance (by this he meant fuel) 7–9–5–6–OH. Temperature minus 47. Acknowledge, Shannon." He listened for a moment, heard the muffled voice at the other end, then flicked the switch. "Report received, Skipper," he announced.

Through the flight-deck door in the rear of the compartment, Jane Braden, the senior stewardess, entered, carrying her one hundred and twelve pounds like a Rockette. Her shoulder-length blonde hair was pulled back severely in a bun, but she still looked like a Rockette and was built, in the memorable words of Flight Engineer Purcell, overheard in a bar one evening, "like a steel-girdered, two-funneled ship of the line on her inaugural sailing day." Jane leaned against the navigator's chair and Craig spoke to her without turning.

"How we doin' back there, Janie?"

"Your passengers are highly content. But on behalf of the stewardesses, we would like to respectfully request that we get to New York as soon as possible." She smiled and the smile was bright and beautiful, much like the rest of her. "One's going to the opera," she continued, "three have heavy dates, and the fourth is available to any honorable and single, male crew member."

There was laughter at this. Purcell half rose in his seat to announce his qualifications in a piping voice that always made him sound like a bosun with a built-in claghorn. Farver, laughing with the rest of them, suddenly broke off and stared out into space.

Like many pilots, somewhere along the line the captain had developed a sixth sense for anything amiss. It could be a slightly laboring engine that skipped once in a thousand revolutions. It could be a stodgy rudder that an engineer wouldn't pick up with a microscope—but a pilot could feel. Or it could be a sensation of something . . . something indefinable . . . something without a precedent that would suddenly blanket him with a packed-ice feeling of impending trouble. And, at thirty-five thousand feet in a six-hundred-miles-an-hour airplane, trouble wore a thousand masks, a million disguises. It could creep out of a crevice at any point along the one-hundred-and-forty-six-foot fuselage of a 707. Farver had that feeling.

"Hold it a minute," he said. He stared off to the left of the instrument panel, obviously listening, then he turned to Craig.

"You feel anything?" he asked.

Craig too listened. "Feel anything? No. What do you mean, Skipper?"

Farver shook his head. "I don't know. I felt something. Something funny. A sensation of speed." His eyes ran hurriedly across the instrument panel. "I . . . I can't even put my finger on it." Then he took a deep breath and seemed to relax. "I guess I'm getting old."

Craig glanced at the instruments. "True airspeed, 540, Skipper. We're level. Do you suppose we picked up a tail wind?"

Farver shook his head. "Maybe. Those jet streams are tricky. I remember a TWA guy once told me he hit one that he figured was adding two hundred knots to his ground speed. This is a crazy feeling I can't shake. You can't *feel* a tail wind. But I *feel* something!"

Craig shook his head. "Everything looks fine, Skipper."

"Magellan," Farver said to the navigator, "give us a speed check with your Loran."

"Right," Hatch answered. He watched the grid lines of the black box in front of him, where the two pinpoints of light appeared and disappeared. His jaw tightened and perspiration appeared on his forehead. "I'd better do it again," he said.

"What's going on—" Jane began.

Hatch waved her quiet. "Hold it a minute." Again he studied the Loran. "Skipper," he said tersely, "Loran indicates a ground speed of 830 knots." He shook his head, mystified. "I've never heard of a tail wind like that."

Farver's voice was tight. "Check it again." Then he turned to Wyatt, "See if you can raise OSV Charlie, air defense radar. Ask them to give us a fix and check our ground speed." Then he turned back toward the navigator. "Hatch, you sure about that Loran?"

Hatch's eyes were glazed with concentration as he studied the instrument. "Skipper, I'm not only sure—but we're still accelerating. 980 now." He hunched closer over the Loran. "1120. 1500." His lips began to tremble and his face suddenly looked white. "Jesus God," he half shouted, "I can't even keep up with it."

"Anything from air defense?" Farver barked at Wyatt.

"No, sir," was the answer. "I can't raise them."

Hatch half rose in his seat, his voice trembling. "2100. Honest to God . . . 2100 . . . and still increasing."

"I hope the wings stay on." It was more than just a statement from Craig. It was like a prayer.

"They will," Farver answered grimly. "Don't worry about the wings. Just watch that true airspeed. Ground speed doesn't mean a Goddamned thing. We're just in one helluva jet stream." He looked down at the instruments and then shook his head in total disbelief which was almost shock. "Magellan," he said, his voice raised. "My needle just reversed on Gander Omni." He looked up. "How in God's name could we get past Gander? Give me a fast position check."

Hatch stood on his seat in order to put his head into the tiny astrodome over the cockpit. He took a fast fix on the sun. For a moment he was silent. Then he said, "Skipper—we *are* past Gander. We must be doing 3,000 knots."

Taut, suddenly lined faces looked at one another and fear, like an airborne virus, infected the room. Farver's voice cut into the silence.

"Try to raise Harmon control," he ordered Wyatt. "If you can't raise them try Moncton or Boston. And at this speed . . . you might as well try to get Idlewild!"

Wyatt again went on the radio. "Trans-Ocean 33," he said, his voice trembling slightly. "Trans-Ocean 33. Harmon Control, come in please . . . Harmon, please acknowledge. Trans-Ocean 33 Moncton. Trans-Ocean 33 Boston control, come in please . . . Trans-Ocean 33 to Idlewild control . . . can you hear us, please?" Wyatt lowered the mike. "No soap," he said quietly. "I can't raise *anyone.*"

Fear was the silence that followed the announcement. It was the sweat on Wyatt's forehead. It was the grim set to Craig's face. It was the panicky fluttering of Jane Braden's heart. And to Captain Farver it was an interloper threatening his coolness, his presence of mind, his ability to think and make decisions. The instruments in front of his eyes told him a lie. They *couldn't* be going that fast. Not and stay in one piece. Not and have the wings remain on the aircraft. Not without being shaken to pieces and disintegrating into so many tons of falling metal.

And yet they were continuing to accelerate. And the big 707 shot through the sky in a denial of logic and truth and mathematical equations. And inside its aluminum hull, the five crew members stared at their instruments. Deep inside they acknowledged their fears and gave silent assent to their helplessness.

A few moments later Jane Braden closed the flight-deck door behind her and went into the lounge. Her assistant, Paula Temple, a short, attractive brunette, was putting coffee in a tray in a small galley adjoining the lounge. Paula looked up and winked.

"I hope you prodded the fly people. I'm seeing the *Ride of the Valkyrie* tonight." Then she saw the look on Jane's face. "What's the matter?" she whispered.

Jane Braden entered the galley and pulled the curtain around them, closing them off from the lounge.

"Janie," Paula persisted. "I've always had a thing about Valhalla." Her voice shook slightly. "Be a good egg and tell me if I'll be there in time for the curtain."

Jane leaned closer to her. "Let me put it to you this way," she said. "It's my most earnest wish that the Valhalla you're talking about is at the Metropolitan Opera in little old New York."

"Instead of?" Paula's voice was a whisper.

"Instead of a . . . conducted tour into the real thing. We're in trouble, Paula."

"How bad?" Paula asked.

"They don't know yet." She looked down at Paula's tray. "Go ahead and serve it."

Paula lifted up the tray in shaking hands and started to pull the curtains apart.

"Paula—" Jane said to her.

Paula turned.

The beautiful blonde winked at her. "Like . . . coffee, tea or milk . . . and with a smile!"

Paula nodded, forcing a tight smile of her own as she gripped the tray tighter. "You got a deal," she announced, "but I wish to God I'd gone to acting school!"

She pulled the curtain apart and carried the tray past the lounge into the first-class compartment. She walked down the aisle conscious of the faces on either side. Men, women, a sleeping infant, an RAF officer. Innocent, guileless faces of human beings who felt a total trust in the omniscient father-figure at the controls of this complex vehicle. They felt safe because the alternative was a panicky insanity.

A stout, mouth-flapping, middle-aged woman, who was every tourist who'd ever complained about cold water in a London hotel and trumpeted America's pre-eminence in the field of plumbing fixtures, spewed out a monologue to the tall, gray-haired RAF pilot beside her.

"It's as my late husband used to say," she gurgled. "The only problem with the British, aside from the fact that you're perhaps a little behind the times, is this awful coldness of you people. You just don't seem to . . . to emotionalize anything. You're such cold fish about everything. And you know it's a fact—a person gets sick holding things in." She swept on without dropping a beat. "You know, you talk about ailments—I had a cousin once in Boise, Idaho. She had one of the worst livers in the medical history of the state. When that woman passed on, rest her soul, would you believe it? There were five medical associations bidding just to get her liver in a bottle on display. But her mother . . .

my father's sister . . . absolutely refused to let them show her liver. And it's like I always said to my late husband—" She broke off suddenly and stared at the epaulets on the officer's shoulders. "What did you say you were?" she inquired.

The officer, with tired eyes, smiled thinly. "A captain, madam. I'm a military attaché to our British Consulate in Los Angeles."

"Now isn't that wonderful," the woman gushed at him. "Nephew of mine was in the navy during the Second World War. He was on a cruiser, or PT boat or something like that. Or was it a battleship?"

The RAF officer suddenly stared straight ahead. He first looked down at the floor then out toward the wing. There was no loss of power. No telltale shimmying. No flame or smoke. Nothing. And yet there was this feeling . . . this feeling that he couldn't describe even to himself. There was something wrong. This he knew. It was simple and unequivocal. There was something going wrong with this plane.

He turned to look down the aisle at the stewardess who was picking up coffee trays. Were her hands shaking as she went by him? Was there an odd look on her face? Imagination can spawn one nightmarish hallucination after another. This he knew. But the sensation persisted. And there *was* an odd look on the stewardess's face as she passed him.

"What's the matter?" his stout seat companion asked. "Air sickness? I've got some wonderful pills in my bag here—"

"Do you feel anything?" he interrupted her.

The woman stared at him blankly. "*Feel* anything? Like what?"

The RAF captain averted her look. "Nothing," he said softly. "I . . . ah . . . I just thought I felt something." He looked at the woman briefly out of the corner of his eye and decided that he'd keep this one to himself. He smiled at her and said, "What about this nephew of yours in the navy?"

In the rear seat of the first-class compartment, a middle-aged man smiled at his wife. "Notice how nervous that little stewardess was? Probably got some kind of big heavy date or something when we land in New York."

His wife nodded sleepily and closed her eyes. The man picked up a magazine and began to read.

* * *

In the cockpit of Flight 33 the tension was like a big block of some material that could be cut with a saw. At intervals each man looked toward Farver, hunched over his instruments, and then to Hatch the navigator who continued to study the Loran, shaking his head in disbelief as each moment passed. Second Officer Wyatt fiddled with the radio and kept speaking quietly into the mike.

"What about it?" Farver asked him.

Wyatt shook his head. "Not a thing, sir. Not a bloody thing. Either they're off whack . . . everybody out there—" his voice was meaningful "—*or we are.*"

Craig whirled around in his seat. "Why the hell don't you check your equipment—"

"I checked it four times," Wyatt shouted back.

"Knock it off," Farver interrupted. "We'll just have to bull it through and see if anything—"

He never completed this sentence. Not then or ever. There was a sudden, blinding flash of hot, white light. For one fragment of a second they seemed caught up in some kind of giant picture negative in reverse polarization. They looked foggy and indistinct. Then the cockpit shuddered and bucked. Purcell was flung from his seat. The clipboards overhead tumbled down on Hatch's head. Both Farver and Craig instinctively reached for the controls, but the light had dissipated and the plane was once again in easy, level flight.

"Did we hit something?" Craig asked breathlessly.

"I don't know," Farver answered briefly. "Check for damage."

Craig looked out the side window. "Numbers three and four are still on the wing," he announced. "They look okay."

Farver turned from studying the left wing. "Ditto one and two," he said tersely. "Everything seems in one piece. Purcell, go aft and check for any cabin damage. Report back as fast as you can. I'll get on the horn and try to calm everybody down if they need calming. Tell the girls to stay with it." He turned back to the instrument panel and his eyes traversed the maze of levers and dials. "We're in trouble," he said softly, as if to himself, "but I'll be Goddamned if I know what *kind* of trouble."

"That light," Hatch said in a strained, tight voice. "That crazy light. What was it?"

"That's something we'll have to find out," Farver said. He turned to Craig. "And quick too."

"What was the shaking?" Craig asked. "Turbulence?"

Farver shook his head. "I doubt it. It was more like a . . . like a—"

"Like a what?" Craig asked impatiently.

"Like a sound wave," Farver said. *As if we'd gone past the speed of sound.*"

Craig was incredulous. "You mean we hit Mach 1? We broke the sound barrier? But how the hell could that happen? We didn't get any Mach 1 warning."

"We probably wouldn't," Farver said, "not with a true airspeed of only 440. I don't know what it was. I just don't know. Magellan's last speed check showed 3,000 knots. We could have broken some kind of sound barrier, but . . ." He hesitated. "But not any sound barrier I've ever heard of before. Magellan, can you give me a Loran fix now?"

Hatch checked his equipment. "Whatever that bump was, Skipper," he said, "it's really knocked out everything. Loran's inoperative."

"Altimeter and rate of climb steady, Skipper," Craig announced, checking the dials in front of him.

Behind them Wyatt fiddled with the radio. "Skipper," he said, "I still can't raise Gander or Moncton or Boston or any place. It's like I said . . . either they're off the air or we are . . . or both!"

Farver took a deep breath. "Hatch—give me a sun fix. I'll need a heading to Idlewild from our last known position. If we can't raise anybody, we'll have to go down and establish visual contact!"

Craig looked at him, amazed. "Skipper," he said, "we can't do that. If we leave this altitude we'll land smack dab in the middle of twenty other flights."

"Anybody got an alternative?" Farver asked. "Sooner or later we're going to have to find a landmark or go VFR. With no radio contact we're like a deaf and dumb man. As long as we stay up here we're also blind."

Purcell entered from the flight deck. "No damage aft, Skipper," he announced. "Everybody's shook up a bit and they're curious. A few of them are plenty scared too."

Farver took a deep breath. "Them and me both!" He reached for the hand mike. "Ours not to reason why. Ours but to do or die . . . into the valley of public relations." He flicked on the cabin P.A. switch and wondered how his voice sounded as he spoke into the mike. "Ladies and gentlemen, this is Captain Farver. I want to assure you that everything is fine."

Craig closed his eyes and shook his head.

Farver grinned, but his mouth looked as if it had been cut out of paper with a scissors. "There is no danger," he continued on the mike. "We encountered a little clear air turbulence back there along with some kind of . . . atmospheric phenomena. There's been no damage to the aircraft."

His eyes moved up over the mike to scan the cockpit. The radio equipment. The silent black box that had once told them precisely where they were and where they were heading.

"I repeat," he said, "there is no cause for alarm. We'll keep you posted. If we run according to schedule, we should be landing in Idlewild inside of the next forty minutes."

He flicked off the switch, put the mike aside. Jesus God, he said to himself, I should put on a gray flannel suit and sell toothpaste. There was a point, he thought to himself, where the passengers and crew should link arms and face whatever there was to face. They could be milk-fed and reassured to a degree. But then you had to come clean and tell them it was altogether probable that catastrophe was about two city blocks away, and all of them had better start making their peace. This is what he thought, but what he said was "Purcell—what's our fuel?"

Purcell checked his instruments. "29,435 pounds," was the answer.

Farver shook his head, scratched his jaw. "With that Loran out I don't know what our ground speed is. But I've got a hunch we've left that tail wind. I don't have that feeling of speed any more. Do you, Craig?"

Craig shook his head.

Farver looked over his shoulder. "How about the heading to Idlewild, Magellan?"

Hatch scribbled furiously on a clipboard, adding, subtracting, estimating and guessing. "Part of this is scientific," he announced finally. "Part of it's Kentucky windage. Try two-six-two. That's as close as I can make it."

Again the silent faces stared toward the Captain. The whis-

THE ODYSSEY OF FLIGHT 33 / 259

tling of the jet engines sounded normal and natural and yet strangely foreboding. Farver took a long, deep breath, like a man heading into an icy shower.

"All right, gentlemen," he announced, keeping his eyes straight ahead. "You know what we're up against. We have no radios. We're apparently out of touch with all ground radar points. We don't know where we are. We don't even know if we're on airways. This beast gulps fuel—you know that only *too* well. We've got one chance—go down through this overcast and look for something familiar. It's very possible, not to say probable . . . we may hit something on the way down, but we've got to take that chance." He paused.

"I just want you to know where we stand. Everyone keep a sharp look out for other traffic and keep your fingers crossed." He reached over and flicked on the seat-belt sign. His fingers tightened on the wheel in front of him and he said quietly, "I don't think a few prayers would be out of order either." Then his voice was a clipped command. "All right, Craig . . . we're going down!"

The 707 raised its right wing and, like a monstrous yet beautiful bird, nosed down through the clouds and headed toward the earth. Inside the cockpit no one spoke a word. Eyes stared through the small windows—eyes that strained like overworked optical machines, desperately trying to x-ray through the billowing clouds. It was as if, by some miracle of concentration and effort, they hoped to see another airplane in time to avoid the blinding hell of a midair collision. But there were no other aircraft. There was nothing—only clouds that gradually became thinner and more transparent. Suddenly they had broken through, and below there was land.

Purcell spoke first. He shook his big, curly head, looked sardonically over toward Hatch and said, "Hatch, you dumb, silly bastard! Who the hell taught you to navigate?"

Wyatt kept shaking his head as he stared out of the window. "I don't under—"

Purcell cut him off. "Two-six-two," Purcell mimicked ferociously, "and that's supposed to take us over New York. Why this dumb bastard couldn't navigate a kite across a living room!"

Hatch was stunned. Before he could answer Farver called the shot. The captain was staring out toward his left wing and the land mass that loomed beneath it.

"Hold it a minute," he said quietly. Then to Craig, "Level her off."

It was incredible. It was really a monstrous practical joke. It was a bad dream that followed a late lobster snack and an extra quart of beer. But there it was down beneath them, stretched out in sharp and clear relief.

"I don't get it," Farver said, shaking his head. *"But that's Manhattan Island!"*

"Manhattan Island," Purcell whispered, standing up to look over Craig's shoulder. "How can it be Manhattan Island? Where the hell's the skyline? Where are the buildings?"

"I don't know where they are," Farver said. "But we're over New York City. There's only one small item amiss here."

Jane Braden entered from the galley. "The passengers are—" she began.

"I don't blame them," Purcell interrupted.

"We're over land," Jane persisted, "but I don't see any—"

Farver turned and stared directly at her. "Any what, Janie? Any city?" He shook his head. "We don't either." He jerked his thumb toward the windshield. "That's Manhattan Island down there. There's the East River and the Hudson River. There's Montauk Point and every other topographical clue we need." He paused. "The problem is . . . the real estate's there. It's just that the city and eight million people seem to be missing. In short . . . there isn't any New York. *It's disappeared!"*

Craig grabbed Farver's arm. "Skipper, verify something for me, would you? And in a hurry? *Look!"*

Purcell and Hatch left their seats to look over the shoulders of the pilot and copilot.

"It's not possible," Hatch announced.

"What in the name of God is going on?" Purcell asked.

Down below, under the left wing of the 707, was a wild, tangled jungle, but something else was clearly visible, even from three thousand feet, through the window of the speeding airplane. It was a dinosaur nibbling some leaves off the top branch of a giant tree. That's what it was. A dinosaur. And, when Flight 33 banked around to make another pass over the area, it looked up with huge, blinking eyes, perhaps thinking in its tiny mind that this was some big, strange bird. But it continued to feed.

In the first-class passenger cabin, the RAF pilot started at what he thought he saw sweep by underneath him. The fat lady asked him what was the matter, but he did not answer her. A tourist passenger in the rear of the plane, a zoology professor coming back from a sabbatical, gulped and marred the bridge of his nose, as he thrust his face against the glass to stare down at what appeared to be an extinct animal he had lectured about a thousand times. But a 707 is a rapid piece of machinery. Within moments it had left Manhattan Island far behind and was headed north toward Albany. But Albany, like New York, did not exist. It was jungle and swamp and a maze of low-slung mountains. The plane headed inland toward what should have been Buffalo, then Lake Erie and Detroit. None of it was there. No cities. No buildings. No people. Just a vast expanse of prehistoric land.

Captain William Farver announced to nobody in particular, "We've gone back in time. Somehow, someway, when we went through the speed of sound . . . we went back in time!"

Silence from the crew.

Silence from Jane Braden who, in this crazy, illogical moment, wanted to cry.

Silence from Farver, though his mind worked and probed and sifted and tried to formulate a plan.

Any eventuality. That, in a sense, was the Hippocratic oath of the airline pilot. Be prepared for any eventuality and be ready to meet it in a fraction of an instant without panic or indecision. But "any eventuality" did not include this. It meant a flameout of an engine. It meant a runaway prop. It meant a hydraulic system gone awry. But the nightmare that was moving underneath the aircraft in the form of the eastern section of the North American continent, five million years earlier—this was an eventuality not planned for in any manual.

It was Craig who finally spoke. "What do we do about it, Skipper?"

Purcell looked at the fuel indicator. "Skipper, we're down to 19,000 pounds," he said.

Farver scanned his instruments. "Here's what we do about it. We rev this baby up until she's going as fast as she can. We'll climb upstairs until we hit that jet stream. And then . . ." He looked at the faces of the men and the girl. "Then we try to go back where we came from." He turned to Craig. "All right, First Officer," he said in a voice just loud enough to be heard, "*Let's do it!*"

The 707 pointed its nose toward the high layer of cumulus

clouds and in a moment was immersed in them, pulling away from the earth that mocked them with its familiarity and with its strangeness.

Hatch suddenly noticed that his Loran was working again and he screamed out the airspeed as the ship climbed. "700 knots," he announced. "780 knots. 800 knots. 900 knots." He looked up excitedly. "Skipper . . . we're doing it, I think. Honest to God, I think we're doing it—"

The plane screamed through the sky like a projectile from some massive gun. In thirty-eight seconds it was up to 4,000 knots. Farver suddenly looked up, the sweat pouring down his face.

"We're picking it up again. Feel it? We're picking it up again."

They all felt it now. A sensation of such incredible speed . . . a feeling of propulsion beyond any experience they'd ever had before. And then the white light flashed in front of their faces. Once again the cockpit bucked and lurched and then the light was dissipated and the plane was level, its jet engines sucking in the air and roaring with unfettered power. But the blinding speed had gone. The plane intercom buzzed furiously and when Craig picked it up, he heard the frightened voice of one of the two stewardesses in the tourists' section at the rear of the plane. The girl was trying to keep the hysteria out of her voice and it took Craig a moment to calm her down long enough for him to tell her that they were all right. It was the jet stream again.

Paula Temple came through the flight-deck door, her face white. "Look, I know you've got your hands full . . . but somebody get on that pipe and in a hurry! I've got at least three people back there who are close to hysteria and—" She stopped abruptly, staring toward the front of the cockpit through the glass. Before she could say anything, Craig was half out of his seat, pointing.

"Look," he shouted. "Skipper, look. We made it! We're back! Look!"

Through a break in the heavy overcast they all saw it then. It was the skyline of New York, its tall spires shooting up toward the sky. Hatch closed his eyes and mumbled a prayer. Farver felt the sweat clammy on his forehead and for the first time noticed that his hands were shaking. He reached for the loudspeaker microphone, grinned around the cockpit, then pushed the button.

"Ladies and gentlemen, this is Captain Farver. We had some momentary difficulty back there, but as you can see we're now over New York and we should be landing in just a few minutes. Thank you."

Paula leaned against the bulkhead, tears in her eyes, her lips trembling. Jane held her tightly for a moment, kissed her on the cheek.

Jane said, "Come on partner, let's go back and make believe nothing happened."

The two girls left and the captain of Flight 33 breathed deeply. He was conscious of a tightness in the chest suddenly unraveling itself. He checked the instruments, made a few adjustments, then spoke to Wyatt.

"How about Idlewild?"

Wyatt was already fiddling with the radio. "Nothing doing." He shook his head. "Our VFH is still out."

"Maybe Idlewild's is too," Farver suggested. "Try using high frequency."

"I did already, Skipper. Nothing from Idlewild."

"How about LaGuardia? Keep using high frequency. Somebody should hear us."

Wyatt spoke into the mike. "LaGuardia, this is Trans-Ocean 33. LaGuardia, Trans-Ocean 33."

There was some static and then a metallic voice that came from the other end. "This is LaGuardia," the voice said. "Who's calling please?"

There was a whoop of unbridled delight from Purcell. Craig pounded the captain on the back, and Hatch kept applauding as if some unseen dance band had just finished a concert on the wing.

Wyatt held up his hand for silence and went back on the mike. "This is Trans-Ocean 33, LaGuardia," he said. "We're on the northeast leg of the LaGuardia range. Both our ILS and VOR appear inoperative. Request radar vector to Idlewild ILS."

There was a pause at the other end and then the voice came back, impatient and belligerent. "What are you, a wise guy? You'd like *what*?"

Wyatt's face sobered. "A radar vector to Idlewild ILS," he repeated.

"What flight did you say this was?" the LaGuardia tower asked.

Wyatt's voice took on a tenseness. "Trans-Ocean 33. Come on, LaGuardia, quit fooling around. We're low on fuel."

The other four men in the cockpit leaned forward toward Wyatt, a tiny, errant fear building in each mind as to what new devilment . . . what new incredible and wild deviation from the norm they were moving against now.

Then the LaGuardia tower voice came back on. "Trans-Ocean Airlines?" it asked. "What kind of aircraft is this?"

"This is Trans-Ocean 33," Wyatt said into the mike. "A Boeing 707 and we—"

The voice interrupted him. "Did you say a Boeing 247?"

Farver bit his lip, feeling anger and impatience surge through him. He plugged in his own mike. "Let me handle it," he said tersely to Wyatt. Then he held the mike close to his mouth. "LaGuardia, this is a Boeing 707, and every five-second period you keep this aircraft up in the air, you're shortening the odds on its ever getting back on the ground. Now don't give us this two-four-seven jazz. You're only about twenty years behind the times. This is a 707, LaGuardia. A jet. Four big, lovely Pratt & Whitney turbines, only they're getting hungry. We're low on fuel and all we want is a radar vector to Idlewild. Now Goddamn it, do you have us in radar contact or don't you?"

There was a pause and then the LaGuardia voice came back on, still sullen, but with just a shade of concern. "I don't know who you guys are," the tower said, "and we don't know anything at all about radar, jets, or anything else. We've never heard of a 707 aircraft. But if you're really low on fuel, we'll clear you to land."

Craig, who'd been consulting an approach chart during this exchange, leaned over to Farver and pointed to it. "Captain," he said, "their longest runway is less than five thousand feet. Can we take a chance?"

The LaGuardia voice came back on. "Trans-Ocean 33, you're cleared to land on runway 22. Altimeter two nine eight eight, wind south 10 miles per hour. The Captain is to report to the CAA office immediately after landing."

"Roger," Farver said tersely into the mike. "We'll stay in touch." He removed the microphone plug, then suddenly frowned. "CAA?" he asked aloud. "Why, they haven't called the Federal Aviation CAA—"

It was part of a pattern, he thought to himself. Part of a

routine they had been going through for the past hour. A jigsaw puzzle perfect in every detail except every now and then a round peg appeared and didn't fit the square hole. Then he shook his head and pushed it out of his mind as he turned to Craig.

"We'll bring her down, Craig," he said. "It'll be like landing in a phone booth, but—"

Hatch, who was standing up between his seat and the two pilots' chairs, suddenly pointed out of the window, his eyes wide.

"Captain," he said, pointing a shaking finger toward the left window. "Circle again, will you?" He wet his lips. "And then look!"

Farver winged the plane over gently, circled in as short an arc as he could and then came back, following the trembling finger of Hatch. And then they all saw it. The scene whisked past their eyes in less than a second, but it registered. It was an indelible shock that made itself known optically, but then entered the mind of every one of the crew members to infiltrate their brains and corrode the lines to sanity.

Yes, they had all seen it. And when Farver turned the aircraft to retrace the flight path, they saw it again. A trylon and perisphere were set in the middle of what appeared from the air to be a giant fair or carnival. And they all knew what it was.

Craig's hands dropped from the controls and he had to press them into his sides to keep them from shaking. "Skipper," he said, "do you know what that is down there? Do you know what—"

Farver, hunched forward in his seat, kept shaking his head from side to side.

Wyatt said in a small, strained voice, "It's the New York World's Fair. That's what it is. The New York World's Fair. But that means we're in—"

"1939," Hatch interrupted him. "We came back . . . we came back . . . but dear God . . . *we didn't come back far enough!*"

They all turned toward Farver. What was happening was more than they could handle. Far more than even their better-than-average minds could assimilate. And they did what any human being would do. They looked up and away, abdicated all decisions, and threw the massive dead weight of responsibility on the number one man in the cabin.

Farver felt it press down on him. The prerogative of command . . . but worse, the responsibility. They all wanted to know what to do and he was the one man who would have to tell them.

And what *do* you tell them? What is the procedure? What is the command that is right and proper to cover a situation that has no precedent, no logic, and no reason. For one panicky moment Farver's mind went blank and he felt like turning on them and screaming, "Goddamn it, don't look at me. Don't wait to hear what I say. Don't hang on the next command that's supposed to come from *this* airplane pilot!"

Holy Mother—it was too much to expect that any human being could rise up in the middle of this nightmare and point the way to an awakening or anything even resembling it. But after a moment, whatever was the invisible challenge that was thrown at him by the frightened faces, he responded. He was the captain of this aircraft. And though reality and logic were cracking up and falling to pieces all around him—*by God he would command!*

"We can't land," Farver said finally, his voice soft. He shook his head. "We can't land in LaGuardia . . . and we can't land back in 1939. We've got to try again. That's all that's left. Try again."

Craig nodded toward the flight-deck door. "What about the passengers?"

"I think we had better let them in on it now." Farver flicked on the P.A. system and reached for the mike. "Ladies and gentlemen," he said, his voice firm, full of resolve, no condescension, no fake optimism. "What I'm going to tell you is something I can't explain. The crew is as much in the dark as you are. Because if you look out on the left-hand side of the aircraft . . . you'll see directly below us an area called Lake Success. And those buildings down there aren't the United Nations. They happen to be . . ." his voice faltered for a moment then came back on. "They happen to be the World's Fair."

Down the length of the plane the loudspeaker carried Captain William Farver's voice and the passengers listened as a nightmare began to close in on them.

"What I'm trying to tell you," Farver's voice told them, "is that somehow, someway . . . this aircraft has gone back into time and it's 1939. What we're going to do now is increase our speed, get into the same jet stream and attempt to go through the sound barrier we've already broken twice before. I don't know if we can do it. All I ask of you is that you remain calm . . . *and pray.*"

In the cockpit, Farver pulled the yoke forward and the 707 once again pointed toward the sky.

The giant aircraft disappeared through the heavy overcast. Its roaring engines grew indistinct and faded out, leaving a silence in its wake and a long jet trail that was picked up by the wind and carried away.

Thirty thousand feet below, it was 1939 and people gaped at the wondrous exhibits. There was the waterfall in front of the Italian building; the beautiful marble statuary that fronted the Polish pavilion; the exquisite detail of the tapestry and wood carvings shown by the smiling Japanese. And the people walked happily through a warm June afternoon, seeing only the sunlight and not knowing that darkness was falling over the world.

She was a Trans-Ocean jet airliner on her way from London to New York, on an uneventful June afternoon in the year 1961. She was last heard from six hundred miles south of Newfoundland, then somehow she was swallowed up into the vast design of things, to be searched for on land, on sea, and in the air by anguished human beings, fearful of what they'd find.

You and I, however, know where she is. You and I know what happened. So if some moment . . . any moment . . . you hear the sound of jet engines flying atop the overcast . . . engines that sound searching and lost . . . engines that sound desperate . . . shoot up a flare. Or do something. That would be Trans-Ocean 33 trying to get home . . . from The Twilight Zone.

DUST

There was a village built of
crumbling clay and rotting wood. It squatted, ugly, under a
broiling sun, like a sick, mangy animal waiting to die. It had a
name, but the name was of little consequence. It had an age, but
few people cared how old it was. It lay somewhere in the South-
west on the fringe of a desert—a two-block-long main street,
lined with squalid frame stores and a few adobe huts. They shook
and wheezed and groaned like tired old men whenever a wagon
went by (which was seldom), raising the dust and leaving it to
hang like a fog.

On this day, even the few stores that were not boarded up
had closed their doors. Scrawled signs announced that each was
"Closed For The Funeral" or "Will Be Open After Funeral." And
also, on this day, the street was empty, save for a swaybacked
horse pushing an aged snout into a water trough and flicking off
the glossy green flies that descended on its flanks by the hundreds. Its switching tail was the only movement on the main
street. Sounds came loudly and intermittently from around the
corner; hammering, the creak of boards, then the sound as of
some heavy object being dropped through the air only to be
caught up short.

They were building a gallows.

Incongruously, here was activity. Here was fresh lumber. Here were men at work. The gallows stood sixteen feet high. Four giant pillars supported a platform with a trapdoor. Over it was a heavy cross beam from which dangled a thick rope, a noose expertly tied at its end.

This village and its people shared an infection. It was the germ of misery, of hopelessness, of loss of faith. And for the faith-less . . . the hopeless . . . the misery-laden . . . there is time— ample time—to engage in one of the other pursuits of men.

They begin to destroy themselves.

Peter Sykes walked down the main street pulling an over-laden pack mule. The animal was sick and overworked. It stum-bled along, head down, eyes half-closed. At intervals Sykes yanked viciously on the rope. The animal would start, then seem to push itself forward, eyes glazed with pain and fatigue, bony body white with sweat. Pots and pans, bottles, magazines, coiled rope, and nondescript boxes protruded from the saddle bags by which the mule was weighted down.

Peter Sykes had small eyes that darted this way and that way from a fat and filthy face. As he moved his massive bulk through the dust, from time to time he produced a bottle from his hip pocket and took a long, luxurious drink. The liquor dribbled from the corners of his mouth and traveled in little rivulets through his beard stubble.

"Awright, ladies and gents," he suddenly shrieked when he got halfway down the main street. "It's Peter Sykes back from St. Louis and stocked up with everything that's needed for kitchen, barn and"—he held up the pint bottle—"the dried throat and the swollen tongue!"

He boomed out his fat man's laughter and shoved the bottle back into his hip pocket. He stopped the mule in front of a wooden building that was the town jail. He dropped the rope in the dust, and climbed laboriously to the wooden plank sidewalk. A barred window faced the street. Sykes peered through the bars into the dark cell. A thin Mexican boy sat on a bench at the far end, his hands resting quietly on his lap, his head bent forward.

"Mr. Gallegos, I believe," Sykes said, bowing from his vast waist. He chuckled. The obese body shook and the folds in his face seemed to come alive like wiggling snakes. "Mr. Gallegos," he repeated. He scratched his jaw in an exaggerated pretense of thought. "Today's a special day, isn't it? Now let's see . . . what's the special day?" He grinned and snapped his fingers. "I remember now! It's just this moment come back to me."

Sykes pointed through the bars. "Today you're gonna get hanged!" Obscene laughter poured out of him. "Today young Mr. Gallegos, killer of children, dangles at the gallows!"

He limped away from the window, tears of laughter rolling from his eyes. Two men were walking down the wooden sidewalk toward him. His laughter died out, his eyes narrowed and took on a different expression. These were customers and Peter Sykes's entire life was built upon commerce. He waddled over to the nearer man, grabbed him in a perspiring fist.

"Good whiskey from St. Louis, Jonesy," he said importantly. He patted his hip pocket. "Eighty-five cents a fifth."

The man looked embarrassed and shook off Sykes's hand. Immediately Sykes turned to the other passer-by, blocked him with his big bulk, shoved his face close to him and rolled his eyes. His voice, almost inaudible, was like a leer.

"Post cards, Eddie," he whispered, wiggling his tongue. "Wonderful post cards this trip. French dancing girls in their native costumes."

Sykes giggled, jammed his elbow in the man's ribs, then laughed aloud as he walked away, head down. Sykes was still chuckling as he went back to the jail and into the Sheriff's office.

It was a bare room with a makeshift desk, a gun rack, and a barred door leading to the single cell. John Koch sat behind the desk, a tarnished badge on his worn and dusty leather vest. His long, lean tanned face, the eyes deep-set and tired, showed forty-seven hard years indelibly imprinted in lines over the cheekbones and on either side of the jaw. Koch barely glanced at Sykes, then busied himself with papers on the desk. He felt the intrusion of the fat man and the sense of envelopment that Sykes carried with him.

"What'll it be for you today, Mr. Koch?" Sykes's shrill voice intruded upon the quiet of the room. "Don't need any more rope, do you?" He called out toward the barred door. "Oughta see the fancy five-strand hemp I sold the town for your party, Gallegos! It could lift about five of you."

He lumbered across the room to stand close to the cell door. The look he threw at Gallegos was as much a part of him as his rolls of fat. There was a meanness to it. A raw prejudice. A naked dislike of other men.

"Not any more at home like you, are there?" Sykes laughed loudly, then asked, "And what do you fancy today, Mr. Koch?"

"What do I fancy, Mr. Sykes?" Koch forced himself to keep his voice steady and low. "I'll tell you what I fancy. I'd like you to take your fat carcass and your loud mouth out into the air. This is a small room and it's the hot time of the morning."

The grin on the fat man's face grew tight and strained. Sykes knew what Koch was feeling. He was not insensitive to the anger he aroused. But he'd lived a life of walking over other people's anger and disgust. It was his own peculiar strength.

"How about you, Mr. Gallegos?" Sykes jeered. "What would be your pleasure this morning? Maybe a nice hacksaw?"

Again his whole body quivered with laughter but it faded when he saw the look on the Mexican boy's face. The black eyes that caught and pierced him held fathomless pools of hate.

"This one I wouldn't miss!" Sykes gloated. "I just wouldn't want to miss this one!" He took the bottle from his hip pocket, uncorked it with his teeth. "There's gonna be a funeral procession down this street, Gallegos. You better look out and watch. They're burying the little girl you mangled under your wagon. You're sobered up now, aren't you, Gallegos? You remember the little girl, don't you? You got stinking drunk, rode a wagon down the street, and what you did to that poor little girl—"

The Mexican boy leaped from the bench, slammed against the bars and thrust an arm out through them, trying to reach the fat man. But Sykes nimbly stepped back a foot and waggled a finger.

"Uh, uh, Mr. Gallegos. You'll get your chance to move around this afternoon. You'll be able to kick and kick and kick."

This struck him as so funny that he threw back his head and roared.

Koch stared at Sykes. God, what an animal, he thought. What a filthy animal. Some men were built for their trade. They were designed to be cheats, hucksters, medicine men. There must be some kind of mold, the thought ran through his mind, which produced the filth that stood in front of him holding the rotgut whiskey.

"You ought to take a drink of this, Sheriff." Sykes's voice patronized Koch. "It's a good tonic." He patted the flab that hung over his belt. "Puts a little grizzle there. Sets you up great for a good hanging. Yes, sir. Makes you feel strong and firm." He held out his vast, flabby arm and made a muscle. "You oughta feel this!"

Koch's mouth trembled. "I don't touch dog meat, Sykes."

The bottle was slammed down on the desk top. "You talk big behind a badge, Mr. Koch."

"It just sounds big to you, Sykes, because you're a midget. You only grew up as high as a money belt and that's a low height for a man."

Sykes's little eyes glittered. "I've always had a question about you, Koch," he said, in a low voice. "Seems you got a thing for foreigners and strays. But you're mighty tight-lipped when it comes to your own."

Koch rose from his chair. "You're not my own, Sykes, so don't claim any kinship." He pointed toward the cell. "And as for the boy in there—he had his trial and today he's gonna swing for it. But there's nothing in his sentence that says he's got to be tormented by a pig who sells trinkets at funerals." He stared at the fat man and Sykes had to turn away. "Go on, get out of here."

Sykes moved toward the door, anger building up inside him. Anger at being despised. Anger at the itchy sweat that rolled down his body. Anger because hatred was his own special province; hatred of people, hatred of all he had to do to stay alive. He wanted to walk out without saying anything more, but found himself turning at the door.

"When the day is over, Mr. Koch," he asked, "which one will *you* weep for?"

Koch looked at the thin Mexican boy whose hands gripped the bars and whose young face suddenly looked so old. "I've got enough tears for both, Mr. Sykes," he answered quietly.

The fat man walked out on to the street and heard the sound of rolling wagon wheels. He shaded his eyes against the blinding sun. The funeral procession was turning the corner at the far end of the street. The long line of people included the black-garbed figures of a middle-aged man and his wife, who walked behind a minister; behind them, in the center of the column, was the wagon with the unpainted pine box. The box was very small.

Sykes moved his fat bulk down to the dusty street and, with a great flourish, removed his hat and held it over his heart. He waited until the middle-aged couple were a few feet from him, and then joined the procession.

"Mr. and Missuz Canfield," Sykes panted as he shuffled along beside them. He was sweating and half out of breath, but his tone was deep and mournful. "I'm real sorry about this. My condolences to yuh. But this afternoon it's gonna be a lot cheerier. We're gonna string up the dirty little animal who done this."

The husband and wife stared at him incredulously and the woman bit her lip and turned away.

Sykes screwed up his face like a little baby beginning to cry. "It's God's will, Mr. and Missuz Canfield," he screeched. "It's God's will. But she's gonna be avenged. *She is going to be avenged.* So you don't have no worries on that score. The Mexican who done it is gonna pay for it."

Koch came up behind Sykes, pulled him by the back of his jacket and half yanked him off his feet. Sykes whirled around, a hand raised. This was knocked aside by the tall sheriff whose face was white and grim.

"Some other time, Sykes, huh?" Koch said quietly. "Some other time act like a man with no brains. But not now. Now you keep quiet."

Sykes glared at him, but the look on the other man's face was the kind you didn't talk back to. This crazy, Goddamned sheriff. This fanatic. Well, what the hell. He'd made his position known. The Canfields had seen him. He had been properly doleful and he'd supplied the rope for the hanging. They'd remember that. His eyes suddenly blinked and narrowed.

He nudged Koch. "Now look at that, will yuh? Now ain't that the most gall you ever seen in one place? There's Gallegos's old man! He got the nerve . . . the honest to God nerve . . . to show himself in broad daylight! And during the funeral procession too! Somebody ought to take a horsewhip to that dirty little—"

The rest of the words never came out. He saw Koch's baleful face, and Sykes forced a smile. Down the street Pedro Gallegos and his little ten-year-old daughter, Estrelita, were standing in the center of the road waiting for the procession.

Pedro Gallegos was sixty-eight years old. He was thin, scrawny, with bent shoulders, and the lines in his face looked as if they'd been hewn in rock. Sun had done it. And toil. And now sorrow—sorrow beyond any kind of words. He held the little girl's hand tightly and as the funeral procession got closer he whispered something in her ear and then gently pushed her forward.

When the Canfields came abreast, Estrelita walked out and stood in front of them. They stopped, looking at the little girl and then over toward the old Mexican, whose lips trembled, whose features worked as he whispered something soundlessly and then motioned toward the little girl to speak.

Estrelita looked at the ground and mumbled something in a low voice.

Gallegos half shouted from a few feet away. "Louder, Estrelita. Tell them, my darling. Tell them, my heart. Speak to them. Go ahead."

The Canfields looked away in white-faced, shocked embarrassment.

"My father wishes me to tell you," the little girl began. "My father wishes me to tell you that . . ."

The words died in her throat. She looked fearfully over her shoulder toward her father. "My father wishes for me to tell you," she tried again, "that his heart is broken. That if he could . . . if he could give . . ."

"His own life in return," Pedro Gallegos whispered. Then it came out louder. "His own life in return. *His own life in return, Estrelita.*"

Mrs. Canfield's eyes were tightly shut and her husband gripped her arm.

"His own life in return," Estrelita said, "he would do so with great willingness." She wet her lips. Her thin, little face looked agonized. "He . . . he understands . . ." Once again the words stopped.

Pedro Gallegos took a stumbling step toward her, tears rolling down his face. "He understands what it is like to lose your flesh," the old man said. "He understands and he is sad for you. He asks now that . . ." The old man sobbed aloud. "Estrelita, tell them. Say it to them."

"He asks that you have no malice for his son, Louis, who did this awful thing. He . . . he did not do it on purpose and he is sick in his heart and his mind because of it."

The little girl scuffled a bare foot in the dust, her hands

tightly intertwined behind her back, her dark little face flushed with pain and misery. Her father walked another few feet toward the Canfields, then with palms outstretched, dropped to his knees in the dust.

"Señor . . . Señora," the old man pleaded, "please do not let them kill my son. He will spend the rest of his life and I, mine, in your service. Anything. Anything you wish. But please . . . please do not let them take my son's life."

The little girl ran to throw herself into her father's arms and bury her face against his shoulder. He held her tightly, stroking her hair and crooning softly into her ear, something in Spanish that the others could not hear.

The Canfields looked at one another and the husband said in a choked voice, "Don't hold us up any further, please. Can't you see . . . can't you see that we're burying our daughter today?"

He took his wife's arm and they continued to walk toward the cemetery at the edge of town, a patch of barren sand dotted irregularly with inexpertly carved, ugly stones and makeshift wooden crosses, as if the squalor of living had its own counterpart in death.

Why couldn't he have stayed away, Canfield thought. Why did he have to come out on this afternoon? Why does he have to throw more pain at us when his son has already supplied the ultimate in pain?

Oh God, Sheriff Koch thought, oh dear God. This place. This ugly town full of ugly people. This sapper of strength and dignity that robs the living and now even the dead with the heat of it and the misery of it.

Peter Sykes squinted after the disappearing procession. It don't make a damn, really, he thought, that they didn't buy the coffin from him. Next time. Next time they would. He'd supplied the rope for the hanging and there was a thirty-eight percent mark up on the rope. Next time the coffin, he thought. Next time he'd be here in time for the bidding.

That was what Sykes thought, as the thin column of people and the wagon with the pine box disappeared into the fields beyond the town, going toward the ugly little cemetery that lay under the hot Southwestern desert sun.

There were no flowers. None at all. It was too hot for flowers.

* * *

Pedro Gallegos, holding tight to his little daughter's hand, walked slowly toward the jail. The ragged, dusty men on the street moved aside as he passed and stared coldly at him. He felt their hostility and forced himself to walk straight ahead. Koch stood near the cell window and he too noticed the angry faces of the townspeople.

Gallegos looked around at these faces, released Estrelita's hand and held out his own in front of him. "Please . . . please . . ." His puckered, weather-beaten old face with the deeply etched lines and sad eyes pleaded with them. "My son did not mean to do it. He is a lover of children just as you all are. He is a lover of children—"

He felt a shocking, tearing pain over his right eye as a stone glanced off the side of his head. It drew blood. Estrelita let out a small scream. Louis gripped the bars of the cell and shouted out at his father.

"Padre, por favor vayase a la casa. No se le necesita aquí."

Peter Sykes grinned. "He'll do you no good here? Is that what you say to this old man, Gallegos? This is a staunch figure of a man, Louis—this father. Look at him. The patriarch of the Mexican community." He rumbled deep laughter from his gut. The others did not share the laughter, but continued to stare at the old man.

"Father," Louis said urgently in a soft voice. "Take Estrelita home. They will hurt you if you stay here. Please . . . go home now."

The old man's eyes were wet. He wiped the blood from his eye, reached in his pocket and took out a coin which he held out toward his son.

"Louis," he said, "a lucky coin. It is said that one can make a wish on it—"

Someone in the crowd laughed, but at that moment Peter Sykes did not laugh. He looked at the coin squinty-eyed, suddenly very interested. Koch stepped in front of the cell window.

"Go home, old man," he said gently. "Make wishes . . . or pray. But Louis is right. You'll do no good here."

"You have never been drunk, Mr. Sheriff?" the old man asked. "You never felt such misery rising in you that salvation seemed to look at you only from out of a bottle?" The blood was running again from the cut over his eye. "You never felt pain . . .

such pain that you had to ride through the night and not look behind you?"

He gestured toward the cell. "My son was hungry and he felt such a pain and he drank too much and he rode down the street not looking . . . not seeing.

"He had a sadness deep inside. Sadness that there was not enough to eat. Sadness that he had no work. Sadness that the earth all around him was growing barren in the sun. And he did not see the little girl. He never saw her for an instant." Pedro Gallegos fumbled blindly for his daughter's hand, gripped it and pulled her closer to him.

Koch said nothing. The old man knew that he had said enough. Perhaps too much. And all of it to no avail. He was a dirty old Mexican and his words carried no meaning to the men who listened to them. He was a dirty old Mexican and he was the father of a murderer. So Pedro Gallegos shuffled away, down the dusty street. Estrelita started to follow him, but stopped when Sykes whistled at her.

"Come over here," the fat man said.

Estrelita stood stock-still.

"Come over here," Sykes repeated urgently. "I won't hurt you."

The little girl went slowly to him. Sykes held her tight by the shoulders and shoved his fat, sweaty face close to hers.

"You tell your Papa," he said softly. "Understand? Comprende? You tell your Papa I want to help him. You tell him that coin of his is worthless. But I have a magic dust that turns hate to love. Understand? Comprende? Turns hate to love. You tell him that. A magic dust, but it is very precious, understand? Very, very dear."

The little girl nodded. Sykes looked around surreptitiously.

"Five hundred pesos," he said. "You tell your Papa to bring five hundred pesos in an hour and I will sell him the magic dust that makes people love and forgive. Understand?"

Wide-eyed, Estrelita nodded. She backed away from the fat man and broke into a run. Sykes watched her until she caught up with her father and they disappeared.

The crowd dispersed and Koch went back into the jail. Sykes sat down on the steps and took out a bag of tobacco from his pocket. He opened it, stared at it, grinned and finally laughed aloud.

Sykes emptied the bag, then went down on his knees and scooped dust into it. He pulled the strings tight with his teeth then swung it back and forth.

"Magic dust," he said aloud. "That's what she is. Five hundred pesos worth of magic dust." Then he threw back his head and laughed.

It was two o'clock in the afternoon when people started to arrive. Battered, makeshift wagons, full of parents and children from outlying districts; townspeople who erupted into the streets and were drawn compulsively toward the jail. It was almost that time.

Koch stood leaning against the whitewashed clay wall of the building, rolling a cigarette. When he finished the cigarette he gave it to Louis Gallegos. Gallegos let Koch light it for him.

"Gracias," he said. "There should be a good attendance today," he added simply.

"When was it that God made people?" Koch asked. "Was it on the fifth day?—He should have stopped on the fourth!"

Louis Gallegos shook his head. "They are tired of hating this place. The sun. The ground that is dead under their feet." His fingers gripped the bars. "So they must go out and find something else to hate."

A wagon creaked slowly to a stop in front of the jail. A farmer and his wife were on the front seat and in the back were six wide-eyed, excited children.

Koch stepped away from the wall toward the wagon. "It isn't a carnival, Rogers," he said. "It's a hanging."

The farmer jerked his thumb toward the children. "You mean the kids?" he asked. "They ain't ever seen a hanging. I figured that it was about time."

"Why?" asked Koch.

"Why not? They'll learn a lesson. This is what happens to drunk Mexicans who kill kids."

Koch smiled. "I guess that's pretty vital." He hesitated. "How do you teach them pain, Rogers? Shoot one of them in the arm?"

The farmer shook his head, and said to his wife, "Tell them to stay together. I'll tie up the horses."

While the farmer hitched his team, his six-year-old son crawled off the back of the wagon and wandered over to peer up

at the young Mexican framed in the cell window. Louis Gallegos
smiled at him.

"Are you the man?" the little boy asked. "Are you the one
they're gonna put the rope on?"

"Sí, little one. I am the man."

"Will it hurt?"

Gallegos closed his eyes. "If God wills it."

Koch gently pushed the boy aside. "Go on," he ordered. "Go
with your Dad." Then he turned toward Louis. "It's about that
time."

Gallegos nodded. "I'm ready, Sheriff."

The townspeople watched as Koch and a deputy led Louis
Gallegos out of the jail, his hands manacled together. They
started a slow walk down the street toward the gallows. The people closed ranks and, as if by common consent, followed them.

A priest stood on the gallows, waiting. He was Mexican and
he knew his clerical garb meant nothing to these people. The
brown skin set him apart, and the fact that he spoke little English. The cross that hung from his neck was no symbol of
peace to the grim men and women who gathered around the
gallows. A Mexican priest was a Mexican. And the priest understood this as he stood atop the platform and watched Louis
Gallegos, his hands manacled in front of him, walk slowly up the
steps toward him.

A man in the first row called out impatiently. "What the
hell? That should have been done in the jail! Let's get on with it!"

There were nods of assent, but no other voices. This was a
quiet crowd, anxious to have happen what had to happen. But
there was no fire under these people. There was no rage. Their
hatred was like themselves. It was quieted down by the hot sun,
measured by the dictates of the climate. So it was a quiet crowd.
But they knew what they wanted.

Peter Sykes stood in front of the jail looking expectantly
down the street until he saw Pedro Gallegos turn the corner at the
far end and run toward him. Sykes's eyes shone. He held up the
little bag and dangled it in the air, then crooked the finger of his
free hand and waggled it toward the old man. Sykes kicked open
the door to the jail. Silently he pointed toward the interior as
Pedro Gallegos came up to him. They went inside and Sykes
closed the door.

"Your daughter told you, old man?"

Gallegos swallowed. His face was wet with a combination of sweat and tears. His voice shook as he answered. "She told me. She said that you had a dust . . . a dust of magic properties."

Sykes smiled. "That's the idea, old man. Sprinkled over the heads of the people . . . it'll make them feel sympathy for your son. It's very rare, you know. It's magic." His face changed and something hard crept in the lines by the mouth. "You brought the money, old man?"

Gallegos reached inside his worn, shabby shirt and took out a small bag of his own, tied at the top with string. He untied it and emptied the contents into his palm. There were three gold pieces.

Sykes felt his palms perspire. "Gold pieces, huh?" he said, taking a breath. "Where did you get them?"

"All my friends . . . all my friends went into the city. One sold a wagon, another sold a horse. Some borrowed. We got many pesos and we converted them."

He reached for the bag of dust, but Sykes pulled it back.

Gallegos wet his lips. "It will work, Mr. Sykes?" he asked. "The magic dust—it will work? You sold the rope to hang my son. Now you sell me that which will save him?"

"I'm a businessman, Mr. Gallegos," Sykes said reasonably. "I sell that which is needed." He shook his head. "I make no distinctions. This will work. Like I told you . . . it's magic!"

Sykes smiled, held out his hand. The old man slowly dropped the coins one by one into it, then held his own hand out for the dust which Sykes very deliberately turned over to him. Gallegos clutched it tightly to him.

"It must work," he said. "It must work. It must be magic!"

Then propelled by urgency and fear and a sudden hope of salvation, he pulled open the door.

"Louis," he screamed as he ran. "Louis, I'm coming, my son. I'm coming."

Sykes stepped outside, holding the three gold pieces in his hand. "Just throw some into the air," he shouted after the old man. "Over their heads." He laughed. "That's right . . . and then watch the magic!"

He rubbed the coins together and liked the feel and the moisture and the scraping sound of them. He sat down on the steps of the jail.

"Magic," he said through his laughter. "You go out there and watch the magic!"

He sat rolling the coins in his sweaty palm and thought that things had a way of coming out all right. He hadn't been around to sell the coffin . . . but he had made something out of the day anyway. He felt warm and good inside. He reached in his hip pocket and took out his pint bottle of whiskey. Yes, things had a way of coming out all right!

Louis Gallegos knelt on the platform, the rope hanging a few feet above him. The priest administered the blessing in a soft, singsong Latin. Intermittently a rumble of impatient voices called for an end of prayer and a commencement of the business of the day.

But the priest kept his eyes fastened on the back of the kneeling boy's head and made himself oblivious to the sounds. Each time he crossed himself and reached another juncture in the blessing another moment had passed, another fragment of Louis Gallegos's life had been pushed aside. So very little remained.

At last the priest could do nothing but stand there, his fingers clenched, while Sheriff Koch went to Gallegos, took his elbow and helped him rise. The deputy placed the noose around his neck and then tightened it. A murmur of approval ran through the crowd.

Only Mrs. Canfield, mother of the dead girl, turned her eyes away, not wanting to see and wishing she had not come. Her husband took her arm and motioned with his head toward the platform. It was a silent and symbolic command. On the day of retribution, they, the bereaved, must not look away. They must stand in the front row and watch as justice was done.

"Magic . . . magic . . ." came the sound of Pedro Gallegos's cracked, old voice. He rounded the corner and ran toward the crowd. He held the bag of dust high over his head. Out of breath, sweating, stumbling, he ran among the people, scattering the dust over their heads, half sobbing his incantations.

"You must pay heed to the magic now," he exhorted them. "You must stop all this . . . and pay heed to the magic."

Back and forth he ran, stumbling, landing on his knees, then rising to run again past the gamut of icy faces. A child laughed at the apparition, but his mother put her finger over his mouth and there was dead silence as the old man continued to fling dust over their heads and shout.

"Magic. You must pay heed to the magic. All of you—it is only for love. It is for compassion. The magic is so that my son can live—as you yourselves would want yours to live. Magic . . . magic . . . magic . . ."

A young man, husky, squat, powerful, thrust his foot out and tripped the old man. He fell face down. The bag dropped from his hands and he scrabbled across the ground after it.

"It's magic," he whispered hoarsely. "Magic . . . it is for love. It is for love. The magic is for love."

The trapdoor creaked open. The rope went taut with the weight of the body. The gasp from the crowd built to a roar. The old man covered his face and screamed.

"No. Oh, no. Por el amor de Dios!"

The ground swayed under him and he turned cold from head to foot. But presently he became aware that the crowd was growing gradually quieter, until at last there was no sound at all. Very slowly his fingers parted and he peered out to see what had so strangely stilled the crowd. He saw a piece of rope hanging down through the trapdoor. Beneath it stood Louis Gallegos, the torn noose around his neck, his face white.

Only Sykes spoke, his voice tremulous. "But it was a new rope. Five-strand hemp!"

The people were silent, baffled. Koch went to Louis Gallegos's side and faced the crowd.

"What about it, Mr. Canfield? Mrs. Canfield?"

Pedro Gallegos, holding the empty bag, made his way toward where the Canfields stood.

"Please," he said. "Please . . . it's the magic. You cannot try to defeat the magic."

"Let's try it again," a man called out.

There was a murmur of agreement.

Koch held tight to Louis Gallegos's arm. "There are only two people here," he said, "who have the right to beg an eye for an eye." He turned purposefully to the Canfields. "What about it?"

Canfield felt the blood drain from his face. The unfamiliar black suit was heavy and uncomfortable. But heavier was the pressure of the eyes that watched him, the sense of ears waiting for him to speak. It was his wife who answered.

"No more today, William," she said softly, shaking her head. "No more."

"He killed our child," Canfield said. "He killed our child."

The woman shook her head. "And a part of himself too." She looked at the suffering face of Louis Gallegos.

"There's been enough pain, William," she said. "Quite enough pain. It has to stop now . . . or we'll die, ourselves."

Her husband's face showed indecisiveness, but this was a gentle man, and she knew it.

Canfield turned to Koch. "Sheriff Koch," he said quietly. "We . . . we withdraw the charges." Then he looked up at the dangling rope. "There must be . . . there must be another hand in all this, to make the rope break like that." He shook his head. "Another hand. Maybe . . . maybe the hand of Providence."

Koch took a deep breath and felt something wondrous stirring inside him. "You want to stop it then, Mr. Canfield?" he asked in an official voice. "You have that right."

A farmer stepped out of the crowd. "William?"

Canfield turned.

"We leave it like this?" the man asked.

Canfield nodded. "We leave it like this. One victim is enough." He faced his fellow townspeople. "I think we should all go home now," he said.

He took his wife's arm and they walked away. By ones and twos, then by groups, the people left the square. Within a few moments it was empty save for Koch, the old man, and the young Mexican boy with the manacled hands, the ugly red mark on his throat, the noose around his neck. Koch released the manacles.

The boy said wonderingly, "I'm . . . I'm free?"

Koch felt a weariness he had never known before. "Are any of us . . . free, Louis?" he asked. "But you can go home." He removed the rope from the boy's neck. "You have *that* much freedom."

The boy rose to his feet and clutched his father for support. His knees were weak and a faintness descended on him.

"It was the magic, Louis," the old man said. "It was the magic dust that brought back love to the people."

The boy kissed him. "Yes, my Father," he said. "It was the magic. Come . . . come, we will go home now."

The old man took the boy's face in his hands, nodded, smiled, and then burst into laughter. After a moment Louis

Gallegos began to laugh too and, arms intertwined, they stood laughing uproariously, laughing at the miraculous salvation that had descended upon them, at the joy of being alive. Still laughing, they started home. Koch went back to the jail, glad that one day's work was done.

Later, Peter Sykes wandered drunkenly back to the gallows, and stared up at the broken rope. He kept shaking his head and mumbling. "I'll be damned," he said to himself. "I'll be God-damned. It was a new rope! It was a brand new rope!"

He still clutched the three gold coins in his hand. When he saw that three small Mexican children were watching him, Sykes turned away, but somehow, in spite of himself, he felt drawn to them. Without conscious volition, Sykes flung the coins on the ground at the children's feet. They stood motionless, almost as if they were not breathing.

"Go ahead," Sykes yelled. "Take them. They're yours!"

Slowly and with great dignity, the children reached down into the dust and each took a coin. Then they watched the fat man as he walked slowly across the square.

Why, the fat man said to himself. Why? Why did I do that? I don't understand. Once he stopped and looked over his shoulder at the Mexican children. He began to laugh. "Must be the magic," he announced out loud. "That's what she is . . . magic!"

The laughter bubbled and gurgled inside him and then burst out into the air. The great noise surrounded him as he walked down the main street past the jail. He had never laughed like that before. And still it came and he couldn't stop. He could be heard blocks away, a fat huckster who waddled through the dust and roared with uncontrollable laughter.

The square was empty; the sun had disappeared over the vast horizon that stretched all around the town. An empty tobacco bag lay near the gallows. Soon it would be swallowed up by the desert as all things were swallowed up.

The town, still ugly and still full of squalor, prepared itself for the night. It was small, misery-laden, and this had been the day of a hanging. Of little historical consequence really. But if there was any moral to be drawn . . . it might be said that in any quest for magic, in any search for sorcery . . . it might be wise to first check the human heart.

For inside this deep place is a wizardry that costs far more than a few pieces of gold. It was, of course, a fact that no one in the town could articulate this thought. But there was a feeling. There was a mood. And there were questions now where before no questions had existed.

So the town let the starry night enfold it, and went to sleep. The next day the town would again give battle to the sun and the sand. The gallows would be torn down. But the day of the hanging . . . this had been committed to memory.

NEW STORIES
FROM THE
TWILIGHT ZONE

THE WHOLE TRUTH

You could say this of Harvey Hennicutt—he was an exceptional liar. When Harvey peddled one of his used cars, his lying was colorful, imaginative, and had a charm all of its own.

Along automobile row it was said of him that he could sell anything that had at least two wheels, one headlight, one unbroken glass, and a semblance of an engine—given ten minutes to make the pitch. Many of his most famous transactions are doubtless apocryphal, but some of them are quite authentic, because I remember them myself.

There was the time he latched on to the old General Sherman tank. Bought it off a junk dealer for twenty-five dollars. Harvey put it on a big wooden platform in front of his lot and offered it as the "Week's Special." Now, you may well ask who in their right mind would buy a fifty-three-ton General Sherman tank, complete with cannon. Most of the scoffers along the row posed the same question. But Harvey had picked up the vehicle on Thursday, and by Friday morning, at 9:12, he had sold it for three hundred and eighty-six dollars!

I happened to be in the neighborhood that morning and I heard part of his pitch: "Ever see a buggy like this? Take this little baby out on the highway and see what kinda courtesy you get! No teenager's gonna try to fender-bender ya with this one! Depreciation? Why, hell! I know four members of the Joint Chiefs of Staff and a C.I.A. guy who drive these things regularly back and forth to the Pentagon. The styles don't change, so it ain't never obsolete—and you know how efficient a diesel engine is. The cannon? It's the most effective turn signal you could ever use. The guy behind you has gotta be blind or three days dead not to notice it! Snow, ice, rain, muck, sleet, hail—why, hell, man!—this thing'll go in any weather. Look at the way it's built. What other car on the road has six and a half inches of bullet-proof armor? Visibility? You mean the slit there—in front of where the driver sits? Why, that makes you keep your eye on the road. Nothin' to detract you—no road signs, scenery, good-lookin' broads in sports cars, or anything else. 'Cause all you see is the road right smack dab in front of ya. Why, hell! If I could've latched onto ten of these during prohibition, I could've retired long ago!"

The buyer was a mild little mailman who had simply dropped by the lot to deliver two circulars and a letter from Harvey's aunt. He drove off in the General Sherman tank, looking a little benumbed by the whole thing—and Harvey Hennicutt watched him pull out and stood at rigid attention, saluting, as the thing rumbled by.

Harvey wasn't an innately dishonest man. He didn't lie because he was some kind of devious bastard. It was just that his entire frame of reference was "the deal." He had to buy, sell, and trade the way most people find it necessary to breathe. It was not the extra sixty-five bucks he ootzed out of a hapless customer but simply the principle of backing someone up against a wall and then slowly bending his opponent's will until it dissolved. In the twenty-odd years I knew Harvey, I never heard him tell a stupid lie. They were all of them bright, well conceived, and rather pure, as lies go. All of which leads to the story that he told me when last I saw him.

Now, normally most of Harvey's stories can be overlooked—but not this one. The Harvey Hennicutt who buttonholed me out in front of his lot on that gray, sullen November day was a different man, and a different storyteller. Even the loud, garish sport coat that was his uniform and that screeched at you with its off-violet checks, the flamboyant hand-painted tie, the Stetson sitting on the back of his head could not disguise the grim, set, almost frightened look on Harvey's face. And this was his story:

It was in September—a beautiful Indian summer late afternoon. A golden sun sparkled through the somewhat faded bunting that surrounded Harvey's used-car emporium. It highlighted one particular banner that read: "Harvey Hennicutt's Used Motors—Not a Dud in the Lot." And there stood the cars—or rather, "lay" the cars. Because Harvey's stock in trade was, and always had been, the antique lemon barely able to wheeze on and off his lot. Harvey was leaning against a car, cleaning his nails and watching a young couple examining a 1928 Buick at the far end of the lot.

You had to see Harvey's face to believe it on an occasion like this. He was a General of the Armies deciding the strategy of the attack. He was the psychiatrist analyzing the patient. Now he put on his most infectious smile—the one he saved up for the initial assault, and he carried it with him over to the antique Buick.

The young man looked up somewhat diffidently and nervously.

"We were just looking—"

"We want you to!" Harvey exclaimed. "We certainly want you to. Nobody rushes you around here. Nossir, young man, around here you can exhale, pause, check and re-check, think, peruse, contemplate, thumb over, wade through, and dip into." He made an expansive gesture at the line of cars. "Be my guest, folks."

The young man and woman blinked as the verbal wave hit them and bowled them over.

"We were . . ." the young man began hesitantly. "We were thinking of . . . you know . . . a nice four-door. Something under five hundred dollars and as late a model as we could go."

Harvey closed his eyes, shook his head with a pained, desperate expression on his face. "You shock me, do you know that?" He then looked toward the girl. "Did you know that your husband shocked me just then?"

The girl's mouth formed an O, and then plopped closed. Harvey tapped the fender of the old car.

"Do you know why you shocked me?" he asked. "Do you? I'll tell you why you shocked me. Because you have succumbed to the propaganda of every cement-headed clod up and down this street. I said *propaganda!*" He pounded on the car and left a dent which he hurriedly covered up with his elbow. "They tell ya to go with the late models. Don't they? They do, don't they?"

Captivated, the young man and woman nodded in unison. "You know *why* they tell ya to go with the late models?" Harvey continued. "Do you think they do that because they're honest, law-abiding, rigidly moral church-goers?" He shook his head and made a face like a minister suddenly observing a crap game in one of the pews. "Let me tell ya something, young man." He waggled a finger in the young man's face. "They push late models because that's where the profit margin is! They'll try to cram the post-fifty-fours down your gullet because they'd rather make a buck than a friend! They'd rather make a profit than a relationship!"

Again he pounded on the fender, forgetting himself—and this time there was the screech of metal as the fender separated from the body of the car. Harvey hid this disaster by deliberately standing in front of it.

"They would rather fill their wallets with cash, than their hearts with the fellowship of men to men," Harvey continued.

The young man gulped and swallowed. "Well, all we're looking for is good transportation, and we figured that the newer the car—"

Harvey threw up his hands, interrupting him. "Now, that's where you're wrong! That is precisely where you have gone amiss. That is the juncture where you have headed off into a blind alley. You don't want a new car. You don't want one of these rinky-dinks slapped together on an assembly line, covered with chintzy chrome, fin tails, idiotic names, and no more workmanship than you can stick into a thimble! I'll tell ya what you're lookin' for." Again he pointed a waggling finger into the young man's face. "What you're lookin' for is the craftsmanship that comes with age! The dependability that comes with a proven performance! The dignity of traditional transportation."

He drew back as if unveiling the Hope diamond, and pointed to the car behind him. "This is what you're lookin' for. This is a 1938 four-door Chevy—and this will get ya where ya want to go and get ya back."

Harvey's voice went on and on. The pitch took another four or five minutes. And while the whole thing sounded spontaneous it was all a practiced routine. He broke down his assault into three phases. First was the slam bang, "back-'em-up-against-a-wall" for the initial contact. The second phase was the one he entered into now—the quiet, rather beneficent, patient phase. Later came part three, the wrap-up. Right now, he smiled beatifically at the two young people, winked at the girl as if to say, "I've got a few little ones like you at home myself"—and then, in a voice much gentler, pointed to the Chevy.

"Look. I don't want to rush you kids. Rushing isn't my business. Satisfaction happens to be my business. And I tell ya what ya do. Spend some time with that automobile. Look it over. Sit in it. Get the feel of it. Relish the luxury of it. Check and see how they built cars when cars were really built. Go ahead, my friend," he continued, leading the young man over to the front door—and then hurriedly reaching out to grab the wife. "Sit in it. Climb right in there and sit to your heart's content. What you really need is some candlelight and a good bottle of wine. Because this baby right here has dignity!"

Harvey heard the sound of a car pulling into the lot at the far end. He slammed the door on the young couple, raising a cloud of dust and an agonized groan of protesting metal, smiled at his victims through the cloudy glass, and then hurried over to the north end of the lot where other commerce appeared to be waiting for him.

The "commerce" in this case was a model A Ford, driven by a silvery-haired old man with a face like Santa Claus and happy, guileless eyes. Harvey had a thing about happy, guileless eyes, because it usually meant a quick, and relatively painless, transaction. He walked up within a few feet of the model A. It chugged, whinnied, backfired twice, and finally came to an uneasy stop. The old man got out and smiled at Harvey.

"How do you do?"

Harvey ran a tongue around the inside of his mouth. "That depends, grandpa. If you're here to park it—I'll charge you nominal rates. If you're here to sell it—you've gotta give me three and a half minutes to have my little laugh." With this, he stepped back and surveyed the car, tilting his head in several different directions, walking around several times with an occasional look at the old man. Finally he stopped, heaved a deep sigh, put his hands behind his back, and closed his eyes for a moment.

"Well?" the old man asked quietly.

"I might give ya fifteen bucks. A junkyard'll give ya twelve, and the Smithsonian might beat us both by a buck or two."

The old man merely smiled a gentle smile. "It's a wonderful old car and they made them better in the old days, I think . . ."

Harvey's eyes rolled wildly, and he shook his head as if struggling for an almost superhuman patience. "Grandfather dear," he said, holding out his hands in a gesture of resignation, "that is the old rhubarb. The saw. The turkey that everybody and his brother tries to peddle on the open market." Then, mimicking fiercely: "'Cars were built better in the old days.' That, sir, is a fabrication beyond belief! Why, ten years ago they didn't know how to build cars. It's the new stuff that sells. It's the new stuff that runs. It's the new stuff that shows the genius of mind, muscle, and the assembly line!"

He very condescendingly, and with a kind of supersecretive air, leaned toward the old man. "I'll tell ya what I'll do—because I love your face." He made a motion encompassing the man's whole figure. "Because you remind me of my own grandfather, rest his soul. A man of dignity right down through his twilight years till the day he died saving a boatload of capsized people on the East River!" His eyes went down reverently for a moment, and then up again very quickly. "I'll give ya twenty-five for it. I'll probably have to dismantle it and sell it wheel by wheel, bolt by bolt, to whatever itinerant junk man comes around. But twenty-five I'll give ya!"

"Twenty-five dollars?" The old man looked at the car with nostalgia. "I . . . I kind of need the money." He turned to Harvey. "You couldn't make it thirty?"

Harvey stuck a cold cigar between his teeth and looked away. "You try me, old friend," he said in a grim voice. "You try me right down to the bare nerve of my most inveterate patience!"

The old man kept looking at Harvey. "Does that mean—" he tried to interject.

Harvey smiled down at him with the same assaulted patience. "That means that twenty-five is going, going, going . . . twenty-five is gone!" With a single motion, his wallet was out of his hip pocket, and from a cash-packed interior, he removed three bills and handed them to the old man. He turned him around and pointed toward the shack in the center of the lot.

"You walk into that little office there," he ordered, "and

bring your car registration papers with you." He looked toward the model A. "Did I say 'car'? I meant . . ." He wiggled his fingers as though searching for a word. "That vehicle! I'll stretch a point as far as the next man! But there are limits, my charming old friend, there are definitely limits." With this, he turned abruptly and walked away, back to the young couple still seated in the 1938 Chevy.

He peered at them through the window, wiggled his fingers, smiled, winked, ran a tongue over his teeth, and then looked skyward with suppressed impatience. In the process, he propped a foot on the rear bumper of the car and it immediately clattered to the ground. Harvey lifted it back into place, secured it with a kick, and then turned to walk over to the shack.

When he went inside, the old man had just finished with the registration papers. He smiled at Harvey. "Signed, sealed, and delivered, Mr. . . ." He looked out of the window toward the giant banner. "Mr. Hennicutt. Here are the keys." He placed a set of ignition keys on the desk, and stared at them for a reflective moment. Then he looked at Harvey with a small, apologetic smile. "There is one other item that I ought to mention to you about the car."

Harvey was examining the registration papers and barely looked up. "Oh—do, do," he said.

"It's haunted."

Harvey looked up at him briefly and gave a kind of "see-what-I-have-to-go-through" smile. "Is that a fact?"

"Oh, yes," the old man said. "Indubitably. The car is haunted. It's been haunted since the day it came off the assembly line, and every single one of its owners can attest to this fact."

Harvey continued to smile as he walked around the desk and sat down in his chair. He winked, puckered up his mouth, ran his tongue around inside his cheeks. His voice was quite gentle. "I don't suppose you'd like to tell me," he asked, "*how* the car is haunted . . . or how I can get it unhaunted?"

"Oh, you'll find out soon enough," the old man said. He rose and started for the door. "And as for unhaunting it—you'll have to sell the car. Good day to you, Mr. Hennicutt. It's been a pleasure doing business with you."

Harvey remained seated in his chair. "Oh, likewise . . . likewise," he said.

The old man paused at the door and turned to him. "I think you'll find that you may have actually gotten the best of the bargain at that."

Harvey laced his fingers together behind his head. "My aged friend," he announced in a hurt tone, "you do me the ultimate injustice. This little transaction, haunted or otherwise, is my charity case of the day. You dwell on that, will you? Just go ahead and dwell on it."

The old man pursed his lips. "No, no, no, Mr. Hennicutt. *You* dwell on it— And I rather think you will." Then he laughed, and walked out of the office.

Harvey looked down at the registration papers, then shoved them untidily into a basket on his desk, already running over in his mind how he could advertise the model A as one of the cars used on the "Untouchables"—or even, perhaps, plugging it as the actual car used by Eliot Ness in his capture of Baby Face Floyd. He'd shoot a couple of .22 holes in the rear fender and point these out as having taken place during the monumental chase. Three hundred bucks easy for a car with this history and tradition of law and order. His daydreaming was stopped by the sound of the young couple's voices approaching from outside. He looked out the window to see them walking toward the shack. He immediately replaced his normal expression of avarice by his "third-phase, wrap-'em-up" look—a mixture of parental affection and rock-ribbed, almost painful, honesty. It was this look he took outside with him.

The young man pointed to a 1934 Auburn. "How much is that one over there?" he inquired.

A pigeon, Harvey thought. An absolute, unadulterated, bonafide, A-number-one honest-to-God pigeon. That Auburn had been with Harvey for twelve years. It was the first automobile and the last one he'd ever lost money on. He cleared his throat. "You mean that collectors' item? That's—that's—" Harvey's eyes bugged. For some crazy reason, nothing more came out. He formed the words—packed them up like snowballs, and tried to throw them, *but nothing came out*!

After a moment something did come out. It was Harvey's voice and they were his words, but he was not conscious of actually saying them. "It's not for sale," his voice said.

The young man exchanged a look with his wife and then pointed to the Chevy that they had been sitting in. "How about the Chev?"

Again Harvey felt his mouth open—and again he heard his voice. "That one's not for sale either."

"Not for sale?" The young man looked at him strangely. "But that's the one you were pushing."

"That's the one I was pushing," Harvey's voice said—and this time he knew he was saying it—"but I'm not pushing it any more. That's a heap! A rum-dum. It hasn't got any rings. It hasn't got any plugs. It hasn't got any points. It's got a cracked block and it'll eat up gasoline like it owned every oil well in the state of Texas."

Harvey's eyes looked glazed and he made a massive effort to close his mouth, but still the words came out of it. "The rubber's gone and the chassis's bent, and if I ever referred to it as a runabout, what I meant by that was that it'll run about a mile and then stop. It'll cost you double what you paid for it the minute you try to get it repaired—and you'll be gettin' it repaired every third Thursday of the month."

The young couple stared at him incredulously and Harvey stared back. His tongue felt like a red-hot poker in his mouth. He stood there forlornly, wondering when this madness would pass from him. The young couple exchanged yet another look, and finally the young man stammered, "Well . . . well, what else have you got?"

Harvey's words came out despite anything he could do to stop them. "I haven't anything to show you that's worth your while," he announced. "Everything I've got on this lot should have been condemned years ago. I've got more lemons per square foot than the United Fruit Company. So, my advice to you kids would be to run along and head for a reputable place where you get what you pay for and be pleased with it, but don't come around here, because I'll rob you blind!"

The young man was about to retort when his wife gave him a sharp nudge with her elbow, motioned with her head, and the two of them walked away.

Harvey remained standing there, absolutely motionless. He found himself drawn to the model A that stood in plain, simple, almost exquisite, homeliness. Harvey blinked, shook himself like a big St. Bernard, and then deliberately, with conscious effort, walked back into the shack.

He sat inside for several hours, asking himself a hundred times just what the hell had happened. It was as if some demon had entered him, fastened itself to his larynx and dictated his language. It was the screwiest odd-ball feeling he'd ever felt. But several hours later the feeling had worn off. What the hell, Harvey thought to himself, what the hell! They looked like the kind of kids who'd be back in the morning, screaming for their money.

But once again, for perhaps the twentieth time, he let his eyes rest on the model A. Haunted, the old man had said. Haunted! Goddamn you, Harvey Hennicutt, you will persist in dealing with kooks.

A few moments later, Harvey's assistant entered the shack. This was a sallow post-teenager named Irving Proxmier. Irving was an undernourished version of his master, affecting the same sport coat, the hat tilted on the back of his head, and a hand-painted tie that showed a hula dancer under a Hawaiian setting sun. But the imitation, of course, was noticeably inferior to the original. The effort showed itself, but only the effort.

"Sorry I'm late, boss," Irving announced, putting a cigar in his teeth in exactly the same manner he'd watched Harvey do it. "I was checking the junkyard for those '34 Chevy wheel disks. I found two of them." He looked behind him through the open door. "What's the action?"

Harvey blinked. "A little quiet this afternoon." Then, shaking himself from his deep reflections, he pointed out the window. "That '35 Essex, Irv. I want you to push that one."

"Push it is right. It'll never get anyplace under its own power."

Harvey lit a cigar. "Knock it down to fifty-five bucks. Tell everybody it's a museum piece. The last of its kind." He rose from the chair, walked over to the open door and peered outside. He noticed then that the hood of the Essex was partially open. "Booby," he announced grievously, "you gotta close the hood, booby." He turned to Irving. "How many times I gotta tell ya that? When ya can't see the engine for the rust—you've gotta play a little hide-and-seek. You don't go advertisin' the fact that you're tryin' to job off a car that carried French soldiers to the first Battle of the Marne."

Harvey's face suddenly looked very white. His lower lip sagged. That strange haunted look appeared in his eyes. He whirled around and retraced his steps over to the desk. "Irv," he said in a strained voice. "Irv . . ."

"What's the matter?" Irving asked. "You sick, boss?"

Harvey felt the words bubble inside and then heard them come out. He pointed out the window. "Put a sign on the Essex. Say it's for sale as is. No guarantees. And open up the hood wider. Let 'em take a look at that engine."

Irving gaped at him. "Ya wanna sell it—or ya wanna keep it around for an heirloom? Why, nobody in his right mind would buy that car if they could see what's under the hood."

Harvey sat down heavily in his chair. He felt the perspiration rolling down his face. He opened up the left bottom drawer of the desk and took out a small bottle of whisky, unscrewed the cap, and took a deep gulp. He looked up into Irving's worried face. "What's goin' on?" he asked in a strange, thin voice. "What's the matter with me, Irv? Irv, booby . . . do I look all right to you?"

Irving's voice was guarded. "What did ya have for dinner?"

Harvey thought for a moment, then made a gesture with his hands, denying any possible gastronomic connection. He set his face, jutted his jaw, let out a laugh dripping with bravado, and reached for the telephone.

"This is nuts," he announced definitely, as he dialed a number. "This is . . . this is power of suggestion or something. That old gleep with the model A! Lemme tell ya, Irv—a real nutsy! Comes in here with this song and dance about a haunted car—"

He heard the receiver lifted at the other end. "Honey," he said into the phone, "it's your ever-lovin'! Listen, baby . . . about tonight . . . yeah, I'm gonna be late. Well, I told ya it was inventory time, didn't I?" He doodled with his free hand, drawing a picture of an old man and a model A Ford. "Of course it's inventory time," he continued, "and what I'm gonna be doin'—" He stopped abruptly. Again his face turned white and again the beads of perspiration came on his forehead and traveled in little rivulets down his face. "As a matter of fact, honey," he heard himself saying, "I'm playin' a little poker with the boys after I close up tonight. And when I told ya last month I was doin' inventory—I was playin' poker then, too!"

At this moment, Harvey thrust the phone away from him as if it were some kind of animal lunging for his throat. He gulped, swallowed, and pulled it to him again.

"Honey," he said in a sick voice, "honey, baby—I think I'm sick or somethin'. What I just told ya . . . well, honey . . . it was a gag . . . what I mean to say is—"

Out came the words again. "I'm gonna play poker with the boys again tonight!" With this, Harvey slammed the phone down and pushed it away. He whirled around to stare at Irving, wild-eyed.

"What's goin' on, Irv? What the hell's the matter with me? I got no control over what I say. I got absolutely no control over—"

Again he stopped, took out his handkerchief and wiped his face. He rose from the chair, went across the room over to the open door, and stared out. There was the model A, sitting all by itself, several feet away from the other cars. Harvey kept staring at it, and finally turned to face Irving.

"Irv," he said, his voice strained, "I'm in the middle of a calamity! That old geezer . . . that gleep I was tellin' ya about . . . he said that car was haunted—and he was right! Ya know what, Irv? Whoever owns that car—*he's got to tell the truth!*"

Harvey clutched at his thick hair, yanking it this way and that. He shook his head back and forth, and his voice was agonized. "Irv, booby . . . do ya dig it? Can ya think of anything more ghastly?"

He released his hair and pounded himself on the chest. "Me! Harvey Hennicutt! From now on—as long as I own that car—*I gotta keep tellin' the truth!*"

Three days went by. The three longest days that Harvey Hennicutt could ever remember spending. Patsies came and patsies went and Harvey watched them go, quietly wringing his hands or pulling on his hair or just sitting inside his dinky shack, constitutionally unable even to whisper an adjective—let alone make one of his traditional vaunted pitches. Irving, he set to work making signs, and it was a few of these that the assistant brought into the shack and rather forlornly placed around the room. He pointed at them and looked up at Harvey, who sat there, head in hands.

"I finished the signs, boss," he said.

Harvey separated two fingers to let an eyeball free. He nodded perfunctorily, then covered up his face again.

Irving cleared his throat. "You want I should put 'em on the cars . . . or ya wanna read 'em?"

Once again, Harvey peeked through his fingers at the signs. "Not Guaranteed," "In Poor Condition," "Not Recommended," they announced in turn.

Irv shook his head. His voice was disconsolate. "I've heard of low pressure before, boss . . . but I mean, let's face it—this is *no* pressure."

Harvey nodded and let out a small groan. "Irv, booby," he said in a hospital-ward voice, "do you know that my wife isn't speaking to me? She hasn't spoken to me in three days."

"That ain't your only worry, boss. Do you know that in three days you haven't moved a car off this lot?" He took a step closer to Harvey. "That old lady," he continued, "who came in yesterday afternoon and wanted to buy the old Auburn? Boss—I mean, let's level now! How do ya start a sales pitch by tellin' a customer that if this car was one year older, Moses could've driven it across the Red Sea?" He shook his head. "I mean . . . there's a limit to honesty, boss!"

Harvey nodded his complete approval. "I used to think that, too," he said.

Irv smiled, changed his weight to the other foot, bit slowly into the end of a cheap cigar, and girded himself for another kind of combat.

"Boss," he said, in a slightly different tone, "I didn't wanna bother ya about this. But . . . well, you know—it's that thing about my raise."

Harvey closed his eyes. "Raise?"

Irv nodded. "It's six months today. I mean . . . I didn't wanna bug ya—but ya promised. You said in six months if I sold three cars—"

Harvey turned in the swivel chair and stared out of the window dreamily, but then his eyes grew wider as he felt another voice rising up within him, just as it had been doing the past three days. He tried to clamp his lips shut and throttle off the oncoming words, but they simply wouldn't be throttled.

"Irving," he heard his voice say, "the day I give you a raise, it'll be below zero on the Fijis!"

The words didn't stop there, though Harvey made a massive, almost inhuman effort to stop them by hurriedly reaching into the bottom desk drawer and pulling out the bottle. But even as he was uncorking it, the rest of the speech spewed out of him like lava out of a volcano.

"Every yokel who's ever worked here starts and stops at the same salary! I just keep dangling a raise in front of 'em for as long as it takes 'em to wise up."

Harvey wanted to say how sorry he was—that he didn't mean it—that he loved Irving like a son—that he certainly *would* get a raise as soon as things got back to normal; but all that came out was a simple sentence.

"For you to get any more dough outta me," Harvey heard himself saying, "would be about as easy as poking hot butter in a wildcat's ear."

Harvey lifted the bottle to his mouth as if it weighed a ton, drank, fought down the nausea, and said—in a strained, quiet voice, "Irving, booby . . . that hurt me a lot more than it hurt you!"

Irving squared his thin bony shoulders, took a few steps around the desk, stuck a fist into his former master's face.

"Correction," he said firmly, in his high, piping squeal. "This is gonna hurt me a lot worse than it's gonna hurt you."

With that, he swung from the floor, and Harvey watched it coming until it cracked on the point of his jaw. In a portion of his tired, bedraggled mind, he felt surprise that thin little Irving packed such a wallop. He was still carrying this thought as he fell over backward and landed on the floor.

Irving picked up a sign that read, "In Poor Condition—Not Recommended," laid it on Harvey's chest like a funeral wreath, and then stalked righteously out of the room.

Late that night, as Harvey tells it, he sat on the stoop of the shack looking out sadly at his car lot—and particularly at the model A, which stood like some metal pariah staring balefully back at him through its ancient headlights. The banner and bunting flapped noisily in the breeze, mocking him with their sound and with their meaninglessness.

A paunchy gentleman walked briskly into the north end of the lot, stopped, and looked down the line of automobiles. In old and better days, Harvey would've been on his feet and shaking hands and beginning phase one of the attack before the prospective buyer had drawn three breaths. But on this night, Harvey just rose slowly, waved halfheartedly, and leaned against the shack while the man eyed him and walked toward him.

The man in this case was a gentleman named Luther Grimbley. He wore a variation of a frock coat and had small beady eyes. He also wore a cigar in his mouth, which was obviously an accouterment, and he looked as if he had been born with it. He grimly nodded back at Harvey and then looked sideways at the model A. Clearly, this was one of those "thinker"-type buyers who was as anxious to engage in a battle of wills and wiles as Harvey himself. This was quite evident in the rather nonchalant way Mr. Grimbley studied the model A, but kept his eye on Harvey's expression.

Harvey himself, seeing that the man was traditionally an opponent, forced himself to walk over to him. He dredged up some of his old charm, lit his own cigar, tilted his hat an inch farther back on his head, and looked, at this moment, like the Harvey Hennicutt of old.

"What'll be your pleasure tonight?" he asked.

Grimbley kept the cigar in his teeth. "Luther Grimbley, here," he announced, and handed Harvey a card. "Honest Luther Grimbley, thirty years in politics, currently up for reelection—alderman, thirteenth ward. You've probably heard of me."

All of this came out as if it were a single sentence. Harvey took the card and read it.

"Delighted," he said. "Something in a—" He gulped. "A nice model A? It's beautiful, isn't it?"

Then Harvey mentally sat back, waiting for the perverse honesty inside of him to come out with the denial of what he'd just said, but no words came—and for the first time in several days Harvey felt hope rising up inside.

Grimbley removed the cigar, picked off a few errant fragments of tobacco, and daintily freed them from his fingertips.

"That depends," he said, his eyes half closed. "If you take twelve aspirin and shut your eyes tight—you might call that car beautiful. But in the cold light of neon, son—" He shook his head and pointed to the car. "It's a wreck! What about its condition?"

Harvey chuckled a deep chuckle and started to retort with a biblical quote that he usually used in answer to that question, and one that he had made up himself not six months before, but he heard himself saying, "The block's cracked!" He shuddered, clamped tight on the cigar, and half turned away, damning himself, honesty, the haunted car, and everything else.

Grimbley's eyebrow rose a little. "Block cracked, you say, son?"

Harvey nodded tiredly and gave up fighting. "Block cracked."

"What else?"

Harvey looked down at the tires. "Rubber's almost gone." He kicked at the tire.

Grimbley went over to the car and also kicked the tire. "It sure is," he said. Then he made a face and scratched his jaw. "Might be a few good years left in it." Then, hurriedly, looking keenly over at Harvey, "Not many, though."

Harvey felt the misery welling up, and also the words. "Many? *This* car's living on borrowed time!"

Grimbley ran his tongue inside one cheek and drummed softly on the fender of the model A. He looked at Harvey squinty-eyed.

"What's she worth?" he asked, and then hurriedly changed his tone. "I mean, assuming some clod wanted a real bum car to use for a gag or something."

He chewed off a little piece of the cigar and spit it out, then walked around the car again. He whistled a continuous low whistle, sucked in his cheeks, again tapped gently on the car's fender.

"Maybe fifty bucks?"

Harvey's eyes looked glazed. "Fifty bucks?"

"All right," Grimbley said, "maybe sixty."

"Why not thirty?" Harvey said. "You don't understand, do you?" He pointed to the car. "It's a bad car. It's a lemon."

Harvey wished fervently at this moment that his tongue would rot at the roots and he could keep his mouth shut. He was cursed, damned, and preordained, so he half turned as if ready to walk away and give it up as a bad thing. He was quite unprepared for Grimbley's reaction, for the fat little man stared at him and began to laugh. The laugh turned into a full-throated roar, until it was uncontrollable. Grimbley just stood there and laughed until the tears came out of his eyes.

"Why, you dirty dog, you! Why, you clever son of a—!"

Harvey began to laugh now, too. He didn't know exactly why. Maybe it was release or relief or something—but he joined Grimbley's laughter until his own was a shriek.

"Isn't it the truth?" he screamed. "Isn't it the honest-to-God truth!"

Grimbley wiped his eyes and gradually the laughter died away, though he still shook his head in respectful amazement.

"I've seen all kinds of routines, honest-to-God . . . all kinds of routines." He winked at Harvey and poked him in the chest. "But you clever little cookie, you—this is the old reverse English, isn't it? The old twist-a-roo! Why, you sharp shootin' sharpie!"

He laughed again and clamped the cigar back in his mouth. "You knew I wanted it, didn't you—you little devil, you!" He poked Harvey again. "You knew I wanted it. I'll tell you what," he announced, taking the cigar out, "I'll give you twenty-five bucks for it—mainly on account of it's good politics to drive an old car. Makes people realize you're not getting rich off them!"

He turned to look at the car again. "Make it twenty-two and a half. I didn't notice the dent in the fender." He put the cigar back, squinted his eyes, and looked at Harvey. "Deal?" he asked. "I mean twenty-two fifty, the car—and no strings."

The ecstatic look on Harvey's face slowly dissolved and he felt cold all over. "No strings," he repeated weakly.

Harvey's tone was quite sufficient for Grimbley. Once again his tongue explored the inside of his mouth and he squinted from Harvey to the car and back again.

"You better trot out the strings, buddy boy. Trot out the strings. I want to know what I'm getting!"

Harvey looked off in another direction and closed his eyes. "Twenty-two fifty—the car as is, and . . . and . . ."

"*And what?*"

Harvey turned to him, his voice ghostlike. "It's haunted," he said weakly.

Grimbley took the cigar out of his mouth again and stared at Harvey, and then the laughter came again, uncontrollable, shrieking. "It's haunted!" he shouted. "The Goddamn car is haunted!" He could barely control himself and just stood there, hands around his vast girth, rolling, wheezing, and half doubled over with hysteria, repeating it over and over again. "It's haunted. The Goddamn thing is haunted."

Finally he stopped and wiped his eyes, and the cigar was back between his teeth. "So it's haunted! I swear to God, you're the cleverest cookie in fifty states! You ought to be in politics." He laughed again. "It's haunted." He wiped his eyes again, and the chuckle was still in his voice when he asked, "How's it haunted?"

Harvey's eyeballs rolled up in his head. "Whoever owns it," he heard himself say, "has to tell the truth!" There, Goddamnit,

Harvey thought, at least it's out in the air. He could stop worrying about it. The honest Satan inside him had performed the ultimate treachery and forced the admission out.

The word "truth" had a telling effect on Mr. Grimbley. It was as if Harvey had said "smallpox" or "venereal disease" or "the black plague." He let out a long, low breath and took the cigar out of his mouth.

"Has to tell the *truth*?" he asked, pronouncing the word as if it were a profanity.

Harvey nodded. "The whole truth. And the only way you can stop telling the truth is to sell the car."

Again Grimbley gave Harvey his squinty-eyed look and then stared at the model A. He walked a few feet away and pointed to a 1935 Dodge with a rumble seat.

"How about this baby?" he inquired, loading the question with the grape shot of the experienced price-knocker-down.

Harvey heaved a huge sigh. "That's no baby! It's a great grandfather. It's got no transmission, no rear end, no axle. That one's shot."

Immediately after saying this, his shoulders slumped and his normally ruddy face took on the color of an off-white sheet.

Grimbley's eyes sparkled. He was on the precipice of a vast and strange knowledge and he perceived it readily. He took a few steps over to Harvey and spoke in a hushed voice.

"That's the goods, isn't it?" he asked. "You *have* to tell the truth, don't you?" He shook his head from side to side. "That's it! That's the reason for the song and dance. *You have to tell the truth.*"

Harvey smiled the kind of smile that on babies is considered gas. He made a halfhearted gesture toward the car.

"What about the model A?" he said. "Outside of the fact that it's haunted, it's a . . . it's a nice conversation piece."

Grimbley held up a beefy hand. "For some people, maybe," he said positively, "but not for old honest Luther Grimbley! Buddy boy, I'm in politics and when you tell me I gotta start tellin' the truth all the time—" He pulled at his jowls and looked horrified. "Holy God!" He looked back over at the car. "Well, do you know something? I couldn't make a single political speech! I couldn't run for office again. Why, old honest Luther Grimbley . . . old honest Luther Grimbley would die on the vine!"

He carefully butted out the cigar on the sidewalk, scraped

off the ashes, and deposited it in his pocket. He started off with a wave of his hand.

"See ya around, buddy boy," he called over his shoulder.

"Hey!" Harvey yelled.

Grimbley stopped and turned to him. Harvey pointed to the car.

"Any suggestions?"

Grimbley looked thoughtful for a moment. "Suggestions? Yeah, maybe one. Why don't ya hang yourself!" Then he turned and walked off.

Harvey leaned against the model A, staring down at his feet, feeling the weight of his depression like sandbags on his shoulders. He took a slow, rather aimless walk over to the shack. He had barely entered the small room when Irving appeared at the door.

He entered silently and picked up a paintbrush from a bucket in the corner. He held it up.

"I came back for this."

Harvey nodded numbly and sat down at his desk.

"It belongs to me," Irving said defensively.

Harvey shrugged again and looked at him blankly. "I'm happy for you." He turned in the swivel chair and looked out the window. "I'm like Dante in the inferno," he announced rhetorically. "I'm absolutely like that fella Dante—doomed, damned . . . bankrupt!"

He turned again in the chair to face Irving. "Booby . . . One man! One clod! One absolute idiot who's got a thing for a pig-in-the-poke! Or one guy whose tellin' the truth all the time might do some good! Irving—is there no such patsy in this city? In this country?"

Irving stared at him, totally without sympathy.

"You're askin' me? You got a helluva nerve! Askin' me about patsies! After I've slaved and worked and broke my back and told lies for ya! You got a helluva nerve even sittin' there talkin' to me! My old man says you're a son of a bitch! And ya know somethin', Hennicutt?"

At this point, Irving slammed his small fist down on the desk. "My old man is right!"

Once again he pounded on the desk for emphasis, and it was then that Harvey noticed the newspaper lying there. He reached over and pulled it to him, turning it so that he could read the headlines. He stared at it for a long moment, then put it down and started to drum his fingers on the desk.

"And, furthermore," Irving's voice squealed, "my old man says that for two cents he'd come over here and give you such a hit in the head you'd never forget it! And, besides that—my sister's husband is goin' to law school at night and I've got every intention of talkin' this whole thing over with him and maybe suing you for contributing to the delinquency of a minor!"

Harvey's head was bent low over the paper. He gave no sign of hearing Irving's soliloquy, much less being moved by it.

Irving slammed his bony little fist on the desk top again.

"When I think . . . When I think of the terrible things you had me do—like sellin' that 1928 hearse and sayin' it was Babe Ruth's town car!"

He shook his head at the enormity of his past transgressions, but still Harvey Hennicutt kept his eyes fastened on the paper. His lips moved soundlessly as he read something in it, and then, very slowly, he looked up into Irving's face.

"Why not?" he whispered. "I ask ya, Irving, *why not*?"

Irving thrust out a belligerent pointed jaw. "Why not what?"

Harvey slapped the newspaper. "Why not sell it to *him*?"

"Never mind *him*," Irving screeched out. "What about my rights? What about my severance pay? What about my seniority?"

Harvey had the phone book in his hand and was riffling through the pages. He looked up briefly at Irving.

"Irving, booby . . . I am about to strike a blow for democracy! I don't know *how* I'm goin' to—but I'm goin' to. You and me, booby," he said, looking down at the phone book. "You and me. This moment is goin' down in history right alongside of Washington crossing the Delaware, the invasion of Normandy, and the repeal of the Eighteenth Amendment!"

Irving gaped at him. "What?" he inquired in a soft voice.

"Exactly!" Harvey said. "*And you are there!*"

He grabbed the phone and pulled it toward him. He started to dial a number, and at the same time looked up at Irving.

"You run out and dust off that Packard—the one with the sawdust in the wheel bearings."

"Check, boss," Irving said, as he turned smartly and headed for the door.

Harvey Hennicutt was functioning again. Irving could hear the great man's voice on the telephone. It rang with some of the old assurance, the verve, and the grandeur of the man who had once actually sold a Mack truck to a midget along with a written guarantee that the midget would grow an inch and a quarter each year just by stretching to reach the pedals.

It was eight in the morning when a long, sleek black limousine pulled into Harvey Hennicutt's used-car lot. Harvey, hearing it stop, left the shack and went over to it. He noticed immediately that it was driven by a chauffeur who had a build like Mickey Hargitay.

There was a huddled figure in the back seat who sat motionless with his coat collar hiding his face, but the front door opened and out stepped a dapper little man with a face like a chicken hawk. He gave Harvey a no-nonsense nod, looked around at the various cars, with a raised eyebrow, then pointed to the model A.

"This is the car, I presume?"

Harvey nodded. "That's the baby."

"Baby?"

"It's an American expression," Harvey explained. "We call everything 'baby.'"

He looked over the little man's shoulder at the black limousine. "That's not a bad-lookin' baby *you're* drivin'. You're not thinkin' of trading that in, are you?"

The little man shook his head decisively. "I am interested only in this so-called model A you described on the telephone."

Harvey smiled at him. Then he winked, and jammed an elbow into the little man's rib cage.

"Got to ya, didn't I?"

He jerked a thumb in the direction of the model A. "Wouldn't that be a blast. You take that car back to your country, tell 'em that this is a sample of what the capitalists drive?" Again he rammed an elbow into the little man's side. "That's worth six points, ain't it?"

The little man dusted off his coat, moved a step back, and surveyed Harvey, half with horror and half with a curious, clinical interest.

"Precisely what we choose to do with the automobile," he said tersely, "is *our* business, so long as we agree on the terms. You said that the automobile was three hundred dollars?"

Harvey noted that the little man was already reaching into his coat for a wallet.

"Three hundred dollars," Harvey explained hurriedly, "is for the car without the extras."

He felt his eyeballs swell as the little man dug into the wallet and started to extract bills.

"The hubcaps are extra—that's twenty bucks. The hand crank—not that you'll probably need it—that I'll practically give away for twelve."

His practiced eye was a gimlet microscope as he looked over at the model A.

"That special window glass—" He felt the truth rising up in him and heard himself say at this point, "It ain't unbreakable, I mean."

"Not unbreakable?" the little man inquired.

"It breaks, is what I mean," Harvey explained, and then deciding that discretion was the better part of valor, he wordlessly pulled out several papers, spread them out on the hood of an incredibly aged Jordan 8.

"Now if you'll just sign here," Harvey said, whipping out a pen. "That's the transfer of ownership, title, and memorandum of sale. Each one is in triplicate and I put an X where you gotta sign each one."

The little man collected the papers and carried them over to the black limousine. He tapped on the rear window and a large, pudgy hand came out to take the papers. It disappeared with them into the dark confines of the rear seat. There was a muffled inquiry in a strange language. The little man turned, called out to Harvey.

"My—my 'employer' would like to know if a guarantee comes with this automobile."

Again, Harvey had that ice-cold feeling. It had come—that moment of truth again. He smiled weakly. Coughed. Blew his nose. Hummed a short selection from *Guys and Dolls*. Looked wildly over his shoulder to see if he could find Irving and change the subject. But the question hung over him like Damocles' sword, and all of his ritual, he knew very well, was simply a delaying rearguard action. He had to make his stand—and make it he did.

"The car's haunted," he said, in a hollow, muffled voice.

The little man looked at him with a raised eyebrow. "Haunted?" he inquired.

Harvey unloaded his caution in one fell swoop. "Haunted it is," he said. "Real haunted. I mean, it's like . . . it's like *haunted*! And that's somethin' you can't say about any other car you've ever seen!"

Harvey's voice went on, buoyed up by truth, propelled out by honesty, and given a lyrical quality by his sheer desperation.

"Lemme tell ya somethin', buddy," he said, walking over to the little man to poke him with a forefinger. "A lot of these cars are real gone. I mean *long* gone. And some of 'em are absolute first-rate bonafide lemons. I got some I keep behind the shack, camouflaged, because they're the old busteroo's!"

He whirled around and pointed dramatically toward the model A. "But that car—that model A— That car is absolutely haunted. I guarantee it. *It is like absolutely haunted!*"

The interpreter, or whoever he was, turned and said a few words into the back seat of the car, and, after a moment, was handed some papers by the person sitting there. He passed these over to Harvey.

"Here you are," he said. "All signed." He looked at the model A over Harvey's shoulder. "Now, I presume the car has petrol?" he inquired.

"Petrol?" Harvey made a face. "You mean like—like—"

"Gasoline," the little man interrupted. "Does it have a full tank of gasoline?"

"She's loaded up," Harvey said. "You can just drive 'er away, buddy."

The little man nodded, satisfied, motioned to the chauffeur, who got out of the limousine. Harvey turned, kicked his heels together in the air, and then waltzed back over to the shack like some ponderous ballet dancer. He took the four steps in one leap, slammed his way into the room, grabbed Irving by the ears, and planted a big wet kiss on his forehead. He held out the papers, and studied them. For the first time in days he felt an incredible lightness of mind and body, as if he had just been removed from a concrete cast.

Irving was both frightened and impressed as he looked out through the open door at the black limousine departing.

"You know what that is, boss? That's what they call a Zis. It's Russian."

Harvey kicked over a wastebasket with sheer animal joy. "That's what she is," he said. "Irving, booby," he gushed, as he

312 / NEW STORIES FROM THE TWILIGHT ZONE

leaped up on the desk upsetting an inkwell and a basket of papers, "this is very likely the happiest day of my life!"

Irving was not listening to him anymore. He was staring, wide-eyed, out the door as the model A chugged past him.

"Boss," Irving whispered, "boss, you sold it!"

He turned to stare at Harvey, then slowly his eyes lowered to the newspaper, still on the desk. The headline read, "Khrushchev visiting UN."

"Khrushchev." Irving barely got it out. "Nikita Khrushchev."

He took a hesitant step toward the desk, where Harvey stood like some offbeat god in a pool of ink and torn papers. Irving looked up at him with awe and reverence.

"That's who you sold the car to, wasn't it, boss? Nikita Khrushchev."

Harvey held out the registration papers in his hand and pointed to a signature. "Irving, booby," he announced senatorially, "from this second on, when that old lard-head starts to walk on his lower lip—it comes out like the truth!"

"Boss," Irving whispered, feeling himself in the presence of some kind of deity, "boss . . . how the hell did ya do it?"

Harvey lowered the papers and placed them on the desk well away from the pool of ink. He thought for a moment and then spoke.

"Acumen, Irving," he finally said, in a gentle voice. "Stick-to-itiveness. Will. Determination. Perseverance. Patriotism. Unselfishness. Resolve." He lit a cigar. "And also the fact that if I had to tell the truth one more time, I'd've had to commit suicide!"

He took the cigar out of his mouth and surveyed it at arm's length. "Know what I told 'em, Irv? I told 'em it'd be a real blast to take the raunchiest-lookin' puddle jumper ever to come ort of Detroit, take it back to the USSR and put it on display. Propaganda! That was the pitch. Show all of them walking Muscovites just what the average American drives—or at least what Nikita would like 'em to *believe* we drive."

Irving's face looked drawn and his eyes narrowed slightly.

"Boss," he said, "that ain't patriotic."

Harvey beamed at him from his Mount Olympus of righteousness and holy zeal.

"Irving," he said patiently, "that's what I *told* 'em they could do with the car, but that isn't what they're gonna be *able* to do with it. When Fatty starts that kind of pitch, it isn't gonna come out that way."

He chuckled softly, got down off the desk, reached for the phone, studied it a moment, then started to dial a number.

"Irving," he said, over his shoulder to the boy standing there like a pilgrim seeing a miracle performed. "Irving, run out there and close the hood on the Essex—and if anybody should come within ten feet of it, you lasso 'em. Tell 'em that that car was formerly owned by a lady embalmer who won it at a raffle at a DAR convention in Boston, but it was only used once a year as a float in Fourth of July parades."

Irving's eyes shone with almost tearful respect and admiration.

"Right, boss," he choked. "I'll attend to it."

He turned and went outside, as Harvey heard the operator's voice on the phone.

"Yes, ma'am," he said, chewing on the cigar. "I think I'll probably need Information. . . . That's correct. . . . Ya see, what I had in mind was that if an American citizen had somethin' real important in the way of news . . . I mean . . . if it affected the policy of the United States . . . what I mean is—if from now on, everything that fat boy over there said was the absolute truth— well, what I'd really like to know is . . . *Can you get me through to Jack Kennedy?*"

Then he sat back, chewing happily on his cigar, as outside the noise of Irving's pounding down the hood of the aged Essex came over the quiet lot like a clarion call to arms.

Harvey Hennicutt, as he tells it, was eminently satisfied.

THE SHELTER

Outside it was a summer night. Broad-leaved oaks and maples caught the lights of the old stately houses that flanked the street. A breeze carried with it the eight o'clock noises of television westerns, kids asking for glasses of water, and the discordant tinkle of a piano.

In Dr. Stockton's house, the meal had been eaten, and his wife, Grace, was bringing in the birthday cake. The people at the table rose, applauded, whistled—and somebody began singing "Happy Birthday to You," and then they all joined in.

Bill Stockton blushed, put his head down, held up his hand in protest, but down deep he felt incredibly happy.

Marty Weiss, a small, dark, intense little guy who ran a shoe store on Court Street, got to his feet and shouted out:

"Speech, Doc. Let's have a speech!"

Bill Stockton blushed again. "Lay off me, will ya—you crazy people. A surprise party is all my heart can take. You want to lose your friendly family physician?"

There was laughter, and then Jerry Harlowe—a big, tall man, who had gone to college with Bill—stood up and held out his glass.

"Before he blows out the candles," Harlowe announced pontifically, "I should like to propose a toast, since no birthday celebration is complete without a traditional after-dinner address."

Martha Harlowe gave him a Bronx cheer and Marty's wife, Rebecca, tried to pull him down by the back of his coat. Harlowe leaned over and gave her a big wet kiss and they all shrieked with laughter. Then he held up his glass again, waved off Grace's protest that first her husband should blow out the candles, and addressed the group.

"And now to get down to the business at hand—that of honoring one Dr. William Stockton, who's grown one year older and who will admit to being over twenty-one."

Again they all laughed, and Grace leaned over to hug her husband.

Harlowe turned toward Bill Stockton and smiled, and there was something in the smile that made them all become quiet.

"We got this little surprise party together, Bill," he said, "as a very small reminder to you that on this particular street, and in this particular town, you're a very beloved guy. There isn't one of us in this room who hasn't put in a frantic phone call to you in the middle of the night with a sick kid or a major medical crisis that turns out to be indigestion. And you'd come out with that antique medical bag of yours, one eye closed and half asleep, but without even a moment's hesitation. And while things like this never appear on a bill under 'services rendered,' you made a lot of hearts beat easier, and you've eased more pain than I'd ever like to feel."

He grinned, then winked at the people who were listening so intently.

"And there also isn't one of us in this room," he continued, "who hasn't owed you a whopping bill for a lot of months, and I expect there are plenty of us on this street who owe you one now."

There was laughter at this. And Marty Weiss banged on his glass with a fork.

"What about his hammering at all hours of the night?" he called out. "That's another thing we owe him for."

Jerry Harlowe joined in the laughter, then held up his hands.

"Oh, yes," he said, with a smile. "The good doctor's bomb shelter. I think we might as well forgive him for that, despite the fact that what he thinks is farsightedness on his part is a pain in the neck to all the rest of us on this street. The concrete trucks, the nocturnal hammering, and all the rest of it."

They all laughed again, and Bill Stockton looked around quizzically, knife in hand.

"I can tell you all this," he said. "You don't get any cake until the windbag is finished."

"Why, Bill Stockton!" his wife said, with gentle admonition.

"Bill's right," Marty interjected. "Go ahead, Jerry, get it over with while we're still sober enough to eat."

Harlowe picked up his wine glass again. "This is the end right here. When Grace mentioned that it was your birthday, we took it on ourselves to handle the proceedings. And just as a little personal aside, let me conclude this way. A toast to Dr. William Stockton, whom I've known for better than twenty years. To all the nice things he's done for a lot of people—and because he's forty-four years old, and because we wish him a minimum forty-four more to keep being the same kind of guy he is, and the way he always has been. Happy birthday, you old bastard."

He took a long swig and Rebecca Weiss suddenly began to cry.

"Oh, my dear God," announced Marty. "Down goes a speech, up come my wife's tears."

Bill Stockton blew out the candles, then looked up with a mock sardonic look. "I don't blame her," he said. "First a surprise party—and I abhor surprise parties—and then a sloppy sentimental speech." He turned toward Harlowe and held out his hand. "But just between you and me and the American Medical Association—you're nice people to have around, whether you pay your bills or not."

He turned and looked down the length of the table, and held up his own glass. "May I reciprocate, my friends. To my neighbors—with my thanks that you're in the neighborhood."

"Amen," whispered Marty Weiss, and turned to his wife. "And if you cry again, I'll belt you." He leaned over and kissed her, and Bill Stockton started to cut the cake.

"Hey, pop."

It was Stockton's son, Paul, who came into the dining room. He was a twelve-year-old mass of freckles and looked like a pint-size version of the doctor.

"The television set just went out."

Stockton held out his hands in dismay. "Gad, crisis, crisis, crisis! And how can the world survive without the *Untouchables* and *Huckleberry Hound*?"

"It was the *U.S. Steel Hour*," the boy said seriously. "And the picture went out and then there was some kind of crazy announcement. Something about . . ."

He continued to speak, but he was drowned out by Martha Harlowe laughing at something Rebecca had said to her. But Marty Weiss, closest to the boy, suddenly looked serious. He got out of his seat and turned to the others.

"Hold it, everybody," he said tensely. Then he turned toward Paul. "What did you say, Paul?"

"The announcer said something about turning to the Conelrad station on the radio. What's that mean? Hasn't that got something to do with—"

He stopped abruptly. There was a sudden absolute stillness.

"You must have heard it wrong, Paul," his father said quietly.

The boy shook his head. "I didn't hear it wrong, pop. That's what he said. To turn on your Conelrad station. Then everything went blank."

A gasp came from Jerry Harlowe. A woman let out a cry. They ran into the living room behind Stockton, who immediately turned the knob on a small table-model radio, and stared down at it grimly. After a moment, there came the voice of an announcer. . . .

"Direct from Washington, D.C. Repeating that. Four minutes ago, the President of the United States made the following announcement—I quote: 'At eleven-o-four P.M. Eastern Standard Time, both our Distant Early Warning and Ballistics Early Warning lines reported radar evidence of unidentified flying objects, flying on a course due southeast. As of this moment, we have been unable to determine the nature of these objects, but for the time being, in the interest of national safety, we are declaring a state of Yellow Alert.'"

There was a moment's silence, and Grace seized the doctor's arm. With her free hand, she reached for Paul and drew him to her.

Rebecca Weiss started to cry, and her husband, Marty, just stood there, his face white.

The voice on the radio continued:

"The Civil Defense authorities request that if you have a

shelter already prepared, go there at once. If you do not have a shelter, use your time to move supplies, food, water, and medicine to a central place. Keep all windows and doors closed. We repeat: If you're in your home, go to your prepared shelters or to your basement. . . ."

The voice of the announcer continued, went on and on, repeating the unbelievable introduction to an incredible horror.

They all stood gaping at the radio, and in one fragment of a moment they thought:

The baby, Rebecca Weiss thought. The tiny baby asleep in their house across the street. Four months old. And they had kidded about it this morning. Marty had said they should send her to Vassar, and she'd chuckled about it all morning. Send the baby to Vassar. And suddenly, in searing agony, it occurred to her, that they would have no baby. This infant thing they had built their lives around—she would cease to exist.

I don't believe it, Marty thought. He shook his head. He rejected it. It simply wasn't happening. It was a magazine story or a movie. It was some idle chatter at a party. It was a pamphlet that some kook had left on a doorstep, but it wasn't happening— it couldn't be happening . . . but all the time he knew it was. It was true. It was happening.

I want to cry, thought Jerry Harlowe. I want to cry. I can feel the tears inside me. But I mustn't cry—I'm a man. But the claims . . . the insurance claims. My God—they'd be enormous! He could go bankrupt! It was like a joke. A cold, formless joke. Humor in an insane asylum. A crazy accountant trying to add up an earthquake. Sure—he'd go bankrupt. The world would turn into a jungle. And he'd go bankrupt.

The roses, Jerry's wife, Martha, thought suddenly. The beautiful American Beauties that she'd so lovingly and painstakingly cared for—and this year they had come up so wonderfully. They were so beautiful. Then she clenched her fists and let her fingernails dig into the flesh of her palms, hating herself for the thought. What about the children? What about Ann and Charley? How, in God's name, could a mother think about a rose garden at this moment when death had just been announced over the radio? She shut her eyes tightly, wishing it all away— but when she opened them, the room was there and all the people in it. She felt a sudden nausea rising up inside her—a wave of sickness that left her weak and perspiring.

The pain, Dr. Stockton thought. The incredible pain. He could remember reading about Hiroshima. The burn cases. The radiation poisoning. The scarred, agonized flesh that sent a protracted scream over the dying city. He remembered it was something the Japanese doctors could not cope with. It had been too sudden, too unexpected, agony on a mass scale. This thing that hovered over them now, was whole streets and cities and states; millions and millions of people suddenly thrust into a maelstrom—a slaughterhouse on a scale that couldn't even be measured by the holocaust that was Hiroshima.

So each stood there with a secret thought, while the voice of the radio announcer, quivering with a barely perceptible tension, kept on repeating the announcements over and over again in the same studiedly dispassionate voice—the well-rehearsed ritual of a modern Paul Revere on a twentieth-century night-ride. One if by land or two if by sea, but there was no opposite shore. They were all in this together. There was no escape. There was no defense. Death was en route to them over the Alaskan snow, and all anyone could do was simply to announce its coming.

They ran out of the Stockton house, frantic, panicky—with vague plans for survival propelling them to their own houses. But then a siren rang out—its eerie shriek piercing the summer night, pinioning their thoughts in the night's darkness and holding them in fear-frozen suspension until once again they could break loose and race toward their homes.

And, in each of them, as they ran frantically across the street and down sidewalks and across lawns, was one single awareness. The street was somehow different. It had no familiarity. It was as if each of them had been away for a hundred years and suddenly returned. It was a vast place of strangeness.

And the siren continued to scream its discordant wail through the summer night.

Bill Stockton had placed the radio in the kitchen where Grace was filling water jugs.

"This is Conelrad, your emergency broadcasting station. You will find Conelrad at either six forty or twelve forty on your dial. Remain tuned to this frequency. We repeat our previous announcement. We are in a state of Yellow Alert. If you have a shelter already prepared, go there at once. If you do not have a shelter, use your time to move supplies of food, water, and medicine to a central place. Keep all windows and doors closed. We repeat: If you're in your home, go to your prepared shelters or to your basement. . . ."

The water dribbled out of the faucet, the pressure growing weaker each moment.

Paul hurried through the kitchen, carrying a box of canned goods, and went down the cellar steps.

Bill Stockton came into the kitchen after him, and picked up two of the filled jugs of water on the floor.

"Fill up as many as you can, Grace," he said tersely. "I'm going to start the generator up in the shelter in case the power goes off."

He looked toward the fluorescent light over the sink. Already it was beginning to dim. Stockton looked grim.

"That may happen any moment," he said.

"There's hardly any water coming through the tap," Grace said, a catch in her voice.

"That's because everybody and his brother is doing the same thing we are. Keep it on full force until it stops." He turned toward the basement door.

"Here," Grace called out after him. "Take this one with you. It's filled."

She started to remove the heavy jug from the sink. It slipped out of her hand and fell, smashing to the floor and sending glass cascading around the room.

Grace let out one sob and shoved a fist into her mouth to hold back any more. For just one moment she felt herself falling into hysteria, wanting to scream, wanting to run frantically somewhere, anywhere, wanting unconsciousness to release her from the nightmare that was going on inside her kitchen.

Bill Stockton took hold of her and held her tight. His voice was gentle, but it didn't sound like his voice at all.

"Easy, honey—easy." He pointed to the broken jug. "Make believe it's perfume and it cost a hundred bucks an ounce." He stared down at the bottle of water at his feet. "Maybe in an hour," he said thoughtfully, "it'll be worth more than that."

Paul came up from the basement.

"What else, pop?"

"All the canned goods down?"

"All that I could find."

"How about the fruit cellar?" Grace asked him, keeping her voice steady.

"I put all those in, too," Paul responded.

"Get my bag from the bedroom," Stockton said. "Put that down there, too."

"What about books and stuff?" Paul said.

When Grace spoke her voice broke and the words came out tight and loud—louder than her son could ever remember, and different, too.

"Dammit! Your father told you to get his bag—!"

The boy let out an incredulous gasp. It was his mother, but it wasn't his mother. The voice wasn't hers. The expression wasn't hers. He gave a frightened sob.

"That's all right," Stockton said softly, pushing the boy out. "We're just frightened, Paul. We're not ourselves. Go ahead, son."

Then he turned to his wife. "We'll need books, Grace. God knows how long we'll have to stay down there." Then, in a gentle tone, almost supplicating, "Honey, try to get hold of yourself. It's the most important thing on God's earth now."

He watched her for a moment, then very deliberately turned to look toward the cupboards to the left of the sink.

"What about light bulbs?" he asked. "Where do you keep the light bulbs?"

Grace pointed. "Top shelf in that cupboard there." Then she bit her lip. "We don't have any. I ran out yesterday. I was going to buy some at the store. There was a sale on—"

She leaned against the sink and felt the tears running down her face. "Oh, my God!" she said. "I'm talking like an idiot. A sale at the store. Oh, God in heaven! The world is about to explode and I'm talking about a sale at the store!"

Stockton reached out and touched her face.

"It doesn't make any difference," he said to her quietly. "You can mouth all the idiocies you want to. Just don't panic, Grace. That's the most important thing now." He held her hand tightly. *"We mustn't panic."*

"How much time do we have?"

"There's no telling. I think I remember reading some place that from the first alarm, we might have anywhere from fifteen minutes to half an hour."

Grace's eyes grew large. "Fifteen minutes?"

He shook his head. "I'm guessing, Grace. I don't know for sure. I don't think anyone does."

He went into the dining room. "Keep getting the water," he said to her over his shoulder.

Paul came down the steps through the front hall and into the living room. He carried an armful of books and magazines, and on top of them his father's medical bag.

"I got everything, pop."

"Let me give you a hand," said Stockton, taking the things out of his arms.

Paul turned, and started toward the front door.

"Paul!" Stockton shouted at him. "Are you out of your mind? Stay inside here."

"My bike's outside," the boy said.

"You won't need it. Go on down to the shelter."

"But if they do drop a bomb or something, it'll burn everything up. I know, pop. I read it. If it's a hydrogen bomb, there won't be anything left standing."

Stockton let the magazines drop to the floor. He walked over to his son and gripped him by the shoulders. There was a fierceness to his voice.

"Don't even think that! Don't let yourself think that—and don't say anything about it in front of your mother. She's counting on us, Paul. We're the men here."

He released the boy with one last gentle squeeze.

"As a matter of fact . . . as a matter of fact, we may be out of the danger zone. We might be two or three hundred miles from where the bomb drops. We may not even *know* that it's dropped—"

"Pop," Paul interrupted. "We're forty miles from New York. If they dropped a hydrogen bomb . . ." He looked into his father's eyes. "We'll know it all right, pop."

Stockton stared at this replica of himself, filled with love and pride.

"If we do, Paul," he said quietly, "then we do, that's all—but for the time being our job is to stay alive and you're not going to stay alive running out in the night trying to find a bicycle."

Grace's voice came from the kitchen, shaky and high. "Bill?" She appeared at the dining-room door. "Bill, there's no more water."

"It doesn't make any difference," Stockton said. "I think

we've got enough now anyway. Bring a jug with you, Grace. Paul and I will come back up for the rest of it."

They carried the jugs and the rest of the things down the basement steps and through the door of the shelter, which was at the far end of the cellar.

Grace put down the jug and looked around the small room. Bunk beds, can-ladened shelves, the generator, stacks of books and magazines, medical supplies. Suddenly their whole existence had telescoped into this tiny place loaded with things that up to half an hour ago had had no great significance. Half an hour ago! Grace suddenly recollected that in thirty minutes everything on earth had turned upside down. Every value, every belief, every frame of reference, had suddenly ceased to exist or had taken on a vast life-or-death importance. She watched her husband and Paul leave the shelter and start up the steps toward the kitchen.

Stockton stopped halfway up.

"I forgot," he said. "There's a five-gallon can of gasoline in the garage. Paul, you run out and get that. We'll need it for the generator."

"Right, pop."

Stockton looked briefly across the cellar toward the open door of the shelter. Grace sat on one of the bunk beds staring at nothing. He hesitated a moment, then hurried up to the kitchen, picked up two of the three remaining jugs of water, and went downstairs again.

Grace looked up as he entered the shelter. Her voice was a whisper. "Bill . . . Bill, this is so incredible. We must be dreaming. It can't really be happening."

Stockton knelt down in front of her and took both her hands.

"I just told Paul," he said to her, "if it's a bomb, there's no certainty that it'll land near us. And if it doesn't—"

Grace pulled her hands away.

"But if it does," she said. "If it hits New York, we'll get it, too. All of it. The poison, the radiation—we'll get it, too."

"We'll be in the shelter, Grace," Stockton said, "and with any luck at all, we'll survive. We've got enough food and water to last us at least two weeks . . . maybe even longer, if we use it wisely."

Grace looked at him blankly. "And then what?" she asked,

in a still voice. "Then what, Bill? We crawl out of here like go-phers to tiptoe through all the rubble up above. The rubble and the ruins and the bodies of our friends . . ."

She stopped, and stared down at the floor. When she looked up at him again, there was a different expression on her face—deeper than panic, more enveloping than fear—resignation, ab-ject surrender.

"Why is it so necessary that we survive?" she asked in a flat voice. "What's the good of it, Bill?—wouldn't it be quicker and easier if we just . . ." She let the word dangle.

Paul's voice called, "I got the gasoline, pop. Is that all you need from out here?"

"Bring the can, Paul," his father said. Then he turned to Grace. For the first time there was a tremor in his voice.

"That's why we have to survive," he said. "That's the rea-son."

They heard Paul's steps.

"He may inherit just rubble, but he's twelve years old. It isn't just our survival, Grace. Sure, we can throw our lives away. Just deposit them on the curb like garbage cans." His voice went higher. *"He's twelve years old.* It's too Goddamn early to think about a boy dying . . . when he hasn't even had a chance to do any living."

Paul appeared at the door with the gasoline can.

"Put it there, next to the generator," Stockton said as he walked out of the room. "I'll go up and get the rest of the water."

He climbed back up the stairs to the kitchen and picked up the last of the jugs. He was about to carry it back down when he heard a knock on the kitchen door. Jerry Harlowe's face peered through the parted curtains.

Stockton unlocked the door. Harlowe stood outside, with a smile on his face that looked as if it had been painted on. His voice was strained.

"How ya doin', Bill?" he asked.

"I'm collecting water, which is what you should be doing." Harlowe looked painfully ill at ease.

"We got about thirty gallons and then the water stopped," he said. His face twisted again. "Did yours stop too, Bill?"

Stockton nodded. "You better get on home, Jerry. Get into your shel—" He wet his lips and corrected himself. "Into your basement. I'd board up the windows if I were you, and if you've got any wood putty or anything, I'd seal the corners."

Harlowe fiddled with his tie.

"We don't have a cellar, Bill," he said, with a lopsided grin. "Remember? The benefits of modern architecture. We've got the one brand-new house on the street. Everything at your beck and call. Everything at your fingertips—" His voice shook. "Every wonder of modern science taken into account . . . except the one they forgot." He put his eyes down and stared at his feet. "The one that's heading for us now."

He looked up slowly and swallowed. "Bill," he said, in a whisper, "can I bring Martha and the kids over here?"

Stockton froze. He felt anger. "Over here?"

Harlowe nodded eagerly. "We're sitting ducks there. Sitting ducks. We don't have any protection at all."

Stockton thought for a moment, then turned away. "You can use our basement."

Harlowe grabbed his arm. "Your basement?" he asked incredulously. "What about your shelter? Goddamnit, Bill, that's the only place anybody can survive. We've got to get into a shelter!"

Stockton looked at him, and the anger that had been just a dull resentment surged up inside. He held it down with effort, wondering to himself how the familiar face, once pleasing and boyish, could be so abhorrent to him now.

"I don't have any room, Jerry," he said. "I don't have nearly enough room—or supplies, or anything. It's designed for three people."

"We'll bring our own water," Harlowe said, eagerly, "and our own food. We'll sleep on top of one another if necessary." His voice broke. "Please, Bill . . ."

He stared at Stockton's impassive face. "Bill, we've got to use your shelter!" he cried. "I've got to keep my family alive! And we won't use any of your stuff. Don't you understand? We'll bring our own."

Stockton looked down at Harlowe's hands, then into his face.

"What about your own air? Will you bring your own air? That's a ten-by-ten room, Jerry."

Harlowe let his hands drop. "Just let us stay in there the first forty-eight hours or so. Then we'll get out. Honest to God, Bill. No matter what, we'll get out."

Stockton felt the water jug heavy in his hand. This could not be prolonged, he knew that. His voice cut through the air like a scalpel.

"When that door gets closed, Jerry, it stays closed. Closed and locked. There'll be radiation—and God knows what else." He felt an anguish rising deep inside him. "I'm sorry, Jerry. As God is my witness—I'm sorry. But I built that for *my* family."

He turned and started for the basement.

Jerry's voice followed him. "What about *mine*? What do *we* do? Just rock on the front porch until we get burned to cinders!"

Stockton kept his back to him. "That's not my concern. Right at this moment, it's my family I have to worry about."

He started down the steps. Harlowe ran after him and grabbed his arm.

"I'm not going to sit by and watch my wife and my kids die in agony!" Tears rolled down Harlowe's face. "Do you understand, Bill? I'm not going to do that!"

He shook Stockton, and started to cry uncontrollably. "I'm not going to—"

Stockton pulled away. The jug slipped out of his hand and bounced down the basement steps, but it did not break. Stockton went slowly down the steps and picked it up.

"I'm sorry," he heard Harlowe say. "Please forgive me, Bill."

Stockton turned to look up. Oh, God, he thought. That's my friend standing there. That's my friend. But then his anger returned. He spoke to the figure standing above him.

"I kept telling you—all of you. Build a shelter. Get ready. Forget the card parties and the barbeques for maybe a couple of hours a week and admit to yourself that the worst is possible."

He shook his head. "But you didn't want to listen, Jerry. None of you wanted to listen. To build a shelter was admitting the kind of age we're living in—and none of you had the guts to make that kind of an admission."

He closed his eyes for a moment and then took a deep breath. "So now, Jerry, now you've got to face the reality."

He took one last look at the white, stricken face on the stairs. "You want help now, Jerry? Now you get it from God." He shook his head. "Not from me."

He walked across the cellar toward the shelter.

* * *

The front door opened and the Weisses hurried through the hall into the living room. Rebecca carried their baby in her arms and stayed close to Marty.

"Bill!" Marty called. "Bill—where are you?"

"They're already in the shelter!" Rebecca cried hysterically. "I told you they'd be in the shelter! They've locked themselves in."

Jerry Harlowe appeared from the kitchen. "It's no use," he said. "He won't let anyone in."

Marty's dark little face twisted with fear. "He's *got* to let us in!" He pointed toward Rebecca and the baby. "We don't even have any windows in half the basement. I don't have anything to plug them up with either."

He started to push his way past Harlowe. "Where is he? Is he downstairs? Is he in the shelter?"

He walked through the dining room into the kitchen, saw the open basement door, and called down.

"Bill? Bill—it's Marty. We've got the baby with us."

He stumbled down the cellar steps, calling, "Bill? Bill?"

The lights dimmed in the basement and Marty groped his way across the cellar floor until he reached the metal door of the shelter, now closed.

Behind him, in the darkness, his wife's voice called out.

"Marty! Marty—where are you? The lights are out! Marty—please . . . come back and get us."

The baby started to cry, and then, from outside, came the sound of the siren.

Marty pounded on the door of the shelter. "Bill! Please . . . Bill . . . let us in!"

Stockton's voice came back, muffled, from the other side of the door.

"Marty, I would if I could. Do you understand? If it didn't mean endangering the lives of my own family, I would. I swear to you, I would."

The last part of his words were drowned out by the siren, and then by the shrill wailing of the baby from the steps. Panic clawed at Marty and he pounded on the door with both hands.

"Bill!" he shouted. *"You've got to let us in!* There isn't any time. Please, Bill!"

On the other side of the door, the generator had begun to

hum and the lights went on in the shelter—two big one-hundred watt bulbs, glaringly white.

Bill Stockton put his head against the steel door and closed his eyes. He shook his head.

"I can't, Marty. Don't stay there asking me. I can't."

His mouth went tight and his voice shook. "I can't and I won't!"

Marty Weiss knew then that the door was to remain locked. He turned and peered through the darkness at the figure of his wife standing on the steps. He felt a surge of tenderness. Of love. And, at this moment—of a loss, final and irrevocable. He turned and stared at the closed door.

"I feel sorry for you, Bill," he said, quietly but clearly. "I really do. You'll survive. You'll live through it." His voice went higher. "But you're going to have blood on your hands. Do you hear me, Bill? You'll have blood on your hands."

Inside the shelter, Stockton stared at his wife. She tried to say something to him, but nothing came out.

Stockton could hear Marty Weiss's footsteps retreating through the cellar and up the steps. His hands shook, and he had to clasp them together to keep them still.

"I can't help it," he whispered. "It's us or it's them. All my life . . . all my life I've only had one function. That was to end suffering. Relieve pain. To cure. But the rules are different now. The rules, the time, the place. Now there's only one purpose, Grace—that's to survive. Nothing else means anything. And we can't afford to *let* it mean anything." Suddenly he whirled to the door. "Marty! Jerry!" he screamed. "All of you—any of you! Get out of here! *Stay* out of here!"

Behind him he could hear his son beginning to cry.

"Goddamn it! Goddamn it! If there's blood on my hands . . . all of you—all of you put it there!"

And then he began to tremble. Fatigue struck him like a blow; he felt as if he could no longer stand up, and he sat down on one of the cots.

Far off there was the sound of the siren.

Bill Stockton closed his eyes tightly and tried to make his mind go blank. But the sound persisted, and he felt a massive pain.

* * *

A group of neighbors collected outside Bill Stockton's house. One of them carried a portable radio, and the voice of the Conelrad announcer supplied an urgent background to the whispered questions and the occasional cry of a child or a woman.

Harlowe came out from the house and stood on the front porch. Marty Weiss and his wife followed him.

Martha Harlowe pushed her way through the group, holding tight to the hands of her children. "Jerry," she called toward the porch, "what happened?"

Harlowe shook his head. "Nothing happened. I think we all better go back and try to fix up the cellars."

"That's crazy!" a man's voice said. "There's no time for that. Bill's got the only place on the street that would do any good."

A woman cried out, "It'll land any minute!" Her voice was frantic. "I know it—it's going to land any minute!"

"This is Conelrad," the radio announced. "This is Conelrad. We are still in a state of Yellow Alert. If you are a public official or a government employee with an emergency assignment, or a Civil Defense worker, you should report to your post immediately. If you are a public official or government employee . . ." The voice continued underneath the flood of voices.

A big, burly man who lived on the corner started up the steps to Stockton's porch. Jerry Harlowe stood in his way.

"Don't waste your time," Harlowe said. "He won't let anyone in."

The man turned helplessly toward his wife, who stood at the foot of the steps.

"What'll we do?" the woman asked, panic building in her voice. "What are we going to do?"

"Maybe we ought to pick out just one basement," Marty Weiss said, "and go to work on it. Pool all our stuff. Food, water—everything."

"It isn't fair," Martha Harlowe said. She pointed toward the Stockton porch. "He's down there in a bomb shelter—completely safe. And *our* kids have to just wait around for a bomb to drop!"

Her nine-year-old daughter began to cry, and Martha knelt down to hold her tightly to her.

The big man, on the porch steps, turned to survey the group. "I think we'd better just go down into his basement—break down the door!"

In the sudden silence the siren wailed shrilly across the

night, and the ten or twelve people seemed to draw closer to one another.

Another man took a step out from the group. "Henderson's right," he said. "There isn't any time to argue or anything else. We've just got to go down there and get in!"

A chorus of voices agreed with him.

The big man walked down the steps and started around the yard toward the garage.

Harlowe shouted at him. "Wait a minute!" He raced down the steps. "Goddamn it—wait a minute! We all wouldn't fit in there. It'd be crazy to even try!"

Marty Weiss's voice called out plaintively, "Why don't we draw lots? Pick out *one* family."

"What difference would it make?" Harlowe said. "He won't let us in."

Henderson, the big man, looked unsure for a moment. "We could all march down there," he said, "and tell him he's got the whole street against him. We could do that."

Again, voices agreed with him.

Harlowe pushed his way through the group to stand near Henderson. "What the hell good would that do?" he asked. "I keep telling you. Even if we were to break down the door, it couldn't accommodate all of us. We'd just be killing everybody, and for no reason!"

Mrs. Henderson's voice broke in. "If it saves even one of these kids out here—I'd call that a reason."

Again, a murmur of assent came.

"Jerry," Marty Weiss said, "you know him better than any of us. You're his best friend. Why don't you go down again? Try to talk to him. Plead with him. Tell him to pick out one family— draw lots or something—"

Henderson took a long stride over to Marty. "One family— meaning yours, Weiss, huh?"

Marty whirled around toward him. "Well, why not? Why the hell not? I've got a four-month-old baby—"

"What difference does that make?" the big man's wife said. "Is your baby's life any more precious than our kids'?"

Marty Weiss turned to her. "I never said that. If you're going to start trying to argue about who deserves to live more than the next one—"

"Why don't you shut your mouth, Weiss!" Henderson

shouted at him. In wild, illogical anger he turned to the others. "That's the way it is when the foreigners come over here. Pushy, grabby, semi-Americans!"

Marty's face went white. "Why, you garbage-brained idiot, you— There's always one person—one rotten, unthinking crumb, who suddenly has to become the number-one big straw boss and decide what ancestry is acceptable that season—"

A man at the back shouted out: "It still goes, Weiss. If we've got to start hunting around for some people to disqualify—you and yours can go to the top of the list!"

"Oh, Marty!" Rebecca sobbed, feeling a surge of a different fear.

Weiss threw off her restraining arm, and started to push his way through the crowd to the man who had spoken. Jerry Harlowe had to step between them.

"Keep it up—both of you," he said, tautly. "Just keep it up— we won't need a bomb. We can slaughter each other."

"Marty!" Rebecca Weiss's voice came from the darkness near the porch. "Please. Go down to Bill's shelter again. Ask him—"

Marty turned to her. "I've already asked him. It won't do any good!"

There was the sound of the siren again—this time closer. And far off in the distance, a stabbing searchlight probed the night sky.

The Conelrad announcer's voice came up again, and they heard him repeating the same Yellow Alert announcement as before.

"Mommy, Mommy!" a little girl's voice quavered. "I don't want to die, Mommy! I don't want to die!"

Henderson looked at the child, then started to walk toward the garage. Gradually, in little groups, the neighbors followed him.

"I'm going down there," he announced as he walked, "and get him to open that door. I don't care what the rest of you think—that's the only thing left to do."

Another man called out: "He's right. Come on, let's do it!"

They were no longer walking. Now they were a running, jostling group, linked by positive action. And Jerry Harlowe, watching them run past him, suddenly noticed that in the moonlight all their faces looked the same—wild eyes; taut, grim, set mouths—an aura of pushing, driving ferocity.

They slammed their way through the garage, and Henderson kicked open the door leading to the basement. Like a mob of fanatics, they shouted their way into the basement.

Henderson pounded his fist on the shelter door. "Bill? Bill Stockton! You've got a bunch of your neighbors out here who want to stay alive. Now you can open that door and talk to us and figure out with us how many can come in there—or else you can just keep doing what you're doing—and we'll bust our way in!"

They all shouted in agreement.

On the other side of the door, Grace Stockton grabbed her son and held him tight. Stockton stood close to the door, for the first time unsure and frightened. Again he heard the pounding—this time by many fists.

"Come on, Stockton!" a voice called from the other side. "Open up!"

Then there was the familiar voice of Jerry Harlowe.

"Bill, this is Jerry. They mean business out here."

Stockton wet his lips. "And I mean business in here," he said. "I've already told you, Jerry—you're wasting your time. You're wasting precious time that could be used for something else . . . like figuring out how you're going to survive."

Again Henderson smashed at the door with a heavy fist, and felt the unyielding metal. He turned to look at his neighbors. "Why don't we get some kind of a battering ram?" he suggested.

"That's right," another man said. "We could go over to Bennett Avenue. Phil Kline has a bunch of two-by-fours in his basement. I've seen them."

A woman's protesting voice, somehow petulant and ugly, broke in. "That would get him into the act," her voice said. "And who cares about saving *him*! The minute we do that, then we'll let all those people know that there's a shelter on this street. We'd have a whole mob to contend with. A whole bunch of outsiders."

"Sure," Mrs. Henderson agreed. "And what right do they have to come over here? This isn't *their* street. This isn't *their* shelter."

Jerry Harlowe stared from one silhouette to another and wondered what insane logic possessed them all.

"This is our shelter, huh?" he cried fiercely. "And on the next street—that's a different country. Patronize home industries! You idiots! You Goddamn fools! You're insane now—all of you."

"Maybe you don't want to live," Rebecca Weiss's voice cried out. "Maybe you don't care, Jerry."

"I care," Harlowe said to her. "Believe me, I care. I'd like to see the morning come, too. But you've become a mob. And a mob doesn't have any brains, and that's what you're proving. That's what you're proving right at this moment—that you don't have any brains."

Henderson's voice spoke—harsh, loud. "I say let's get a battering ram!" he shouted, like a cheerleader. "And we'll just tell Kline to keep his mouth shut as to why we want it."

"I agree with Jerry." Marty Weiss's voice was tentative and diffident. "Let's get hold of ourselves. Let's stop and think for a minute—"

Henderson turned to face Weiss's small dark form. "Nobody cares what you think!" He spit it out. "You or your kind. I thought I made it clear upstairs. I think the first order of business is to get you out of here."

He moved in on Marty and lashed out with the force of two hundred pounds. His fist smashed against Marty Weiss's cheek and Marty fell backward, landing first against a woman, then stumbling against a child, and finally winding up on his back. His wife screamed and started running toward him—and the whole dark basement echoed and re-echoed with the sound of angry shouts and frightened cries, sparked by the wail of a terror-stricken child.

"Come on!" Henderson's bull voice carried over the noise. "Let's go get something to smash this door down."

They were a mob, and they moved like a mob. Fear had become fury. Panic had become resolve. They stormed out of the basement onto the street. Each was willing to follow his neighbor. Each was content to let someone else lead. And while they marched wildly down the street, the voice of the Conelrad announcer darted like a thin menacing needle in and out of their consciousnesses.

"We have been asked to remind the population once again," the announcer's voice said, "that they are to remain calm. Stay off the streets. This is urgent. Please remain off the streets. Everything possible is being done in the way of protection, but the military cannot move, and important Civil Defense vehicles must have the streets clear. So you're once again reminded to stay off the streets. *Remain off the streets.*"

But the crowd continued down the block. They were not listening to the words that the radio said. There was an emergency, and the radio made it official.

Less than five minutes later, they were back in front of Stockton's house. They had found a long board and six men were carrying it. They took it into the garage, breaking a window in the door as they entered. Then they used it to smash the door into the basement. They carried it through the basement over to the shelter door and began to pound against it. The shelter door was thick—but not thick enough. The weight of the board, with six big men at it, first dented and then punctured the metal. And once the first rip appeared, others followed it, until, within moments, the top hinge had been smashed away and the door began to buckle.

Inside, Bill Stockton tried to pile cots, a chair, other furniture, and finally the generator, against it. But with each smashing, resounding blow, the barricade was pushed back.

The door finally gave and crashed into the shelter. The impetus of the final blow carried board and men into the room, and the side of the board grazed Stockton's head, tearing out a chunk of flesh.

Suddenly everyone was silent, and over this sudden silence came the sound of the siren—a long, piercing blast which gradually died away—and then the voice of the radio announcer came on again.

"This is Conelrad," the announcer's voice said. "This is Conelrad. Remain tuned for an important message. Remain tuned for an important message."

There was a silence for a moment, and then the voice continued. "The President of the United States has just announced that the previously unidentified objects have now been definitely identified as being satellites. Repeat. There are no enemy missiles approaching. Repeat. There are no enemy missiles approaching. The objects have been identified as satellites. They are harmless, and we are in no danger. Repeat. We are in no danger. The state of Yellow Alert has been cancelled. The state of Yellow Alert has been cancelled. We are in no danger. Repeat. There is no enemy attack. There is no enemy attack."

His voice continued, the words at first having no sense to the listeners, then gradually taking on form and meaning.

And then men turned to look at their wives and slowly took

There came the sound of a roar. It was at first distant, like a far-off growl, then it built up until it was a full-throated shriek—and around the corner came a red Jaguar, chrome-spoked wheels churning their way through the dust, and screaming their protest as the car turned more sharply and headed down the main street. It threw up tons of dust as once again the driver jerked it abruptly to the right and slammed on the brakes. The car plowed to a stop a foot from the porch of the saloon, squatting there like some low-slung red animal. A horse tethered next to it stared at the driver, snorted, and looked away.

Rance McGrew climbed carefully out of the front seat, swiped the dust off his cream-colored whipcord pants and white silk shirt, straightened the black and yellow ascot around his neck, and carefully tilted the brim of his white Stetson. He kicked the car door shut and started up the steps of the saloon.

"Howdy, Mr. McGrew," one of the cowboys said.

"Howdy," Rance answered, clutching at the post at the top of the steps as one of his boots turned inward, and he teetered momentarily.

Rance wore the only elevator boots in the business, with two-inch lifts inside and three-inch heels on the bottom. This shot him up to five feet seven.

The door to the saloon opened and Sy Blattsburg came out. He was a bald, dapper little man in a sport shirt. The shirt was soaked with perspiration. He looked worriedly at his wristwatch and then at Rance.

"You're an hour and fifteen minutes late, Rance," he announced with suppressed anger. "We should've had this scene all shot by now."

Rance shrugged his shoulders under their padding, and swaggered past him through the swinging doors into the make-believe saloon, where a camera crew and a party of extras sat around looking relieved and bored at the same time.

Sy Blattsburg, who had spent twenty years directing all kinds of phony-balonies, followed this particular phony-baloney into the saloon. "Makeup," he called, as he padded after the star.

The makeup man hurried onto the scene. Forcing a beatific smile at the "cowboy," he pointed to the wooden stool in front of the makeup mirror.

"Right over here, Mr. McGrew," he said pleasantly.

Rance sat down on the stool and surveyed his reflection.

"Make it kind of quick, will you?" the director said, his lips twitching ever so slightly. "We're quite a bit behind, Rance—"

Rance turned, knocking the powder puff out of the makeup man's hand. "Don't bug me, Sy," he said with a fast burn. "You know what emotional scenes do to me just before we shoot!"

The director smiled and closed his eyes, then patted the star on his padded shoulders. "Don't get upset, Rance baby. We'll try to knock this one out in a hurry. What do you say we get started—huh? Okay, baby? This is scene seventy-one."

He snapped his fingers and the script girl handed him the manuscript. "Here it is, right here," he said, pointing to one of the pages.

Rance languidly held out his hand and Blattsburg gave him the script. Rance looked at it briefly, then gave it back. "Read it to me," he said.

Blattsburg cleared his throat. His hand shook as he clutched at the script. "Interior saloon," he read. "Cover shot of two badmen at bar. Rance McGrew enters. He walks to bar. He glances sideways left and right."

Rance pushed the makeup man's arm away and turned slowly to stare at the director. "'He glances sideways left and right'? Is my head supposed to be built on a swivel?"

He grabbed the script out of the director's hand. "I'm gonna tell you something, Sy," he announced. "When a cowboy walks into a bar, he walks to the far end of the room. He takes his drink. He looks at it. Then he looks straight ahead. He doesn't look left and right."

With this, Rance McGrew turned back toward the mirror, his face white under the powdered makeup, his lips twitching. His large baby-blue eyes clouded like those of a high-school sophomore cheerleader whose megaphone had just been dented.

Sy Blattsburg closed his eyes again. He knew only too well the tone of Rance McGrew's voice and he was also familiar with the look on the face. It boded no good—either for that moment or for the day's schedule.

"All right, Rance," he said softly. "We'll shoot it your way. Anyway you want." He wet his lips. "Now can we begin?"

"In a moment," Rance said, his eyes half closed in what appeared to be a very special and personal agony. "In just a moment. My stomach's killing me. These scenes," he said, as one hand massaged his belly. "These miserable emotional scenes."

He pointed to a large hide-covered box on the floor near him. There, in hand-stitched elegance, was the name "Rance McGrew." Two stars were underneath it. A prop boy opened it up and rummaged through its interior. There were bottles of medicine, throat lozenges, sprays, and a large stack of autographed publicity pictures of Rance fanning a six-gun. The prop boy took out one of the bottles of pills and brought it over to the makeup chair.

Rance opened the bottle and popped two of the pills into his mouth, swallowing them whole. Then he sat quietly for a moment—the makeup man waiting motionless. Rance slowly opened his eyes and nodded, whereupon the makeup man continued his ministrations.

Fifty-odd people began quietly setting up the scene. The cameraman checked the position of his camera, nodded his approval to the operator, and everyone turned to look expectantly toward Sy Blattsburg.

Sy checked the angle of the camera, and then called, "Second team out! The star is here!"

Rance McGrew's stand-in left his place close to the swinging doors and Sy turned toward Rance.

"All set, Rance baby," he said diffidently. "And we'll shoot it just the way you want."

Rance McGrew rose slowly from his wooden stool and stood looking at himself in the mirror. The makeup man put on the final touches of powder. A wardrobe man puttered around his leather vest.

Rance, still looking at himself, cocked his head, snapped his fingers, and pointed to one shoulder. The wardrobe man hurriedly inserted an inch of additional padding. Again Rance stared into the mirror and then snapped his fingers again. "Holster," he said tersely.

A property man trotted to his side and began to tie on his holster.

Rance checked it by holding one arm straight down at his side and sighting down at it. "An inch more hang," he ordered.

The property man quickly obeyed, loosening the belt one notch as Rance checked himself again in the mirror, moving his head around so that he could survey himself from several different angles. He stepped away from the mirror and then advanced on it, arms held away from his body in the manner of every fast gun since the beginning of time.

It might be parenthetically noted here that there was a point in history when there actually were top guns. They were a motley collection of tough mustaches who galloped and gunned their way across the then new West. They left behind them a raft of legends and legerdemains. But heroics or hambone—it can be stated quite definitely that they were a rough and woolly breed of nail-eaters who in matters of the gun were as efficient as they were dedicated. It does seem a reasonable guess, however, that if there were any television sets up in Cowboy Heaven, so that these worthies could see with what careless abandon their names and exploits were being bandied about—not to mention the fact that each week they were killed off afresh by Jaguar-drawn Hollywood tigers who couldn't distinguish between a holster and hoof and mouth disease—they were very likely turning over in their graves or, more drastically, getting out of them.

None of this, of course, occurred to Rance McGrew as he swaggered across the set to the bat-wing doors, losing his balance only once or twice as his boots gave slightly to the left—much in the manner of a nine-year-old Brownie wearing her mother's high heels.

When Rance reached the swinging doors he squared his padded shoulders, snapped his fingers again, and ordered tersely: "*My gun.*" This, of course, was the final item in the ritual of Rance McGrew's preparation, and it occurred at the same time each morning. The prop man pitched underhanded an ugly-looking six-shooter which Rance caught deftly, spun around on the trigger finger of his right hand, and then with equal deftness flipped it to his left hand. He then let it spin over his shoulder, putting his right hand behind him to catch it. The ugly-looking six-shooter didn't know about the plan. It sailed swiftly over Rance, over the cameraman, over the bartender, and slammed against the bar mirror, smashing it into a million pieces.

Sy Blattsburg shut his eyes tightly and wiped the sweat from his face. With a heroic effort, he kept his voice low and untroubled. "Dress it up," he ordered. "We'll wait for the new glass." He pulled out a five-dollar bill and handed it to the cameraman.

He had now lost four hundred and thirty-five dollars over

the three-year span of Rance McGrew's television show. In one hundred and eighteen films, this was the eighty-fourth time that Rance had broken the bar mirror.

Twenty minutes later the set had been dressed and a new mirror put up. Blattsburg stood alongside the cameraman. "All right," he said, "ready . . . action!"

The camera began its quiet hum. Outside a horse whinnied, and through the swinging doors swaggered Rance McGrew in simple, powdered elegance, a noncommittal sneer on his face. The two "bad guys" stood at the bar and watched fearfully as he approached them. Rance went up to the bar and slammed the palm of his hand down on top of it.

"Rotgut whisky," he said in a deep voice, perhaps one octave lower than Johnny Weissmuller's. And while he may have walked like a Brownie, Rance's ordinary speaking voice was that of a grocery boy in the middle of a voice change.

The bartender yanked a bottle from the shelf and slid it down the length of the bar. Rance nonchalantly held out his hand for it and looked mildly surprised as the bottle sped past him to break against the wall where the bar ended.

Sy Blattsburg jammed both his thumbs into his eyes and stood shaking for a moment. "Cut," he said finally.

There was a murmur of reaction from the crew. It was traditional that Rance missed at least one bottle that was slid toward him, but this usually occurred toward the end of the day when he was tired.

The sneer on his face turned a shade petulant as he waggled a finger toward the bartender. "All right, buddy boy," he said warningly. "You try to gag it up one more time and you'll wind up plucking chickens at a market!"

He turned toward the director. "He put an English on that, Sy. He deliberately made it curve."

The bartender gaped at the two "bad guys."

"English on a bottle?" he whispered incredulously. "That guy needs a catcher's mitt!"

With masterful control, Blattsburg said quietly, "All right. Let's try it again. From the bottle. Positions, please."

"Scene seventy-three—take two," a voice called out.

Again the bartender pulled down a bottle and very carefully nudged it so that it slid along the bar slowly and stopped dead, a hand's length away.

Rance's lips curled in one of his best sneers. He reached for the bottle, picked it up, slammed it against the edge of the bar, and then raised the jagged neck to his mouth, drinking thirstily. He threw the bottle over his shoulder, probed at one of his back teeth with his tongue, and finally, rather showily, removed a large fragment of fake glass from his mouth. This he flipped toward the bartender and his mail-order sneer returned to his face.

He leaned against the bar, wiggling his shoulders, and surveyed the two "bad guys." At the same time, he carefully checked his reflection in the mirror and tilted his Stetson an inch or so to the right.

"I guess you boys know I'm the marshal here," he announced in his best Boot Hill voice.

The two "bad guys" were visibly shaken.

"We heard tell," the first one said, not daring to meet Marshal McGrew's gaze.

"We heard tell," the other cowboy chimed in.

Rance lifted one eyebrow and stared from one to the other. "And I guess you know that I know that Jesse James is due here, aimin' to call on me."

The first cowboy nodded and his voice shook.

"I knew that, too," he said fearfully.

"Likewise," his companion added.

Rance stood there for a quiet moment, moving his head left and right, the sneer coming and going.

"Somethin' else I know that you two don't know," he said, "is that I know that both of you know Jesse James. And I'm waitin'—I'm jus' gonna stand here waitin'."

The two "desperadoes" exchanged horrified stares, and with all the subtlety of a grade C wrestler they looked worriedly toward the swinging doors. This was Rance's cue to move away from the bar, hands held down and ready at his sides.

The sneer now came with a smile. "I figgered I'd bluff ya," he said triumphantly. "Jesse's here all right, ain't he?"

"Marshal . . ." the bartender pleaded. "Marshal McGrew . . . please . . . no killin' in here!"

Rance held up his hand for quiet. "I ain't aimin' to kill 'im," he announced gently. "I'm jus' gonna maim 'im a bit. I'm jus' gonna pick off his pinky!"

The first "desperado" swallowed and gulped. "J-J-Jesse ain't gonna take kindly to that," he stuttered.

Out on the street there was the sound of hoofs, the creak of leather, and then boot-steps across the wooden floor of the saloon porch.

The swinging doors opened, and there stood Jesse James—evil incarnate. Black mustache, black pants and shirt, black gloves, black scarf, and black hat. His particular sneer was closely related to Rance's, though not worn with the aplomb of the marshal.

He walked across the saloon with catlike grace, hands held down and away from his body.

"It's Marshal McGrew, ain't it?" he asked, planting his legs far apart, his hands still out—elbows bent.

Rance McGrew sneered, sniggered, clucked, and breathed heavily, and finally said, "Yup."

"You're about to breathe your last, Marshal."

Then Jesse went for his gun. Halfway out of the holster a simulated bullet drew simulated blood from his hand, which he clutched in agony as his gun flew off to one side.

The prop man blew smoke out of the chamber of the blank-cartridge pistol.

Sy Blattsburg nodded approvingly.

The two cowboys at the bar reacted with proper horror.

The extras sitting at the tables jumped to their feet and moved slowly backwards toward the wall.

Meanwhile, back at the bar, Rance McGrew was still tugging at the gun in his holster. It finally came out, left his hand, and kept going over his shoulder, over the cameraman, over the bartender, smack dab into the mirror, breaking it into a million pieces.

Sy Blattsburg looked as if someone had told him that he had just become engaged to a lizard, he opened his mouth and a noise akin to a sob—a protest, a throttled roar—came out. When he got control of himself, he said quite clearly, "Cut!"

He turned toward the cameraman and giggled. Then he just sat down and began to cry.

And so it went through the day. They shot Rance grappling with Jesse until Jesse hauled back to let the marshal have it on his sneer. Rance's stand-in took his place to receive the blow, and then fell backward to land on top of a collapsing table.

There was some exceptional footage of Rance throwing Jesse over the bar to smash against a shelf full of bottles; then the action called for Jesse to climb up on top of the bar and dive over it into the on-coming Rance. Rance's stand-in again took the brunt of this assault, stepping in in time to receive the full weight of Jesse James hurtling through the air at him.

By late afternoon Rance began to show the effect of four hours of mortal combat. Sweat showed through his powder. His stand-in had half his shirt ripped off, a large mouse under his left eye, and three dislocated knuckles.

Rance patted him on the shoulder as he passed by. "Good show," he said bravely, like a Bengal Lancer talking to a doomed drummer boy.

"Yes sir, Mr. McGrew," his stand-in said through bruised lips.

Sy Blattsburg checked his watch, then walked to the center of the room. "All right, boys," he announced. "This is the death scene—Rance stands at the bar, Jesse lies over there. Rance thinks he's unconscious. Jesse picks a gun off the floor and fires at Rance's back."

The actor playing Jesse James looked up startled. "At his *back*?" he said.

"That's right," Blattsburg responded.

"I don't want to fight you, Sy," the actor said, "but that's not the way Jesse James used to operate. I mean . . . everything I've read about the guy, he fought pretty fair. Why can't I yell something?"

Rance McGrew's upper lip curled. "That's thinking," he said with devastating sarcasm. "Oh, that's thinking. Yell something. Warn the fastest gun in the West that he's about to be shot at."

Rance took a step over and poked a finger against the actor's chest. "You happen to be up against Rance McGrew," he snarled. "And when you're up against Rance McGrew you've got to play it dirty or you're gonna play it dead. Now quit arguing and let's get to it!"

The actor looked over at Sy Blattsburg, who made a gesture of a finger to his mouth.

As the actor walked past him, Sy said, "Jesse James might not fight that way—but," he continued in a whisper, "Rance McGrew would!"

Once again the extras took their places at the tables. Jesse James lay down in a chalked-off spot on the floor and Rance McGrew stood by the bar, his back to his adversary. The property man put a bottle in front of him and Rance sniffed at it. Once again his upper lip curled.

"I told you ginger ale!" he screeched. "This Goddamn stuff is coke!"

The property man looked worriedly at the director. "It's supposed to look like whisky though, Mr. McGrew, and—"

Rance's shriek cut him off. "Sy! Will you fire this oaf—or straighten him out—one or the other?"

Sy Blattsburg stepped in front of the camera. His voice was gentle. "Mr. McGrew would prefer ginger ale."

The property man heaved a deep sigh. "Yes sir, Mr. McGrew."

Jesse James, lying on the floor, whispered to the director: "I don't care what he says—Jesse James wouldn't shoot anybody in the back."

Sy gritted his teeth. "Yeah, I know, but Rance McGrew would. Rance McGrew would also fire anybody and his brother. So do me a favor—play it Rance McGrew's way or we'll never get this picture finished."

"All right. You're the boss, but I can just see Jesse James turning over in his grave now. I don't mean just once. I mean about four hundred revolutions per minute."

Sy Blattsburg nodded and shrugged. "All right," he called out. "Let's get with it. Scene ninety-three, take one."

The camera began to hum and Blattsburg called out "Action!"

Rance McGrew reached for the bottle, smashed it open, held it out, and looked in the mirror. He could see the reflection of the crew, the cameramen, the director, and, naturally, Rance McGrew. He put the shattered bottle to his mouth and took a long, deep swig. Then the bottle fell from his hands. His eyes bulged. He choked, gasped, and clutched at his throat.

"Why, you stupid bastard—that's whisky! *That's real whisky!*"

Again he looked up toward the mirror, and this time what made him gasp was not the burning liquid pouring down his throat. It was what he saw in the mirror. Just himself. Himself and two strangers—two dirty-looking cowboys standing a few feet away from him.

One of the hostesses sat with customers at the table, but it wasn't the long-legged blonde who was there before. It was a fat, dumpy, frowsy-looking babe on the corseted side of fifty-five.

Rance kept opening and shutting his eyes, then started to say something to the bartender when he realized that this gentleman, too, had changed. He was no longer the fat, waddling, bald-headed man cast in the role. He was a thin, chicken-chested little guy with his hair parted in the middle. He stared back at Rance questioningly.

Rance stumbled back from the bar and stared upward. There had been no real ceiling—just a series of catwalks where some of the lighting men had been positioned. Now there was no catwalk—just a plain old ceiling.

Marshal McGrew continued to walk backward until he felt the swinging doors behind him. He kept on going and wound up on the street just as an old man ran breathlessly toward him. An old man he'd never seen before.

"Marshal," the grizzled octogenarian wheezed at him, "Jesse's gunnin' for you. He's comin' right now!"

"Cement head!" Rance shrieked back at him. "He already came in—scene seventy-three. Goddamn it—will my agent hear about this! Will the head of the studio hear about this!" He pounded on his small chest. "Try to get *me* for another benefit! Boy, am I gonna tell you something!"

He pointed toward the old man and then stopped breathing before his words came out, for down the street a horse ambled slowly toward him. And on the horse was a tall lean man in a black costume—his hawk face shadowed by the black broad-brimmed hat.

Any real student of the West would at this moment have died of a coronary, because the face was that of Jesse James. Not the actor—but Jesse James.

The horse stopped a few feet from where Rance stood and the rider dismounted, looked up and down the street, and then slowly came over toward the marshal.

The marshal, meanwhile, found himself sitting on the steps of the saloon unable to move.

The tall dark man stood over him and surveyed him intently.

"They call me Jesse James," the deep voice said. "I mean the *real* Jesse James—not that side of pork that's been play-actin' me!"

Silence—except for the plop-plop sound of Rance McGrew's

sweat, which kept running down the bridge of his nose and landing in the dust. Finally Rance looked up, his eyes glazed.

"Cut?" he inquired. "Shouldn't we cut?" His voice was tearful. "Please somebody—cut already!"

But nothing happened. The apparition under the black hat remained. No makeup man came to dab off the marshal's perspiration. No stunt man stood on the periphery ready to save him from the least damage. Marshal McGrew was all alone.

"I'm lookin' fer the marshal in town," Jesse James said. "Fella named McGrew. Rance McGrew."

Rance very slowly tipped his hat down over his face and stuck out his left hand, pointing down the street. "That-away," he announced.

"You wouldn't be him, huh?" Jesse asked.

Rance shook his head and continued to point down the street, but suddenly Jesse lashed out with both hands, grabbed Rance by the front of his vest, and yanked him to his feet. Holding him with one hand, he tapped the shiny badge adorning Rance's costume and looked accusingly into the pale, perspiring face of the lawman.

Rance gulped, swallowed, and started to take off the vest—looking wildly around. "Where's the fellow who lent me this?" he inquired weakly.

Jesse stopped him in the middle of his activities and pulled him closer.

"I think you and me better have a talk, marshal. Mebbe a long talk, mebbe a short talk—but a talk."

He slowly released Rance and continued to stare at him.

"You're supposed to be tough," he said thoughtfully. "Ya don't look very tough. Wanna know what ya look like?"

"I haven't been well," Rance answered in a thin little voice.

Jesse nodded. "You look like a marshmallow." Then he paused and stepped back. "Don't that rile ya none?" he asked.

Marshal McGrew smiled at him with a wispy "when-are-they-gonna-let-me-commit-suicide?" kind of smile.

Jesse shrugged. "C'mon," he ordered. "First we'll have a drink, and then we'll have a talk." There was a meaningful pause. "Then we'll have a showdown."

He herded Rance up the steps and into the saloon. Once inside, he shoved him up against the bar.

"Two whiskies," Jesse said, "and leave the bottles."

The bartender slid one bottle down the bar and Jesse backhanded it like Roy McMillan. The other bottle Rance laboriously stopped with both hands. Habit made him instinctively smash it against the bar—not once but five times, with no tangible results. This bottle was made of sterner stuff than the marshal was accustomed to. On the sixth smash, however, he finally managed to crack it, and on the seventh he wound up holding a small piece of glass and a cork. The rest of the bottle, and its contents, were in a puddle at his feet.

Rance looked up guiltily toward Jesse James, who stared at him like a scientist checking a bug under a microscope.

"Marshmallow!" Jesse spat in disgust.

He tilted his own bottle to his lips and took a long draught. He threw the bottle over his shoulder and reached inside his vest for a sack of tobacco and a pack of cigarette papers. He opened the sack and expertly poured an exact amount on the paper, rolled it between thumb and two fingers into a neat cylinder, licked the edge, rolled it again, caught the string of the tobacco sack in his teeth and pulled it closed, twisted one end of the cigarette shut, pasted the other to his lower lip, scratched a big wooden match with his thumbnail, and lit up. He then threw the makings—sack, paper, and another match—over to Rance McGrew, who immediately started to open the sack with his teeth, got the string caught between two of his molars, sneezed, and after much laborious finagling managed to spill a small thumbnailful of tobacco onto the paper. He then kneaded, pressed, tamped, and licked, put the cigarette to his mouth, and discovered that the tobacco had run out of the open end.

Rance shamefacedly pried the string out of his teeth, then stopped to think about what to do with the empty piece of paper stuck to the side of his mouth.

Jesse decided it for him. He backhanded the paper into the air, then looked a little dolefully at McGrew, shook his head, and said, "You don't do nothin' well, do ya, McGrew?"

He took a deep luxurious drag on his cigarette and blew the smoke into Rance's left eye. After waiting a moment for some reaction—and there was none except a small tear—he shook his head again.

"Don't that rile ya?" he asked.

Rance smiled at him and coughed out a piece of tobacco.

"Nothin' riles ya, does it?" Jesse James said. "You're the most even-tempered dude I ever did meet. However," he continued, blowing smoke out again, "I ain't got no more time to be social, Marshal. I believe it's time to come to a meetin' of the minds."

He took a step away from the bar and immediately the people at the table made a collective dash to neutral corners.

It was, Rance thought to himself, like every movie he'd ever seen—and he reflected further that this couldn't be happening. Eventually he'd wake up. But he couldn't wake up, because the thing went right on happening.

Jesse James nodded toward the frightened onlookers. "Why d'ya suppose they're gettin' under cover, marshal?"

Rance gulped. "I think the place is closing." He looked around a little wildly. "Yep—it's curfew time!"

Again he gulped, winked, smiled, and then with a kind of skipping gait headed toward the door. "Mighty nice meetin' ya, Mr. James . . . Jesse."

He was at the swinging doors when Jesse's voice stopped him.

"Marshal," Jesse said, "jus' stop right there!"

The voice was like a lasso that circled around Rance's legs and held him tightly. He slowly turned to face Jesse, who had reached out with his foot and pulled a chair over.

"You wasn't leavin', was ya, Marshal?" Jesse asked as he sat down. "I mean . . . you wasn't jus' gonna up and walk out, was ya?"

Rance smiled at him like some village idiot. "Nope," he answered, "I was just wonderin' if it was gonna rain."

He turned to stare out very professionally toward the street, then turned back to Jesse. "Nope," he said firmly, "it ain't gonna rain."

Jesse laughed, and then tipped his chair back. "D'ya know what I thought, Marshal?" he said. "I thought you was gonna play some kinda trick on me. Remember the time that bad guy had ya covered in the back and ya started out the swingin' doors and ya swung one door back and knocked the gun outta his hand?"

"That was the opening show last season," Rance interjected.

"Or how about when that rustlin' gang had collected in here to bushwhack ya—ten or eleven of 'em?"

Rance smiled in fond recollection. "Thirteen," he said. "I was up for an Emmy on that one."

Jesse nodded, and when he spoke he sounded grim. "That was when ya shot from the hip and brung down the chandelier." He shook his head. "That was some shootin', Marshal."

Rance was wistful. "I did better the next week. Horse thief named McNasty. Shot a glass outta his hand, bullet ricocheted and hit his confederate out there on the porch. I got thirteen hundred pieces of mail on that one."

Jesse nodded again. "I bet you did. I bet you did, indeed. Why, folks jus' couldn't help admirin' a man of your talents."

Then he laughed again—first a low chuckle, and then a tremendous booming explosion.

Again Rance smiled back at him—with the kind of smile that on a baby indicates gas.

"Thing of it is, Marshal," Jesse James continued, "thing of it is, I don't reckon you ever fired a real gun in your life, did ya? Or hit a man in anger? Or mebbe even got hit in anger, yourself?" He leaned forward in the chair. "Tell me true, Marshal. Ever ride a horse?"

Rance cleared his throat. "On occasion."

"A real horse?"

"Well—" Rance fidgeted, scratching himself. "I happen to be allergic—hives."

"Hives?"

Rance went through a series of extravagant gestures, indicating the torture of urticaria. "You know—itching. Cats give it to me, too."

Jesse leaned back in his chair. "So ya don't ride," he said, "ya don't shoot, ya don't fight. Ya jus' strut around wearin' a phony badge and goin' through the motions of killin' off fellas like me."

"Oh, I wouldn't say that," Rance said. "There was one episode when we let one of the James boys get off. It was kind of . . . kind of a complicated plot."

He walked over toward Jesse James and pulled a chair up close to him. "It seems that there was a kid sister going to school in the East. She came out to visit him on the day he was supposed to be hanged. She appealed to me and I saw to it that he got a suspended sentence."

Jesse stared at Rance, unsmiling. "I know about it," Jesse said. "I also know how you captured 'im. Jumped eight hundred feet off a cliff to land on the back of his hoss when he wasn't lookin'." He shook his head from side to side. "Now, c'mon, Marshal. You ever jump eight hundred feet off a cliff to land on a man's hoss?"

Rance looked pale. "Heights . . . heights bother me," he said weakly.

Jesse nodded. "That figgers. So ya see, Marshal—we had this meetin', up there and all of us decided—my brother Frank and me, Billy the Kid, the Dalton boys, Sam Starr . . . quite a few of us—and the consensus was, Marshal . . . was that you wasn't doin' a thing for our good names. We had a little election up there and they chose me to come down and mebbe take a little shine offa your pants!"

Rance stared at him. "How's that?" he asked.

"Don'cha get it? We see ya week after week shootin' down this fella, shootin' down that fella—capturin' that bushwhacker, capturin' that rustler—but alla time winnin'! Man, you jus' don't never lose. You're the winnin'est fella ever come down the pike, and that's for sure. So, me 'n' my friends—well, we figgered how it was about time that mebbe you lost one time!"

Rance swallowed hard. "That's not such a bad idea. I could take it up with the producer." His voice was hopeful.

Jesse shook his head. "I don't think there's time fer that," he said firmly. "I think that mebbe if you're gonna lose, you're gonna have to lose right now!" He rose from the chair slowly and then kicked it away. "But I'll tell ya what I'm gonna do, Marshal. I'm gonna play it square with ya. A whole helluva lot squarer than you ever played it with us. Face to face and no—how you call 'em?—stunt men."

He pointed out toward the street. "Right out there on the main street—you 'n' me."

Rance pointed to himself with a limp hand. "Me?" he asked.

"Right outside," Jesse continued. "Me comin' down one side of the street—you comin' down the other."

Rance gestured a little forlornly. "It's been done before. You didn't happen to see *Gunfight at O.K. Corral*, did you?"

Jesse James spat on the floor. "Lousy!" he said, like a judge pronouncing sentence.

"Didn't care for it, huh?" Rance cleared his throat, tapped his fingertips together. "It's always been my belief," he said, "that when shooting a western—"

Jesse James lifted him up off his chair and placed him hard on his feet. "Let's go, Marshal," he said.

He gave him a shove and Rance stumbled out through the swinging doors, followed by Jesse and by the crowd in the saloon. Jesse shoved him again and he tumbled down the steps.

Again Rance thought: This must be the tail end of a bad dream. He'd wake up sleeping in his Jaguar. There—right there in front of those steps was where he had parked it. Only it wasn't there now, of course.

Jesse gave him a push and pointed toward one end of the street. "You come around that corner," he directed Rance, "and I'll come around that one." He jerked his thumb over his shoulder. "I'll let ya make the first move. Now, nothin' could be fairer than that, Marshal, could it?"

"Oh, my, no," Rance answered. "No, indeed. Nothing at all." Then he very busily looked at his wristwatch. "How about tomorrow afternoon—same time?"

This time Jesse pushed him with more verve and Rance fell over his own elevator boots, banging his knees as he landed.

"This afternoon!" Jesse said to the U. S. Marshal in the dust. *"Right now!"*

Rance was reasonably sure that he could never rise to his feet again, let alone get through the long walk to the spot where he would make both his entrance and ultimately his exit. But, utilizing some hidden will power, he did manage to right himself and was surprised to find himself walking toward the end of the street. True, his legs felt like two pillars of cement and his heart beat so loudly he was sure Jesse James could hear it. And true, too, he had no intention of coming back. He was quite certain that when he turned the corner at the far end of the street, he'd find a way to get the hell out of there.

A moment later, his plans went to pot. A barbed wire fence sealed off the area around the corner. There was simply no place to go. Rance peeked out around the corner and saw Jesse coming toward him, a few hundred feet away. "Stunt man," Rance whispered. "Oh, stunt man!"

Then, inexplicably, Rance found himself making the big move around the corner. It was like stepping into an icy shower. But something had given him momentum and he found himself walking down the street. He'd done it a hundred times before, but this was different. Good had always triumphed, because evil had always faced him with one of its arms tied behind its back. He was conscious, too, that he was completely unable to swagger at this moment, and swagger had been one of the hallmarks of Rance McGrew. No one in the business—Wyatt Earp, Paladin, Marshal Dillon—none of them could swagger like Rance McGrew—and he'd had the added handicap of uplifts and extra-high heels.

Through the sweat, the dust, and the blinding sun, Rance could see Jesse getting closer to him. They were perhaps twenty feet apart now. "Go ahead," Jesse invited. "Reach!"

Rance's look was positively dyspeptic. His momentum stopped. He started to back up.

"I'm gonna count to three," Jesse said.

"This is ridiculous," Rance responded, continuing to back off. "It *never* happens this way."

"One . . ." Jesse said incisively.

The sweat poured down Rance McGrew's arms. "In over a hundred episodes," he said plaintively, "Rance McGrew never got shot down—not even nicked."

"Two . . ." Jesse James's voice was a bell tolling.

"I didn't even want to be in this series," Rance said as he backed up against a black horse-drawn hearse. "I wouldn't have even taken it on if it hadn't been for the residuals."

"Three!"

Rance looked briefly over his shoulder to see what had impeded his backward motion, and sweat showered off his face when he saw the hearse.

"The residuals, plus the fact that they used my own name as the central character."

"Reach!" Jesse said. "I mean right now!"

"Oh, my God!" Rance sobbed. "What you're going to do to the youth of America!" Then he half closed his eyes and went grabbing with both hands for the gun in the holster, fully expecting the hot screaming impact of a bullet in his stomach. He heard the gasp of the onlookers, and, still fumbling for his gun, he looked up briefly to see Jesse James holding his own six-gun out, pointing straight at him.

Jesse shook his head. "Jus' like I figgered," he said—almost with disappointment. "This guy couldn't outdraw a crayon."

Tears rolled down Rance's face. "Jesse," he said, holding out his hand supplicatingly, his own six-gun now dangling from his finger, "Jesse . . . give me a break . . . Will you give me a break, Jesse?" He sank to his knees, crying softly. "Jesse . . . I'm too young to die, and I've got a mother, Jesse. I've got a sweet little old mother who depends on me for her support." He let his gun fall to the ground, then he pushed it through the dust toward Jesse James. "Here . . . take it—genuine pearl on the handle. It was sent to me by a fan club in the Bronx. Take anything, Jesse—take everything."

Jesse looked at him coldly. "Ya say ya got nominated fer an Emmy? Man—you can't act any better'n ya can draw!"

Rance felt a surge of hope when no bullet plowed through his body. "What about it, Jesse?" he entreated. "Will you give me a break? I'll do anything you say. Anything at all. I mean it—anything. You name it—I'll do it!"

The gun in Jesse's hand was lowered to his side. He stared at Rance thoughtfully. "Anything?" he inquired.

"Name it!"

Jesse looked off reflectively and rubbed his jaw with the back of his hand. "Marshal," he said quietly, "we ain't a long ways off from a bargain." He picked tentatively at his teeth. "I ain't jus' sure exactly what it is that I want—but I'll think about it some."

Rance held his breath. "You mean . . . you mean you're not going to shoot me down?"

Jesse James shook his head. "Nope. But I'll tell ya what I *will* do. I'll see to it that you're gonna have to play it mighty careful from now on." He made a gesture toward the sky. "We may be stiffs up there—but we're sensitive."

Again he took out the makings, and as he walked back toward his horse he deftly and gracefully fashioned a cigarette. Once he stopped and looked back toward Rance. "I'll think about it some," he said, and lighted the cigarette. "I'll think about it some." And right in front of Rance McGrew's eyes he disappeared.

"Jesse!" Rance screamed. "Jesse—"

"Jesse!" Rance screamed, and the crew looked up, startled.

There was Rance standing at the bar, staring at his reflection in the mirror. Above him he could see the lighting men, and behind his own reflection was that of Sy Blattsburg and the cameraman.

Sy hurried up to him, his face worried. "You all right, Rance?"

"Yeah," Rance answered weakly. "Yeah, I'm all right." Then, looking around, "But where'd you all go?"

The director exchanged a nervous glance with several of the crew. His voice was even more concerned. "Where did we go? We didn't go anywhere, Rance. Nowhere at all, baby. Are you sure you're all right?"

Rance gulped. "Sure . . . sure, I'm fine—I'm just fine."

Sy turned to face the set. "All right," he said. "Let's get back to business now. Scene one hundred thirteen. Jesse's on the floor—"

Rance gave a startled gasp. He almost had to force himself to turn from the bar to where the ersatz Jesse was lying.

"You think he's unconscious," Sy continued, "but he tries to get you in the back. You fall to the floor, turn over with your gun in your hand, let him have it from on your belly."

At this moment there was the loud honk of a Jaguar horn.

"Somebody wants to see you, Mr. McGrew," one of the grips called from outside. "Says he's your agent."

Rance looked bewildered. "My agent?"

Sy Blattsburg closed his eyes and counted slowly to five under his breath. "Look, Rance," he said, a slight tremor in his voice, "I don't know what your chain of command is. So you go out and talk to your agent. Find out what it is that he wants, and what it is that you want, and what it is we can shoot."

Trancelike, Rance walked out of the saloon and stopped dead in his tracks on the top step of the porch. There was his red Jaguar, just as if nothing had happened. Even the steer horns on the front of the hood were a reminder to him of the reality of Rance McGrew, idol of young and old. But standing alongside of the automobile was an apparition. It was the real Jesse James.

He wore Bermuda shorts, an Italian printed silk sport shirt, and a mauve beret. He was rolling his own cigarette but when he'd finished, he stuck it into a four-inch cigarette holder. He took a deep drag, flicked off the ash, then winked at Rance, who stood swaying between numbing fright and oncoming coma.

"Howdy, Marshal," Jesse said warmly. "You said 'anything,' so 'anything' is the following: I'm jus' gonna stick around from picture to picture and make sure you don't hurt no more feelin's." He took out the cigarette holder and studied it thoughtfully, then he looked up and smiled. "Now, in this here scene, the guy that plays me don't fire at your back. He's lost a lot of blood and he's weak as tea, but he manages to git up to his feet, knock you through the window, and then make his getaway out the back." He put the cigarette holder between his teeth. "You dig, Marshal?"

Rance stared at him wide-eyed. "Knocks *me* through the window? *Rance McGrew?*"

Jesse's eyes narrowed into slits, not unlike the openings in a Mark III tank. His pupils were the business ends of atomic cannons. "You heard me, Marshal," he said. "Knocks you through the window and makes his getaway out the back."

Rance heaved a deep sigh, turned, and reentered the saloon.

Jesse could hear the mumble of voices from inside. There was one piercing wail that belonged to Sy Blattsburg, and some jumbled colloquy that sounded like "Areyououtofyourmothergrabbingmind? JesseJamesdoeswhat?!"

Jesse smiled and deftly plucked the cigarette out of the holder, stamping it under his patent-leather loafers.

Another voice came from inside. "Scene one hundred thirteen—take two."

There was the sound of a scuffle, and then Rance McGrew came through the window in a welter of shattered glass.

Jesse walked over to stand above him, but in the process took a script from the front seat of the Jag. "I was readin' next week's episode, Marshal. The one where ya knock a gun outta Frank James's hand from a fourth-story window half a block away, usin' the base of a lamp."

Rance slowly and painfully got to his feet. "No good?" he inquired softly.

"Stinks!" said Jesse. "The way I see it, Frank hears ya, whirls around, fires from the hip—knocks the lamp outta your hand."

Jesse opened the car door and motioned Rance inside. Then he walked around to the driver's seat, got in, turned the key, and stepped on the gas. The car zoomed backward three quarters of the way across the street, stopped, and then roared forward.

Jesse's voice could be heard over the sound of the engine. "Now, two weeks from now," the voice said, "I think we oughta give Sam Starr a break. He's a nice fella—awful good to his mother—"

The rest of his voice was drowned out by the engine's roar as the car disappeared down the dusty street.

* * *

While nothing is certain except death and taxes—and even these may be somewhat variable—it seems reasonable to conjecture that the range riders up in Cowboy Heaven felt appeased. Jesse James used his mandate well, and from that moment on, Rance McGrew, a former phony-baloney, became an upright citizen with a preoccupation with all things involving tradition, truth, and cowboy predecessors.

THE NIGHT OF THE MEEK

It was Christmas. There was absolutely no question about that. Festive good will filled the air like the smell of maple syrup—sweet, sugary, and thick with insistence. There was one more day to complete Christmas shopping and this item of information was dinned into the minds of the citizenry like a proclamation of impending martial law—"One More Shopping Day until Christmas!" It was the war cry of the big sell, and on this twenty-fourth day of the twelfth month of the one-thousand-nine-hundred-and-sixty-first year of our Lord, it served as a warning that just a few hours remained for people to open up their wallets and lay rather tired fingers on dog-eared credit cards.

"One More Shopping Day until Christmas." The words were strung in tinsled lettering across the main floor of Wimbel's Department Store. Mr. Walter Dundee, the floor manager of Wimbel's, glanced at them briefly as he did his rounds up and down the aisles, casting businesslike eyes at the organized mayhem surrounding him.

He was a balding little fellow in his fifties, inclined to paunchiness, but briskly efficient in his movements and atti-

360

tudes. Mr. Dundee could spot a shoplifter, a bum credit risk, or a grimy little child breaking a mechanical toy—he had an abhorrence of children of all ages—in one single all-pervading glance. He could also spot an ineffectual salesperson just by listening to a couple of sentences of the opening pitch.

Mr. Dundee walked through the aisles of Wimbel's that December 24th, barking out orders, snapping fingers, and generally riding herd on these last few moments of Yuletide humbuggery. He extended watery smiles to harried mothers and their squalling children, and he gave explicit and terse directions to any and all questions as to where merchandise could be found, where rest rooms were located, and the exact times of delivery for all purchases over twenty-five dollars, no matter how far out in the suburbs they went. As he walked up the aisles past Ladies Hand Bags, toward the Toy Department, he noted the empty Santa Claus chair. One of his sparse little eyebrows, set at a rakish tilt over a tiny blue eye, shot up in fast-mounting concern. There was a sign over the chair which read, "Santa Claus will return at 6:00 o'clock."

The large clock on the west wall read "6:35." Santa Claus was thirty-five minutes late. An incipient ulcer in Mr. Dundee's well-rounded abdomen did little pincer things to his liver. He belched, and felt anger building up like a small flame suddenly blasted by a bellows. That Goddamn Santa Claus was a disgrace to the store. What was his name—Corwin? That Goddamn Corwin had been the most undependable store Santa Claus they had ever hired. Only yesterday Dundee had seen him pull out a hip flask and take an unsubtle snort—smack dab in the middle of a Brownie troop. Mr. Dundee had sent him an icy look which froze Corwin in the middle of his tippling.

Mr. Dundee was noted for his icy looks. As a boy, thirty-odd years before at military school, he had become Sergeant Major of the Fourth Form—the only non-athlete ever to achieve this eminence—because of the icy look that he carried with him throughout his professional career. It made up for the fact that he stood five feet four inches tall and had a figure like a coke bottle.

Now he felt frustrated that his rage had no outlet, so he scanned the store until he spotted Miss Wilsie, Ladies Inexpensive Jewelry, primping in front of a mirror. He stalked over to her, pinioned her with his look, and then announced:

"You have nothing better to do, Miss Wilsie? Preparing

yourself for a beauty contest? There are customers waiting. Be good enough to attend to them!"

He waited only long enough for the color to drain out of the girl's face as she hurried back to her place behind the counter, then he turned again toward the empty Santa Claus chair and cursed the errant Santa Claus, now thirty-eight minutes late.

Henry Corwin sat at the bar, a moth-eaten Santa Claus outfit engulfing his sparse frame. Discolored whiskers hanging from a rubber band covered his chest like a napkin. His cocky little cap, with the white snowball at the end, hung down over his eyes. He picked up his eighth glass of inexpensive rye, blew the snowball off to one side, and deftly slipped the shot glass toward his mouth, downing the drink in one gulp. He looked up at the clock over the bar mirror and noted that the two hands were close together. Precisely where they were he couldn't tell, but he did feel a sense of time passing. Too much time.

He suddenly noticed his reflection in the mirror and realized that he was not drunk enough, because he still looked like a caricature. The Santa Claus uniform, which he had rented from Kaplan's Klassy Costume Rental, had seen not only better days but many earlier ones. It was made out of thin cotton, patched and repatched. The color had faded to a kind of ailing pink and the white "fur" trim looked like cotton after a boll weevil assault. The cap was several sizes too small, and was actually a reconverted Shriner's fez with the insignia taken off. The face looking back at him had gentle eyes and a warm smile that was slightly lopsided. It crinkled up at the ends and made you want to smile back.

Corwin was neutral to the face. He rarely took note of it. At this moment he was more concerned with the costume, fingering it and noting considerable lollipop stains, week-old ice-cream spots, and some brand-new holes, sizable enough to reveal the two pillows he had strapped over his union suit. He took his eyes away from the reflection and pointed to his empty glass.

The bartender walked over to him and gestured at the clock. "You told me to tell yuh when it was six-thirty," he announced. "It's six-thirty."

Corwin smiled and nodded. "That's exactly what it is," he agreed.

The bartender picked his teeth. "What happens now? Yuh turn into a reindeer?"

Corwin smiled again. "Would that that were so." He held up his empty glass. "One more, huh?"

The bartender poured him a shot. "That's nine drinks and a sandwich—that's four-eighty."

Corwin took a single five-dollar bill from his pocket and put it on the counter. He started the shot glass toward his mouth. But as he did so, he noticed two little faces staring at him through the frosted glass of the front door. Big eyes looked at him in rapt attention and breath-catching worship—the eyes of every kid who, with the purest faith, had known that there *was* a North Pole, that reindeer *did* land on rooftops, and that miracles *did* come down chimneys. Even kids like this had this faith on grimy One-hundred-and-eighteenth street, where Puerto Ricans crowded into cold dirty rooms to gradually realize that poverty wore the same clothes both on lush islands and in concrete canyons a thousand miles away.

Corwin had to stare back at the little faces, and then he had to smile. They looked like slightly soiled cherubs on some creased and aged Christmas card. They were excited that the man in the red suit was looking at them.

Corwin turned his back to them, and quickly gulped the contents of the shot glass. He waited a moment, then looked at the door again. The two little noses pressed against the glass suddenly disappeared. But before they went they waved to Santa Claus at the bar and Corwin waved back.

He looked thoughtfully at the empty shot glass.

"Why do you suppose there isn't really a Santa Claus?" he asked, speaking partly to the glass, partly to the bartender.

The bartender looked up tiredly from drying glasses. "How's that?" he asked.

"Why isn't there a *real* Santa Claus"—Corwin nodded toward the front door—"for kids like that?"

The bartender shrugged. "What the hell am I, Corwin—a philosopher?" He stared at Corwin for a long moment. "Do you know what your trouble is?" he said. "Yuh let that dopey red suit go to your head!"

He picked up the five-dollar bill, rang up the cash register, then put the change in front of Corwin.

Corwin looked at the coins and smiled a little crookedly. "Flip yuh—double or nothing."

"What the hell do yuh think this is, Corwin—Monte Carlo? Go on—get outta here!"

Corwin rose somewhat unsteadily, testing soggy legs. Then, satisfied that they were serviceable, he walked across the room to the front door and out into the cold, snowy night, buttoning the top button of his thin cotton jacket, squeezing his cap down as far as it would go. He put his head into an icy wind and started across the street.

A big Caddie, with a Christmas tree protruding from the trunk, shot past him, honking. A red-faced, angry chauffeur shouted something as the car sped away. Corwin just smiled and went on, feeling the wet flakes cool on his hot face. He stumbled on the opposite curb and reached for the lamppost which was several feet away.

His arms encircled nothing but snowflakes and he pitched forward on his face, landing on a pile of snow next to a garbage can. With great difficulty he got to a sitting position, and became suddenly aware of four ragged little legs standing close by. He looked up to see the two scrawny Puerto Rican kids staring down at him, their little faces dark against the snow.

"Santa Claus," the little girl said, catching her breath, "I want a dolly and a playhouse."

The silent little boy alongside nudged her with an elbow.

"And a gun," she continued hurriedly, "and a set of soldiers and a fort and a bicycle—"

Corwin looked up into their faces. Even their excitement, their exuberance, the universal Christmas look of all children, couldn't hide the thinness of their faces—nor could the sweetness of them, and the gentleness, hide the fact that their coats were too small for them and not nearly heavy enough for the weather.

Then Henry Corwin began to cry. Alcohol had unlocked all the gates to his reserve—what flooded out of him were the frustrations, the miseries, the failures of twenty years; the pain of the yearly Santa Claus stints in moth-eaten costumes, giving away fantasies that he didn't own, imitating that which was only make-believe to begin with.

Henry Corwin reached out and pulled the children to him, burying his face first against one and then the other, the tears cascading down his cheeks, impossible to stop.

The two little children stared at him—incredulous that this red-coated god, who dealt in toys and unbelievable wonders, could sit on a snowy curb and cry just as they did.

"*Por que Santa Claus esta llorando?*" the girl whispered to the little boy.

He answered her in English. "I don't know why he's crying. Maybe we have hurt his feelings."

They watched him for a while until his sobs subsided and he released them, stumbling to his feet and heading down the street away from them—this thin shabby man with the wet face, looking as if he believed that all the anguish of the world was of his doing.

An hour later when Mr. Dundee saw Corwin come in through the side door, he felt that perverse pleasure that is one of the parts built into mean men. Here was someone he could vent his wrath on—a wrath that at this moment was anointed with inflammable oil. He waited for Corwin to walk toward him, drumming his fingertips together behind his back and then deftly grabbing the Santa Claus by the arm as he walked past.

"Corwin," Dundee said through clenched teeth, "you're almost two hours late! Now get over there and see if you can keep from disillusioning a lot of kids that not only there *isn't* a Santa Claus—but that the one in the store happens to be a bar-hopping clod who'd be more at home playing Rudolph the Red-Nosed Reindeer!" He gave Corwin a shove. "Now get with it—Santa Claus!" This last was spat out like an epithet.

Henry Corwin smiled wanly and started toward the Santa Claus section. He paused by the electric trains and watched two little colored boys staring at them as if they were a collection of miracles. Henry winked at them, went to the control panel, and started to push buttons.

Three trains started up simultaneously, racing around the tracks, over bridges, through tunnels, past station platforms. Little men came out and waved lanterns or threw mail sacks, or did any one of a dozen marvelous things that toy trainmen do. But after a moment it seemed evident that Henry Corwin was not mechanically minded. The two little boys looked at each other with growing concern as a Union Pacific Flyer raced down the tracks on a collision course with a Civil War supply train.

Henry Corwin hastily pushed a few more buttons, but the collision was inevitable. The two trains met head-on in a welter of dented metal, ripped tracks, and flying toy trainmen.

Never one to leave well enough alone, Corwin pushed two more buttons which made the damage total. He switched another set of tracks that sent the heavily laden freight train piling into the wreckage of the first two. Toy trains flew through the air, bridges collapsed; and when the noise had subsided, Corwin saw the two little boys staring at him.

"What do yuh think?" Corwin asked them, smiling a little sheepishly.

The first little boy looked at his companion, then back toward Corwin. "How are yuh on erector sets?" he asked.

Corwin shook his head a little sadly. "About the same."

He tousled the two little heads, and then climbed over the velvet rope that was strung around the Santa Claus chair.

There was a line of waiting children and clock-watching mothers and they surged forward when the slightly moth-eaten Kris Kringle mounted his throne. He sat there for a moment, shutting his eyes briefly as he felt the room start to spin around him. Christmas decorations and colored lights whirled round and round as if he were riding a merry-go-round. He tried to focus on the faces of the children as they kept streaming past him; tried to smile and wave at them. He shut his eyes again, feeling nausea rising inside of him. This time, when he opened them he was face to face with the blurred image of a small gargoyle being pushed toward him by a bosomy, loud woman with a set of shoulders like Tony Galento's.

"Go ahead, Willie," the woman's voice screeched, "climb up on his lap. He won't hurt you, will you, Santa Claus? You go ahead, Willie, you tell him—" She gave the seven-year-old another insistent push toward Santa Claus. Corwin half rose, weaving unsteadily and extending a wavering hand.

"What's your name, little boy?" Corwin asked, and then hiccoughed loudly. He tilted sideways, grabbed for the arm of the chair, and then pitched forward to land on the floor at the little boy's feet. He sat there smiling a little wanly, unable to get up or to do anything else.

The small gargoyle took one look at Corwin and in a blaring voice, similar in pitch to his mother's, shrieked, "Hey, ma! Santa Claus is loaded!"

The gargoyle's mother immediately screamed, "You've got some nerve! You ought to be ashamed!"

Corwin just sat there and shook his head back and forth. "Madam," he said very quietly, "I *am* ashamed."

"Come on, Willie." She grabbed the boy by the arm. "I hope this isn't going to be a traumatic experience for you." She looked over her shoulder toward Corwin. "Sot!"

People, hearing the tone, stopped and stared.

Mr. Dundee hurried up the aisle toward Toyland. He gave an all-pervading glance, and then his voice assumed that unctuous, placating quality of every hard-pressed floor manager.

"Is there some trouble here, madam?"

"Trouble!" the big woman spat back. "No, there's no trouble, except this is the last time I trade in this store. You hire your Santa Clauses out of the gutter!"

She pointed toward Corwin, who was struggling to his feet. He took a hesitant step toward one of the brass poles flanking the entrance to his "throne."

"Madam," he said very gently, "please. It's Christmas."

Willie's mother's face twisted, and in the light of an illuminated sign which read, "Peace on Earth—Good Will to Men," she looked like a cross between the Wicked Witch of the North and a female Ebenezer Scrooge.

"Don't rub it in," she said tersely. "Come on, Willie."

She barged into two people, pushed them bodily out of the way, and dragged the child down the aisle.

Dundee turned to stare toward Corwin, then at the salespeople and customers who had congregated. "All right!" he said grimly. "Back to work! Back to your positions."

He walked toward Corwin, stopping by the velvet rope. His thin lips twitched as he waggled a finger at Corwin and waited for him to come over to him.

"Yes, Mr. Dundee?"

"Simply this," Dundee said, "Mr. Kris Kringle of the lower depths. Since we are only one hour and thirteen minutes away from closing, it is my distinct pleasure to inform you that there is no more need for your services. In other words, you've had it. Now get out of here!"

He turned to face the row of mothers and children, smiling beatifically. "All right, kiddies," he gushed, "free lollipops! Just go over there to the candy counter. Go right ahead!"

He smiled, winked, and looked benevolent as the disappointed children and the hard-pressed mothers moved away from the Santa Claus with the sagging shoulders.

Corwin stared down at the floor, feeling the looks of the children, and after a moment turned and started to walk toward the employees' locker.

"A word of advice," Dundee said to him as he passed. "You'd best get that beat-up red suit back to whatever place you rented it from, before you really tie one on and ruin it for good and all."

Corwin stopped and stared into the twitching angry little face. "Thank you ever so much, Mr. Dundee," he said quietly. "As to my drinking—that is indefensible and you have my abject apologies. I find of late that I have very little choice in the matter of expressing emotions. I can either drink . . . or I can weep. And drinking is so much more subtle."

He paused and looked briefly at the empty Santa Claus chair. "But as for my insubordination"—he shook his head—"I was not rude to that fat woman. I was merely trying to remind her that Christmas isn't just barging up and down department store aisles and pushing people out of the way and screaming 'foul' because she has to open up a purse. I was only trying to tell her that Christmas is something quite different from that. It's richer and finer and truer and . . . and it should allow for patience and love and charity and compassion." He looked into the frozen mask that was Mr. Dundee's face. "That's all I would've told her," he added gently, "had she given me the chance."

"How philosophical!" Mr. Dundee retorted icily. "And as your parting word—perhaps you can tell us how we go about living up to these wondrous Yule standards which you have so graciously and unselfishly laid down for us?"

There was no smile on Corwin's face. He shook his head and shrugged his narrow shoulders. "I don't know how to tell you," he said quietly. "I don't know how at all. All I know is that I'm a defeated, aging, purposeless relic of another time. That I live in a dirty rooming house on a street that's loaded with kids who think that Christmas is a day to stay out of school and nothing more. My street, Mr. Dundee, is full of shabby people where the only thing to come down the chimney on Christmas Eve is more poverty." He smiled crookedly and looked down at his baggy red jacket. "That's another reason I drink. So that when I walk past the tenements I'll think that they're the North Pole and the children are elves, and that I'm really Santa Claus carrying a bag of wondrous things for all of them."

He fingered the worn cotton "fur" around his neck. "I wish, Mr. Dundee," he said as he started to turn away, "I wish that on just one Christmas . . . only one . . . I could see some of the have-nots, the shabby ones, the hopeless and the dreamless ones . . . just on one Christmas . . . I'd like to see the meek inherit the earth."

The crooked smile came again as he looked down at his bony hands and then up at Mr. Dundee. "That's why I drink, Mr. Dundee, and that's why I weep."

He took a deep breath, the strangely twisted little smile still on his face, then turned and shuffled down the aisle past the whispering salesgirls and the tired shoppers, who looked at this symbol of Christmas who was so much more tired than they.

Henry Corwin walked down the avenue past 104th Street. He felt the cold snow on his face and looked vaguely at the festive windows of the stores as he passed. When he reached his block he headed toward the saloon, walking very slowly, hands buried in his armpits. He turned a corner and headed down an alley toward the rear door of the bar, and it was then that he heard the sound.

It was a strange sound. Sleigh bells—or something like them. But very odd. Somehow muffled and indistinct. He stopped and looked skyward. Then he smiled to himself and shook his head, assuring himself that sleigh bells or anything else could be found only in his mind—that tired, whiskey-dulled brain. But after a moment he heard the bells again, this time more persistent and louder.

Corwin had stopped near a loading platform of a wholesale meat plant. He looked up at the sky again and wondered. He started at the caterwauling dissonance of a night-prowling cat that suddenly leaped out from behind a barrel and scurried past him in the snow. It raced across the alley to another loading platform on the other side, leaping to the top of a garbage can and in the process knocking over a burlap bag that rested precariously on top of it. Then the cat disappeared in the darkness.

The burlap bag landed at Corwin's feet and spilled open, depositing half a dozen dented tin cans in the snow. Corwin reached down and righted the bag, shoving the cans back inside.

Then he lifted the burlap bag over his shoulder and started to carry it back to the platform. Halfway there he heard the bells again. This time much clearer and very much nearer.

Again he stopped in his tracks and stared up toward the sky, wide-eyed. Another sound joined that of the bells. Corwin couldn't describe it except to make a mental note that it was like the sound of tiny hoofbeats. He very slowly let the burlap bag drop from his shoulders, and once again it fell over and spilled its contents on the ground. Corwin looked down at it, blinked his eyes, rubbed them, and stared.

Protruding from the open bag was the front end of a toy truck, an arm and a leg of a doll, and evidence of other toys of every description. He fell to his knees and started to reach into the bag, taking out truck, doll, playhouse, a box marked "Electric Train," and then stopped, realizing that the bag must be filled with all such things. He let out a cry of surprise and jammed the toys back in the bag. He hoisted it to his shoulder and started a slow, stumbling trot toward the street, occasionally stopping to pick up a toy that fell, but feeling the words bubbling up inside of him and finally coming out.

"Hey," he shouted as he turned the corner onto 111th Street. "Hey, everybody! Hey, kids—Merry Christmas!"

The 104th Street Mission was a big, ugly, barren place, sullen to the eye and deadening to the spirit. Its main room was a naked square full of straight-backed, uncomfortable benches, with a small platform and organ at the far end. Large signs dotted the walls with little homilies like, "Love Thy Neighbor," "Do unto Others as You Would Have Others Do unto You," "Faith, Hope and Charity."

Seated up and down the rows of benches were perhaps fifteen shabby old men. A few of them held cheap china mugs filled with watery coffee. They cradled them in cold hands, feeling the warmth and letting the steam rise up into their bearded tired faces. They wore the faces of poverty and age, each encrusted with layer after layer of the hopelessness of lonely old men whose lives had somehow swiftly and silently disintegrated into false teeth, and cheap coffee mugs, and this ugly, drafty room that traded religion and thin gruel in exchange for the last remaining fragments of dignity.

Sister Florence Harvey headed the Mission. After twenty-four years, she had begun to blend with the walls, the benches, and the miserable atmosphere. She was a tall, sour-looking spinster with deep lines imbedded at the corner of her mouth. She pounded the organ with a kind of desperate verve, playing badly but loudly an obscure Christmas carol that had spirit if not melody.

An old man rushed in from the outside and began whispering to another old man who sat on the rear bench. After a moment all the old men were whispering and pointing toward the door. Sister Florence noted the disturbance and tried to drown it out by playing even louder, but by this time some of the men were on their feet, talking loudly and gesturing. Sister Florence finally struck a discordant chord on the organ, rose, and glared at the old men in front of her.

"What's all this about?" she asked angrily. "What's this noise? Why the commotion?"

The old man who had brought the original message took his cap off and rolled it nervously in his hands. "Sister Florence," he said diffidently, "I ain't touched a drop since last Thursday and that's the gospel truth! But I swear to you right now, on account of I seen him with my own eyes—Santa Claus is comin' up the street headin' this way and he's givin' everybody their heart's desire!"

There were mumbled exclamations from the other old men. Dull and saddened eyes turned bright. Tired old faces became animated, and their voices punctuated the room.

"Santa Claus!"

"He's comin' here!"

"And he's bringing us whatever we like!"

The door leading to the street burst open and in walked Henry Corwin, his face red, his eyes shining, and over his shoulder he carried the bag, brightly wrapped packages protruding from its top.

Corwin put the bag down on the floor, looked up, twinkling, and made a Santa Claus gesture of a finger to nose tip. He looked around the room, smiling—his voice absolutely gurgling with excitement.

"It's Christmas Eve, gentlemen, and I'm in business to make it a merry one." He pointed to one of the old men. "What'll be your pleasure?"

The scrawny little old man pointed to himself, amazed.

"Me?" he asked in a toothless wheeze, then he wet his lips. "I fancy a new pipe." He almost held his breath as he said it.

Corwin reached into the bag without even looking. He withdrew a curved Meerschaum. There were "Oh's" and "Ah's" as the old man took the pipe in trembling fingers and stared at it numbly.

Corwin pointed to another old man. "How about you?" he asked.

This little old man opened and closed his mouth several times before a sound came out. "Maybe," he croaked, "maybe a woolen sweater?"

Corwin made a sweeping theatrical gesture. "A woolen sweater you shall have," he trumpeted. He stopped as he reached into the bag and looked up again. "Size?"

The old man held out two thin blue-veined hands. "Who cares?"

Out of the bag came a turtleneck cashmere, and at this point the old men crowded around Corwin, their frail voices filled with hope.

"Another sweater maybe?"

"How about some pipe tobacco?"

"A carton of cigarettes?"

"New shoes?"

"Smoking jacket?"

And at each request, Corwin produced the desired item by simply reaching into the bag. He was unaware of Sister Florence looking at him angrily from the fringe of the crowd. Finally she pushed her way through to stand over Corwin.

"Now, what's this all about?" she asked acidly. "What's the idea of coming in here and disrupting the Christmas Eve music service?"

Corwin laughed aloud and slapped his hands together. "My dear Sister Florence," he bubbled, "don't ask me to explain. I can't explain. I'm as much in the dark as everybody else, but I've got a Santa Claus bag here that gives everybody just what they want for Christmas. And as long as it's puttin' out . . . I'm puttin' in!"

His eyes were wet as he reached into the bag again. "How about a new dress, Sister Florence?"

The thin bony woman turned on her heel disapprovingly,

but not before she caught a flash of a huge beribboned box that Corwin pulled out of the sack.

Again came the voices of the old men, gentle, plaintive, persistent, and Corwin spent the next five minutes taking things out of the bag, until the room looked like the aftermath of an inventory in a department store.

Corwin was unaware of Sister Florence bringing the policeman in. She pointed to Corwin from the door and the cop made his way over to him. He reached Corwin and hovered over him like a symbol of all the law and order in the world. He put his hand on Corwin's shoulder. "It's Corwin, ain't it?" he asked.

Corwin got to his feet, the grin so broad that his jaw ached. "Henry Corwin, officer," he announced, and then laughed in a spasm of delight. "At least it *was* Henry Corwin. Maybe now it's Santa Claus or Kris Kringle—I don't know."

The policeman regarded him blankly and then sniffed the air. "You're drunk, ain't yuh, Corwin?"

Corwin laughed again and the laugh was so marvelously rich and winning and infectious that all the old men joined in. "Drunk?" Corwin shouted. "Of course I'm drunk! Naturally I'm drunk! I'm drunk with the spirit of Yule! I'm intoxicated with the wonder of Christmas Eve! I'm inebriated with joy and with delight! *Yes, officer—by God, I'm drunk!*"

A toothless old man looked around bewilderedly. "What was them things he was drinking?"

The policeman held up his hands again for quiet and kicked at the burlap bag meaningfully. "We can settle this one in a hurry, Corwin," he said. "You just show me the receipt for all this stuff."

Corwin's smile became frayed at the edges. "The receipt?" he gulped.

"The receipt!"

The old men smiled among themselves, nodded and winked, and turned, smilingly confident, toward Santa Claus.

Corwin didn't nod. He simply swallowed hard and shook his head.

"No receipt, huh?" the policeman asked.

"No receipt," Corwin whispered.

The policeman let out a single snort and kicked at the bag again. "All right," he announced, "collect all the stolen goods and put them in a pile over here. I'll see that they get claimed after I find out where he took the stuff from." He turned to Corwin. "All right, Santa, let's you and me take a little trip down to the precinct." He grabbed Corwin's elbow and started to push him toward the door.

Over his shoulder, Corwin got a last look at the old men. Each was depositing his gift on a pile on the floor. They did it quietly, with no complaints and no sign of disappointment. It was as if they were quite accustomed to miracles being fragile, breakable things. They had spent their lives trying to hold onto illusions, and this was no different.

Sister Florence went back to the platform and shouted out the name of the next carol. "A one, a two, a three," she screeched, and then gave mortal combat to the music while the old men began to sing in sad, cracked little voices. Every now and then one of them would cast a wishful look over his shoulder at a Meerschaum pipe or a cashmere sweater on the pile of gifts that sat a million miles away from them.

In the small detention room at the station house, Officer Flaherty guarded the burlap bag and his prisoner, who sat despondently on a bench, his eyes staring at the floor. The brisk footsteps from outside sounded familiar to Corwin. He knew who they belonged to, and sure enough it was Walter Dundee who was ushered into the room.

Dundee wore a look of contented ferocity. He rubbed his hands together briskly, like a happy executioner. "Aah," he murmured, "here he is." He pointed toward Corwin. "And here we are." He made a gesture encompassing the room, and then pointed to the bag. "And there *that* is! And you, Mr. Corwin, my wistful St. Nicholas, are soon going up the river!" He turned toward Officer Flaherty, his voice hopeful. "Do you suppose he could get as much as ten years?"

The officer looked somber. "It don't look good, Corwin," he said. "Of course they might lop off a few months if you was to tell us where the rest of the loot was." He looked at Dundee and jerked his head in Corwin's direction. "He's been givin' away stuff for two and a half hours. He must have a warehouse full of it."

Corwin looked first toward Dundee, then at the policeman,

and then at the burlap bag. "I'm glad you brought that up," he said quietly. "There's a little discrepancy here."

Dundee's lips twitched. "Listen, you moth-eaten Robin Hood—the wholesale theft of thousands of dollars' worth of goods is not a 'little discrepancy'!" He moved over to the bag and started to open it. "Though I can tell you right now, Corwin, that this whole affair has come as no surprise to me! I happen to be a practical judge of human nature."

He dipped into the bag and started to remove things— garbage bags, tin cans, broken bottles, and a large black cat that leaped out, squalling, and ran out of the room.

"I perceived that criminal glint in your eyes," Dundee continued, as he wiped some catsup off his cuff, "the very first moment I laid eyes on you! I'm not a student of human misbehavior for nothing. And I can assure you—"

Suddenly, Dundee stopped talking and gaped at the pile of garbage he had heaped on the floor. Quite abruptly he realized what he had been removing. He stared at the bag, incredulous. Officer Flaherty did the same.

Corwin smiled ever so slightly. He waggled a finger at the bag. "Mr. Dundee," he said softly, "you've kind of put your finger on the problem!" He waggled his finger at the bag again. "It can't seem to make up its mind whether to give out garbage or gifts."

Flaherty's face turned white and his mouth worked before any sound came out. "Well . . . well . . ." he spluttered, "it was givin' out gifts when I seen it." He turned to Dundee. "Whatever they wanted, Corwin was supplying it, and it wasn't tin cans neither! It was gifts. Toys. All kinds of expensive stuff. You might as well admit it, Corwin."

Corwin smiled. "Oh, I admit it all right. When I put in—it put out." He scratched his jaw thoughtfully. "But I believe the essence of our problem here is that we're dealing with a most unusual bag—"

Dundee waved him quiet. "My advice to you, Corwin, is to clean this mess up and get out of here."

Corwin shrugged, went over to the bag, and started to put the debris back inside.

In the meantime Dundee turned to the policeman. "And you, Officer Flaherty," he said devastatingly, "call yourself a policeman! Well, I suppose it's a demanding task to distinguish between a bag full of garbage and an inventory of expensive stolen gifts."

The policeman's lower lip sagged. "You can believe me, Mr. Dundee," he said plaintively, "it's just like Corwin says—we're dealing with somethin' . . . somethin' supernatural here."

Dundee shook his head. "You know . . . you amaze me, Officer Flaherty. You really amaze me. In other words, all we need to do is ask Mr. Corwin to make a little abracadabra for us and no sooner said—done!" He looked up toward the ceiling. "Well, go ahead, Corwin. I fancy a bottle of cherry brandy, vintage nineteen-o-three." He threw up his hands in disgust and shut his eyes.

Corwin was halfway to the door. He paused, smiled a little thoughtfully, and then nodded. "Nineteen-o-three. A good year." He reached into the bag for a gift-wrapped package which he placed on the bench. Then he hoisted the bag over his shoulder and walked out of the room.

Dundee opened his eyes, took out a cigar, pointed it at the policeman. "Now, as for you, Officer Flah—" He stopped abruptly, staring at the beribboned box on the bench.

The policeman walked over to it and with shaking fingers pulled out a large bottle—a gift card hanging from it. His voice wavered slightly as he read it aloud. "Merry Christmas, Mr. Dundee."

The cork suddenly and inexplicably popped out of the bottle, and the policeman sat down on the bench because his legs could no longer support him.

Dundee's mouth was wide open as he stared at the bottle.

The policeman finally picked it up, wiped the neck, and held it out. "After you, Mr. Dundee."

Dundee took a couple of shaky steps over to Flaherty. He accepted the bottle and tilted it to his mouth, then he handed it back to the policeman. The two men sat side by side taking turns, doing honors to an oddball gift that they were both sure was a figment of their imaginations, just as the sudden warm feeling in their stomachs must also be illusory. But sit there they did. And drink they did. And the make-believe liquid in the imaginary bottle was the best-tasting brandy they'd ever had.

A light snow drifted gently down through the glow of a

street corner lamp where Henry Corwin sat, the burlap bag between his legs. People came and went. But they came empty-handed and left with whatever precious little thing they had asked for. An old man carried a smoking jacket. A sad-faced immigrant woman in a shawl gazed lovingly at fur-lined boots that she cradled in her arms as she walked away. Two little Puerto Rican children loaded their gifts onto a brand-new red wagon and, chattering like bright-eyed squirrels, ran through the snow. A rheumy-eyed Bowery bum clutched happily at a portable television set. And still people came and went—a tiny Negro girl, barely able to walk, an eighty-year-old ex-First Mate from a banana boat that hadn't sailed in twenty years, a blind gospel singer who stared, unseeing, into the snow-filled night, crying softly as two of his neighbors helped pull a new organ down the sidewalk toward his tenement room.

And Henry Corwin's voice carried over the traffic noise and his hands flew in and out of the bag. "Merry Christmas . . . Merry Christmas . . . Merry Christmas . . . Here's a sweater for you. What's that, darling—a toy? Here you are. An electric train? Got lots of them. Smoking jackets? Lots of them here. What do you want, sweetheart—a dolly? What color hair would you like, darlin' . . . blonde, brunette, red, or what have you?"

And still the gifts came, and Henry Corwin felt a joy, a fulfillment, a sense of contentment he had never before known. It was when bells on a distant church steeple rang out midnight that Henry Corwin realized that most of the people had disappeared and that the bag was empty burlap lying limply at his feet.

The toothless little old man with his smoking jacket worn over his shabby coat looked off in the direction of the chimes. "It's Christmas, Henry," he said softly. "Peace on earth, good will to men."

A little Puerto Rican child, setting up toy soldiers in the snow, smiled at Santa Claus sitting on the curb. "God bless us," he whispered, "everyone."

Corwin smiled and felt a wetness on his cheeks that wasn't snow. The smile persisted as he touched the burlap sack. "A Merry Christmas to all." He got to his feet and looked at the old man standing close to him. He straightened the phony beard and started to walk down the street.

The old man touched his arm. "Hey, Santa! Nothin' for *yourself* this Christmas?"

"For myself?" Corwin said quietly. "Why, I've had the nicest Christmas since the beginning of time."

"But with nothin' for yourself?" the old man persisted. He pointed to the empty bag. "Not a thing?"

Corwin touched his make-believe whiskers. "Do you know something? I can't think of anything I want." He looked toward the empty bag. "I think the only thing I've *ever* wanted was to be the biggest gift-giver of all times. And in a way I've had that tonight." He walked slowly along the snowy sidewalk. "Though if I did have a choice . . . any choice at all . . . of a gift"—he paused and looked back toward the old man—"I guess I'd wish I could do this every year." He winked and grinned. "Now, that *would* be a gift, wouldn't it!"

The old man smiled back at him.

"God bless you," Corwin said, "and a Merry Christmas."

"To you, Henry," the old man said, "to you."

Henry Corwin walked slowly down the street, feeling a sudden emptiness—a dullness, as if he had traveled through a land of lights only to enter suddenly a gray limbo. He didn't know why he stopped, but then he realized he was standing at the entrance of the alley. He looked into it and, double-taking, looked in again and caught his breath. All his brain, his logic, his understanding of what could and couldn't exist told him in this one flashing instant that this was simply an illusion added to a night full of illusions. But there it was.

Set back deep at the far end of the alley was a sleigh and eight diminutive reindeer. And even more incredible, there was a tiny pipe-smoking elf standing alongside.

Corwin jammed his knuckles into his eyes and rubbed hard, but when he peeked through his fingers there was the scene just as he'd seen it.

"We've been waiting quite a while, Santa Claus," the elf said, taking a puff of his pipe.

Corwin shook his head. He wanted just to lie down in the snow and go to sleep. The whole thing was make-believe—of this there could be no doubt. He smiled foolishly and then giggled as he pointed to the pipe. "That'll stunt your growth." Then he giggled again and decided there was no point in going to sleep, since obviously that's precisely what he *was*—asleep.

The little elf's voice carried with it just a tinge of impatience. "Did you hear me? I said we've been waiting quite a while, Santa Claus."

Corwin let it sink in and then very slowly raised his right hand and pointed to himself.

The elf nodded. "We've got a year of hard work ahead of us to prepare for *next* Christmas, so come on awready!"

Henry Corwin walked slowly into the alley and, as if in a dream, mounted into the tiny sleigh.

Officer Patrick J. Flaherty and Walter Dundee walked down the steps of the station house arm and arm, feeling no pain at all. They stopped at the foot of the steps.

"Going home now, Officer Flaherty?" Dundee asked.

Flaherty smiled happily back at him through glazed eyes. "Goin' home, Mr. Dundee. And you?"

"Going home, Officer Flaherty. This is quite the nicest Christmas Eve I've ever had."

There was a sound and both men looked up into the night sky.

Dundee shivered. "Flah . . . Flah . . . Flaherty? I could have sworn that—" He looked at the policeman, who was blinking and rubbing his eyes. "Did *you* see it?"

The policeman nodded. "I thought I did."

"What *did* you see?"

"Mr. Dundee—I don't think I'd better tell you. You'd report me for drinking on duty."

"Go ahead," Dundee insisted. *"What did you see?"*

"Mr. Dundee . . . it was Corwin! Big as life . . . in a sleigh with reindeer . . . sittin' alongside an elf and headin' up toward the sky!" He closed his eyes and heaved a tremendous sigh. "That's about the size of it, ain't it, Mr. Dundee?"

Dundee nodded. "That's about the size of it, Officer Flaherty." His voice sounded small and strained. He turned to the big cop. "I'll tell you something. You'd better come home with me. We'll brew up some hot coffee and we'll pour some whiskey into it, and we'll . . ." His voice drifted off as he stared toward the snow-filled sky, and when he looked back at Flaherty he wore a smile that somehow shone. "And we'll thank God for miracles, Officer Flaherty. That's what we'll do. We'll thank God for miracles."

Arm and arm, the two men walked off into the night—and over the disappearing sound of tiny bells came the deep resonant ringing of the church bells as they ushered in the next day. The wondrous day. The joyous day above all joyous days—the day of Christmas.

THE MIDNIGHT SUN

"The secret of a successful artist," an old instructor had told her years ago, "is not just to put paint on canvas—it is to transfer emotion, using oils and brush as a kind of nerve conduit."

Norma Smith looked out of the window at the giant sun and then back to the canvas on the easel she had set up close to the window. She had tried to paint the sun and she had captured some of it physically—the vast yellow-white orb which seemed to cover half the sky. And already its imperfect edges could be defined. It was rimmed by massive flames in motion. This motion was on her canvas, but the heat—the incredible, broiling heat that came in waves and baked the city outside—could not be painted, nor could it be described. It bore no relation to any known quantity. It simply had no precedent. It was a prolonged, increasing, and deadening fever that traveled the streets like an invisible fire.

The girl put the paintbrush down and went slowly across the room to a small refrigerator. She got out a milk bottle full of water and carefully measured some into a glass. She took one swallow and felt its coolness move through her. For the past week just the simple act of drinking carried with it very special reactions. She couldn't remember actually *feeling* water before. Before, it had simply been thirst and then alleviation; but now the mere swallow of anything cool was an experience by itself. She put the bottle back inside the refrigerator and looked briefly at the clock on the bookcase. It read "11:45." She heard footsteps coming down the stairs outside and she walked slowly over to the door, opened it, and went out into the hall.

A little four-year-old girl stared up at her soberly, her eyes fixed on Norma's glass of water. Norma knelt down and put the glass to the child's lips.

"Susie!" a man's voice cut in. "Don't take the lady's water."

Norma looked up at a tall, sweat-drenched man in an unbuttoned sport shirt. "That's all right, Mr. Schuster," Norma said, "I have plenty."

"Nobody has plenty," the man said as he reached the bottom of the stairs and moved the little girl aside. "There's no such thing as 'plenty' anymore." He took the little girl's hand and crossed the hall to knock on the opposite door. "Mrs. Bronson," he called, "we're leaving now."

Mrs. Bronson opened the door and stepped out. She was a middle-aged woman in a thin housecoat, her face gleaming with sweat. She looked frowsy and dumpy, although Norma could recollect that she had been a petite, rather pretty woman not too long ago—much younger-looking than her years. Now her face was tired, her hair stringy and unkempt.

"Did you get gas?" Mrs. Bronson inquired in a flat, tired voice.

The tall man nodded. "I got twelve gallons. I figured that'd take us at least to Buffalo."

"Where are you going?" Norma asked.

The tall man's wife came down the stairs. "We're trying to get to Toronto," she said. "Mr. Schuster has a cousin there."

Mrs. Bronson reached down to stroke the little girl's hair, and then wiped some of the perspiration from the tiny flushed face. "I'm not sure it's wise—you trying to do this. The highways are packed. Bumper to bumper, the radio said. Even with the gas shortage and everything—"

Schuster cut her off. "I know that," he said tersely, "but we gotta try anyway." He wet his lips. "We just wanted to say good-by to you, Mrs. Bronson. We've enjoyed living here. You've been real kind." Then, somehow embarrassed, he turned quickly to his wife. "Let's go, honey." He picked up the single suitcase and, holding his little daughter's hand, started down the steps. His wife followed.

"Good luck," Mrs. Bronson called down to them. "Safe trip."

"Good-by, Mrs. Bronson," the woman's voice called back.

The front door opened and closed. Mrs. Bronson stared down the steps for a long moment, then turned to Norma. "And now we are two," she said softly.

"They were the last?" Norma asked, pointing to the steps.

"The last. Building's empty now except for you and me."

A man, carrying a tool kit, came out of Mrs. Bronson's apartment.

"She's runnin' again, Mrs. Bronson," he said. "I wouldn't sign no guarantee as to how long she'll run—but she shouldn't give yuh any trouble for a while." He looked briefly at Norma and fingered his tool kit nervously. "Was you gonna pay for this in cash?" he asked.

"I have a charge account," Mrs. Bronson said.

The repairman was ill at ease. "Boss said I should start collectin' in cash." He looked a little apologetically toward Norma. "We been workin' around the clock. Refrigerators breakin' down every minute and a half. Everybody and his brother tryin' to make ice—then with the current bein' cut off every coupla hours, it's tough on the machines." With obvious effort he looked back at Mrs. Bronson. "About that bill, Mrs. Bronson—"

"How much is it?"

The repairman looked down at his tool kit; his voice was low. "I gotta charge yuh a hundred dollars." He just shook his head disconsolately.

The quiet of Mrs. Bronson's voice did not cover her dismay. "A hundred dollars? For fifteen minutes' work?"

The repairman nodded miserably. "For fifteen minutes' work. Most outfits are chargin' double that, and even triple. It's been that way for a month. Ever since . . ." He looked out the hall window toward the street. "Ever since the thing happened."

There was an embarrassing silence and finally Mrs. Bronson took off her wedding ring. "I don't have any money left," she said quietly, "but this is gold. It's worth a lot." She held the ring out to him.

The repairman failed to meet her eyes. He made a jerky spasmodic motion that was neither acceptance nor rejection.

Then he looked at the ring and shook his head. "Go ahead and charge it," he said, keeping his face averted; "I ain't takin' a lady's weddin' ring." He went over to the stairs. "Good-by, Mrs. Bronson. Good luck to you." He paused at the top of the stairs.

The yellow-white sun was framed in the window above him. It was constant now, but somehow an evil thing that could no longer be ignored.

"I'm gonna try to get my family out tonight," the repairman said, staring out the window. "Drivin' north. Canada, if we can make it. They say it's cooler there." He turned to look back toward the two women. "Not that it makes much difference—just kind of . . . kind of prolonging it." He smiled, but it was a twisted smile. "Like everybody rushin' to fix their refrigerators and air conditioners . . ." He shook his head. "It's nuts. It's just prolonging it, that's all."

He started slowly down the steps, his big shoulders slumped. "Oh, Christ!" they heard him say as he turned at the landing and went down again. "Christ, it's hot!" His footsteps crossed the downstairs hall.

Norma leaned against the side of the door. "What happens now?" she asked.

Mrs. Bronson shrugged. "I don't know. I heard on the radio that they'd only turn the water on for an hour a day from now on. They said they'd announce what time." She suddenly stared at Norma. "Aren't you going to leave?" she blurted.

Norma shook her head. "No, I'm not going to leave." She forced a smile, then turned and went back into her apartment, leaving the door open.

Mrs. Bronson followed her. Norma walked over to the window. The sun bathed her with its heat and with its strange, almost malevolent light. It had changed the entire city. The streets, the buildings, the stores had taken on a sickly oyster color. The air was heavy and soggy.

Norma felt perspiration rolling down her back and her legs. "I keep getting this crazy thought," she said, "this crazy thought that I'll wake up and none of this will have happened. I'll wake up in a cool bed and it'll be night outside and there'll be a wind and there'll be branches rustling—shadows on the sidewalk, a moon."

She turned her face to stare directly out of the window and it was like standing in front of an open oven. The waves of heat struck at her, pushed into her flesh, poured through her pores. "And traffic noises," she continued in a softer voice, "automobiles, garbage cans, milk bottles, voices." She raised her hand and pulled at the cord of the venetian blind. The slats closed and the room became shadowed but the heat remained. Norma closed her eyes. "Isn't it odd . . ." she said, reflectively, ". . . isn't it odd the things we took for granted . . ." There was a pause. ". . . *while we had them?*"

Mrs. Bronson's hands were like two nervous little birds fluttering. "There was a scientist on the radio," she said, forcing herself to be conversational. "I heard him this morning. He said that it would get a lot hotter. More each day. Now that we're moving so close to the sun. And that's why we're . . . that's why we're . . ."

Her voice trailed off. She couldn't bring herself to say the word. She didn't want to hear it aloud. The word was "doomed." But unspoken or not, it hung there in the still hot air.

It was just four and a half weeks ago that the earth suddenly, inexplicably, changed its elliptical orbit, and began to follow a path which gradually, moment by moment, day by day, took it closer to the sun.

Midnight became almost as hot as noon—and almost as light. There was no more darkness, no more night. All of man's little luxuries—the air conditioners, the refrigerators, the electric fans that stirred up the air—they were no longer luxuries. They were pitiful and panicky keys to temporary survival.

New York City was like a giant sick animal slowly mummifying, its juices boiling away. It had emptied itself of its inhabitants. They had trekked north toward Canada in a hopeless race against a sun which had already begun to overtake them. It was a world of heat. Each day the sun appeared larger and larger; and each day heat was added to heat until thermometers boiled over; and breathing, talking, moving, came with agony. It was a world of a perpetual high noon.

It was the next afternoon, and Norma walked up the steps carrying a heavy bag of groceries. A can and some wilted carrots protruded from the top. She stopped on the landing between two floors and caught her breath. Her light cotton dress clung to her like a wet glove.

"Norma?" Mrs. Bronson's voice called out. "Is that you, honey?"

Norma's voice was weak and breathless. "Yes, Mrs. Bronson."

She started up the steps again as the landlady came out of her apartment and looked at the bag in Norma's arms. "The store was open?"

Norma half smiled. "Wide open. I think that's the first time in my life I've been sorry I was born a woman." She put the bag on the floor and pointed to it. "That's all I was strong enough to carry. There weren't any clerks. Just a handful of people taking all they could grab." She smiled again and picked up the bag. "At least we won't starve—and there are three cans of fruit juice on the bottom."

Mrs. Bronson followed her into her apartment. "Fruit juice!" She clapped her hands together like a little child, her voice excited. "Oh, Norma . . . could we open one now?"

Norma turned to her, smiled at her gently, and patted her cheek. "Of course we can."

She started to empty the bag while Mrs. Bronson kept opening and closing drawers in the kitchen area.

"Where is the can opener?"

Norma pointed to the far drawer on the left. "In there, Mrs. Bronson."

The landlady's fingers trembled with excitement as she opened up the drawer, rummaged through its interior, and finally pulled out a can opener. She carried it over to Norma and abruptly grabbed a can out of the girl's hand. And then, her hands shaking, she tried to get the point of the opener firmly into the can, breathing heavily and spasmodically as she did so. Can and opener fell from her fingers and landed on the floor. She dropped to her hands and knees, emitting a childlike wail, and then suddenly bit her lip and closed her eyes.

"Oh, my God!" she whispered. "I'm acting like some kind of an animal. Oh, Norma—I'm so sorry—"

Norma knelt beside her and picked up the can and the opener. "You're acting like a frightened woman," she said quietly. "You should have seen *me* in that store, Mrs. Bronson. Running down the aisles. I mean, *running*. This way and that way, knocking over things, grabbing and throwing away, then grabbing again." She smiled and shook her head, and then got to her feet. "And at that," she continued, "I think I was the calmest person in

would be like an oven in here—as hot as it is now, as unbearable, it would be so much worse." She put her hands to her mouth. "Norma, it would be so much worse."

Norma didn't answer her. Mrs. Bronson drank a little more of the grapefruit juice and put the glass down. She walked around the room aimlessly, looking at the paintings that lined the room. And there was something so hopeless in the round, perspiring face, the eyes so terribly frightened, that Norma wanted to take her into her arms.

"Norma," Mrs. Bronson said, staring at one of the paintings. Norma moved closer to her.

"Paint something different today. Paint something like a scene with a waterfall and trees bending in the wind. Paint something . . . paint something cool."

Suddenly her tired face became a mask of anger. She seized the painting, lifted it up, and then threw it down on the floor. "Damn it, Norma!" she screamed. *"Don't paint the sun anymore!"* She knelt down and began to cry.

Norma looked at the ripped canvas lying in front of her. It was the painting she'd been working on—a partially finished oil of the street outside, with the hot white sun hovering overhead. The jagged tear across the picture gave it a strangely surrealistic look—something Dali might have done.

The old woman's sobs finally subsided but she stayed on her knees, her head down.

Norma gently touched her shoulder. "Tomorrow," she said softly, "tomorrow I'll try to paint a waterfall."

Mrs. Bronson reached up to take Norma's hand and held on to it tightly. She shook her head; her voice was a hoarse whisper. "Oh, Norma, I'm sorry. My dear child, I'm so sorry. It would be so much better if—"

"If what?"

"If I were to just die." She looked up into Norma's face. "So much better for *you.*"

Norma knelt down, cupping the old face in her hands. "Don't ever say that again to me, Mrs. Bronson. For God's sake, don't ever say that again! We need each other now. We need each other desperately."

Mrs. Bronson let her cheek rest on Norma's hand and then slowly got to her feet.

A policeman came up the stairs and appeared at the open door. His shirt was unbuttoned. His sleeves had been cut off and were ragged and uneven at the elbows. He looked from Norma to Mrs. Bronson and wiped the sweat off his sunburned face. "You the only ones in the building?" he asked.

"Just me and Miss Smith," Mrs. Bronson answered.

"You had your radio on lately?" the policeman asked.

"It's on all the time," Mrs. Bronson said, and turned to Norma. "Norma, honey, what station did we—"

The policeman interrupted. "It doesn't make any difference. There're only two or three on the air now and they figure by tomorrow there won't be any. The point is—we've been trying to get a public announcement through for everyone left in the city." He looked from one face to the other and then around the room, obviously reluctant to go on. "There isn't going to be a police force tomorrow. We're disbanding. Over half of us have gone already. A few volunteered to stay back and tell everyone we could that—"

He saw the fear creep into Mrs. Bronson's face and he tried to make his voice steady. "Best thing would be to keep your doors locked from now on. Every wild man, every crank and maniac around will be roaming the streets. It's not going to be safe, ladies, so keep your doors locked." He looked at them and made a mental note that Norma was the stronger of the two and the more reliable. "You got any weapons in here, miss?" he asked, directing the question to her.

"No," Norma answered, "no, I haven't."

The policeman looked thoughtful for a moment and then unbuckled his holster, removing a police .45. He handed it to Norma. "You better hang onto this. It's loaded." He forced a smile toward the landlady. "Good luck to you."

He turned and started down the steps, Mrs. Bronson following him out. "Officer," she said, her voice shaking, "Officer, what's going to happen to us?"

The policeman turned to her from halfway down the steps. His face was tired, drained out. "Don't you know?" he asked quietly. "It's just going to get hotter and hotter, then maybe a couple of days from now"—he shrugged—"four or five at the most, it'll be too hot to stand it." He looked over Mrs. Bronson's shoulder at Norma standing in the door, still holding onto the gun. His mouth was a grim straight line. "Then you use your own judgment, ladies." He turned and continued down the steps.

It was the following day or night. The current had gone off, and with it the clocks, so that the normal measurement of time was no longer operative. A sick white light bathed the streets and chronology had warped with the heat.

Norma lay on the couch in her slip, feeling the waves of heat, like massive woolen blankets piled on top of her. It was as if someone were pushing her into a vat of boiling mud, forcing the stuff into her mouth, her nose, her eyes, gradually immersing her in it. Between the nightmare of sleep and the nightmare of reality, she groaned. After a moment she opened her eyes, feeling a dull, throbbing ache in her temples.

She forced herself to rise from the couch, feeling the same ponderous heaviness as she walked across the room to the refrigerator. She opened the door, took out the milk bottle full of water, and poured herself a quarter of a glass. This she sipped slowly as she retraced her steps across the room to the window. She gasped as her hands touched the sill. It was like touching hot steel. Her fingers went to her mouth and she stood there licking them, and finally she poured a few drops of water from the glass onto them. She listened for sounds, but there was absolute stillness. At last she turned and crossed the room, opened the door, and went out into the hall. She knocked on the door of Mrs. Bronson's apartment.

"Mrs. Bronson?" she called. There was no answer. "Mrs. Bronson?"

There were slow footsteps behind the door and then the sound of a door chain. The door opened a few inches and Mrs. Bronson peered out.

"Are you all right?" Norma asked.

The landlady unhooked the chain and opened the door. Her face looked pinched and ill, her eyes watery and too bright. "I'm all right," she said. "It's been so quiet. I haven't heard a sound." She moved out into the hall and looked over the landing toward the steps. "What time is it?"

Norma glanced at her watch and shook her wrist. "It's stopped. I'm not sure what time it is. I'm not even sure whether it's morning or night."

"I think it's about three o'clock in the afternoon," Mrs. Bronson said. "It feels about three in the afternoon." She shook her head. "I think that's what time it is."

She closed her eyes very tightly. "I lay down for a while," she went on. "I tried shutting the curtains to keep the light out, but it gets so stifling when the curtains are shut." She smiled wanly. "I guess that's psychological, isn't it? I mean, I don't think there's much difference between out there and in here."

From up on the roof came the sound of glass breaking, and then a loud thump.

Mrs. Bronson's hand shot out and grabbed Norma. "What was that?" she whispered.

"Something . . . something fell."

"Oh, no . . . it was *someone*."

Norma looked up the steps leading to the top floor. "Didn't you lock the roof door?" she whispered, feeling a nightmare moving in on her.

"Yes," Mrs. Bronson said hurriedly, then clapped a hand to her mouth. "No," she corrected herself, and shook her head wildly. "I don't know. I don't remember. I thought I did."

A door above them squeaked open and Norma didn't wait to hear anymore. She took Mrs. Bronson by the arm and pulled her into her apartment, slamming the door and locking it. The two women barely breathed as the sound of footsteps came down the stairs. They stopped outside.

Mrs. Bronson turned to Norma. Her mouth opened as if ready to say something, but Norma clamped her hand over it and warned her with her eyes to be silent.

There was the sound of movement in the hall, and footsteps came to the door. "Hey!" a man's voice called out. "Who's in there? Somebody in there?"

Norma felt all the muscles in her body constrict. Neither of them made a sound.

"Come on out," the voice said. "I know you're in there. Come on out and be friendly." The voice sounded impatient. "Come on—I ain't got all day. You come out or I'm gonna come in!"

Norma, her hand still on Mrs. Bronson's mouth, looked desperately around the room. She saw the policeman's gun on the coffee table, moved over, and picked it up. She went to the door and held the gun close to the keyhole. She cocked it and then put her face against the door. "Did you hear that?" she asked in a loud voice. "That was a gun. Now get out of here. Go down the steps and go out the front door. Leave us alone."

Heavy breathing sounded on the other side of the door. Whoever was out there was thinking it over very carefully.

"Okay, honey," the voice finally said. "I never argue with a lady who has a gun."

Shuffling footsteps started down the stairs and Norma moved quickly to the window, craning her neck so that she could see the front steps below. She waited, but no one came out of the building.

"I don't think he went down the stairs—" she started to say, and then, hearing the click of a key, she whirled around to see Mrs. Bronson opening the door. "Mrs. Bronson!" she cried. "Wait a min—"

The door was pushed open and a man stood there—a hulking, heavy-featured giant of a man in a torn undershirt, his face and body grimy. Mrs. Bronson screamed and started to rush past him. He caught her by the arm and threw her aside.

Norma held up the gun, clawing at it, trying to find the trigger. The man lashed out, knocking the gun aside, and backhanded her across the face. Norma was stunned by the jolting pain. The man kicked the gun across the floor, then walked over and put his foot on it. He stood there breathing heavily, looking from one to the other.

"Crazy dames! It's too hot to play games. It's too damn hot!"

He reached down and picked up the gun, then looked around the room. He saw the refrigerator and went over to it. One bottle of water was left in it and he smiled with relief as he took it out. He threw his head back and drank, the water running out the corners of his mouth and dripping down the front of him. When he had finished the bottle he threw it to one side, where it broke on the floor with incredible loudness.

He walked slowly across the room, still holding the gun, and looked at the pictures, studying them carefully. He looked at Norma and pointed to one of the paintings. "You do this?" he asked.

Norma nodded, not daring to speak.

"You're good," the man said. "You paint real good. My wife used to paint."

The terror overflowed from Mrs. Bronson. "Please," she

moaned, "please leave us alone. We didn't do you any harm. Please—"

The man just stared at her as if her voice came from far away. He turned, looked at the painting again and then down at the gun, as if he had suddenly become aware of it. Very slowly he lowered it until it hung loosely from his hand and then he dropped to the floor. His mouth twitched and his eyes kept blinking. He went over to the couch and sat down.

"My wife," he said, "my wife was having her baby. She was in the hospital. Then this"—he motioned toward the window— "this thing happened. She was . . . she was so fragile—just a little thing." He held out his hands again as if groping for the right words. "She couldn't take the heat. They tried to keep her cool but . . . but she couldn't take the heat. The baby didn't live more than an hour and then . . . then she followed him." His head went down, and when he looked up again his eyes were wet. "I'm not a—I'm not a housebreaker. I'm a decent man. I swear to you— I'm a decent man. It's just that . . . well, this heat. This terrible heat. And all morning long I've been walking around the streets trying to find some water."

His eyes pleaded for understanding; and underneath the dirty sweat, his face suddenly looked young and frightened. "I didn't mean to do you any harm, honest. I wouldn't hurt you. Would you believe it?" He laughed. "I was scared of *you*. That's right—I was just as scared of you as you were of me."

He rose from the couch and started across the room, his foot hitting a fragment of the broken glass from the bottle. He looked down at it. "I'm . . . I'm sorry about that," he said. "I'm just off my rocker. I was just so thirsty." He moved toward the door past Mrs. Bronson. He held out a hand to her. It was a gesture that was almost supplication. "Please . . . please forgive me, will you? Will you please forgive me?"

He went to the door and leaned against the frame for a moment, the sweat pouring down his face. "Why doesn't it end?" he said in a low voice, almost unintelligible. "Why don't we just . . . why don't we just burn up?" He turned to them. "I wish it would end. That's all that's left now—just to have it end." He went out.

When Norma heard the front door close, she went over to Mrs. Bronson, helped her to her feet, and cradled her head in her arms, petting her like a mother.

"I've got a surprise for you," she said. "Mrs. Bronson, listen to me, I've got a surprise for you."

She went across the room and pulled out a canvas from a group of others. She turned it around and held it in front of her. It was a hurriedly done waterfall scene, obviously rough work and painted with desperation.

Mrs. Bronson looked at it for a long moment and slowly smiled. "It's beautiful, Norma. I've seen waterfalls like that. There's one near Ithaca, New York. It's the highest waterfall in this part of the country, and I love the sound of it." She went over to the canvas and touched it. "That clear water tumbling over the rocks—that wonderful clear water."

Suddenly she stopped and looked up, her eyes wide. "Did you hear it?" she asked.

Norma stared at her.

"Don't you hear it, Norma? Oh, it's a wonderful sound. It's so . . . it's so cool. It's so clear." She kept listening as she walked across the room to the window. "Oh, Norma," she said, her smile now a vapid, dreamy thing, "it's lovely. It's just lovely. Why, we could take a swim right now."

"Mrs. Bronson . . ." Norma said in a choked voice.

"Let's take a swim, Norma, at the bottom of the waterfall. I used to do that when I was a girl. Just sit there and let the water come down on you. Oh, the lovely water," she murmured, as she leaned her face against the burning-hot glass. "Oh, the beautiful water . . . the cool nice water . . . the lovely water."

The white-hot rays of the sun clawed at her face, and slowly she began to slump to the floor, leaving a patch of burnt flesh on the window, and then she crumpled in a heap silently.

Norma bent down over her. "Mrs. Bronson?" she said. "Mrs. Bronson?" Norma began to cry. "Oh, Mrs. Bronson . . ."

It happened rather quickly after that. The windows of the buildings began to crack and shatter. The sun was now the whole sky—a vast flaming ceiling that pressed down inexorably.

Norma had tried to pick up the gun but the handle was too hot to touch. Now she knelt in the middle of the room and watched as the paint began to run down the canvases, slow rivulets of thick sluggish color like diminutive lava streams; after a moment, they burst into flames that licked up the canvases in jagged, hungry assaults.

Norma didn't feel the pain when it finally came. She was not aware that her slip had caught fire or that liquid was running out from her eyes. She was a lifeless thing in the middle of an inferno, and there was nothing left inside her throat or mind to allow the scream to come out—

Then the building exploded and the massive sun devoured the entire city.

It was black and cold, and an icy frost lay thick on the corners of the window. A doctor with thin lips, his overcoat collar turned high, sat alongside the bed and reached over to touch Norma's forehead. He turned to look across the room at Mrs. Bronson, who stood by the door.

"She's coming out of it now," he said quietly. Then he turned back toward the bed. "Miss Smith?" There was a pause. "Miss Smith?"

Norma opened her eyes and looked up at him. "Yes," she whispered.

"You've been running a very high fever, but I think it's broken now."

"Fever?"

Mrs. Bronson moved to the bed. "You gave us a start, child— you've been so ill. But you're going to be all right now." She smiled hopefully at the doctor. "Isn't she, doctor? Isn't she going to be all right?"

The doctor didn't smile back. "Of course," he said quietly. Then he rose and motioned to Mrs. Bronson. He tucked the blankets tighter around the girl, picked up his bag, and moved out into the hall where Mrs. Bronson was waiting for him.

A cold air whistled up through the landing—and through the window over the stairway snow came down in heavy ice-laden gusts.

"I hope she'll be all right," the doctor said to Mrs. Bronson. "Just let her sleep as much as she can." He looked down at his bag. "I wish I had something left to give her," he said disconsolately, "but the medicine's pretty much all gone now." He looked toward the window over the landing. "I'm afraid I won't be able to come back. I'm going to try to move my family south tomorrow. A friend of mine has a private plane."

Mrs. Bronson's voice was quiet and sad. "They say . . . they say on the radio that Miami is a little warmer."

The doctor just looked at her. "So they say." Then he stared at the ice-encrusted window. "But we're just prolonging it. That's all we're doing. Everybody running like scared rabbits to the south, and they say that within a week that'll be covered with snow, too."

Through the partially opened door to Mrs. Bronson's apartment a radio announcer's voice could be heard. "This is a traffic advisory," the voice said, "from the Office of Civil Defense. Motorists are advised to stay off the highways on all those routes leading south and west out of New York City. We repeat this advisory: *Stay off the highways!*"

The doctor picked up his bag and started toward the steps.

"There was a scientist on this morning," Mrs. Bronson said as she walked beside him. "He was trying to explain what happened. How the earth had changed its orbit and started to move away from the sun. He said that . . ." Her voice became strained. "He said that within a week or two—three at the most—there wouldn't be any more sun—that we'd all . . ." She gripped her hands together. "*We'd all freeze.*"

The doctor tried to smile at her, but nothing showed on his face. He looked haggard and old and his lips were blue as he tightened the scarf around his neck, put on a pair of heavy gloves, and started down the steps.

Mrs. Bronson watched him for a moment until he disappeared around the corner of the landing, then she returned to Norma's room.

"I had such a terrible dream," Norma said, her eyes half closed. "Such an awful dream, Mrs. Bronson."

The older woman pulled a chair up closer to the bed.

"There was daylight all the time. There was a . . . a midnight sun and there wasn't any night at all. No night at all." Her eyes were fully open now and she smiled. "Isn't it wonderful, Mrs. Bronson, to have darkness and coolness?"

Mrs. Bronson stared into the feverish face and nodded slowly. "Yes, my dear," she said softly, "it's wonderful."

Outside the snow fell heavier and heavier and the glass on

the thermometer cracked. The mercury had gone down to the very bottom, and there was no place left for it to go. And very slowly night and cold reached out with frozen fingers to feel the pulse of the city, and then to stop it.

THE RIP VAN WINKLE CAPER

The tracks of the Union Pacific were reptile twins snaking their way south of the Nevada line into the vast torrid valleys of the Mojave desert. And once a day when the crack streamliner, City of St. Louis, thundered along these tracks past the needle-like volcanic crags, the distant sawtoothed desolate mountains, the dead sea of ash and brittle creosote brush, it was the intrusion of a strange anachronism. The screaming power of the diesel pushed aside the desert winds. It shot past the white and arid wastes of the ancient land as if afraid of being caught by the jagged, crumbling spurs of rock that surrounded the great quadrangular desert.

And once . . . just once . . . the impossible happened. The steel cord that tied the train to the earth was parted. Too late, the giant wheels sent up protesting sparks and agonized metal shrieks, trying to stop that which could not be stopped—fifty tons of engine and train moving at ninety miles an hour. It thundered off the broken tracks and smashed against a sloping sand dune with an explosive roar that shattered that still desert with earth-shaking reverberation. Cars followed the engine off the tracks like nightmares piling atop nightmares until the carnage had spent itself. The City of St. Louis was a dying metal beast with fifteen broken vertebrae stretched across the desert floor.

The moving van lumbered up the side of the desert slope toward the lonely ledge above. It groaned and wheezed in the heat, while behind it a small sedan followed closely. When it reached the ledge the van pulled to the left and let the sedan go by, stopping a few hundred feet away. Then the van reversed until it had backed against the opening of a cave—a yawning mouth in the face of the rock. Two men got out of the van and two out of the sedan. They wore unmarked white coveralls, and all four met near the tailgate of the van. They were like a committee of quiet generals meeting for a critique after a giant battle—sweaty, dead-tired, but victorious.

What they had just accomplished *had* been a victory. It was an operation that needed the precision of a stopwatch combined with the timing, logistics, and power of a full-scale invasion. And everything had worked beyond their wildest, most sanguine dreams. For inside the moving van, neatly piled in heavy motionless lumps, was two million dollars in gold bullion.

The tall man with the thin face and the steady, intelligent eyes, looked like a college professor. His name was Farwell and he had a doctorate in chemistry and physics. His specialty was noxious gasses. He turned toward the others and held up his thumb in a gesture of victory.

"Clockwork, gentlemen," he said with a thin smile. His eyes moved slowly left and right, staring into the faces of the other three.

Next to him was Erbe, almost as tall as Farwell, with thin sloping shoulders, a pale nondescript face—perhaps a little younger-looking than his years. He was the expert in mechanical engineering. He could make anything, fix anything, manipulate anything. With probing eyes and surgeon's fingers, he would gently caress a maze of gears, cogs, wheels, cylinders—and coax them into a hum.

Alongside him was Brooks. Broad and stocky, partially bald, with an infectious grin and a Texas accent, he knew more about ballistics than almost anyone alive. Someone had said that his brains were made out of gunpowder, because in the area of firearms and other weaponry he was a dedicated genius.

And to his right was DeCruz—small, mercurial, handsome—a shock of unruly black hair hanging over deep-set, probing dark eyes. DeCruz was the expert in demolition. He was a master at destruction. He could improvise anything and blow up everything.

Two hours earlier these four men, in an incredible blending of talent, timing, and technique, had executed a heist unlike anything ever performed in the annals of crime. DeCruz had planted the five one-pound blocks of TNT that had blown up the tracks and sent the train to its destruction. Erbe had almost single-handedly put the two vehicles together from the parts of a dozen others—with parentage untraceable. Brooks had developed the grenades. And Farwell had come up with the sleeping gas. And in precisely thirteen minutes every occupant of the train had been asleep—the two engineers forever. Then the four men had moved quickly and quietly into one of the cars to remove the rotary-locked pouches carrying the bullion. Again DeCruz had utilized his talents to blow the locks apart, and the bullion had been transferred to the van.

It was part of their natures that none of them was concerned with the two dead engineers or the twenty-odd badly wounded human beings they'd left behind. Expediency was the one gospel that they all recognized and paid homage to.

It was DeCruz who hopped over the tailgate and started to push the treasure toward the rear of the van.

"Apples in the barrel," Erbe said, and he grinned as he started to carry one of the bars of bullion toward the cave.

Brooks took another bar of bullion and let his fingers run over it. "So far," he said, "but we ain't spent nothin' yet."

DeCruz paused and nodded thoughtfully. "Brooks is right. Two million dollars' worth of gold, but I'm still wearing dungarees and I got a dollar and twenty cents in my pocket."

Farwell chuckled and winked at them. "That's *this* year, Señor DeCruz. Today this . . ." He pointed to the tailgate and then nodded toward the cave opening. "But tomorrow! Tomorrow, gentlemen, like Croesus! Midas! Rockefeller and J. P. Morgan all rolled into one." He patted the gold piling up on the tailgate. "Perfection, gentlemen. That's how you performed. With perfection."

Brooks laughed. "Man, did you see that train engineer when he hit those brakes! Looked like he thought the world was comin' to an end."

"Why not!" DeCruz said, his voice shrill, his eyes flashing.

He pointed to himself proudly. "When I blow up tracks, I blow up tracks!"

Brooks stared at him. There was a rooted dislike, an undisguised contempt in his look. "Find a foundry for me, DeCruz—I'll cast a medal for you."

DeCruz's black eyes returned the dislike. "What's *your* trouble, Brooks? That wasn't any easy thing tying up those tracks like that. You coulda done better, huh?"

Farwell, the catalyst, looked from one to the other. He motioned DeCruz back into the van. "May we get to business now?" he said. "We're on schedule and I'd like to keep it that way."

They continued to move the gold off the van and into the cave. It was torturously hot and the ten-inch cubes were deadweight in their arms as they slowly emptied the van.

"Man!" said Brooks as he moved into the cave with the last of the bars. He put it on top of the pile next to the deep pit that had been dug days before. "You're a heavy little bastard. Any more at home like you?"

Erbe came up beside him. "Yeh, one million nine hundred and eighty thousand bucks' worth . . . just like him." He turned to Farwell. "It worked just like you said it would—car full of gold, train derailed, sleeping gas puts everybody out . . ." He looked down at the gas mask hanging from his belt. ". . . except us," he said pointedly.

Farwell nodded. "Except us, Mr. Erbe. It was not our time to sleep. It was our time to enrich ourselves." He looked briefly at his watch. "All right, gentlemen, the gold is in the cave. Next on the agenda—we destroy the van and Mr. Erbe wraps up the car with cosmoline."

He walked across the cave to the far end. There were four glass-covered boxes, the size of coffins, lined up evenly. Farwell touched the glass top of one of them and nodded his head approvingly.

"And now," he said in a whisper, "the *pièce de résistance*—the real culmination—the ultimate ingenuity."

The three men stood behind him in the shadows.

"It's one thing," Farwell's quiet voice continued, "to stop a train on its way from Los Angeles to Fort Knox and steal its cargo. It's quite another thing to remain free to spend it."

DeCruz squatted down in the dirt. "When?" he asked. "*When* do we spend it?"

"Don't you know, Señor DeCruz?" Farwell's voice was faintly disapproving. "I would have thought that this aspect of the plan would be particularly clear in your mind."

DeCruz rose and walked over to the glass boxes. He stared at them with obvious trepidation. "Rip Van Winkles," he said, "that's what we are . . ." He turned toward the others. "We're four Rip Van Winkles. I'm not sure—"

Farwell interrupted him. "What aren't you sure of, Mr. DeCruz?"

"Getting put to sleep, *Mr.* Farwell. Just lying down in these glass coffins and getting put to sleep. I like to know what I'm doing."

Farwell smiled at him. "You know what you're doing. I've explained it very precisely to you." He turned, taking the other men into his conversation. "All four of us will be placed in a state of suspended animation. A protracted . . . rest, Mr. DeCruz. And when we wake up," he pointed toward the pit and the gold stacked alongside, "that's when we take our gold and enjoy it."

DeCruz turned from the glass box and faced him. "I say everybody should get their cut now and take his own chances!"

Brooks took out a large switchblade that gleamed in the dim light. "That's what *you* say, DeCruz." His voice was quiet. "But that ain't what we agreed on. What we agreed on was that we'd stash the gold here and then do what Farwell tells us to do. And so far he ain't been wrong. Not about anything. The train, the gold, the gas—everything. Just like he said. And all we had to do was walk over a lot of horizontal people and transfer a fortune like it was cotton candy."

"Amen to that," Erbe said.

"Amen to that, sure," DeCruz said excitedly, "but how about *this!*" He swiped at one of the boxes with the back of his hand. "None of you mind being helpless and closed up in these?"

Brooks went very slowly over to DeCruz, the knife still held in his hand. "No, Mr. DeCruz," he said softly, "none of us mind."

The two men faced each other, and in this moment of challenge it was DeCruz who wavered and turned away. He continued to stare at the semi-opaque glass of the box, and he took a deep breath. "How long, Farwell?" he asked in a different voice. "When we each push the button inside and the gas comes out, and this . . . this suspended animation thing takes over. How long?"

"How long?" Farwell answered him softly. "I don't know exactly. I can only surmise. I would say that we would all wake up within an hour of each other—no more." He looked again down the long row of caskets. "I would say approximately one hundred years from today's date." He looked around the circle of faces. "One hundred years, gentlemen, and we shall walk the earth again." He turned and went over to the pit, then looked at the gold bullion. "As rich men, however," he continued, "as extremely rich men."

DeCruz's lips trembled. "One hundred years." He shut his eyes. "Just like Rip Van Winkle."

It took them the rest of the day to pile the gold into the hole and cover it with earth. The moving van was blown up with the last remaining block of TNT. The sedan was pulled into the cave, covered with cosmoline and then with a large tarpaulin. And then Farwell closed the giant steel door covering the opening, its outside a twin to the rock walls on either side.

The four men stood in the shadowy light of the lanterns set around the cave and their eyes were drawn to the four glass boxes that waited for them with quiet invitation. On a signal from Farwell each man climbed into his box, closed the lid, and locked it from inside.

"All right, gentlemen," Farwell said over the intercom system linking the four boxes. "First of all, I want to know if you can hear me. Knock once on the side as I call your name." There was a pause. "DeCruz?"

DeCruz moved a shaking hand and knocked on the side of the glass.

"Erbe?"

There was a muffled sound from Erbe's coffin.

"Brooks?"

Brooks, grinning, tapped his fingers on the glass and tossed a salute.

The lantern light flickered weakly and the room was filled with an orange dusk in the last few moments before the darkness.

Farwell's voice was cool, deliberate. "Now I'm going to give you, in sequence, precisely what will happen," he said, his voice hollow in the silence. "First, you're to check the air locks located on your right. Do you see them there?"

Each man looked up to a spot just above his eyes.

"All right," Farwell's voice continued. "The red arrow should be pointed toward 'closed and locked.' Now you each count to ten very slowly. When you come to the end of the count, reach up with your left hand to the shelf just above your head. There's a small green button there. Do you all find it?"

There were movements within the other three coffins.

"You're to press this button. When that's done, you'll hear a slight hissing sound. That will be the gas being measured into the enclosures. Take three shallow breaths, then a long, deep one. After a moment you'll begin to experience a heavy, drowsy feeling. Don't fight this. Just continue to breathe regularly and try to remain as still as possible. A good idea would be to count backwards from twenty. This will occupy your mind and keep you from any excess movement. By the time you reach eight or seven you should lose consciousness."

There was another silence.

"All right," Farwell's voice continued. "Check your air locks first, gentlemen."

The other three men followed his directions, and then three sets of eyes turned in their confinement to look across the cave toward the first coffin.

"Now begin to count," Farwell's voice said, "and on ten, release the gas."

The lips of the four men moved as the quiet countdown took place—then, very slowly into each glass enclosure came a white stream of milky gas until the bodies inside were no longer visible.

"Good night, gentlemen." Farwell's voice was heavy and indistinct. "Pleasant dreams and a good sleep. I'll see you . . . in the next century." His voice became weaker. "In the next century, gentlemen."

There was no more movement and no more sound. The lamps around the cave flickered out and there was nothing but darkness.

Inside the glass caskets the four men breathed deeply and regularly, unconscious of the quiet *or* the darkness, oblivious now to the time passing outside the cave ninety miles from a wrecked train in the Mojave desert.

Time passed. The wrecked skeleton of the moving van turned brown with rust, and then disintegrated into little pieces of metal that mixed with the sand and was eaten by it. Winds blew; the sun crossed the sky day after day.

And time continued to pass, until there came a moment when a small lever inside the first glass box went "click" and the top started to open.

Farwell opened his eyes. For a moment he looked puzzled; gradually awareness flooded into his face. His body seemed heavy and sluggish and it was a while before he could move. Then very slowly he sat up and reached for a flashlight beside him. He had built this with a set of batteries of his own design, set in a welded case made of steel and magnesium. When he pushed the switch a beam of light shone up toward the ceiling of the cave. There was movement down the line as two other caskets opened and Brooks and DeCruz could be seen sitting up inside their caskets. The last box in line remained closed.

DeCruz climbed out of the box, his legs stiff and unfamiliar. There was a tremor in his voice. "It didn't work." He felt at his face, then moved his hand up and down his body. "We don't have any beards," he said. "Our nails haven't even grown." He stared accusingly at Farwell. "Hey! Mastermind with the big brain and all the answers—*why didn't it work?*"

"It must have worked," Farwell said. "It was foolproof. All the body functions stopped—there wouldn't be any growth of beard or nails or anything else. I tell you, it worked. It *had* to work."

DeCruz moved across the dim cave and felt around the wall. He found a giant lever half surrounded by rocks. There was a clank of rusting chains, and after a moment the steel partition moved on its tracks. It let in blinding daylight that made the three men shut their eyes. It was several moments before they could become accustomed to the light. Then DeCruz walked out to the broad ledge and stared out over the horizon.

"Look," he said, his voice shaking, "there's the Goddamn highway. It hasn't changed. It hasn't changed a bit." He whirled around, and grabbed Farwell by the shirt. "Mastermind! Big brain! So instead of a hundred years, it's maybe an hour—and we're still hot. And all that gold back there is so much garbage, because everybody and his brother's going to be looking for it—"

Farwell flung off DeCruz's hand and turned around, staring back into the cave. "Erbe," he said. "We forgot Erbe."

The three men ran to Erbe's coffin. Farwell was the first to see what had happened. He picked up a large rock and stared at it. Then he looked up toward the ceiling and then down to the crack in the glass cover of the coffin.

"This is what did it," he said softly. "It cracked the glass and the gas escaped."

He looked down at the skeleton in the glass coffin.

"Mr. Erbe has proven my point, gentlemen. He's definitely proven my point . . . *the hard way.*"

Brooks and DeCruz stared. Neither of them spoke for a moment. Finally DeCruz asked, "How long . . . how long would it take"—he pointed toward the skeleton—"for this to happen?"

Farwell made a gesture. "A year, or a hundred years." He looked toward the entrance to the cave. "But the odds are, Mr. DeCruz, that we're now in the year twenty sixty-one."

The three men walked into the sunlight.

"Now the next step, huh?" DeCruz's voice was urgent. "We get the gold into the car and we take it into the first city we find. And we either find a fence, or we melt it down some way." He faced Farwell. "That's the deal, isn't it?"

Farwell stared at him, and then looked at DeCruz's hands. There was something in the look that made DeCruz drop them to his sides.

"Why is it, Mr. DeCruz," Farwell asked him, "that greedy men are the most dreamless—the least imaginative—the stupidest?"

DeCruz's lips tightened. "Listen, Farwell—"

Farwell jerked his head toward the horizon. "For the first time, DeCruz," he interrupted him, "for the first time in the history of men we've taken a century and put it in our hip pockets. We've taken a lease on life and outlived our stay. We've had our cake, but we're still going to eat it." His voice became thoughtful and quieter. "That's quite an adventure out there, Mr. DeCruz. Though you're a little insensitive to it, that's quite an adventure. That's a world we've never seen before. A brand-new exciting world we'll move into."

DeCruz's features twisted. "But with gold, Farwell," he said, "with two million bucks' worth of gold. That's how we're going to move into it."

"Of course," Farwell said quietly. "Of course." He continued to stare across the vast expanse of desert. "I wonder what kind of a world . . ."

He turned and went slowly across the ledge toward the cave, conscious of this incredible moment; feeling an almost wild exuberance as his awareness whispered to him that they, of all men, had conquered time.

DeCruz followed him and began to scrabble in the pit. Each time he found another bar of gold, he gave an exclamation of excitement and joy. Brooks helped him, and the two men shared enthusiasm as they continued their digging.

But to Farwell the gold seemed no longer important. He watched them pile it up and then remove the cosmoline from the car. There was a tense moment when DeCruz sat in the front seat and turned the ignition key. The car engine roared back to life. It purred as if it had been parked not an hour ago—a belated testament to the dead Erbe's efficiency. But Farwell was only vaguely aware of the engine noise or of the gold being loaded. What preoccupied him was what lay beyond the desert, beyond what they could see—the hidden new world waiting for exploration.

DeCruz shut off the ignition and asked, "All set?"

Farwell looked at him. "All loaded?"

DeCruz nodded. "She's all ready." He turned away, his eyes unsubtle reservoirs of deception. "Maybe," he suggested, "I oughta drive her up and down a little. See if she runs okay."

Brooks, stripped to the waist, sweat pouring from him, took a step over toward the car. "Ain't you the most thoughtful little fella that ever come down a pike! You wanna take her for a little ride, huh," he mimicked, "and see if she's okay. Just you and the gold. Why, I wouldn't trust you with gold if it was the filling in your own mother's tooth. No, buddy boy—when we move outta here, we move out together." He turned to Farwell. "Where's the water can? We might as well load that up."

Farwell pointed toward it a hundred feet away. "It's over there where we buried Erbe," he said.

Brooks nodded and started across the sand toward the metal can that sat beside a freshly filled grave.

DeCruz watched him, his eyes narrowed. He very carefully and unobtrusively turned the ignition key and started up the engine.

Farwell was closing the entrance to the cave when he saw the car shoot ahead across the ledge. Brooks saw it at the same moment and his initial surprise gave way to a wild fear as he saw the car, like some malevolent beast, close in on him.

"DeCruz!" he screamed. "DeCruz! You dumb bastard—"

DeCruz's eyes remained set, focused directly in front of him, staring through the windshield. He saw Brooks make a frantic sideways leap—but too late. He heard the thump of metal hitting, jarring, tearing. And with it the scream of the mangled man. He let the car surge forward, keeping his foot on the accelerator. Then he glanced over his shoulder to see Brooks's body face down in the sand a hundred feet behind him. He took his foot off the accelerator and put it on the brake.

Nothing happened. DeCruz's throat constricted as he realized the far ledge was only a few yards ahead of him. Again he slammed on the brake, and reached desperately, frantically, for the emergency. Too late. The car was doomed, and it was during the few seconds before it plunged over the far ledge that DeCruz managed to open the door and fling himself out. The impact knocked the breath from him and he felt sand, harsh and gritty, in his mouth. And at the same time he heard the sound of the car smashing hundreds of feet below against the rocks.

DeCruz got to his feet and went over to the far end of the ledge, staring down at the car, which now looked like a toy destroyed in a child's fit of anger. He looked back at Farwell, who was standing over Brooks's broken body. Their eyes met and Farwell came over to him.

"DeCruz . . . DeCruz, what in God's name!" Farwell looked down at the car lying on its side, and then back toward the dead man. "Why?" he whispered. "Tell me. *Why?*"

DeCruz stared back intently into Farwell's face. "Brooks had an accident . . . or hadn't you noticed?"

"Why did he have an accident? Why did you do it?"

DeCruz nodded perfunctorily at the car. "That I didn't plan to do. I wanted Brooks dead—not the car." Then, challenge in his voice: "Deadweight, Farwell. So much deadweight."

He smiled, the corners of his thin mouth drew up—and Farwell noted the evil in his face. He remembered when DeCruz had joined them. This was the one man who would bear watching, he had thought. But he had remembered too late.

He looked at the battered body of Brooks, half buried by the sand, both legs sticking out at incredible angles. Too late for Brooks. Again he looked into the dark eyes that continued to challenge him. Maybe too late for himself too. He turned deliberately and started to walk back toward the cave. "I keep underestimating you, Mr. DeCruz," he said as he went.

"Farwell!" DeCruz shouted at him.

Farwell stopped without turning around.

"We do it my way now, huh? Take all we can put in two knapsacks and then hit the road."

Farwell was silent for a moment as his mind worked. Then he shrugged. "I can't think of any other alternative at the moment." He thought of the car far down in the gorge lying on its side, then he began to laugh. "The obvious," he chuckled. "The simple idiotic ridiculous obvious."

He laughed again and kept shaking his head as DeCruz stared at him, puzzled. "Even if it had run, Mr. DeCruz," he explained, "even if you hadn't wrecked it"—he motioned toward the gorge—"the license plates are a hundred years old. We would've been picked up the moment we hit the highway." He chuckled again, this time more softly, and looked up at the hot sun. "We'll load what we can, but it's going to be very warm walking. Very warm."

He smiled at DeCruz. "So you're quite right, Mr. DeCruz. Now we'd better hit the road."

The two men walked for hours down the sandy slopes toward the highway. They plodded along silently, each carrying a knapsack full of gold bullion; each feeling the hot sun beating down on them. Early in the afternoon they reached Highway 91. It crossed the flats of Ivanpah Lake, running east and west. Farwell and DeCruz paused briefly on one of its shoulders, and it was Farwell who pointed east. They hoisted their knapsacks higher and started walking along the side of the road.

An hour later, Farwell, stumbling, held up his hand and stood there slumped over—his face a red mask of pain and deadening fatigue. "Hold it up, DeCruz," he said, breathing heavily. "I've got to rest."

DeCruz looked at him and smiled. Anything that took strength, will, resolve, resilience—this was what he understood and could conquer. He was a young animal with no breaking point. "How're you doing, Farwell?" he asked with an enigmatic smile.

Farwell nodded, not wanting to talk, his eyes glazed with overexertion. "The map said . . . the map said twenty-eight miles to the next town. At this rate we won't reach it until tomorrow afternoon sometime."

DeCruz continued to smile. "At this rate, you may *never*

reach it. I told you you should've stayed back there and watched the gold. I kept telling you, Farwell."

This time it was Farwell who smiled. "Oh, yes—you did, didn't you, Mr. DeCruz?" His own smile now was twisted. "But I don't think I'd have ever seen you again. I think I'd have died back there."

He looked down the limitless stretch of highway and his eyes narrowed. "There hasn't been a car," he said thoughtfully, "not a single car." He let his eyes scan the distant row of mountains and there was a hint of incipient terror creeping into his voice. "I hadn't thought of that. I hadn't even thought of that. Just like with the license plates. What if—"

"What if what?" DeCruz's voice was harsh.

Farwell stared at him. "What's happened these past one hundred years, DeCruz? What if there's been a war? What if they dropped a bomb? What if this highway stretched to—" He didn't finish. He simply sat down on the sandy shoulder of the road and removed his knapsack, turning his head from side to side as if trying to slough off the heavy weight of heat and sun and the desperate tiredness.

DeCruz came up close to him. "Stretched to what?" he said, and his voice sounded frightened.

Farwell half closed his eyes. "Stretched to nothing, DeCruz. Stretched to nothing at all. Maybe there *isn't* any town up ahead. Maybe there *aren't* any people." He began to laugh, shaking uncontrollably until he fell over on his side and lay there, the laughter still pouring out of him.

DeCruz shook him, then took hold of him and forced him upright. "Knock it off, Farwell!" he said tightly. "I told you to knock it off!"

Farwell looked into the dirty, sweaty face that was close to hysteria and shook his head. "You're a frightened little man, aren't you, DeCruz? You've always been a frightened little man. But it's not your fear that disturbs me. It's your greed. It's because you're so greedy that you have no appreciation of irony. None at all. And wouldn't that be the irony of *all* ironies to walk until our hearts burst, carrying all this gold."

He stopped abruptly as a distant sound suddenly broke the quietness of the desert. It was so faint that at first Farwell thought it might be his imagination. But it grew in intensity until it took on its own dimension. DeCruz heard it too, then, and both men looked up toward the sky. First it was a speck, and the speck became a form—a jet aircraft with a vapor trail stretched across the blue desert sky. Then it disappeared far off in another direction.

This time DeCruz laughed. "There's a world left, Farwell," he said triumphantly. "That proves it. And that means there's a city up ahead. And we're gonna make it, buddy. We're gonna make it. Come on, Farwell, let's get moving."

He went back to his own knapsack and hoisted it to his shoulder; then he reached down for his canteen, uncorked the top, and took a long gurgling drink, the rivulets of water pouring down his chin as he sucked greedily on it. But halfway through his enjoyment he took a look at Farwell and smiled.

Farwell's hand had rested on his belt, but now he was staring down at a small chain attached to nothing. Farwell looked up. His voice shook. "My canteen came loose," he said. "I must've left it back on the dunes the last place we stopped. I don't have any water."

He tried to keep his voice even—his face unrevealing; but no pretense, however subtle, could cloak this kind of reality. He knew it, and the thin smile playing on DeCruz's face told him that his companion was well aware of it.

DeCruz hoisted his knapsack higher on his back. "That's tragic, Mr. Farwell," he said, the smile persisting. "That's the saddest story I've heard all day."

Farwell wet his lips. "I need water, DeCruz. I need it desperately."

DeCruz's face took on a look of exaggerated concern. "Water, Mr. Farwell?" He looked around like a bad actor. "Why, I believe there's some water around that you could drink." He looked down, farce-like in his concern, at his own canteen. "Why—here's water, Mr. Farwell." He looked across the shimmering heat at the parched face of the older man. "One drink— one bar of gold. That's the price."

"You're out of your mind," Farwell said, his voice cracking. "You're out of your Goddamned mind."

"One drink—one bar of gold." DeCruz's smile faded. These were the ground rules and he was laying them out.

Farwell stared at DeCruz, and then slowly reached into his knapsack, hoisting out a gold bar. He threw this on the road. "I continue to underrate you, Mr. DeCruz," he said. "You're quite an entrepreneur."

DeCruz shrugged, unscrewed the cap of his canteen, and carried it over to him. "Ain't it the truth, Mr. Farwell," he said, offering the canteen.

Farwell started to drink, but after a few swallows DeCruz pulled the canteen away from him. "One drink—one bar of gold," he said. "That's the going rate today, Mr. Farwell. It may go up tomorrow. I haven't checked the market. But for today, it's one for one." Then, in a different tone, the tone of a man who's suddenly taken charge, "Let's go, Mr. Farwell!"

He jammed Farwell's gold bar into his own knapsack, turned abruptly, and started down the highway. Over his shoulder he could see Farwell stumble to his feet, dragging the knapsack along the road like some recalcitrant pet reluctant to follow him.

At four o'clock in the afternoon Farwell felt that he could no longer breathe. His heart was like a lump of lead smashing back and forth inside his body. The late afternoon sun stayed hot and persistent as it slowly nose-dived toward a distant mountain peak.

DeCruz, several yards ahead of Farwell, turned to smile at him. It was his voice that Farwell could no longer stand. The corroding contempt in it, the insufferable superiority of the strong surveying the weak.

"What's the matter, Farwell?" DeCruz asked. "You poopin' out already? Hell, we've got another four or five hours of daylight."

Farwell stopped and shook his head. His lips were cracked, and just to touch them with the salt-tipped end of his tongue was a torture. "Stop," he said, his voice a mumble. "Have to stop. . . . Need water, DeCruz. . . . Must have water." He stood there swaying on his feet, his eyes sunk back in his head.

DeCruz grinned at him. It had reached the point where the gold actually meant nothing to him. What was of the essence was his prerogative. The juxtaposition of leader and follower dictated now not by brains but by the elements. He stood over Farwell, enjoying the other man's agony. "I've got about a quarter of a canteen left, Farwell," he said. He held up the canteen and shook it, then took a drink. "That's good," he said, the water driveling out of the corners of his mouth. "That was very good."

Farwell held out a shaking hand. "Please, DeCruz," he said through cracked lips, his words coming out distorted from a swollen tongue. "Please . . . help me."

DeCruz deliberately held the canteen up. "The rate of exchange has changed a little bit this afternoon, Mr. Farwell. It's two bars of gold—for one swallow."

Farwell's legs gave out and he sank to his knees on the ground. He slowly, painstakingly, removed the knapsack from around his neck and with a massive effort spilled out the gold bars. There were four left. He was unable to lift the two in his hands and finally wound up pushing them across the sand over toward the other man. DeCruz lifted them easily and put them into his knapsack. The weight of them started a tear along one side, but this was of no concern to DeCruz. He looked down at the bulging container, and then into the face of Farwell. He could see the hatred behind the tired eyes and, perversely, this pleased him.

"You angry, Mr. Farwell?" he asked smoothly. "You're not angry, are you?"

Farwell did not speak. He very slowly, with thick, sweaty fingers, tied up his knapsack and then rolled over to lie on his side, his breath coming in tortured gusts from an overworked set of lungs in a body pushed beyond its endurance.

They slept the night, and at seven in the morning started out again. DeCruz's stamina was unchanging, and he deliberately set a pace too fast for Farwell, who stumbled and lurched behind him. Several times DeCruz paused and looked back over his shoulder, smiling. Twice he took a drink of water, doing it flamboyantly and obviously until the moment Farwell came up beside him; then he screwed on the cap and hurried ahead.

Farwell was like a ghost—dead, lusterless eyes set in a filthy sand-covered face, lips and skin cracked like some aged parchment.

At noon the sun was a broiling mass overhead and Farwell suddenly turned white and dropped to his knees. DeCruz waited for him, but he saw that this time the older man was not getting up. He walked over to him and pushed him with his foot.

"Farwell?" he asked. There was a pause. The man looked lifeless. "Come on, Farwell. We've got some miles to go yet."

A groan came from the man on the ground. He lifted his head, his eyes closed, his mouth open, his swollen tongue off to one side. "No." The voice came like an animal's. "No," he said again. "I can't go any further. I need water."

DeCruz chuckled and handed him the canteen. "One swallow, Mr. Farwell. One swallow."

Farwell's hands trembled as he gripped the canteen and put it to his mouth. He could hear the water swishing inside, and all his instincts, all his desires—the absolute key to his own survival—were funneled into this one action as he put it to his lips. DeCruz's hand came down hard and swift, pushing the canteen away. Its top gashed Farwell's tender lips, drawing blood, as he looked up unbelieving.

"We hadn't figured out the contract, Mr. Farwell," DeCruz said, his eyes two dark pinpoints. "Today the rate's gone up again."

Farwell's eyes were almost closed, as painfully, he took the knapsack from around his neck and let it drop to the ground. He kicked it across.

DeCruz chuckled and went down on his knees to retrieve it. In doing so, his own knapsack was left in the road and one of the gold bars spilled out of it as it tilted over. His back was to Farwell as he started to pick up the gold.

Farwell stared at him, marveling that he could feel hatred at this moment—that he could feel anything beyond his own suffering. But the hatred brought awareness that this was the final moment, his last chance.

He stared at DeCruz's broad back, hating its youth, hating the muscles that rippled underneath the shirt, hating the fact that DeCruz was going to win, while he himself would succumb. He felt his anger surging underneath, and for just one instant it dredged up strength and resolve. His fingers closed on a gold bar and he slowly lifted it. Then, rising to his feet, somehow incredibly, he managed to raise the gold bar high. He lurched sideways at DeCruz, just as the other man looked up at him. Farwell let the bar drop from his hands. It struck DeCruz on the temple.

DeCruz let out one small gasp and fell backwards. Again Farwell picked up the bar and let it smash into DeCruz's upturned face. This time there was a crunching sound as DeCruz's skull caved in. And through the bloody mangled face the eyes looked up. They retained the last emotion the man ever felt. Surprise. Absolute, incredulous surprise.

Farwell felt weakness return to him. He stood there wavering, his legs like rubber bands, his body a mass of pain. He turned and stumbled over to the canteen that was lying on its side. The water had spilled out into the sand. The canteen was empty.

Farwell started to cry, the tears coursing down his filthy

beard-stubbled face. He fell to his knees, his shoulders shaking, his fingers caressing the empty canteen—as if he might be able to milk liquid from it.

After a while he got to his feet, looked at the gold bars spread out around him, and shook his head. They were meaningless lumps of deadweight. But he knew that they were all that remained to him. He went down on his knees again and struggled with them, trying to pick them up, then trying to push them across the sand toward the knapsacks. But he had no more strength left and it was only with a superhuman effort that he was finally able to lift one up by cradling it against his body and hoisting it with both arms. This one he carried with him down the highway—a lurching stumbling figure of a man who moved by reflex and nothing else. There was no liquid left in throat or mouth, and each breath he took was a hot bolt of pain coursing through his body. But still he walked and continued to walk until late afternoon.

He fainted, and was unaware of the side of his face hitting a rock as he pitched forward. He just lay there, his eyes closed, feeling a dreamy contentment flow over him. Then he forced his eyes open as he heard the sound. First it was a distant indistinct hum, then it became the sound of an engine. He tried to move his arms and legs, but they were beyond command now. Only his eyes had life. He tried to turn his head, but it was only his eyes that moved, and through one corner he could see an approaching vehicle—a metallic low-slung thing that shrieked toward him and then slowed down, the noise cutting off abruptly.

He heard footsteps cross the road over to him and he looked up. It was a tall man in a loose-fitting garment, but the figure was hazy and indistinct; and Farwell could not get his swollen tongue or cracked lips to function. He felt terror as he realized that no words were coming from him. But then, from deep inside him, came a voice. It was like the sound of a record player slowly running down. The words were grotesque and almost unformed, but they came out.

"Mister . . . mister . . . this is gold here. This is real gold. I'll give it to you if you'll drive me into town. If you'll give me water. I must have water." He forced one hand to move across the sand where it pointed to that last bar of gold a few feet from him. "Gold," the voice came again. "It's real gold. And you can have it. I'll give it to you. I'll give it to you. . . ." The fingers clutched convulsively, and suddenly the hand opened. There was a spasmodic jerk, and then there was no movement at all.

The man knelt down to listen for Farwell's heartbeat. When he rose to his feet he shook his head. "Poor old guy," he said. "I wonder where *he* came from."

The woman in the vehicle rose from her seat to look across the road. "Who is it, George?" she asked. "What's the matter with him?"

The man walked back to the vehicle and got into the driver's seat. "Some old tramp," he said, "that's who it *was*. He's dead now."

The woman looked at the gold bar in her husband's hand. "What's that?"

"Gold. That's what he said it was. Wanted to give it to me in exchange for a ride into town."

"Gold?" The woman wrinkled her nose. "What in the world was he doing with gold?"

The man shrugged. "I don't know. Off his rocker, I guess. Anybody walking in this desert at this time of day *would* be off his rocker." He shook his head and held up the bar of gold. "Can you imagine that? Offered that as if it was worth something."

"Well, it was worth something once, wasn't it? Didn't people use gold as money?"

The man opened the door. "Sure—a hundred years ago or so, before they found a way of manufacturing it." He looked at the heavy dull metal in his hand and then threw it onto the shoulder of the road. He closed the door. "When we get back into town we'll have the police come back and pick him up." He pushed a button on the dashboard, setting the automatic driver control, then looked over his shoulder at the figure of Farwell, who lay in the sand like a scarecrow blown down by the wind. "Poor old guy," he said thoughtfully, as the vehicle started to move slowly forward. "I wonder where he came from." He put his hands behind his head and closed his eyes.

The woman pushed another button and a glass top slid forward, shutting off the heat. The vehicle started down the highway, and after a moment disappeared.

Fifteen minutes later a police helicopter arrived, hovered over the scene, and landed. Two uniformed men walked over to the body of Farwell, gently placed it on a stretcher, and carried it over to the aircraft. The officer in charge noted down on a small pad the particulars. "Unidentified man. Age approximately sixty. Death from overexposure and exhaustion." Three scrawled lines on a policeman's pad, and it comprised the obituary for one Mr. Farwell, a Doctor of Chemistry and Physics.

Weeks later they found DeCruz's body, almost decomposed; and not long after, the body of Brooks and the skeleton of Erbe.

All four men were minor mysteries, and their bodies were consigned to the earth without mourning and without identity. The gold was left where it lay—stretched across the desert and piled up in the back seat of a disintegrating ancient car. It soon became imbedded in the landscape, joined the sage, saltbrush, pearlweed and the imperishable cacti. Like Messrs. Farwell, Erbe, Brooks, and DeCruz, it had no value. No value at all.